RED SECTOR

DOUBLE HELIX

BOOK THREE OF SIX

RED SECTOR

DIANE CAREY

Double Helix Concept by John J. Ordover and Michael Jan Friedman

POCKET BOOKS
New York   London   Toronto   Sydney   Tokyo   Singapore

An *Original* Publication of POCKET BOOKS

POCKET BOOKS, a division of Simon & Schuster Inc.
1230 Avenue of the Americas, New York, NY 10020

STAR TREK is a Registered Trademark of
Paramount Pictures.

This book is published by Pocket Books, a division of
Simon & Schuster Inc., under exclusive license from
Paramount Pictures.

ISBN: 0-671-03257-7

First Pocket Books printing July 1999

10 9 8 7 6 5 4 3 2 1

POCKET and colophon are registered trademarks of
Simon & Schuster Inc.

Printed in the U.S.A.

Chapter One

"ATTENTION! THIS IS A STARFLEET SPECIAL SECURI-
TY FORCES EVACUATION SQUAD! WE ARE ABOUT TO
LAND A DIPLOMATIC COACH AND FIVE FIGHTER
ESCORTS. ALL CIVILIANS MUST CLEAR THE COURT-
YARD IMMEDIATELY! ANYONE REMAINING WILL BE
STUNNED AND REMOVED TO A SECURITY BRIG! ALL
PERSONS ... ATTENTION! ... THEY'RE NOT CLEAR-
ING OUT. CAN THEY EVEN HEAR ME? PERRATON, IS
THE TRANSLATOR ON? PECAN, GET YOUR WING
BACK INTO FORMATION! WHERE'S THE BROADCAST
GREENLIGHT? WHAT KIND OF DUNSELS INSTALLED
THIS SYSTEM?"

"AH, PERRATON HERE ... STILES, BE AWARE THE
BROADCAST SYSTEM IS GREEN AND TRANSLATING.
YOU JUST CALLED THE WHOLE PLANET A BUNCH OF
DUNSELS."

"SHUT IT DOWN!"

"OAK ONE, THIS IS BRAZIL. FORMATION'S SHIFT-
ING STARBOARD. THE EMBASSY'S GOT A BIG GAR-
GOYLE ON IT AND I'M ABOUT TO CLEAN ITS TEETH."

"LATERAL THRUST. ABORT LANDING PATTERN—

PERRATON, WOULD YOU RED THE P.A. BEFORE I COUGH UP A LUNG?"

"Copy that. Public address speakers are shut down. Fighter formation's still too cramped for diamond grid, Stiles. Acorn just bumped a water tower."

"All wings, pull up! We'll modify formation and try our approach again. Did the whole city hear us arguing?"

"They heard *you* arguing."

"Ahhh, I should've become a medic . . . Nuts, Oak One. Go to Ruby formation. Pecan, move two degrees port. Brazil, get off his tail. Acorn, keep your wings trim. Why can't you people hold a hover grid?"

"Oak One, Acorn. It's not us. Stiles, it's you. You have to put the coach down and vertical your stabilizers to give us enough room to land in that courtyard."

"Stabilizers . . . I hate stabilizers . . . I was supposed to go in for multi-vehicular flight school this week, but nooo, I had to grab a mission. Listen up! I'll land the coach first, then all wings settle around me five seconds later. Keep it sharp!"

"What's the matter with you, Stiles?" Pilot Andrea Hipp's German accent seemed crisp over the comm. *"This isn't synchronized swimming, you know."*

"I said no chatter! The ambassador's watching!"

A prattle of aye-ayes settled the issue for the moment, but did nothing for Eric Stiles's stomach, or his icy fingers, or his tingling feet. This command stuff left a lot to be wished for. And his hair was in his eyes . . . he was looking through a blond curtain. Didn't help.

On the screens of his fully carpeted cockpit, Stiles saw the platinum glitter of the Federation Embassy at PojjanPiraKot seem to rise up to meet him. Actually, he and the coach he piloted were descending into the brick city courtyard, but the illusion of a floating building disoriented him briefly. On the secondary side monitors, the five fighter escorts regrouped into Ruby formation and found the space to wiggle into the brick court, settling around the main coach vessel like baby ducks crowding a drake.

"Doesn't look like I expected it to," he commented. "What are those metal bands on all the buildings?"

"The city's all reinforced." Ensign Travis Perraton's blue eyes peered with fresh curiosity at a smaller monitor as he adjusted the coach's shields to let them land, irritating Stiles with his eternal good mood. "They've got some kind of gravitational problem on this planet. All the buildings have had to be structurally rebuilt over the past few years since it started."

"What kind of gravitational trouble?"

"Something like high tides or earthquakes, I guess. That's what I've heard, anyway."

Stiles wanted to comment, but was busy settling the coach onto its extender pads. The fantasy of brilliant artisanship in moving spaceborne vessels into an atmosphere and landing them in a surefooted, graceful manner had shriveled in his hands. At least that part was over. He trembled with irritation as the system's check barberpoled. Perraton had managed to clear the belly shields. Otherwise, the coach would've sat in the air like a beachball on the water—and probably rolled over.

"You're down," Perraton confirmed. "You can unclench now."

"I'm fine!"

"Yeah, sure you are. You worried about coming in shielded for the whole twenty hours it took us to get here from the starbase."

Stiles bristled at the suggestion that he wasn't in control. "Emergency diplomatic evacuations have certain *regulations* attached. Not getting a second chance is just *one* of the assumptions. Evac regs *assume* the situation is hostile and precautions have to be—"

"Don't quote the book."

"Give me a view of the whole courtyard."

Screens around the cockpit flashed views of all six lander pads with irritated civilians scooping dirt out of huge potted plants and dumping it on the ship's pads. So much for respect.

"Are they throwing rocks?" Stiles asked.

"It's garbage." Eying the same screen, Perraton stood up and pulled on his torso armor, buckling the padded vest over his chest. "Some of 'em are throwing balls of mud from those pots."

Stiles straightened. "Secure the coach and scramble the evac squad. Nuts, Oak One. Remain in your cockpits. Do not get out, understood? Sit tight and let Oak Squad flush the dignitaries. I'll escort Ambassador Spock personally."

"They're pushing on my struts. Our light-stun phasers can—"

"Negative!" Stiles broiled. "Let 'em crowd you. Keep finger shields activated in case they touch the wings. And all of you shut up! I don't want the ambassador to hear the slightest disrespect."

"Oh, we respect you. Don't you respect him, Cashew?"

"I drip respect."

"As you were!"

"As I was? Did I change? I like me this way. Did you change, Acorn?"

"Animals," Stiles grumbled. "I'd like to get you disrespectful slugs on starship duty for five minutes, just five minutes. . . ." He buried himself in padded insulation as he pulled his flak vest over his head, then slipped into his gauntlets, adjusted his sidearm, and led Perraton out into the coach's main seating area.

Here, six other members of Oak Squad were already suited up and looking at him from inside their red-tinted helmet shields. Travis Perraton, Jeremy White, Bill Foster, Dan Moose, Brad Carter, Matt Girvan—their names and faces swam before his eyes like a manifest, and for a moment he thought the blood was rushing out of his head. Midshipmen and ensigns, all in training for what would eventually become specialties, for now they were assigned to Starbase 10 in the Security Division, under their senior ensign—Stiles. At twenty-one, Eric Stiles was the old man of the outfit. Perraton was next, at twenty years old and forty-two days junior to Stiles' ensign stripes. Knowing that they had heard the ribbing he took from the wings, Stiles felt his face flush. He had to lead the mission. He'd gotten himself into this on purpose. He had to address them as a commander. Nobody to hide behind. They'd seen the landing. His dream of a crisp textbook military approach and regulation landing had gone up in an ugly puff. Now the squad members were blushing and snickering, burying grins, trying not to look right at him—that was hard to take!

"Heads up." His voice cracked. "There's a riot going on outside. Some kind of local political trouble. The embassy is beam-shielded, so we have to go in the security door. As we approach, the guard will drop the door shields. We'll have to go in and come out in single file. We're going to put the dignitaries between us, at two or three in a row. There are about twenty of these people, so the seven of us'll be just about right. I'll go last, with the ambassador right in front of me. He's the primary person to guard, and if he gets so much as a hangnail, somebody's gonna answer to me in a dark alley. After we get—shut up, Foster!"

"I didn't say anything!" Bill Foster protested.

"Quit snickering! This is . . . this is—"

"Serious," Perraton supplied.

"I know, Eric," Foster muttered.

"You call me 'Ensign,' mister!"

"Aye aye, Ensign Mister."

"I want this mission to go like clockwork! I don't want a single twitch that isn't in the rule book! Don't snicker, don't slip, don't do anything that isn't regulation!"

A hand was pressed to his shoulder and drew him backward a step on the plush carpet.

"Everything'll go fine, Eric," Perraton mildly interrupted. "We're ready when you are." His short dark hair was buried under a white helmet with Starfleet's Delta Shield printed on the forehead, now obscured by the raised red visor. The shield glowed and sang at Stiles. Starfleet's symbol.

And Stiles had to make it look good. In the wake of Perraton's mental leashing, the symbol now lay heavily upon him. If he couldn't yell at his men, how would he keep them in shape?

He huffed a couple of steadying breaths, but didn't lower his voice. Now that he'd gotten up to a certain level of volume, it was hard to reel in from that. He took a moment to survey the squad—bright white helmets, black leggings, white boots, red chest pads against the black Starfleet jumpsuits, and the bright flicker of a combadge on every vest. Elbow pads, chin guards, red visors . . . looked fair. Good enough.

Time to go.

"There are riots going on," he repeated, "but so far nobody's tried to breach the embassy itself. Our job is to clear a path

5

between the coach and the embassy and get all Federation nationals out. These people don't have a space fleet, but their atmospheric capabilities are strong enough to cause a few problems. I won't consider the mission accomplished until we're clear of the stratosphere. When we get out of the coach, completely ignore the people swarming around unless they come within two meters or show a weapon. Clear?"

"Clear, sir!" Carter, Girvan, Moose, and Foster shouted. Perraton nodded, and White raised his rifle. Had they accented the "sir" just a little too much?

Stiles stepped between them and the hatch. "Mobilize!"

Perraton took that as a cue, and punched the autorelease on the big hatch. The coach's loading ramp peeled back and lay neatly across the brick before them. Instantly, the stench of burning fuel flooded the controlled atmosphere inside the coach. At Stiles's side, Perraton coughed a couple of times. Other than that, nobody's big mouth cracked open. Stiles led the way down, his heavy boots thunking on the nonskid ramp.

They broke out onto a courtyard of grand proportions with colonnades flanking it on three sides and the diplomatic buildings on the fourth side—a battery of fifteen embassies, halls, and consulates. Most of them were empty now. The Federation was the last to evacuate. Two of the colonnades were in ruins; part of one was shrouded in scaffolding while being rebuilt. Most of the buildings showed signs of structural damage, but generally the Diplomatic Court of PojjanPirakot was a stately and bright place, providing a sad backdrop for the ugliness of these protests.

A quick glance behind showed him the positions of the five fighters landed around the coach. Their glistening bodies, streamlined for both aerodynamics and space travel, shined in the golden sunlight. There was Air Wing Leader Bernt Folmer, their best pilot, code "Brazil," parked like a big car in front of Greg "Pecan" Blake. Behind the coach the tail fin of Andrea Hipp's "Cashew" fighter caught a glint of sun. On the other side, hopefully parked nose to tail, were Acorn and Chestnut, brothers Jason and Zack Bolt—but Stiles didn't bother to check their position. He only hoped they were in sharp order.

All around were angry people waving signs, some in a language he didn't understand, others scrawled in English, Vulcan, Spanish, Orion Yrevish, and a few other languages familiar from courtesy placards all over Starfleet Command where multitudes wandered.

The ones in English jumped out instantly before Stiles's racing mind. OUT ALIENS . . . LEAVE OUR PLANET . . . GET OUT STRANGERS . . . ALIENS UNWELCOME . . . CURSE ALIENS ALL. . . .

Some of the people were calling out in English, too, though clumsily and without really understanding the arrangement of nouns and verbs. The anti-alien message, though, arrowed directly through to the team.

To the music of enraged shouts from the people rattling gates and creating a din by banging small silver knives on the iron posts, Oak Squad broke into a jog and flooded into a broad shield of sunlight glaring between the embassy and the consulate next door. The doorways and lintels were heavily reinforced with titanium T-girders, and titanium bands swept around every building, two on each story, like shiny ribcages. Stiles glanced around at his squad, making sure nobody pulled ahead of the formation. This had to be crisp. The ambassador was watching from some window inside that embassy. Everybody was watching.

Fifty meters . . .

Oak Squad thundered forward relentlessly, their phaser rifles tight against their chests. As Stiles led his men across the patterned brick, he saw that just the raw heat from the coach's VTOL thrusters had scorched some of the bricks nearly black and pitted them beyond repair, destroying the geometric design in the historic courtyard.

His boots felt secure and thick as he crunched over the litter of broken glass, smashed fruit, and rocks that had been thrown by the rioters, who were now milling around the fighters and the coach. These Pojjan people were stocky and thick, with strong round cheekbones and bronze complexions tinged with an olive patina, reminding Stiles of Aztec paintings seen under a green filter. They wore various clothing, from the men's ordinary shirts and pants or the women's shiftlike dresses to the brightly beaded tribal tunics and leggings he'd seen on travel posters.

The travel agencies might as well rip those posters up. Nobody was going to want to come to this dump anymore.

He cast the rioters a threatening glance or two, but although some were touching the ships' landing struts they weren't doing anything destructive. Not yet anyway. If anything happened, the escort pilots would zap them. So he kept moving forward at a pace, letting the natives swerve out of his way. He led the squad manfully through a large puddle of fuel, some of which was still gulping out of a discarded and dented container. Their boots splattered it and freshened the stench.

Thirty meters.

Cries of anger, protest, and insult at Starfleet's intrusion into their courtyard grew louder, as the squad jogged across the brick plateau. Stiles didn't understand the Pojjan language, but some of these people were shouting in English or Vulcan and waving get-out-of-town banners in English, apparently smart enough to know how to get to the Federation personnel.

It's getting to me. I'm allowing it to shake me. Just do the job, get the people out of the embassy, into the coach, and lift off. Ignore the crowd. Just ignore them.

At his right elbow, Travis Perraton was watching a gang of Pojjan teenagers on the other side of the embassy fence. A flash of flame—the teenagers were lighting up a fuel-soaked towel.

"They can't throw that this far, can they?" Blake asked from behind Stiles.

"They don't have to," Perraton said. "We're jogging toward puddles of kerosene."

"Gasoline," Midshipman Jeremy White corrected from the flank.

"Stinks," Dan Moose added, then cast to the man on his left, "Make room, Foster."

"Sorry."

"Bag the noise," Stiles snapped, turning his head briefly to the right. "Don't splash through the gas. If we get it on our uniforms, we're in big trouble."

And that was his error—that one glance over his shoulder. A stunning force struck his left shin just below the kneepad, driving his entire leg out behind him. Blown forward by the force of his own movement, Stiles let out a single strangled yell, leaped forward over a slick of gasoline, and crashed to the bricks just beyond the slick. Though he evaded the gas, he slid sidelong into a pile of garbage dumped on the courtyard. Managing to thrust his arms out, he somehow kept from landing on his phaser rifle, which instead clattered to the brick and butted him in the face shield, then scratched across his bared jaw. If his visor had been up, the rifle would've taken out his teeth.

A blunt force rammed into his lower back—a boot—as Carter tumbled over Stiles, crumpling to the bricks on top of the garbage. Carter rolled and ended up on one knee.

With his jaw and knee throbbing, Stiles tightened his body, twisted onto his side, and brandished his weapon at the laughing crowd as his face flushed with humiliation. They were laughing at him. His fantasy of a clockwork mission had just cracked and blown up before his eyes.

Bile rose in his throat, a rashy heat down his legs. His lungs tightened as he felt slimy garbage soak into his uniform and the stench of petroleum knot his innards. The sky wheeled above him, cluttered with white helmets and flashing red visors reflecting the afternoon sun.

Smiling, Perraton reached to pull him to his feet. "Nice going, lightfoot."

"Don't help me!" Stiles blurted.

As if bitten, Perraton retracted his hand. Stiles rolled to his feet, now smudged with the gummy remains of garbage and mudballs.

When he got to his feet, Stiles staggered a few steps in the wrong direction and was forced to endure the foolish chicken-scratch of turning around and struggling back to the front of his squad, and the further embarrassment of realizing his men were deliberately slowing down so he could get in front. He slammed his way between them, elbowing Perraton and White cruelly out of his path. He didn't need their charity!

At the gates, two Pojjan guards immediately opened the iron grid and let them in without a word. The embassy's medieval-looking carved wooden door, three guys wide and set between two gargoyles, also opened automatically.

No, not automatically—this door was manual. Another

guard or servant of some nationality Stiles didn't recognize was now peeking around the door's iron rim like a shy cow peeking out of a barn. He was an elderly man, with bent shoulders and bright green eyes set in a jowly dark face with stripes painted on it. More tribal weirdness.

Moving further into the heavily tiled foyer, Stiles suddenly felt ridiculously out of place. The foyer was splendid, its mosaics of gold-and-black chipped stone and glossy ceramics portraying some kind of historic battle scene and the coronation of somebody. Must be from way back, because this wasn't a monarchical culture anymore.

Was it?

The guard pushed the big door shut and swung a huge titanium bolt into place to lock them safely inside, then turned to the clutch of evac troopers and gasped, "One minute! I'll get the ambassador's assistant!"

And he disappeared into a wide archway that was two stories tall.

Oak Squad stood in the middle of the gorgeous tile floor, their uniforms scuffed and stinking, and looked around.

"I'd hate to be the guy who cleans the grout," Perraton commented.

White grunted as he scanned the mosaic on the ceiling. "How long you think we'll have to wait?"

"Not long," Stiles filled in. "They called for us to come get them, so they're probably ready to leave. And they're Vulcans, so you know they're efficient."

"How do you know they'll be stiffs?" Moose asked.

"Because Ambassador Spock's a st—a Vulcan. They like to have their own kind around. They understand each other better than we do."

"Oh, right," White drawled. "They do everything better than we do."

Stiles scoured him with a glare. "Don't start on me, Jeremy."

He turned away, but in his periphery he noted Perraton's quick motion to White, erasing any further annoying comments.

Though they stood in this wide foyer feeling dirty and small, they were not alone. Sounds of footsteps and voices leaked from the depths of the embassy halls, and twice Stiles saw ethereal forms slip from one office to another. Did they trust him to get them out safely? Had they seen the botched choreography of the landing? Did they wonder whether the ensign in command was competent enough to handle this?

He gripped his phaser rifle until his hands hurt and shifted from foot to foot, halting only when a young woman—a human—skittered through the grand main door and into the huge foyer. Stiles didn't pay attention. . . . The small-boned woman, with tightly wrapped brown hair, tiny pearl earrings, and a twitch in her left eye, went directly to the tallest of them—Jeremy White—and breathily said, "I'm Miss Karen Theonella, Ambassador Spock's deputy attaché. Are you Ensign Stiles?"

She had a tight foreign accent that sounded Earth-based, but Stiles couldn't pinpoint the country.

"He's over there, ma'am," White told her, and gestured.

Stiles stepped through the cluster of Starfleeters and took his helmet off, revealing his sweat-plastered blond hair. "Eric Stiles, ma'am. I'm here to evacuate the entire embassy. Nobody should be left behind."

"We understand." Miss Theonella rubbed her tiny pink palms as if kneading bread dough between them. "All embassy envoys, functionaries, ministers, delegates, and clerks will be going, as well as four Pojjana defectors who lost their homes in the last Constrictor. They're being given asylum here and we have clearance for them to be evacuated with us. In all there are thirty-five of us."

"Thirty-five!" Perraton blurted. Then he instantly clammed up, but the number twenty kept flashing in his eyes like beacons.

How could seven of them safely escort thirty-five dignitaries through fifty meters of rioting?

"We're prepared, ma'am," Stiles shoved in, more loudly than necessary, before anyone else could speak up. "About the landing . . . the ambassador is probably wondering why we were so . . . out of formation. . . ."

"What?" Miss Theonella's white temples puckered and her brows came together like pencil points. "We can't see the courtyard from here. There are only reception rooms on the court side of the building. Was there some reason you wanted us to be watching you? Was there a signal?"

He stared at her, caught between relief and disappointment that nobody had been watching. "Uh . . . no, no signal."

Preoccupied, the thin young woman simply said, "Continue to wait here, please, Ensign. I'll get the ambassador."

Again the evac squad stood alone, holding their rifles, standing in the middle of the gleaming tile floor, listening to the drumming chants of angry people outside in the square and trying to imagine how they were going to hustle thirty-five dignitaries through that. The unpleasant possibility of rushing half of them out to the coach, then coming back for the second group—Stiles winced. Two trips through that courtyard full of alien-haters? Was that safer than one big rush? If he ordered two separate groups, would the angry people see that as their last chance to get them and attack the second group?

"Wonder why they hate aliens," Dan Moose voiced.

Stiles noted that his men were looking at the windows and doors, but his own eyes were focused on the long hall of offices into which Miss Theonella had disappeared. The ambassador was in there somewhere.

All the men turned to face the hall to their left as a crowd of elegant dignitaries bobbed toward them. In the midst of them was the tall, instantly recognizable figure of the famous Ambassador Spock.

Bow? Kneel? Handshake?

"Don't faint! Eric, stand at attention!"

Perraton's anxious whisper boomed in Stiles's ear like a foghorn.

"Stand at attention!"

"Attention. . . ." Stiles planted his boots on the tile, but wasn't able to get them together. He squared his shoulders, raised his chin, held his breath, clutched his rifle, and forced an appearance of adept steadiness and control. Cool. Calm. Military. Crisp. In control. In charge. Confident. Smelly.

The ambassador and his party approached them, but Spock wasn't looking at them. Instead his dark head was bowed as he spoke to Miss Theonella, who was clipping along at his side. The ambassador listened, nodded, then spoke again while a male attendant slipped a glossy blue Federation Diplomatic Corps jacket onto the boss's shoulders.

The sight was a shock—Stiles had expected the flowing ceremonial robes that Vulcan seniors were usually seen wearing, but now that he saw Spock in the trim gray slacks and dark blue jacket with the UFP symbol on the left side, that outfit seemed to make more sense for a spaceborne evacuation. Robes might be harder to handle on boarding ramps and in tight quarters.

Why hadn't he thought of that?

Though Spock—tall, narrow, controlled—possessed all the regal formality common to his race, his famous form was somehow less imperious in person than Stiles had anticipated, his angular Vulcan features more animated, and framed by the fact that he was the only Vulcan in the bunch. Of course, Stiles had only seen still photos or staged lecture tapes. Seeing Spock in real life was very different—he wasn't stiff at all.

As they approached, he could hear Miss Theonella's thready voice.

". . . and the provincial vice-warden will be sending his prolocutrix as proxy to speak for the entire hemisphere at Federation central. Also, sir, the consul general's wife and children are waiting in the Blue Room, and Chancellor De Gaeta's wife is in his office."

Miss Theonella finished her sentence just as she and the ambassador and their party came into the foyer.

"Thank you, Karen, very good work," Ambassador Spock said gently, countering her quivering report with his silky baritone voice. "Suggest to the Sagittarian military attaché that he post a Pojjana communications sentry, and that person must speak both Bal Quonnot and Romulan."

That voice! That famous voice! Stiles had been hearing it all his life! Historical documentaries, training tapes, mission interactives, holoprograms—now he was here, in person, right in the same room with that voice!

"This is Ensign Stiles," Miss Theonella added with a gesture. "And the evacuation escort men, sir."

The ambassador scanned the team, then fixed his gaze at Stiles. Directly *at* him. Right in the eyes! He was looking right at him!

Those eyes—like blades! Black blades!

Stiles tried to take a breath, but all he got was a gulp of garbage fumes from his soaked trouser leg. As his lungs seized up, he felt the boink-boink of Perraton's finger poking him in the back.

Report, you idiot!

"Ev . . . Evacuation Squad reporting as you requested, sir! Ensign Eric J. Stiles, Starfleet Special Services reporting, sir! One G-rate transport coach, evacuation team, and five fighter escorts, sir!"

The ambassador's black-slash brows went up like bird's wings. The chamber fell to silence. Stiles' fervid report echoed absurdly.

Calmly Spock said, "At ease, Ensign."

His deep mellow voice took Stiles utterly by surprise.

"Aye aye, sir!" Stiles choked.

"We'll be ready within five minutes," the ambassador told him fluidly, then turned to the attendant who'd put the jacket on him. "Edwin, please bring out the consul general's family and Mrs. De Gaeta and turn them over to Ensign Stiles."

"Right away, Ambassador."

As the man left, Spock turned again to Miss Theonella. "You have our records and diplomatic pouches? The legal briefs and service files? Personnel manifests?"

She held up a stern black pilot's case with a magnetic lock, hanging from a strap on her shoulder. "All here, sir."

"Very well. We should also bring the jurisdictional warrants. They could be confiscated and used to gain passage into restricted areas."

"I'll get them, sir."

"No, I'll get them." The ambassador turned to leave, then paused and gazed briefly at the tiled floor, thinking. "Stiles . . ."

"Here, sir!"

Spock looked up at the inflamed response. Coolly he repeated, "At *ease*, Ensign."

Stiles shivered, glanced at Travis Perraton, and again met the ambassador's eyes. "Yes, sir. . . ."

"Are you by chance related to—"

"Yes, sir, I am, sir! Starfleet Security Commander John Stiles, Retired, is my grandfather, sir! He served with you under Captain James T. Kirk, Stardates 1709 to 1788 point 6 as Alpha-Watch navigator aboard the *U.S.S. Enterprise*, NCC 1701, commissioned stardate—"

"I recall the ship, Ensign."

"Oh . . . oh . . . aye, sir. . . ."

"You have a long line of Starfleet service officers in your family heritage, I also recall."

"Yes, sir! Several active-duty servicemen lost in the Romulan Wars, sir! A captain, two lieutenants, two—"

"Commendable, Mr. Stiles. Carry on." Spock turned to the little gaggle of people behind him and said, "All of you please stand by until everyone else arrives. Then you'll take your instructions from Ensign Stiles as to how you will arrange yourselves during the actual evacuation. As you know, the building is beam-shielded, and therefore we must go out the door and board the transport coach on foot. Unfortunately, our general safety compromises our safety during emergency evacuation. Karen, keep them in order. I will return momentarily."

With that he disappeared down a different hallway and into an office, leaving a confused clutch of embassy persons standing here in the foyer, wide-eyed and obviously frightened. By nature, the two groups divided to opposite sides of the foyer, embassy folks over there, Oak Squad over here.

Stiles let himself be tugged aside, and barely registered the low mutters of his men around him through the afterglow of his meeting with Spock.

"Beam-shielding," Matt Girvan grumbled. "There's planning. What if they had to get out under more dangerous conditions than mudballs and molotovs?"

"It's beam-shielded so assassins or terrorists can't beam *in.*"

"Why couldn't they make it one-way?"

"Too unstable. Sucks too much energy to maintain over time."

"Doesn't matter. We'll get 'em out. Eric'll carry them all on his back if he has to."

"If he doesn't choke up a lung first."

"We'll be lucky if he doesn't make us bow backward out of the room."

The team laughed. A cluttered sound, muffled . . . like a storm coming.

Beside Stiles, Perraton raised his helmet visor and smiled with genuine sympathy.

"You okay, Eric?" he asked.

Stiles felt his lips chapping as he breathed in and out, in and out, like a landed fish. He'd just met his hero and he didn't know if he'd liked it.

And it wasn't over. In fact, it was just beginning. He'd have to do everything perfectly from now on. No more botched formations. No more stammering. He had to be perfect. Smooth.

"Ease up, lightfoot," Perraton suggested privately. "He's just a guy."

"Just a guy," Stiles rasped. "He's a hero, Travis . . . a Starfleet icon . . . the first Vulcan in Starfleet . . . Captain James Kirk's executive officer . . . I've heard every story a hundred times all my life—do you know how many times he participated in saving the *whole* Federation? And even the Klingon Empire?"

"Doesn't matter now. Anyway, the hard part's over. You met him, you survived, and the experience didn't suck out your brains. He was a Starfleet man for half a century. He knows the drill. So get a perspective. Here he comes."

Do the job. Do the job.

The ambassador flowed back into the foyer, now carrying a slim red folder and followed by more than a dozen people and his attendant Edwin. Suddenly the foyer was swarming with civilians. At least they were mostly adults, a few teenagers— Stiles didn't relish the prospect of herding toddlers through that mess out there. He stiffened as the ambassador came directly to him.

"We're ready, Mr. Stiles."

"Yes, sir . . . how would you like to do this?"

Spock handed the folder to Miss Theonella. "Pardon me?"

"I . . . I figured you'd have some preference about . . . what order you want them in and . . . how to do it."

The ambassador thought about that briefly, his dark eyes working, as if he hadn't considered such an option. After a moment he vocally shrugged. "Your mission, Ensign."

Over Spock's shoulder, Perraton smiled and gave Stiles a thumbs-up.

Sustained by that, Stiles forced himself to rise to the demand. "Uh . . . if you people would form a line, two by two, and Oak Squad situate yourselves between them, uh, one every . . . uh—"

He paused, tried to do the math, but couldn't remember how. His brain *had* been sucked out!

Maybe he wouldn't have to count and add and divide—his men were already arranging themselves into position. Perraton was taking the lead, and motioning the others into the queue at intervals.

"I'll take the rear guard," Stiles said. "Ambassador, would you mind coming back here with me, sir?"

"Thank you, Ensign, I will."

"All right, let's—no, no, you can't do the door." Stiles motioned to the funny-looking butler who was still standing his post at the door, waiting to open it for everybody. "Travis, put that man in line behind Girvan and you do the door. Then fall in."

"Copy that."

"Okay, phaser rifles ready."

"Ready!" his men shouted.

"Rifles up!"

"Up!"

"Very well!"

Stiles took one more look at Ambassador Spock's steady form in line before him, at the large UFP shield printed on the back of the blue jacket. The stars of the United Federation of Planets swam before his eyes.

He drew a breath. His voice echoed under the high tiled ceiling.

"Mobilize!"

Chapter Two

BRASH SUNLIGHT BLARED into Stiles's eyes, smashing his dream of frictionless success. The sun courted the horizon now, directly ahead of them, as they charged the protesters crowding the courtyard. Curtains of fire roiled around them where the gasoline puddles had been ignited by molotovs. On the other side of the licking flames stood the coach and fighters and a half-dozen unconscious rioters. Apparently Brazil had needed to enable his stun phasers to back them off.

Now the rest of the protesters were giving the fighters a wider berth, and turned instead on the jogging queue of embassy personnel and their six Starfleet guards trying to wend through the pockets of stenchy flame.

A fist shook in his face—and Stiles rammed his rifle butt into somebody's chest. Mudballs slogged through the line, striking the civilians. One caught Moose in the helmet. He staggered, but got back in line before Stiles could react.

Crack!—a molotov bottle smashed in front of the ambassador. New flames broke out, flooding the bricks, dividing Spock, Stiles, and one woman from the rest of the line. Spock instantly veered sideways, caught the woman in front of him, and steered her around the flames and back behind Moose's protective form.

"Oak Squad!" Stiles shouted over the noise. "Phasers on stun, fire at will!"

He didn't know whether or not they heard him until White and Perraton opened fire on a group of protesters blocking the way to the coach. The rifles blanketed the area with a red bulb of energy, and the rioters went down in a heap.

"Wish we could just toast 'em," Stiles grumbled, tactlessly boiling with contempt for this civil unrest. Why couldn't they just follow rules and stick within the law? Why'd they have to cause trouble?

"Stiles Oak-One! Ramp!"

The coach's automatic ramp opened before them with a whine. Perraton led the frantic evacuees right to it, then angled to one side and shouted warnings to the crowd as the diplomatic people clomped up the ramp. Luckily nobody had to yell at them to stay in line. They were perfectly satisfied running for the cover offered by the coach's maw. Just as the middle of the line was swallowed by the coach, Jeremy White veered away from the queue to drive back the same herd of angry teenagers that had harassed them on the way in. Now those teenagers were armed with iron bars—and the bars were red hot. White held back on firing his weapon, instead using it to bash away the iron bars threatening him.

"Jeremy!" Stiles called. "Stun 'em!"

But White couldn't get enough room to turn his phaser rifle barrel down and take aim. He tried twice, and each time was pummeled by a hot iron bar—the teenagers were too close, surrounding him so he couldn't move forward or back. If he tried to stun them at hand-to-hand range, he'd end up stunning himself too. And White was getting angry. Stiles could hear his furious grunts and barks as adrenaline took over and defensive/offensive training got a grip on him. Step by step he drove the teenagers back, inch by inch, but not enough for rifle stun. And they were hitting him with their hot bars until his protective padding smoked and sparked.

"On board, on board!" Stiles shouted to the civilians. He couldn't help White until these people were all present and accounted for in the safety of the coach. When Ambassador Spock was finally on the ramp, Stiles wheeled around, jumped off the footboard, and rammed through the enraged teenagers. He drove one of them to the ground, then rammed his rifle butt into the ribs of another, until he could see White's scratched helmet and smell the burning padding of his uniform.

"Jeremy! You're covered! About face!"

White tried to turn, but was caught in the neck by a vicious blow and tumbled to the brick at Stiles's feet. Stiles stepped over him, aimed his rifle, and fired.

A burst of bright energy engulfed four of the teenagers, so close that Stiles felt his skin go numb even under the protective gear.

"Get up!" he ordered, kicking White uncharitably. "On your feet! Board the ship!"

White rolled out from under him, possessing the presence of mind to keep a grip on his weapon, because they sure didn't dare leave it here, and stumbled to the ramp. Perraton skidded down and caught him, then shoved him into the coach and shouted, "All clear, Stiles! Stiles! Eric!"

"Acknowledged! Power up!"

"Aye aye!"

"Nuts, Oak One, power up for liftoff!"

"Copy, Oak One."

Instantly the fighters began humming with power buildup. Perraton disappeared back inside, and Stiles was two steps behind him, scrambling up the ramp on two feet and a hand, his weapon clutched in his other hand. Perraton was there to yank him inside, and backhanded the ramp control. The ramp whined upward and clacked shut, then the hatch bolts slammed into place.

Inside, Bill Foster was collecting the phaser rifles and slamming them back into their wall rack while the other men dumped their helmets into the reception locker.

"We're secure," Perraton reported. "Dan's powering up for you." He hit the hatch lock for takeoff, turned to Stiles and shrugged. "Wasn't so hard."

"It wasn't?" Stiles gasped, scanning the crowd of frightened evacuees. "Is anybody hurt?"

They all looked at each other, but no one spoke up. They were bruised, dirty, coughing, no longer the prim bunch he'd seen in the embassy, and one woman was sobbing, but most of them were in their seats and belted in. Now he saw that Ambassador Spock was buckling up two of the family members. So Spock was responsible for the organization. No surprise there.

Stiles dumped his helmet on the carpet and peeled out of his flak vest. "Where's Jeremy?"

"I'm over here."

Jeremy White's lanky form, smeared with dirt now, was sprawled in one of the crew seats, pressing a hand to his neck. His helmet was off too, and his uniform was still smoldering. Stiles stuffed his vest into Perraton's hands and hurried forward to Jeremy White .

"You all right?" he asked.

White blinked up at him. "Affirmative, more or less."

"Why'd you break formation?"

White's glare roughened. "Gosh, Eric, I got this irresistible crush on a girl way over there and figured to ask her out if I could just get through those terrorists with the hot irons and broken bottles—what the hell kind of a question is that?"

"You follow orders from now on, have you got that?"

Slumping back a little more, White grimaced. "Put a leash on it, will you? We're doing everything you say!"

Stiles almost snapped a reprimand, but what good would that do? And all the dignitaries were looking at him. Should he throw a tantrum?

Instead he surveyed White's dirt-flecked face and sandy hair, and decided on a better choice.

"You're all right, though?" he asked. "Not burned?"

The anger flowed out of White's heat-blotched cheeks. "Except that now I have to tell my mother I scratched the little body she cooked for nine months."

"Then take the portside defense guns. Let's get off this planet."

"Aye aye." White pushed out of his seat and made sure his neck wasn't bleeding.

"Girvan, starboard gun."

"Starboard, aye."

"Travis, navigate. We got a mountain range in our liftoff path."

"Right."

The three men went in three different directions, two to the defense pods and Perraton to the cockpit. A second later, Dan Moose came out of the cockpit and said, "We're powered up. I can't pilot this thing, though. You're the only one who can fly it in an atmosphere."

"I know, I'm coming. Sir, are you comfortable?" He paused before the ambassador on his way to the cockpit and asked a silly question. What difference did comfort make?

"I'm sorry about the trouble out there, sir," Stiles babbled. "If it were up to me, we'd sweep the whole courtyard with wide stun. Why do people have to behave that way?"

Spock straightened from helping Edwin buckle up. "Those people are frightened, Ensign, and disheartened. The political situation here is volatile. This was our last chance to evacuate Federation personnel. Prudence dictated that we get out while we can. The Pojjana have abandoned any overtures toward Federation membership, despite our efforts to help them protect themselves. This is an interplanetary squabble between them and the Bal Quonnot now, lacking clear rights and wrongs. Federation policy will now be hands off. The sector will be declared 'red.' "

"Then why were they trying to stop us from leaving? If they don't want us here—"

"A number of factions on this planet may find advantage in preventing our leaving. I should warn you," Spock added, and lowered his voice, "they never attacked the embassy itself because that would have been an act of war according to the Articles of Confederation. The embassy building is Federation soil. However, once we're in the atmosphere, they can shoot us down and claim any number of scenarios. We must be on our guard and ready to fight."

"We're ready, sir! I've got five fully armed fighter escorts, and this coach has two defense guns and a detachable midwing utility jump-plane."

Spock raised one eyebrow and drawled, "Yes . . . of course it does."

Now what did that mean?

Stiles was about to ask, then realized that all these innocent civilians were looking at the two of them, hanging on every word. From the ambassador's expression, Stiles got the idea he wouldn't get any answers even if he did ask. He shouldn't have asked anything. Gum stuck on your shoe doesn't ask, "Where are we going?"—it just sticks to the shoe.

Spock, having been around humans all his life, seemed to recognize the look. Stiles was instantly mortified that the ambassador had read the questions in his eyes. Why hadn't he taken the time to study the political climate here? Wasn't that his job as mission leader? Thirty-five diplomatic persons including the famous adventurer Ambassador Spock—killing them would send vibrations across the quadrant. Kidnapping them would be an even bigger coup—for somebody. A shipload of diplomatic hostages, and Stiles had to make a fool of himself by needing the most elementary facts explained to him.

Shriveled like a prune, he glanced around at all the people watching him, judging him, and croaked, "Prepare for lift-off."

"Very well." Spock simply took a seat in the first row, next to Miss Theonella and Edwin.

Feeling completely shrunken, Stiles threw off his gauntlets and stepped through the hatch to the cockpit and into the pilot's seat. Stinking of garbage, his jaw swelling up like a melon, he kicked the foot controls and threw the coach into antigrav so abruptly that the fighters were left below. Too bad. They'd catch up.

On his cockpit screens he noted all five Nuts coming up quickly on his flanks.

"Nuts, Oak One, I want some maneuvering room out of the city. Spread out. Attempt Emerald formation."

They each acknowledged with a green light, and he knew he was free to maneuver the bulky craft out over the countryside and toward the mountains. It would take the coach about five miles to reach escape velocity and make it up to an altitude at which they could veer up and out of the atmosphere. Soon the city pulled away beneath them, and he steered around two water towers and a radio antenna and was clear. Now for the mountains.

Since the mountain range surrounded the city on all sides, there was no way to avoid them. Coming in for a landing was less of a problem than accelerating to escape velocity, especially since they had to get up to speed as quickly as possible. This planet had an air force. He knew that much.

"Several Pojjan fighter aircraft just scrambled on an intercept course, Eric," Perraton reported.

"Behind us?"

"Angle two-five zero, port side and closing. Spreading out across our aft flanks."

"I'm increasing speed. As the atmosphere gets thinner, we'll get faster. They'll never catch us."

"Don't you want some defense back there?"

"Yes—yes, I do. Nuts, Oak One. Take up Diamond formation. Guard our aft flanks. Fall back, repeat, fall back. Acknowledge as you take position."

In his side ports he saw Pecan and Brazil fall away toward the aft, and soon all five green lights flashed in acknowledgement.

"Nothing'll get by our guys," he muttered with satisfaction.

"The Pojjan planes are trying to come around, Eric," Perraton warned. "All four of them coming around on the starboard side."

"Moving to port," Stiles accepted, and steered the coach out of the way so the nuts on the starboard flank could deal with the encroaching Pojjan fighters. "I don't know why they're even trying. In two minutes they won't be able to catch up with space-ready vessels."

"Oak One, Chestnut."

"Oak One. Go ahead, Zack."

"The Pojjans aren't firing on us yet, but they're trying to slip by us. Don't they know what our weapons can do?"

"Maybe not," Stiles said. "They don't have a space fleet."

"I don't know—it's like they're touring or something here. Should we open fire?"

Determined not to ignite a situation the ambassador already described as volatile, Stiles tried to use reserved judgment. He'd looked idiotic enough already. He had to make Spock proud of him.

"As long as they're not shooting," he said, "just stay between me and them. They can't catch me now."

"Understood."

"Ensign?"

Stiles glanced over his shoulder at the chilling sound of that voice. Ambassador Spock stood at the hatchway, gripping the rims and peering through to the wide forward screen.

"Yes, sir?" Stiles responded. "Is there a problem? We're almost to flank speed. The mountains are coming up under us. We'll be in space in about ninety seconds. I've positioned all my fighters in a rearguard, between us and the pursuit fleet, just in case the bad guys have more speed than they seem to. Nobody can catch us now, sir."

"Unlikely," Spock accepted, deliberately not stepping into the cockpit. "Ensign, may I make an observation?"

Stiles almost fainted with the depth of that question. An "observation" from Science Officer/Captain/Ambassador Spock? A Starfleet superior for as long as Stiles and his whole team had collectively been alive? That was virtually a direct order!

Stiles steered the coach through the first mountain peaks that reached toward them from a skirt of low snowclouds. "Of course you can, sir!"

Spock now stepped through the hatchway and knelt beside Stiles to get a better view of the mountains.

Why was he looking at the mountains?

"As I am sure you know," Spock began, "it is unlikely those planes pose any danger to us."

"Yes, sir. I mean, no, sir."

"And it is likely that the Pojjana know their planes cannot overtake us."

"Well . . . they might know it, sir. . . ."

"Then perhaps you should consider," the ambassador quietly advised, "that while the Pojjana do not possess strong space-faring, their atmospheric capabilities are formidable. Those planes behind us could be diversionary."

Stiles heard the words, but for a moment they made no sense. Then, gradually, the picture of reality crystallized in his mind and he abruptly understood the ugly mistake he was making.

"Oh . . . oh!" Stiles's mouth suddenly went completely dry, and he gripped his controls. "Oh, God!"

Suddenly Travis Perraton tensed at his own console. "Tactical display shows something in front of us! Coming up through the clouds! It's an A/I! They've got an A/I blocking our way! There are mountains on both sides! Eric, can we climb?"

By not taking any chances, by pretending to be a topnotcher who knew how to do his job and going for finesse instead of humility, Stiles had left everything wide open. Eric Stiles, man about town, citizen of the galaxy, had left the ship without forward protection. No vanguard!

Now he was coming into the targeting sights of whatever the Pojjans wanted to throw in his way—he'd let those planes steer him into its firing range, and all his defensive fighters were five miles behind him, guarding him from planes that couldn't catch up. The Pojjan planes didn't have a chance of catching him, but they sure had a chance of steering the coach toward an assault net hidden in the mountains!

Stiles felt his throat close up around the realization that he'd been completely duped. Spock hadn't interfered until it became obvious that Stiles was being suckered into a vulnerable position.

And no, he couldn't climb yet. Not that high—not yet.

He stared at the forward screen as a huge, nasty-looking assault/interceptor moved merrily through the mountain pass, essentially a giant gun platform, on an intercept course with the coach. And certainly that would happen, because in this short space there was no way to gain enough velocity to rise any higher, and there were mountains funneling them on both sides. All that Pojjan A/I had to do was move toward them in the sky and let the cricket fly into the web.

There were only moments left before the two craft would intersect. Seconds—

Stiles bolted to his feet, driven by a rash decision.

"Ambassador, can you pilot this coach? Ah—what am I saying! I'm so—I'm such—of course you can!"

As Stiles stepped through the hatch, Spock stood aside as if he were clairvoyant about Stiles' intentions.

"I understand, Ensign," the ambassador said as he slid into the pilot's seat. "You know your nominal weapons will be ineffective against an assault/interceptor."

Stiles yanked open the equipment locker and pulled out an air mask and gloves. Dry-mouthed and ashamed, he rasped, "It's my duty to try, sir."

"Commendable."

Perraton twisted around in his seat. "What's going on? Eric? What're you doing? Where do you think you're going?" Then his blue eyes flashed with shock. "You're not going out in the Frog!"

Harnessed by his failure to master the savoir-faire of command, Stiles didn't respond. He yanked on his gloves and slipped the air mask's strap over his head.

"Oh, no!" Thrusting to his feet, Perraton grasped Stiles's arm, forcing Stiles to shake him off in order to yank on a thermal jacket. "Eric, you're not serious!"

"As you were, Mr. Perraton," Spock advised, steering the coach masterfully through the angry mountains.

Perraton shrank back into his seat, cold with astonishment, his lips working as he tried to think of something to say.

Spock adjusted his pitch controls, but continued speaking to Stiles. "The midwing is unlikely to be able to divert a craft of that mass," he attempted again.

Was he trying to talk Stiles out of going?

"I know that, sir," Stiles said. "But by my calculations you only need an additional fifteen seconds to get up enough speed to break out of the atmosphere over that thing."

"Eleven seconds."

"Oh . . . well, I'll try to get it for you. Good luck, sir."

Even in the midst of piloting the heavy coach, Spock bothered to turn and give him the gift of eye-to-eye contact, a deeply meaningful effort that Stiles didn't miss.

"And to you, Mr. Stiles," he said.

Stiles closed his thermal jacket around his chest as he ran down the aisle through the glances of frightened passengers. He wanted to forget about the jacket, but training had kicked in. If he didn't have the jacket, he'd been too cold to be effective inside the uninsulated midwing.

As he passed the side-gunner pods, Jeremy White cranked around with surprise. "Eric, where do you think you're going? Who's piloting?"

Stiles ran past him. "Mind your gun, Jeremy."

Spock hadn't tried to stop him. Why not? Travis was right—this was hopeless. A twelve-foot one-man defense plane against a hundred-foot assault/interceptor?

As Stiles crawled into the Frog, the smallness of the utility craft struck him like a club. The little detachable was a holdover from previous technology, just something people expected to see on a transport coach and could be used now and then to scout a landing area or as a spotter. It had phasers, yes, but hardly more powerful than a hand phaser, and not very useful against large targets. It was amphibious, hence its nickname, but was almost never used in water; mostly it gave passengers the illusion of safety and options which it really couldn't deliver. It hung from the belly of the big coach, more of a wart than anything useful in a battle situation.

And he was about to launch himself in this crackerbox and pretend he could do something about a hundred-foot A/I platform.

He had to do *something*. This was something.

They didn't need him anyway. Spock could pilot the coach, probably better than Stiles could, so he was useless here. Might as well take a wild shot at clearing the coach past the platform out there. The A/I was big, but not maneuverable. It was made to do exactly what it was doing—hover out there, block the path, and pounce on whatever those planes funneled through to it. If the coach could just get past it, the A/I couldn't chase them.

One chance . . . one chance. . . .

He dropped into the pilot's seat, which accepted his backside like a big hand, and didn't bother buckling himself in. No—better buckle in, just in case he had to spiral or yaw hard. Wouldn't help to fall out of the seat onto his head, would it?

The belts were hard and stiff over his shoulders and around his chest. His feet fell upon the lower trim controls. His gloved hands gripped the yoke. The Frog's comm system would automatically tie in with his combadge . . . he could still communicate with his team, with the ambassador . . . they'd be able to both see and hear him making a further fool of himself.

Though it seemed minutes were going by, in fact it was only seconds before he had yanked the release and the Frog had drifted away from the coach, instantly going to its own power once it felt itself let go.

Stiles rammed the throttle, and was suddenly rushing out from under the belly of the big gray-white transport as if bursting out of a cloud.

"Mr. Stiles, Spock here."

The voice in his ear startled him.

"Stiles, sir," he responded automatically.

"You are at full throttle. You realize that the Frog will burn itself out quickly at that speed. In less than three minutes, you'll have nothing left."

"I know that, sir. I figure there won't be much point in doing any less."

"Your choice, Ensign."

"I'm coming into range, sir. I'm opening fire. I'll try to distract them enough that you can get by."

"Understood."

Oh, that was charity. What were the chances his little popgun phasers could do any damage to the enormous assault craft rushing toward him between the snowy crags of the mountain belt?

He opened fire anyway.

Shoot! Shoot! Again! Direct hit!

Bolts of red energy cut through the mist and skittered across the big gunladen maw of the A/I. He was way ahead of the coach now, in range of those guns, but they weren't firing at him. Why not? He was firing on them, so why weren't they returning fire?

No point. They knew the Frog wasn't worth the trouble, couldn't pose a threat to them, couldn't possibly stop them from taking down the coach.

And judging by the way his phaser energy sparked and fizzled on that ship's shielded skin, they were right. In seconds he wouldn't have any power left, at this speed, this effort.

The Frog rocketed over the top of the A/I, treating Stiles to a vision of bristling guns just waiting to skin the coach to death. All he had to do was distract them for eleven seconds, but they weren't playing. His last chance to be a hero was fizzling just like his phaser shots. They were ignoring him.

"They're ignoring me," he muttered. "Sir, how close are you to escape velocity?"

"Twenty-five seconds, Ensign."

"Sir . . . they're not paying any attention to me. How can I get them to chase me instead of you?"

"It's unlikely that you can," Spock bluntly told him.

Oh, why not? He'd come this far into the valley of the stupid. One more step couldn't do any worse.

"Sir," Stiles began, "I need a suggestion. I'll do anything for that eleven seconds."

"Very good, Ensign. Consider this—that interceptor is not a space vessel. It depends upon lift."

"Thank you, sir!"

"You'll be in extreme danger, Ensign."

"Doesn't matter, sir. In a couple of minutes, the Frog won't have anything left anyway. Here I go. . . ."

Spock didn't respond to that. Stiles waited for the zing of heroism to strike him, but nothing happened. He was too laden with the silliness of his mistakes to take much credit for what he was about to do. Pulling back on the Frog's steering mechanism, he vectored full about and once again streaked toward the interceptor when he heard the decisive Dutch accent of Fighter Wing Leader Bernt Folmer.

"Oak One, Brazil. Stiles, what're you doing? You can't fight that thing off with a Frog!"

"Maintain position, wing leader," Stiles told him. "Never mind me."

"Eric, you're making the wrong decision."

"No, it isn't. Cut the chatter."

Before him he saw the A/I piercing the clouds on its way down the natural path formed by mountains on both sides, and beyond that the rushing coach heading directly toward him, its nose up slightly as it tried to reach up and over the A/I and gain escape velocity. Not being a fighting craft of any kind, rather the kind of vessel that would be protected rather than protect itself, it did nothing fast, nothing fierce. Everything was slow and steady—eleven seconds too slow.

In just a moment the coach would be in range of the blunt force of the A/I's guns, and be driven down with its precious payload.

Stiles aimed the nose of his Frog downward, directly at the A/I's tail fins. A slave to lift . . . to the air it rode upon. Not a space vessel . . . why hadn't he thought of that himself?

Like a mosquito buzzing a raven, he shot downward from the high peaks until all around him became a spiky blur. The A/I's big black body grew before him with stunning speed until it filled his forward canopy and he could see nothing but the interceptor and the nearing form of the coach beyond it. All he could see of the coach was the gleaming underbelly—what an angle Spock was piloting! The stresses—could the coach take that?

"Didn't know it could do that," he gasped, but there was hardly any sound. "Ambassador, this is Stiles. If I disable that interceptor, the five fighters can drive it out of your way. Do you copy?"

"Understood. Three fighters would probably be sufficient, Ensign. The other two can effect rescue—"

"No," Stiles said. "Not again. Keep them in formation, all five of them."

"Explain your plan."

"I'm gonna clip that thing."

He was surprised when Spock didn't argue. Stiles found himself both gratified and humiliated by his hero's silence.

Then, abruptly, a giant hand reached out and slapped him blind. A crash like thunder deafened him.

Collision!

Chapter Three

THE FROG RAKED its port wing hard across the A/I's tail pectoral, shearing the fin off halfway down. With a sickening pitch, the tiny defender skidded over the metal top of the interceptor, then scraped off to one side like water sheeting off, now hopelessly damaged, and for a silly moment hung side by side in the sky with its enemy. As Stiles watched, the big interceptor almost casually yawed and lost altitude, falling away beneath the coach and rolling almost on its side, which prevented it from firing its forward guns at anything but the nearest mountain. The A/I took a couple of shots, but missed the coach entirely.

As if in a dream, Stiles listened to the reactions of his fighter pilots.

"The interceptor's falling off! All wings, attack formation! Get under the coach and drive the A/I down!"

"Affirmative. Formation Attack-Alpha."

Brazil's voice—giving the strike order.

Falling apart around Stiles, the Frog shook violently and rattled enough to make a man insane. Nothing responded as Stiles fought for trim—hopeless. The big interceptor was veering out of control, but unfortunately so was he.

"I'm going down!" he shouted, more to himself than anyone listening. He was glad when Spock didn't try to give him last-minute instructions. The Frog was croaking and there was nothing to be done about it.

"The A/I is veering off. They've got no control. Beautiful . . . Stiles, you did it. Eric?"

"I can't see him anymore! Bernt, have you got visual?"

"That's negative. He's off my screens. No visual."

"No visual, Travis."

"Oak One, do you copy? Do you copy!"

"Pecan, Chestnut—stay in formation! We're not out yet!"

Then, Spock's voice, like an oasis amid the youthful cries of the others. *"Coming to flank speed. All wings maintain formation."*

Without control he skimmed through the mountains, past knives of rock and white slopes of snow, scratching and plowing through whatever scooped up into his path, buffeted fiercely by winds and the force of his own fall. Around him the Frog cracked, broke, screamed, until finally an insurmountable crag caught the starboard wing and whipped him into a snow drift.

"Formation Emerald, all wings."

"I saw where he went. Right into the snow crest on the sun-side of mountain on the starboard beam. Permission to break formation and effect search."

"Negative. Maintain formation."

Spock's voice. Stiles clung to the low steady tone. It was the last thing he heard as his craft smashed into a snowy crevasse, as if the boot of a giant had scuffed a sandcastle. As the Frog plowed through fresh snow at flight speed, the impact knocked Stiles roughly left and right, held in place by the straps he almost hadn't bothered putting on. He saw only a spray of white pitted with rocks as the Frog's nose drove itself into the mountainside. The din of contact with mountainous matter and hard-packed snow muffled his helpless shouts and gasps. He crammed his eyes closed and waited to die. Pain raced up his left arm so hard, so sharp that he tried to turn away from it. His left arm tingled, went numb. Had it been cut off?

And suddenly, sharply, like a flat stone dropping, there was silence.

No . . . not quite. He could still hear the skitter of bits of ice and rock settling outside. He opened his eyes.

Nearly dark . . . the Frog was completely buried in snow. Entombed . . . and where? On top of an Alp? Even if he could get out, he could never survive.

Blood ran down the side of his face. Into his eye . . . and stung a little.

He was lying nearly on his back, with his knees up before him and the cockpit controls where the open sky should be. Just lucky to have landed on his ass instead of his head . . . could've been worse, could be hanging here upside down with the blood rushing to his head, looking dopey and unable. . . .

"Spock to Stiles. Can you hear me, Ensign?"

The voice from the comm unit jolted him as if he'd been stricken bodily. He flinched. "What . . . ?"

"Ensign Stiles, this is Spock. We've reached escape velocity. Sensors indicate you've crashed and are stationary, but intact. Is that true? Are you down?"

Stiles coughed and tried to focus his aching on the instrument panel. Yes, he could still see . . . tiny emergency lights cast a soft red glow, just enough to see by.

"Yes, I, uh . . . I'm crashed," he muttered, coughed again, then winced at the searing pain in his arm. "Down behind the lines. . . ."

"Are you stable?"

"No idea."

Above him, the canopy was completely darkened to a severe gray by a ton of snow and ice and dirt, only the tempered windshield preventing him from being crushed or suffocated.

How much fallout was he buried under? No way to know. Should he try to push out? Would it hold him here or let him slip down into a fissure? Was snow heavier than soil?

"Snow. . . ." he murmured, perplexed. Then a gurgling laugh rose in his throat. "I'm from Port Canaveral."

The sound of his voice drummed in his ears. Should he be doing something? Trying to get out?

There was no getting the canopy open under that much weight, and he sure couldn't do it with only one arm.

Still numb?

Yup.

"All wings, come to stratospheric formation. Transfer to space thrust."

"Coach, Brazil. Copy that. All wings comply."

"But I can still get down there. I can land on that mountain—"

"Don't take action until I get a fix on him. These readings aren't steady."

That was Travis's voice. He sounded strange. . . .

Several seconds went by, long ones. Almost a minute. Well past the time when the coach should've been clear of the mountains. What was happening?

Then Ambassador Spock's smooth words broke through the crackling sounds of the pilots. *"The pursuit aircraft are moving away. They have given up. The coach is no longer in danger, Mr. Stiles."*

Stiles cleared his throat and muttered, "Thanks for telling me, sir."

"One of the wings can now break formation and effect rescue with relative dispatch."

"Rescue? . . . oh . . . me. . . ."

With a grunt, Stiles pushed off his helmet, surprised to see a crack in it, and realized his head had been driven into the canopy's side support strut. No wonder his head hurt.

"They may want us to try that," he decided. "There might be other hostiles out there. One ensign against five pilots and thirty-five dignitaries . . . Leave the fighters where they are, sir. I'll just . . . stay here."

It was all bravado. If Spock insisted, Stiles knew he wouldn't stand up to him. He could feel his friends listening, see Travis Perraton's friendly face blanked with astonishment that they were leaving a man behind, see Perraton's European features turn ruddy, his blue eyes widen. Suddenly Perraton—and all of them, really—seemed too young for this job. Maybe Stiles was fooling them, but he wasn't fooling the ambassador.

No one said anything. Nobody wanted to interrupt with the ambassador talking.

Glad they didn't say anything . . . that would've been even harder. Hearing their voices . . .

Spock . . . a half-dozen Starfleet officers rolled into one. An ambassador of high standing and galactic respect. A name known in the farthest reaches, on the tiniest colonies, on the lips of every Federation enemy. Spock and Starfleet were almost the same word. He could've insisted on a rescue attempt. Stiles would've backed down, let himself be rescued. Looked like a dopey kid being pulled out of the water because he'd showed off and fallen in.

Was he refusing rescue to avoid that moment?

Spock didn't press him. Stiles knew what that meant—he was being given something. Spock wasn't countermanding Stiles's decision to sacrifice himself. Ensign or not, Stiles was in charge, even if only in a token way. Nobody thought this would be a hard mission. He felt a little silly that Spock was giving in to him, handing him some kind of lollipop. On the other hand, was Spock going out of the way *not* to take something away from him? Maybe . . .

A hard bump made the mountainside vibrate. He felt it, through the Frog's skin, through the snow, through his jacket.

"There's somebody outside," he spoke up. "Something just landed near me . . . it's got to be them! They're here—they found me!"

"Yes, we have them on sensors. A Pojjana jump-jet just settled on the mountain near you."

Stiles's mouth went suddenly dry. "How long . . . do you think they'll take to get through to me?"

Spock didn't answer him. Maybe he was busy up there, steering that coach into space, avoiding the three Pojjan moons that looped the planet so far away, so much farther than Earth's moon.

"I didn't know the coach could take that much stress," he sighed. "You put a lot of angle on it. Why didn't it stall? How do you do that?"

"Simply, but the Academy prefers not to teach the trick. I forced the P/T levels over tolerance so the thrusters had more power."

"Why didn't the tanks blow from the extra pressure?"

"Tolerance levels are standardized at point of safety. Going

over tolerance only means that measurement becomes unreliable."

"You mean you were just taking a chance?"

"Exactly."

"Wow . . ."

Listening to thumps and thuds from the deep outside, Stiles saw a picture in his mind of the transport coach, piloted by Spock instead of himself, angling more steeping into the late-day sky than Stiles thought it possibly could. He never guessed a ship like that could take so much lift stress. He wouldn't have known to take the chance of added stress, wouldn't have been able to get the coach up fast enough to make use of the eleven seconds.

"I can hear them outside." He gazed up, only seven inches, to the snowed-over canopy. "They're looking for me in the snow. They're digging through . . . I hear the shovels . . . Maybe they're putting explosives on me. Maybe they're not going to dig me out at all. Why should they?"

"Steady, Ensign. You will not be killed."

"Respectfully suggest you don't know that, sir."

"Of course not. Ensign, this sector is now red. Some time may pass before the Federation can negotiate for your release. Do you understand?"

A tremor ran down Stiles's spine. "You mean . . . it might take a couple of months?"

"Or longer."

"Well . . . six months?" His hands chilled even beyond the cooling temperature in the cockpit. Sweat broke out on his brow in spite of the chill.

Spock didn't answer him. That meant something. Longer than six months?

"Sir, tell my family . . . tell them I didn't . . . or just say . . ."

"I will, Mr. Stiles. Be assured of that."

With a sudden groan, Stiles shut his eyes. His request suddenly seemed silly, melodramatic. But more than anything else it was pointless. He reviewed in his mind the faces of his father and grandfather, his aunts and uncles, the wide extended legacy of Stiles service to Starfleet and several other notable planetary corps within the structure of the Federation. Wherever they lived, wherever they were, the Stiles family made a show for themselves.

He shifted this way and that, but there was no room for movement. He was denied even that pitiful comfort and was forced to sit here and look back.

"Sir," he began again, "never mind about my family. Don't tell them anything. Just tell them I'm . . . not around anymore."

There was a brief silence, heavy and notable, like the pause between movements of a symphony. The baton remained in the air, the audience didn't applaud, the instruments were up.

"I shall tell them you performed your duty most admirably, young man," Spock slowly promised. *"You rose to an unforeseen challenge."*

A mirthless chuckle broke from Stiles's chest. More charity. Good words for a pathetic slob, so he wouldn't feel so pathetic.

Too late.

"Rose to it? I caused it. It was only unforeseen because I didn't foresee it." He shivered deeply, to his bones. "Don't bother with my family. Starfleet'll send them the official report. Don't tell them anything else . . . they won't be impressed. This story isn't that good. Doing duty's not enough for them. I'd be better off just lost at sea. No stories."

"Ensign," Spock began again, *"you needn't cheat yourself. You fit into an age-old tapestry of military valor. Even the small deeds are knightly."*

"Oh, please, sir, I've heard that since I was six. We take an oath . . . we wear uniforms . . . we take action . . . when there's trouble, we go toward it instead of away from it. We're military. Can't argue with that. It's got to mean something. If it means I stay here, then that's what it means."

A mechanical whine, muffled by the snow, found its way down to him. Drilling. Or cutting, maybe. He must be trapped under rocks or—were there trees up this high? He hadn't bothered looking.

His cold face cracked with a sorry smile as he reviewed the last few seconds. "I hope the other guys can't hear you talking to me this way."

Spock's voice crackled. Growing more faint. Distant. *"I sent*

Ensign Perraton to tend to the passengers. I have no need of a navigator. We are quite alone."

Overhead, the scratching sound was louder now, more deliberate. The diggers weren't searching anymore. They were purposefully digging. They'd pinpointed this spot. Maybe a fin or wing was sticking out of the snow. Or maybe they had sensors that had caught him. They'd sure found him fast. Things sure could change suddenly.

Stiles let his head fall against the high seat back. "So . . . how'd you know I wanted to be alone? All my life I've heard how Vulcans don't have intuition . . . y'know, no . . . hunches. No emotional anchors, like us fallibles do."

"And you have believed the stories," Spock said.

Stiles touched a swelling on the side of his head and laughed minimally. "Oh, you're making fun of me now."

"With you, Ensign," the ambassador offered gently, *"not of you."*

"Everybody always says Vulcans can't joke."

"Of course not. Nor do we love, fear, lie, or doubt."

Stiles laughed again. Strange that he could laugh . . . strange that this particular person could make him feel better when none of his friends had been able to.

The shovels, diggers, drills . . . getting closer now. Something scratched the nose of the Frog. Stiles saw a finger of golden sunlight appear in front of his left knee. They were almost here. In minutes, he'd be in the hands of the enemy. Would they kill him?

They had a lot of options. He had none. Here he was, trapped in his capsule, probably about to die, and even though his mission was successful, he crashed because of his own lack of foresight. His family was going to be disappointed in him . . . all those commanders, captains, lieutenants, heroes of the Romulan Wars—and one kid who never made it past ensign because he made a mistake on his first mission and got himself shot down.

He'd blown it. Allowed himself to be distracted. Put all his fighters behind him and figured nobody would think to come up in front. He was ashamed that Spock had been forced to point out something so obvious. That's what would go in the report, and on top of it all, after everything else, Spock was seeing that he was afraid.

"It's hard to breathe," he wheezed. Life support off?

"The blue marker dot on the upper left of your emergency grid, ensign. Push it upward."

"Blue dot . . . oh. Got it—I hear the fan now. That's better . . ."

Fresh air, siphoned from outside. Not warm, though. In fact, the incoming air was frigid. But air was air and it cleared his head.

At the very least, he'd be captured now. Maybe tortured. Maybe killed. Would it be better to get killed right now, here on this mountain?

A crawling aneurysm of mortal fear moved through his brain, infecting his body until he was cold and shuddering. He felt it working on him even as he tried to keep it in check. It tightened his throat and changed the timbre of his voice. Could Spock hear that in his voice? Hear that he was afraid?

The sound of shovels scratched the top of his packed snow prison.

"It's getting cold. . . ."

Stiles shuddered through a sigh and this time saw his breath, as the chill from outside permeated the cockpit.

Another scratch—broader, brighter. They'd have him in a minute or two. Now he could hear voices above. Bootsteps. Shouts.

"Sir . . ."

"Yes?"

"I don't know . . . how well I'm going to do," he admitted.

"This is hardly routine for you," Spock offered. *"You are twenty-two."*

"Twenty-one." Miserable now, beginning to feel the pain in his shoulder through fading numbness, he tried to shift his feet but failed even to do that.

What did Spock mean? So he was twenty-one. So what?

Old enough to control simple fears. Old enough to put fear aside. What was a veteran like Spock really thinking of him?

He sank more deeply into his seat, let his legs go limp, flexed his good hand, and touched the frosted canopy near his face. "I guess this is where you tell me everything'll be all right eventually, and I'm brave and ought to be proud of myself."

"I hesitate to quote poetry," Spock said, and Stiles could almost see the hint of a smile.

So he smiled too. "Sir, I wouldn't know what to do with it if you did. I don't even read the insides of my birthday cards."

For a moment there was no sound from the now-distant coach, no response, no coddling. The comm unit crackled, struggling to pull in the spaceborne signal through systems that were probably broken or fried.

"I'm losing you, sir," Stiles said.

"Yes, your reception signal is thready."

"Should I try to boost?"

"Distance is a factor. No need to strain yourself. I'll boost from here."

Stiles's hand fell back to his side and he let himself go limp, trying to ease the ache in his head. A little shaving of frost fell from the canopy where he'd touched it. The flakes landed on his right cheek and stuck there, like a frozen tear. His face was too cold even to melt it.

"The Federation will negotiate for your freedom," Spock told him placidly. *"I'll see to it personally."*

"Don't make a spectacle," Stiles grumbled. "I don't want to be known as the little goof with the big rescue. Then somebody else'll be the hero and I'll just be the jerk who crashed in enemy territory and cost a mint to get back. I don't need that . . . God, my shoulder hurts . . . think they know how to set a human arm?"

"Yes, they know how."

Spock's voice was small now, but clear of static, patient and gentle, laden with understanding of what he was feeling. How could that be?

"I have worked with many humans in my lifetime. There is great comfort for me among them, and much to admire. Above all traits, I believe, I most admire their resilience. Be pliant, Eric. Once you survive this, you'll be a more valuable officer. And a better man."

Stiles heard the words, but it was as if he were listening to wind. Substantial, effective . . . but he didn't understand what

41

made it happen. An instant later he could barely remember what Spock had just said—all he remembered was the sound of his own name spoke so adaptably by that famous voice.

"What do you think I should do?" he asked simply. His throat was raw now. There were fumes in here. "If they don't kill me . . . what do I do to change? I already try so hard . . . how can I be better?"

Now that the question was asked, he steeled himself to listen, to remember a long sermon, the kind his grandfather used to lay on him when there was some lesson to be learned or some grave social gaff to be corrected. All the way home from wherever they were, talk, talk, talk, preach, preach, preach.

And that was why he was surprised. As sunlight broke through above his face and the snow was scraped away from the cockpit's canopy, as he saw the faces of Pojjana soldiers peel back the rocks and crud from his Starfleet coffin, Stiles absorbed Spock's final word. Only one word . . . it echoed and echoed, rolled and settled, it chimed a resonant bell tone. He would hear it for the rest of his life.

"Relax."

Chapter Four

HARD TO BREATHE. STUFFY.

Metal banging against metal. The whine of mechanical treads. Lower pitch than the aircraft. A hatch breaking open— and Stiles fell inelegantly forward and landed on a stone floor.

His head throbbed, his left shoulder and arm ached . . . at least the paramedics, or whatever they were, had bandaged the arm before stuffing him into the brig box on their plane. He'd thought it might've been broken, but it wasn't. His shoulder had been jammed into the side of the cockpit, numbing his whole arm. They'd given him a drug he thought might be poison, but turned out only to be a pain pill. For some reason, probably leverage, they didn't want him dead. Not yet.

Now he was here. He knew a prison cell when he saw one. Unlike Starfleet's fancy bright brigs, this one just had the old-fashioned titanium bars. Sure. Why use expensive energy beams to hold prisoners in when plain metal would do the same job and couldn't be shorted out?

Pressing his right hand to the stone floor, Stiles pushed himself from his knees to a sitting position. Tile, not stone. Big squares of rough-glazed tile. What was it his mother had called that color? Terra cotta.

Over his shoulder, the oval door or hatch or whatever it was that he'd come through clanked shut and barked loudly as it was locked from outside. Nobody had talked to him, nobody had counseled or advised him, nobody had told him what was going on or how long he would be here, or what the legal process would be. Did the Pojjans even have a legal process? How much of a coup was going on here? Was there a government in place at all?

Ashamed of his failure to do simple mission homework, Stiles realized he had no idea what to expect or any way to judge what had happened to him. The Pojjan soldiers had pulled him off the top of the mountain, bandaged his arm, run some kind of scanner over him, flown him back and dumped him into this cell. Was this a prison? Or just a holding cell? Would he be here for six months, or moved to a trial, a sentence, a hotel room?

"I'm not a criminal," he murmured, trying to sort all this out. "Not a rebel or terrorist . . . so what am I?"

With notable effort, he stood up on shaky legs. His head throbbed relentlessly. The cell was dry at least, and warm enough. Well, at least they weren't barbarians. And there was light. Not much—enough to see by, not enough to disturb sleep. All the lights were outside his cell, beyond the titanium bars. Probably they had learned that light fixtures could be cannibalized into lock-blowing bombs. He remembered that from the Academy alternative-energy course.

A bunk and mattress, a woolly blanket, a toilet, a sink.

"Welcome to Alcatraz," he grumbled with a sigh. "Hope they feed me."

"You'll be fed."

Stiles flinched back a step. His heart drummed.

"Who's talking?" he yelped. "Where are you?"

"In the next cell."

Stiles pressed against the bars, trying to see, but the cells were side by side and there was no doing it. The bars were cold against his cheek.

"Are you a prisoner?" he asked.

"Seems obvious."

A male voice. Sounded young. Not old, anyway. Sounded like it could be one of his own team.

"Are you a criminal?"

"My incarceration is political."

"Political . . . so's mine, I think. What're they going to do to us? Have they got courts on this planet? Are there laws?"

"Yes, they have laws."

"How soon will they—"

"Not soon. They're in turmoil here. The Federation is leaving."

"Yeah, I've heard that rumor . . ."

This was getting him no where. He couldn't see the other guy, and if he asked too many questions, that guy would be justified in asking questions also and Stiles would feel obliged to answer.

Then again, why not?

"Who are you? What's your name?"

"Zevon."

"Just 'Zevon'?"

"Yes. Who are you?"

"Eric Stiles."

"Human?"

"Uh-huh."

"Starfleet, then."

"How do you know that?"

"The only humans on this planet are either Starfleet personnel or Federation diplomatic corps workers. The Pojjana would never put diplomatic staff in prison."

"Ah . . . they'll harass the military but not the civilians. There's brainy."

"The military understands that capture is part of the job. The Pojjan know that."

Stiles shuffled to his cot and sat stiffly down, then sank back against the wall. "Are you saying that if I weren't Starfleet, they wouldn't put me wherever we are?"

"That's correct. They wouldn't have captured you at all. The Federation would be hostile if civilians were made political pawns. Starfleet is fairer game."

"Oh, that's great. . . ."

Lying back as he was, Stiles gazed at his uniform, at the black field of shirt and pants, the ribbed waistband, and the poppy-red shoulder band under his chin. It looked strange with the combadge missing. They'd taken it. So they knew it wasn't just jewelry.

"But wait a minute," he began. "I was guarding a coach full of civilians and the Pojjana tried to shoot us down. Why would they do that? Isn't that making them political pawns?"

"The Pojjana could have claimed the coach crashed. If they gained possession of the civilians alive, they probably would have put them back in the embassy and claimed some delay or other."

"Buying time?"

"Most likely. The Pojjana are clumsy with politics. They do things without knowing why."

"Just hedging their bets?"

"Perhaps. The lingering of a thousand civilians is easier to justify than the disappearance of one soldier."

Stiles flexed his legs and winced at the stiffness. "What you're saying is that I'm small potatoes."

"I would suspect so," Zevon confirmed quietly. "If that means what I infer."

"Yeah . . . mmm . . . ow . . ."

From the other cell, the man called Zevon quietly asked, "Are you injured?"

"My ship crashed. I got knocked around. I thought my shoulder was broken, but it's not. Mission was simple . . . if headquarters . . . if they'd just cued me in to the situation, none of this would've happened. They should've briefed me. I'm just an ensign. I'm not supposed to know everything. Somebody should've known this would happen . . . so they can have it. They don't come and get me? Fine. I'll stay here. I don't need Starfleet if they don't need me." Staring at the floor tiles between the frame of his bent knees, he sighed. "I have a date tomorrow night. . . ."

Prison. Prisoner of war? But there was no war. Why was he a prisoner? Did a cold war have prisoners? How long?

Ambassador Spock hadn't told him how long this might last. Now Stiles understood—the ambassador had just not known. He had deliberately evaded answering. The answer was bad. More than six months?

How long would it be before his hair got long enough to braid? How much longer before he actually started braiding it, just for something to do?

Staring ahead at the next few minutes, with an aching shoulder and a throbbing head, somehow the concept of months eluded him. Right now even the concept of lunch was eluding him. How long before he got hungry? Would they feed him? Was deprivation part of the torture regime? How much did this Zevon really know about Pojjan habits? If Zevon himself was Pojjan, he might not really know how they'd treat a human prisoner.

I'm on my own.

"I wouldn't be here if I'd had a better team," he complained. "Travis was the only one with any off-station experience. It's not my fault what happened."

"You were in command of a landing party?"

"It wasn't my fault!"

The other prisoner fell to silence. Stiles's own protest echoed briefly, then died. Ashamed and angry, he sat up and stared at the floor tiles, memorizing the grout. As if framed in each octagonal tile, scuffed and scratched, he saw his teammates' faces.

"Sorry . . ." he whispered. The faces all merged into one face, his own—scarred and shriveled like the picture of Dorian Gray sitting in the attic, hidden, corrupted with excesses.

He pressed a moist palm to his forehead, brushed back his hair, now gritty and sweat-matted, closed his eyes. Thoughts tumbled. Blames and guilts blended into a single nauseous mass.

"I shouldn't. . . ."

His voice pierced the tomblike quiet, then dissolved. He clamped his lips shut before he lost control of what popped out of them. Didn't know whether Zevon could hear him. Hoped not.

Hot in here. It hadn't been hot when he'd been dumped here. Was somebody playing with the temperature controls? Trying to break him down?

"It won't work!" He vaulted to his feet, skidding on the tile. When nothing changed, he paced. Across the cell, around the perimeter, along the bars, to the toilet, back to the bunk. There, he faced himself again.

He turned and continued pacing. His arms and legs ached. Why was he hurting more now than when he'd crashed?

"Do you feel anything?"

"I feel insulted. I feel like I'm being laughed at. I feel—"

"That's not what I mean. Do you feel anything unusual—anything physical?"

Stiles paused at Zevon's sudden return to the conversation. "Like what?"

"Pressure . . ."

"I've got a headache, if that's what you're asking."

"No! Are you standing?"

"What?"

Suddenly his eyes began to sting fiercely, his head to throb horridly, as if he'd fallen into a vat of acid. Had he been shot? Phasered? Some kind of Pojjan weapon? Cramps gripped his midsection and he grabbed the titanium bars of his cell, contracting against them until his knees couldn't fit between them anymore and he began to slip toward the floor. The floor was shaking! The walls were rumbling!

As he forced his eyes open, he saw the stone wall across from his cell now tattered and flaking before his astonished gaze.

Over a whine in his ears he shouted, "What's happening! What is this? An earthquake?"

"Lie on the floor! Quickly!" The other prisoner called over the increasing roar of collapsing stone and cracking mortar. "Lie face up! Put your arms flat at your sides! Breathe deeply!"

"What is this? What is this! Why is this happening!"

"It's the Constrictor! Lie down!"

Stiles pushed off the bars and rushed to the hatch through which he'd been dumped in here. He pounded until his fist rang with numbness. "Hey! Let us out of here! The building's coming down on us! Let us out of here!"

"Lie down, you fool," the other man said one more time.

"Ow—ah—ah—!" Grasping at his ringing head with both hands, Stiles staggered across the tiled floor, insane with new agony. As if iron bars were hanging from his limbs, brute force, like sheer invisible tonnage, pushed him to his knees. The floor came up to meet him and he collapsed forward, pressed physically to the cold tile as if crushed by a giant's palm.

With one last effort he dragged his right arm under him and managed to turn halfway over, then partially onto his back. After that he gave in to the rule of sheer might. He gasped as his flesh flattened against the tiles with such duress that he could feel the edges of the tile and the shape of the grout lines creasing his body. He stared, consumed with fear, at his own arms stretching out before him.

As his face lay against a tile, he saw a crack develop in the floor, small at first and then larger, running through the bars and out into the corridor, then up the wall. The building—

Trapped on his side, Stiles tried to raise his head, to follow the crack with his eyes, but his skull alone weighed a hundred pounds. His arms, sprawled out before him, actually began to bow into the shape of the floor over the indentation of a drain he hadn't even noticed until now. Insane with shock, he witnessed the surreal horror of his right arm breaking, his unsupported limb molding itself to the squared-off shape of the drain. His lips peeled back with sheer agony.

There, where his right arm lay shattered and compressed into the shape of the drain, a fissure opened in the floor, swallowing the drain's metal grate, dismembering the tiles, uncoupling the titanium bars as shriveling compression took over and the planet opened up.

Stiles felt himself fall, deadweight, strong-armed through a cracking floor, and saw in his last glance the mangled building unravel itself and cleave down upon him.

Beneath the grind and roar of utter demolition, he listened as if disconnected to the echo of his own cries.

Chapter Five

"CAN YOU HEAR ME?"

"You don't have to yell, Eric."

"We're doing whatever you say."

"Stiles?"

"The Federation will negotiate for your freedom. I'll see to it personally."

"Wasn't so hard."

"This is hardly routine for you. You needn't cheat yourself."

"Eric Stiles! Can you hear me?"

"Relax."

Voices pumped through a haze of agony. Had to answer them. How else would they find him?

Cold stuffy air lay against tons of crushed stone and the sharktoothed edges of cracked and disrupted floor tile that now formed more of a wall, bracing one side of a deep fissure.

Faint light swam above, dusty shafts of light, offering no comfort but instead framing the ugliness of what lay above and around.

Water dripped somewhere nearby. Hear it, smell it.

Feel it—his left thigh was soaked.

At least I've still got a leg.

Eric Stiles tried to raise the leg he'd just rediscovered. The knee came up a few inches, which forced him to balance by raising his head and shoulders—agony searing through his right arm, shoulders, and right side. He threw his head back and gritted his teeth. The effort drove him all the way to consciousness, suddenly, like hitting a rock, and his eyes shot open. The light he had seen as a blur now focused far overhead. It must be . . . forty feet up. Had that been the cell, up there? Was that the same light in the corridor outside his bars?

"I hear you. I'm trying to reach you."

Who was that?

Until he heard the other voice, this one clear and not far away, Stiles hadn't been aware that he was moaning, wincing out the sheeting pain in his right arm. Broken. He remembered now. It had been sucked into the shape of the tile drain, broken in at least two places.

Were the bones popping through the skin? Would he bleed to death from a broken arm?

"Eric Stiles, speak if you can."

No, leave me alone. I'm almost dead. Let me finish. Complete one thing. Follow through on this one thing.

Slowly, more slowly than the trickling of thought or water, his body adjusted to the constant pain. As he stopped struggling, stopped trying to lift himself, gradually his arm settled from searing mind-numbing agony to an acceptable throb with his fingers numb. The numbness itself hurt, but after a time he was able to concentrate on the hazy light far overhead and play mental games with it. He endured its mockery, accused it of fickleness, fielded its insults, and claimed it was impotent. Surging in and out of awareness, he conducted a conversation with the faint light and imagined that it was singing to him.

At that point, the fleeting thought that he might be delirious finally settled home and he cleared his throat just to hear his own voice. Just as he began to drowse again, something crashed—the sound of brick and tile falling.

Stiles flinched bodily and raised his head. "Who's there?"

"Zevon."

"Where are you?"

"Making my way to you. Can you come toward me?"

"My leg," Stiles gasped roughly, "it's pinned under something."

Only now did he comprehend that his leg was caught, only when he actually heard the words, even though he'd spoken them himself. Was the leg cut off? Just an imagined sensation? He could feel his toes. Was that important?

"Did the building collapse?" he asked. His words echoed slightly, enough to offer a sensation of cave dwelling.

Zevon's response filtered uneasily from far away. "A sinkhole has opened beneath the jail building. We fell into it. It may have saved our lives by relieving the stress at the critical moment."

"What stress?"

"The Constrictor. A particularly harsh one this time."

Stiles paused and concentrated on breathing. He'd heard that Constrictor word before. Where?

Resting his left hand on his chest, he felt himself breathe. In, out, in, and a sigh.

"This is . . . this is really . . . what's the word—ironic?"

"What is?" Zevon sounded closed-in, muffled.

"I pulled rank to get this mission."

"How did you?"

"The ensign who was up for duty that night, he was on my watch rotation. When I heard about somebody getting a chance to evac Ambassador Spock . . . what an opportunity! I rotated the other guy to an escort mission off the starbase. When the name for duty officer came up, it was mine."

Glancing around his jagged stone prison, Stiles noted with clearing eyes the truly freakish surroundings which would now only in the most generous of mists have resembled a building. Twisted pipes and structural supports lay in tatters around him, the walls of former street-level chambers now fractured in dozens of places, so that plasterwork, concrete sections, brackets, lathe, joists, and support rods showed their gory broken edges. His jail cell had been on the street level. Now he was forty feet below the street, in what could be described as a wide well-shaft walled in on all sides by the remains of the floors above.

"Still in the cell," he muttered.

Stone and metal collided somewhere in the dimness, behind a huge slab of concrete that must be the remains of the wall between his cell and Zevon's. How much of the broken building had wedged itself between them?

"Is there anybody else in here?" Stiles raised his head. "Wish I could move . . . I'm so . . . cold . . ."

"Can you see your bunk?"

Bunk? Oh—Stiles blinked and forced himself to figure out his surroundings. There was the toilet, standing on its head with a piece of support rod piercing the bowl. What if he had landed over there? What would that rod have done to his body?

"Has your bunk fallen somewhere near you?" Zevon asked again, more forcefully despite the muffling of the wall material between them.

Stiles turned his head to the left. "It's right next to me."

"Pull the blanket or the mattress on top of you. Cover yourself with it."

"Why?"

"Because you're going into shock."

"Oh, I'm just . . . it's just that my leg's stuck and . . . I can't. . . ."

"You're getting cold. The temperature down here is still—"

"Look, I don't even know you! You could be some kind of a murderer or a criminal. Why should I listen to you? You're coming over here to kill me, aren't you?"

"Pull the blanket over you. Cover your body."

"You just don't want me to see what you're going to do to me."

"Cover yourself, Stiles. Do it immediately. This is an order!"

His right arm shivered violently, transferring the shivering to his chest, his neck, and he suddenly tensed. The collapsed cell around him echoed with a grievous moan. He couldn't disobey orders. Starfleet officers had an obligation. Set a good example. He was older than all the others.

His left hand cramped briefly, shifted—he forced it upward. The bunk lay on his left, tipped up on one of its points and leaning against whatever was behind it. Supported by something he couldn't see . . . supported, as he had been by Travis,

Bernt, Andrea, the Bolt brothers, the whole team. The Evac Team.

"Come on, Eric, lift your hand. You can do it."

Travis Perraton stood up behind that bunk, holding the metal rim, edging the bunk toward his hand until Stiles's fingers touched the blanket.

"Pull it down." Jeremy was there too.

The woolly fabric was cool, but warmed almost immediately as he clutched it. Looking down at him, Travis and Jeremy detached the blanket from where it was tucked under the thin mattress, and the blanket fell onto his arm and shoulder with just a tug.

"Thanks," he murmured. "I knew you'd get here."

Travis nodded and looked at Andrea Hipp and Bernt Folmer. They reached down through the rubble and pulled the blanket over Stiles's chest.

Jeremy White's hand floated forward and tucked the blanket around Stiles's right ribs. "There you go, chief."

"What took you guys so long?" Stiles grumbled, smiling. "My right arm's broken . . . you guys really butchered this building. What'd you have to hit it so hard for? You could've just blown one wall. I could've walked right out. I guess you didn't want to take any chances. What a team . . . you're so great to me . . . I'm sorry I yelled at you."

"You always yell," Travis told him. "We quit listening a long time ago."

"*Long* ago," Andrea Hipp agreed with a grin.

"I'm glad to see you," Stiles told them. "There's some guy in the next cell . . . I think he's going to kill me."

"Why should he?" Andrea asked.

Bernt Folmer shook his head. "You're just nervous. Don't worry about him."

"But he's a criminal or something," Stiles protested.

"How do you know?"

"He's in jail, isn't he?"

Travis smiled and jiggled Stiles's knee. "So are you, light-foot."

Heartened by the presence of his team, Stiles raised his head again and surveyed the sheered-off slab of wall that pinned his right leg. "Why don't you lift this off me? I think I can stand up if you do. My toes are moving."

Uneasily Jeremy White glanced at Bernt. "Well . . . we can't."

"Why not?" Stiles blinked at him, then looked at Andrea and Bernt, then finally at Travis, from whom he would get the straight answer. "What's wrong?"

Travis Perraton leaned against a jagged rock piercing a crack in the wall. "We didn't make it."

"We tried to get you," Andrea added. "But they got us instead."

"What?" Shoving up on his one good elbow, Stiles almost immediately collapsed in a surge of shock and misery. "Aw, Travis . . . how'd you and Jeremy get out of the coach? Why'd you leave? Bernt, the fighters were guarding the coach! You were the Wing Leader . . . you had your orders. . . ."

"We didn't want to leave you," Bernt said.

"You're such a bag of emotions, Eric," Travis commented.

Jeremy splayed his hands in a shrug. "So we're ghosts. Could be worse. Eric, you're going into shock."

"Stay awake, Eric." Travis knelt beside him. "Eric, stay with me, lightfoot. Don't go to sleep. Are you listening? Open your eyes."

"Cover up," Andrea reminded.

"Okay, I've got my own orders, I get it." Pulling the blanket over his chest again, Stiles felt a series of moans run through his body. The sound was detached, as if made by a wheezing wind or a sighing pipe deep in the plumbing.

"Stay awake, Eric," Bernt warmly repeated. "That's an order."

"Aye aye," Stiles murmured. "I feel better now. I'm warming up. Thanks for looking after me."

Travis offered his continental maitre-d' smile. "Sure, lightfoot."

"We've got to go," Bernt said.

Stiles forced his eyes open again. "So soon?"

Andrea shrugged. "It's just that they hate aliens."

"See ya," Jeremy threw in.

Stiles sighed. "See ya. Hey, what about my arm?"

"I can set your arm, ensign." Another voice. Soothing and stable.

He turned his head to his right, and there in the haze of feeble light saw the one person who could sustain him in any crisis.

"Ambassador . . . you came," he rasped, as if thanking the famous man for dropping in at a party. "And I'm just gum on your shoe. . . ."

Spock tilted his elegant head accommodatingly and with his long hands caressed Stiles's demolished arm. "You're under great strain, ensign. I shall set your arm before I go. I have a splint here, but the arm will have to be lifted briefly. Relax."

The words were clear and inspired confidence. Stiles closed his eyes, understanding that there would be terrific pain and he would do better if he relaxed as ordered. Spock pressed a reassuring hand to Stiles's chest, as comfortingly as Travis or Jeremy might have done, then cradled Stiles's shattered limb. His expression became studious and determined.

Stiles closed his eyes tighter, turned his face away, and braced for punishment. When it came, the gripping anguish took him completely by surprise despite his preparation. To a young man in the prime of youth who had never had a broken bone, pain's sheer overdrive utterly disemboweled him. His head cranked back into the stone, his teeth gritted, and he was dimly aware of his body as it wrung and twisted. With every shred of self-control he possessed, he forced his right shoulder to relax and his arm to disengage from the cruelty as he felt his own bones grating.

A disembodied voice phasered gasps into the cool cellar, but he barely registered the sound as his own. Why was it taking so long? Did it take hour to set a bone? Why didn't Spock just cut the arm off? Stiles dealt with the loathsome pain and the sudden heaving of his stomach at this, his first taste of dynamic physical torment.

"Another moment . . ." Spock's voice was his lifeline, but for the first time he didn't believe the hollow reassurance. "Almost finished, ensign."

"Why do you have to hurt me?" Stiles moaned. "You're the only one I ever respected. . . ."

"One more wrap . . . relax now. Let me secure this. Your arm will adjust in a few minutes. Relax, Ensign . . . relax."

A gentle hand pressed to the hollow of his shoulder, poised there, and beneath the steadiness and reassurance of that contact Stiles let his neck and shoulders go limp, and finally convinced his legs to lie quiet. Then the nausea set in. His brow furrowed and his lips clamped against the surging in his stomach and throat. Moans shuddered through his body. He heard them, felt them, but could no more control them than harness the shattered building that now cradled him so far below the street.

His own groans wakened him from the drowse brought on by pain. The first concrete thing he noticed was that the searing jab of broken bones in his arm had drained to a manageable ache. Or perhaps it hurt more than he thought it did, but he was conditioned now to the racking and this was better than that. Desolation of spirit sank in on him, and he opened his eyes and looked to his right.

A narrow form stood over him, plucking at the wrappings on his arm. The slick dark hair seemed so familiar . . . the features somewhat less angular than he remembered, but close enough . . . soft light from overhead dipping into the curves of those famous pointed ears, which had come to represent such style and trust to anyone in the Federation. . . .

Stiles blinked his eyes clear and moved his right leg. The knee came up where he could see it. Torn pants.

His right leg? Wasn't it pinned under a rock?

"Did you move that by yourself?"

"With a lever," the other man said. The voice was different. "A piece of rod from the broken wall." He held up a three-foot remnant of wall rod, then set it down again. "It broke, but it did serve to move the slab from your leg. You're free now. Don't move, however. You're injured."

"I'll be fine," Stiles protested. "Takes more than an earthquake to get a Starfleeter down."

"Of course. Try not to move. I've splinted your arm with two bent pieces of linoleum and strips of my blanket. I hope it holds. Does it seem to pinch at all?"

57

"Where's everybody else?" Stiles asked, ignoring the other question. "Where'd they go?"

"Who?"

"The Evac Team. They were here . . . sit me up, will you, sir?" Stiles drew a full breath, the first one in a long time that wasn't cramped and tight. Oxygen surged into his body, clearing his head.

"You need not call me 'sir.' "

"But I can't just . . ."

"You may call me Zevon. I don't care for the other."

Stiles gazed briefly at the long fingers holding him gently in place. Now that his eyes were adjusted to the dimness and no longer blurred by pain, he surveyed that hand, the long dark red sleeve, the velvety padded jacket of gunmetal gray and with a turtleneck collar of the same dark red, and above that a stranger's face with somehow familiar features. The upswept eyebrows, dark eyes, becalmed face—but a young face. And the hair was not cut in the typically Vulcan slick helmet, but instead a rather roughly cut shag of cordovan brown, longer than Spock's, less orderly, tucked behind the lovely shell-shaped ears, the left of which had a small but noticeable scar, a slight nip out of the side edge. So he'd been through something, some time in the past.

Young, though. Not a hundred-plus-year-old ambassador with a stunning history spanning back to the first openings of deep space—someone else. Stiles struggled briefly with trying to figure Zevon's age, but in his condition he couldn't compute human years against anybody else's.

"Did I lose consciousness?" Stiles asked.

"Briefly," Zevon admitted. "I have no anesthetic to give you, nor any pain medication. Sad thing, for a scientist to be unprepared."

His expression was efficient, as one might expect, yet somehow unashamedly sympathetic. Odd . . .

"I guess we've been down here alone the whole time." Stiles glanced past Zevon, just to make sure he wasn't seeing Travis or Jeremy anymore. Or even the ambassador he so deeply revered. Somehow they'd gotten him through the worst, and retired.

"In fact," Zevon confirmed, "I believe we were alone in the jail building when the Constrictor came."

"Constrictor . . . so what are you doing here, anyway?"

"I am a political prisoner. I was hunted and kidnapped."

"You personally? They wanted you?"

"No. Anyone of my race."

"Why? I mean, I'm just here because my ship crashed. That's how they got me. Nobody hunted me down. Why would they hunt you down? Is it just because they hate aliens?"

"Some, but I command a particular kind of ship. They thought my presence here would give them leverage."

"You *command* a ship? You said you were a scientist, not a captain!"

"Primarily I am a scientist. The command is a position of royal favor."

With a small shake of his head, Stiles frowned. "I never heard of anything like that in the Vulcan fleet."

"Not Vulcan." Zevon passively adjusted the position of Stiles's right arm. "Romulan."

Stiles drew one breath, sharply, and heaved himself to a partially sitting position, up on his right hip. The blanket slipped from his body and fell to one side. He reached over his own form, fished for the piece of rod he knew was here. His fingers struck the rod, knocked it a few inches, and he found it again. In a single swipe he raised the rod, knocked the Romulan along the side of his face, drove him away, and pointed the sharp end of the rod.

"You get away from me!" he shouted. "Stay away from me!"

Zevon backed off, said this once above a murmur of exhalation, not in pronounced pain. The numbness each shove. The muscles are the last ones they'll cut. You can't be willing ... to move ... to sacrifice. Maybe you can take a single step

"I'll take all the steps I need," Stiles held the rod steady between them, like a divining wand, ready to use it either way.

His right shoulder and arm ached dismally now as he cranked upward. Throbbing inside the striped wrapping, Zevon had managed to grind the part with the elbow bone into the blanket on Stiles's side, and that would prove an advantage as he struggled to get out of this place.

Chapter Six

FROM ACROSS THE RAGGED REMAINS of their two crushed cells, Zevon pressed a hand to his face where Stiles had struck him.

"I am not your enemy," he said. "I have no reason to hurt you. We'll both die if you hold me off like this for long."

"All Romulans are our enemies," Stiles blistered. "You just keep your distance!"

"But I freed you from the stone. I set your arm."

"To use me as some kind of hostage! I've been stupid enough for one day! I'm not being stupid again. You stay back. I'm getting out of here."

Zevon lowered his hand. His face showed a single bruised cheekbone, but no open wound. "We must help each other. The prisoners are the last ones they'll dig out. You can't possibly climb out of here, ensign. I doubt you can take a single step."

"I'll take all the steps I need." Stiles held the metal rod between them like a club or sword, ready to use it either way. His right shoulder and arm pumped fiercely now as he exerted himself, throbbing inside the splinted wrapping. Zevon had managed to splint the arm with the elbow bent instead of straight at Stiles's side, and that would prove an advantage as he tried to get out of this hole.

The nasty pit of broken rock wall and plaster sheets and plumbing spun around him suddenly, jagged edges and smooth sheets blending into a single blue-gray cylinder.

"Lie down," Zevon suggested, "before you pass out."

"I don't listen to Romulans!"

His chest heaving with effort, Stiles let his body rest slightly on the edge of a folded bolt of linoleum flooring. He had no idea where the flooring had come from—there had been nothing like this in the holding area. Probably from one of the floors above. How many stories had collapsed on them? Since he had never seen the building from the outside, he had no way of knowing.

Thinking of something else, he looked at his right arm. One irregularly cut sheet of linoleum had been formed around his lower arm and another around the upper arm, held in place by strips of wool. A single wedge of metal slat, some kind of corner brace, had also been strapped there, and was holding his arm in a bent position. By resting the arm on his lap, he could relieve the strain in his shoulder.

"We'll just wait," he gasped. "Somebody'll come to rescue us. They'll come for us . . . they'll get here."

"Ensign Stiles," Zevon attempted slowly, "we are prisoners. There's been a Constrictor, a bad one. The Pojjana will be cleaning up for months. They'll be digging the survivors and bodies out for at least two weeks. Two of your weeks, I should specify. While we may live that long, certainly you can't hold that rod against me for so long. Is there a point in holding it now?"

"There is," Stiles forced through a tight throat. "You're a Romulan. I'm Starfleet. I don't have to believe a thing you say. Maybe this wasn't an earthquake at all. Maybe you bombed the building, you or your people. The Pojjans could dig us out in an hour."

"And so a standoff begins?" Zevon folded his arms, shook his head, and offered a parental gaze. "You make yourself suffer for nothing. I am no soldier."

"I know what you are." His hand and arm shuddering under the weight of the metal bar, Stiles drew his legs up under him and tried to maneuver to a better position. The effort exhausted him, made his head spin. A dark tunnel formed on either side of his vision and he realized he was passing out. With a single heave he rearranged himself. Fighting a sudden clutching muscle spasm in his back, he twisted sideways and managed to shift until he could lean back against the tilted mattress on the bunk he had never yet slept upon.

Sleep . . . sounded so nice right now . . . deliberately he drew long, steady breathes until his head cleared and the tunnel-vision faded back. "We'll starve in here, like this."

Zevon nodded. Had he just said something like that? Stiles thought the conversation sounded familiar.

"I hear water," the Romulan said. "If we have water, we can survive."

"Yeah? How long's a week on your planet?" Stiles blinked to focus his eyes. He saw his bandaged left arm shiver as it held the metal rod toward Zevon. One arm bandaged, the other broken and splinted.

Tightening his folded arms, Zevon leaned back against the cracked wall behind him. "I'm counting in your weeks. I know how humans think."

Stiles raised his head from where he had allowed it to rest back on the upright mattress. "Oh? And how is that? Just how do we think? Since you know us so well, you who've never met one of us before, how do humans *all* think? For your information, soldier, humans are the least like each other of all the races around. That's what my grandfather told me, and he got it from nobody less than Captain James Kirk himself. So you just tell me again how all humans think."

"I meant no insult."

"Stay away from me."

Zevon held up a peaceable hand and nodded. "You must pull the blanket back over yourself. You'll go into shock again if you fail to stay warm."

"I'll take care of myself, thanks." Trying to appear in control, Stiles held the rod higher between himself and the Romulan, doing his best to convey an ongoing threat. "Spock expects me to act right . . . get along here and . . . be an officer. I won't let him down. Somehow he'll know how I did. I've got to make him proud. . . ."

Tilting his head, Zevon asked, "The ambassador? Is that who you were evacuating?"

"Sure was. Did it, too. He's out and you can't have him."

"We don't want him, ensign. Please try to relax and put that—"

"Don't you tell me to relax! Don't you say that word to me! That isn't your word."

"Very well . . . I'll find another word . . . with whom did you have a date tomorrow night?"

"Huh?" Stiles narrowed his eyes. Was this man telepathic? "How'd you know . . . her name's Ninetta. Ninetta Rashayd. She works down in atmospheric control at the starbase. Y'know, the base life support. Air. Took me two weeks to pronounce her name right so she wouldn't give me that look when I asked her out. Not that it matters much now. . . ."

"What kind of look?"

"Well . . . *that* look. The one that tells you to keep your mouth shut and don't even ask." His quivering left arm sagged a little, the rod now resting on his knee. "Travis used to rib me about it. Jeremy used to imitate the look. He was really good at it . . . really funny. I wonder if they're really dead. . . ."

"I beg your pardon?"

"I shouldn't have yelled at them," Stiles murmured, scouring the recent past, smelling his mistakes. "They were doing everything I said to do . . . they were with me. And I gave them hell because I couldn't take a little ribbing."

"Hardly matters now. Please put the blanket back on yourself. Your face is going pale—"

"What did you say made this Constrictor thing happen? Did you tell me? If you did, I forgot it all."

"Graviton waves," Zevon patiently explained. Clearing a place for himself, he sat down on something Stiles couldn't see. "They originate in space and bathe the planet. A recurring disaster for the Pojjana. As unpredictable as lightning-lit wildfires. When the waves strike the planet, everything suddenly gets two, three, or even five hundred percent heavier. What you felt was the pressure of yourself suddenly weighing several hundred pounds. Blood trying to slog through compressed veins, muscles screaming for relief. . . ."

"I remember that part."

"The Constrictor causes massive shifts in tectonic plates, tidal waves, earthquakes, as you call them. Buildings collapse, air vehicles crash . . . some people suffocate if it lasts more than a few seconds . . . elderly people are crushed to death by their own weight. . . ." Waving his hand at their surroundings, Zevon glanced up into the cylindrical pit that trapped them. "Sinkholes and fissures open up under people while they're pinned helplessly to the ground. . . ."

The rod sagged a little more, finally resting against Stiles' leg with his limp hand upon the close end. He gazed at Zevon, listening to the ghastly narrative just as he had listened all his life to the stories of trial and triumph with Captain Kirk and Mr. Spock at the helm of their legendary starship. This story, though, had a glaze of the horrific. It was real. He'd just been through it.

How many other people out there were suffering? What had happened to those rioters in the courtyard? The people in the other embassies lining that brick area?

"How long's this been going on?"

"Nine years," Zevon said. "The first Constrictor wiped out a fifth of the planet's population. Nearly a billion people died."

"A *billion?*" The word pulsed in Stiles' head, cooling down the throbbing of his arm and back. How many million was a billion? Why couldn't he do the mathematics? He was a pilot . . . he could multiply figures . . . do the trigonometry for atmospheric . . . for . . . landing. . . .

A *billion.* The number grew and grew, pressing him down beneath the utter oppression of its swelling. If so many could die, he could endure some discomfort. A broken arm abruptly seemed surmountable, his moans and winces petty.

"Yes," Zevon said. "At first I could scarcely absorb such a number. Now I can put a face to each one."

"Why would you care so much about this Constrictor thing?" Stiles asked.

But Zevon did not answer that. "Half the buildings were destroyed," he continued instead. "Countless trillions of tons of planetary material suddenly heavier for a few critical, deadly moments . . . even the most stoic among us was disturbed to his core. The people of the planet worked valiantly to rebuild. Then it came again, and we knew it was a recurring phenomenon. After the second time, they gave up rebuilding and concentrated on structural shoring of the buildings and bridges which had been strong enough to survive the first two. They've constructed pressure-tolerant housing and connected buildings so the structures could hold each other up . . . I could liken this to a meltdown in a nuclear plant. Now the Pojjana hate all aliens, who brought this thing upon them. If they could put the aliens off the planet, perhaps the Constrictor would go with them. They've scrubbed their planet clean of all who were not native, and still the blight from space has struck on. It will continue to strike, and they will continue to hate you and me and all aliens for what we have done to them. Periodically the Constrictor will send out a roaring burp of radiation into subspace, which causes waves of gravitons. There is no turning it off . . . it will go on indefinitely now. Our meager lifetimes will never see the end of it."

Something in the Romulan's voice, something in his bearing and the set of his shoulders caught Stiles with an unexpected wave of empathy. Zevon's arms were still folded, as if to protect himself, and he gazed not at Stiles but at a nearby pile of russet tiles that no longer resembled a floor. He seemed resigned to the facts, but troubled by hearing them so clinically reviewed in his own voice.

Again, with a different tone, Stiles raised the question that his clearing mind insisted needed asking.

"How do you know so much about this?"

In a clear silence that now fell, moisture dripped from an unseen pipe, draping its solemn percussion on Stiles' question and Zevon's answer.

"I caused it."

"Nobody told me the Romulan Empire was at war with these people!"

At such a declaration, the walls crackled and vibrated, pebbles shivered down the tilted slabs into the sinkhole that had trapped the two unfortunate prisoners.

Across the well, the young Romulan's brows rose at Eric

Stiles' abrupt statement. "War? Oh . . . no, no, there is no war. This was . . . utterly unintentional."

Curbing a lifetime of parochialism for the moment, Stiles reined in his assumptions. "Well . . . what happened, then?"

"This sector is run by the Bal Quonnot, on another planet in this system. They allowed us to conduct quantum-warp experiments here."

"Us? The . . . Romulan Empire?"

"Yes."

"You?"

"Yes. The Pojjana have been struggling for identity amid the Bal Quonnot administration. The Pojjana did not want to deal with the Empire."

"I don't think I'd deal with you either," Stiles said. "If you caused this thing."

Zevon actually nodded, perhaps in agreement, but certainly in understanding. "The Pojjana let the Federation court them for membership, to see if an alien science could retract what another alien science had done to them. The Federation went so far as to establish a planetary outpost."

"How many of these things have happened?"

"Six, now. In nine years. Not in predictable intervals. The Pojjana led the Federation along, but avoided committing to membership, hoping you would help. They wanted the benefits but not the obligations."

"It's happened before," Stiles confirmed. "I've heard of planetary governments trying to get the best of both worlds, refusing to make the decision but still accepting Federation protection and help."

"The Federation is disappointed," Zevon went on. "To your credit, you practice what you preach. The sector is red now."

Stiles paused to fill his lungs with a full breath. His shoulders squeezed in a muscle spasm, and he closed his eyes briefly. "That's what Spock said . . . red sector. I don't know what it means. . . ."

"It means many things. Many banishments, many edicts, many restrictions."

Stiles cleared his throat, and the effort made his ribs ache.

"How do you know so much about . . . stuff I'm supposed to know?"

"All Imperial royal family members are well-schooled in astral politics."

Raising his head sharply, Stiles blurted, "Royal family!"

"Yes."

He stared, but Zevon did not meet his eyes. "How close . . . how high . . ."

"The Emperor is my mother's brother. I am fourteenth in line for the throne."

"Is that . . . close?"

"In a population of two hundred billion inhabiting ninety planets, it is considered very close. However, it's unlikely that I shall ever actually take the throne. Certainly I have no desire to take it."

A cold rock formed in Stiles's chest as he digested the fact that he was involved in something with far more depth than he had first imagined. What moments ago had been two minor players in somebody else's huge drama now became something entirely different.

"How did they capture you?" he asked. "If you're so . . . royal."

"I made the error of accompanying a landing party to take measurements of—not that it matters. I forgot I'd been declared a public enemy. There were bounty hunters. They turned me over to the government. That riot out there . . . it was sparked by my presence here in the city."

"And the government is holding you here? Sounds like they wanted the riots to spark. Why else would they keep you here?"

With a nod, Zevon congratulated him. "Very possibly. This is not a usual holding area for political prisoners. They're usually held in the mountains."

"So we're hostages?"

"Certainly we carry some incendiary value for leverage," Zevon contemplated, "but neither the Empire nor the Federation can cavalierly enter a sector declared red by any major power. That is one of the few agreements between the Federation, the Empire, the Klingons, Orions, Centaurans, and others that has in fact stood the test of time and trouble. Compromise of that is considered irremediable. Relations, friendly or strained, would change instantly. The Pojjana may hope to tempt all that, but . . ." The young Romulan shook his head, a gesture of clear understanding of the situation. "You and I . . . we are on our own here for some time, I should think."

"Alone," Stiles echoed, "on a planet full of people who hate everybody who isn't them."

Shift the legs again. He forced himself to adjust. His shoulders seemed like water now. In his hand the metal rod was like ice and suddenly heavy. His elbow quivered as he tried to continue holding the rod up.

"You're a captain?" he asked, fighting for concentration.

"Centurion. I have . . . I *had* command of a science vessel. My command was a royal favor. It's common to give lower royalty command of royal barges. I thought myself very lucky not to be carting one of my own relatives about in a barge. I always remained aware that I hadn't earned command. I ceded most ship responsibility to my subcommander. The crew understood . . . they never spoke ill of me. What I earned was status as a fully qualified astrophysicist. I was supervising the unit conducting quantum-warp experiments that set up a sympathetic subspace vibration of free-floating gravitons. Now the Constrictor breaks on the shores of the Pojjan planet. And no one will ever stop it."

Zevon dropped his gaze to the messy excuse for a floor. He didn't look up anymore.

"I'm something of an embarrassment to my family," he went on, so quietly that Stiles could barely hear him. "I'm not . . ."

"A 'leader of men'?" Stiles supplied.

As odd as it now seemed to see someone who looked like Zevon return a smile, the Romulan did in fact grin mildly. "Just to prove it, if you said that to any of my uncles or brothers, they would kill you just to prove differently."

Returning the grin, Stiles chuckled. "Call my mother a sow, but don't tell me I'm no leader of men?"

"Something like that."

As Stiles felt his small troubles shrink to inconsequence, he gazed at Zevon and absorbed what he had heard. A hundred questions—none good—crackled in his mind.

"Well, here we are then," Stiles groaned. "A senior duty ensign who finagled his way into command of a landing party because of a family connection with Ambassador Spock. Big me, I thought I could distinguish myself. You know what I see when I look up the ladder? Captain Stiles, Lieutenant Stiles, Lieutenant Commander Stiles, heroes of the Romulan wars, officers on starship service . . . and little Ensign Stiles, who died in the pit after botching a simple evac." He let his head drop back and gazed up, far up, to the patch of dim light at the top of the hole. "I wish I were Ensign Anybody Else."

"Surrounded by giants," Zevon offered. "No wonder you could barely see."

Registering only slightly the favor just done him, Stiles clung instead to the sorrow and shame. "So here I am," he trudged on, "trapped in a sinkhole with a Romulan duke who doesn't want the command he's got, and a collapsed building's about to come down on us. Aren't we pathetic? If you had any emotion, you'd probably cry."

Sharply Zevon kicked at a plank that lay between them, sending it clacking into another position. His eyes hardened. "I am *not* Vulcan," he snapped, and instantly looked away again.

The reaction was so sincere that Stiles almost reached out physically to yank back his words. "Sorry," he offered. "You can pretty much count on me to say the wrong thing. Look, if you were in the sector conducting experiments—everybody does that. Quantum warp . . . that's tricky business. There's nobody who knows everything about that. It's almost not even science. It's practically magic. If something went wrong, it's not your fault."

"It was my fault," Zevon insisted. He pressed a hand to his left thigh and seemed to hurt himself with his own touch. "I should've stood up to my superiors when I first saw what the result might be. The graviton impulses were too erratic. I knew that. I knew it before we started. I should never have condoned the switch-on. As senior scientist, I had the right to postpone."

"Why didn't you, then?"

"I was . . . timid. Yes, I was the senior authority, but only because of my bloodline. There were other scientists who were more qualified quantum specialists. They warned me . . . but I was afraid to fail."

So familiar. Why did everybody have to go through this? Just doing their jobs, and all this had to happen. Sitting here in the near-darkness, three levels below the street, cradled in wreckage and out of the line of sight of any judgmental forces, Eric Stiles released himself from the bondage of prying eyes and pointless opinions. How foolish did he have to be to keep holding this weapon on Zevon?

If only he could put it down.

With a cleansing sigh, he muttered, "Listen, I . . . I feel. . . ." In his left hand, the metal rod wobbled between them, stubbornly holding its position. "Do me a favor, will you? Come over and . . . hold this for me."

Across the wreckage, Zevon blinked, stood up stiffly, and moved toward him.

Stiles parted his lips and started to say something else, but in sudden punctuation of Zevon's dire prophesy, a loud crumbling noise erupted over their heads. Buried in a gray cloud burping from above, Zevon disappeared as several large chunks of building material and a gout of rubble shattered through the hole in the floors above them, chittering like a rockslide, and came sheeting down into their chamber. The rain of rock and pebbles hissed furiously and crashed in a million pieces onto the desk of their little area. Stiles threw his working arm over his face and bent to one side, but he couldn't move far enough to avoid being painted with dust and grit. The metal rod he had claimed as a weapon flew out of his hand and clanked somewhere in the dimness. Cold, stinging debris sheeted his body. The Pojjan guards had taken away his padded vest, gloves, and knee pads, leaving only his daywear uniform to fend off the sharp bits. He felt himself being cut in a hundred tiny places.

As soon as the sound faded, he shoved himself up on his left elbow and twisted around. "Zevon? Where are you?"

In response, he only heard the sound of Zevon coughing somewhere in the cloud of dust. Alive, at least.

Stiles pushed up on his elbow. "Are you okay?"

Out of the puff of stone dust, shimmering paint fragments

and insulation, Zevon finally and slowly came to his feet. Rock bits sheeted off his back and shoulders as he stood and limped over the jagged wreckage to Stiles' side, where he braced himself on the thing Stiles was sitting upon.

"You okay?" Stiles asked again.

Zevon wiped dust from his face. "What is 'okay'?"

"You don't know? Something tells me you speak English, right?"

"Classroom English."

"Oh. I guess it got started with two alphabetical letters, O and K. It means . . . agreement. All right. Well. No idea why it would mean that."

"I see . . . yes, then, I am both O and K."

"But you're limping."

"A piece of this rod went through my thigh. I pulled it out."

"What? You got speared by a piece of that stuff?"

"Yes, when we first fell—"

"Come here! You could be bleeding to death! Let me see your leg."

Turning to show Stiles a crudely bandaged part of his thigh above the knee, Zevon winced and tolerated Stiles's tucking the strips of blanket which now bound each of them. "A few moments ago you were willing to spear me with a piece of this material."

"Well, never underestimate the capacity of Eric Stiles to make a dunderhead of himself. You're still bleeding here. That stuff's blood, isn't it? The green, uh—"

"Yes. I thought it had stopped."

"It hasn't. Let me—come a little closer. Your pant leg is soaked with blood. God . . . we gotta stop this. Pad the wound with something . . . just a minute."

As Zevon gripped a standing slab and winced, Stiles ripped apart the edge of the mattress near him and pulled out a wad of stuffing. He folded the stuffing into a crude pad, then worked it between the blanket strip and the wound on Zevon's leg, unfortunately causing considerable pain, until Zevon could barely stand when it was over.

"That'll help," Stiles hoped. "Come here. Take the weight off it. Sit here next to me."

He smoothed a place on his slab and pulled Zevon to his side. They sat leg to leg, facing each other, as Stiles adjusted the knot on Zevon's bandage. "It didn't pierce through your leg, did it? You could be bleeding in two places. I can't tell—"

"No," Zevon told him, his voice weak now. "No . . . a simple puncture . . ."

Stiles looked at him and paused. "You dragged yourself all the way from your cell to mine, through that wreckage, with your leg impaled like this?"

"I thought you would die if I didn't come." As pebbles continued to trickle around them, Zevon dug through the rubble to the blanket that had fallen off Stiles. Without meeting Stiles's eyes, he pressed the blanket back around the ensign's chest and hips and tucked it as well as possible. "We must keep you warm. You could still go into shock."

Surveying his companion, Stiles allowed himself to be cared for by these unlikely hands. "Don't take this wrong," he began a moment later, "but why would you care? We don't know each other. I could've been just a garden-variety criminal. Why would it matter so much to you if I died?"

For many moments Zevon was silent, though obviously troubled. He tucked and retucked the blanket two or three times before the ringing question demanded attention.

"Because the count is crushing me," he said.

Stiles frowned. "What count?"

Settling his hands in his lap, Zevon sat suddenly still. He sighed roughly, and his expression took on a shield of burden. His eyes crimped. He couldn't look at Stiles.

Again he sighed.

"Tyrants have made names for themselves by murdering a thousand people," he slowly said. "Ten thousand, a hundred thousand . . . a million. I have surpassed them all. There are no Hitlers, no Yum Nects, no Stalins or Li Quans who can compete with me. Among all the men and women of the galaxy, you have the privilege of sitting with someone who is utterly unique. You see, I'm the only person, anywhere, on any world, living or dead . . . who has killed a billion people."

* * *

As he sat on his rock, gazing at Zevon and hearing the echo of true burden, feeling as if he had known this man all his life, Eric Stiles grew up ten years in ten seconds. The urge to say something, to trowel away the grief with mere words, failed him entirely. There were no words for this. Not this.

Rather than flapping his gums as usual, he was completely disinclined to speak at all. Instead he shifted his good hand a few inches and gripped Zevon's forearm in a sustaining way, and did not shrink from the contact. Empathy flowed through the simple touch. The concept of billions of people dead at a single sweep overcame them both and seemed oddly tangible. For an instant or two, critical instants, Stiles totally comprehended the number.

Then, as all huge things do, the grasp of such volume fled and he was left only with the tremendous drumming regret that Zevon must have borne all these years. It wasn't the kind of thing that got better with time. Some things didn't.

There had to be another effort, a different one. One that looked forward for a change.

And that view was tricky for Eric Stiles, but for the first time in his life he didn't care what had happened in the past. For the first time, the future was everything.

With his hand still pressed to Zevon's arm, Stiles spoke quietly, firmly.

"I'm here now. This is where I am. Things are going to be different for both of us. We're getting out of here eventually, and when we do, everything's changing. You and I have both been dragged along by our situations like being caught in a river current or something. It's all we've been able to do just keeping our faces up out of the water all our lives. This . . . it's got to stop. We have to get our own grip on things."

Zevon gazed at him with all the fascination and confusion of a child looking into a kaleidoscope. "How can we?"

"By making sure that things are different because we're here." Stiles hitched himself up to a better position, still holding firmly to Zevon's arm. "When they pull us out of this hole, we're going to still be alive. Then we're going to go to work. We're gonna pay back the universe for all the goofs and gaffs we've made before. We're not going to think about escaping or fighting. This is our planet now. We have a lot to do before the next Constrictor hits."

Mystified, perhaps wondering if his companion were delirious, Zevon narrowed his eyes. "What?"

Heartened by his own words and by the new determination welling in his heart, Stiles willed his conscience into line and saw the future as a clear tunnel of purpose.

"I'll tell you what," he said. "We're going to *save* a billion people."

Chapter Seven

Four Years Later,
Federation Standard Time

"ZEVON, I THINK WE'VE GOT something this time! Look at this!"

"If I'd had the right equipment, this could've been found months ago."

"It reads like a Richter scale! We're actually picking up spaceborne disruption. Watch this."

"But not focused. No way to tell if we have minutes or hours, or even days."

"But we know this time that it's coming. That's something!"

"There hasn't been a Constrictor in more than two years. We've predicted it twice before. The first time we predicted the Constrictor would come in three weeks. It came in three hours. The second time, nothing happened at all."

"But we learned from those mistakes!"

"They won't believe us, Eric."

"But this time we *know!*"

"They won't believe us."

The lab smelled of a burning circuit. Off to Stiles's right, in the corner, the tired dust collector clacked and whirred, creating a sense of action where in fact there was little.

His taxed back muscles shuddered as he sank back in his

chair. "How can we convince them? What do you think we should do? It's not like we can threaten Orsova, and he's got the keys to all the telephones."

Beside him in the only other chair, Zevon seemed more troubled than vindicated by their good work today and the breakthrough they'd been waiting for, which now blinked before them on the overworked spectrometer, its flickering screen data reflected in the cold contents of their two soup-bowls.

"You need to eat," Zevon said, his voice a rasp of fatigue and frustration.

Only now did Stiles realize that his partner was looking not at the glimmering jewels on the screen, but at the filmy soup.

Stiles pressed back and stretched his arms. "Four years of horse-drool soup. So I skip it once in a while. So what? *Limosh t'rui maloor.*"

Zevon looked at him. *"Telosh li cliah maheth."*

Stiles felt abruptly self-conscious and guilty about his appearance. He almost never looked in the mirror over the sink back in their cell anymore—he even trimmed his beard without looking. If he didn't look, he could convince himself from moment to moment that his cheeks were not so sunken beneath the scruffy yellow beard he'd allowed to grow there, his eyes not dull, he could imagine the fullness of youth and the sheen of health he had once possessed and not even noticed in those days. He could ignore the bruises on his temples and the black blotches under the sleeves of his sweater. At least they'd given him a sweater.

He'd stopped looking in mirrors a long time ago, right about when the beard had stopped helping him hide his deteriorating physical condition. All he could tell from the beard was that he was still blond and hadn't gone prematurely gray from the daily stress and struggle.

Over the past four years the Pojjana behavior had been frequently baffling, inconsistent, sometimes maddening, sometimes solicitous, as political temperatures surged or chilled. Things changed every few months—except for a couple of things. The most consistent parts of his life and Zevon's were this lab and the prison's assistant warden, who unfortunately did not have enough to do.

"They've let us come to the lab almost every day," he voiced, shifting from just thinking to also speaking his thoughts. "Why wouldn't they listen to what we find out?"

Weary, Zevon simply gazed at him, seeing something other than the problem of convincing the Pojjana that there might be a way to save lives from the Constrictor. Lately Zevon had had more trouble concentrating, and Stiles was worried. They needed this breakthrough, not just for the billion, but for the two of them. They needed sanity and purpose, some reason to rise above the endless sense of being broken down and dull as barbells. After four years, they needed a win.

Stiles shifted uneasily under Zevon's toil-worn gaze, knowing that the Romulan saw him clearly and hated the sight. A shaft of burning pain ran through Stiles's innards, but he battled to keep it out of his face. He knew Zevon didn't miss it, though. He wasn't fooling anybody.

"Stop watching me," he protested when he could speak again.

"You're in pain, aren't you?"

"No."

"You should eat. It always helps."

"It helps because it makes me throw up, and then I'm too weak to feel anything. Typical Romulan logic."

"Typical Eric defiance," Zevon muttered, his eyes deeply solicitous and sad.

For a moment they simply looked at each other. Eventually, in his mind Stiles stopped seeing his own demolished physical condition and started seeing Zevon's. Zevon had started out typically lean, as was natural for his genetics, but four years ago he'd been strong and well-nourished, with good muscle tone in his arms and shoulders and a glow of privilege in his face. Now his complexion was sallow and his arms were thin. His hair had lost its mahogany luster and had grown below his shoulders. He kept it out of his way by simply pushing it behind his ears. Being Vulcanoid ears, they did the job very well. He was less inclined to bother cutting his hair, though Stiles occasionally offered a trim when he was cutting his own. Strange—Stiles, so used to Starfleet spit-and-polish, had made a silly effort to cling to neatness during their four years as political prisoners, even trimming his nails and cuticles just to have something to do. He was the one who did their laundry and mended the rips in their clothing.

He would've expected the same, even more, from a prince of the Romulan royal line, but Zevon didn't really care what he looked like. His long-suffering uniform, stained and tired, would've dissolved from his shoulders if Stiles hadn't bothered keeping the seams stitched. The only echo of civilization offered them here was their privilege to use the lab, and the fact that every couple of days they got showers. The Pojjana hadn't built a new jail. They'd just pushed the old one back up from the pit and nailed it together. A concrete floor now replaced the tiled one Stiles had first seen when he'd been thrown in here. Generally speaking, though, the food stunk, the quarters were dank, the mattresses sagged, the floor was cold, and the light was bad. Otherwise, home sweet home.

"I wish I had a communicator," Stiles mentioned. "Just one, and I could broadcast this new information to the whole planet. *Somebody'd* listen." Shifting his weakened legs, he added, "I don't miss home very often, but at moments like this I do."

Zevon rubbed his chilly hands. "The silence from home is an old story now. The royal family must not know I'm here, or they would have come by now. They must think me dead. The Pojjana must not be communicating with the Romulan government, or word of my presence would filter out."

"The Pojjana aren't about to tell the empire you're here. You're their trump card. Why should they stir up trouble? And if it comes, they want you here as leverage."

Uneasy with this line of talk, Zevon grew irritable. "My people would come if they knew. We've discussed this enough before."

"Well, mine wouldn't," Stiles concluded. "Obviously. Because they sure as hell know I'm here."

"The Federation declared the sector red, so they have to observe it or they can't expect anyone else to. It has nothing to do with you personally, Eric. Ambassador Spock would've had you out of here if influence mattered."

"If they made it away from the planet alive. They could all be cosmic dust for all we know."

Zevon turned to him. "Eric, you must cling to better hopes. I've had to watch you deteriorate physically, it's taken its toll on us both, but I refuse to watch your hopes turn to dust. Spock expects you to behave like an officer and a gentlemen. I expect that also."

Stiles grinned. "Talk, talk." He gestured at the vibrations playing out on the data screen. "Look at that . . . here we sit with information that could save the billion, and we can't figure out how to get the word to anybody farther up than Orsova. He'll eat it, probably choke, then hit me."

"He is a victim of alien backlash. The Pojjana no longer know whom to trust. You and I are convenient representatives of all the trouble brought down upon these people by the Constrictor. If they knew it was I personally who had—"

Defying the numbness in his legs and shoulders, Stiles launched forward and grasped Zevon's arm. "Quiet! Shut up. Don't take chances."

Zevon's gaze fell. "I wish, now and then, just to tell them and be done with it. I deserve whatever they do."

"You keep your alien mouth shut. You want to risk these plush surroundings? If they knew, they might put us someplace . . . oh . . . tacky."

Now Zevon looked up, and his expression tightened. "We have to risk a change, Eric. You can't stay here much longer. You can't stay on this planet, much less in this prison complex—"

He was interrupted by the sharp clack of the lab door lock. They both tensed visibly, though Stiles was too weak to do much more than uncross his legs.

"Uh-oh—"

Assistant Warden Orsova came in first, as he always did. He was a typical Pojjana northern-hemisphere male, built like a brick, a head shorter than Stiles or Zevon, but nearly as wide. His coppery complexion shimmered in the lab light. His eyes were black as the drawer knobs around the lab. Following him was one of the guards of the lower ranks, with an infantry symbol emblazoned on his uniform front and the colors of an unfamiliar unit.

"Hello, you men." Orsova slurred the words as he drawled his way through his own language.

He was drunk. They recognized the signs. Orsova held his liquor well, but there was a certain lingering odor, and his behavior would change, submerged anger bubbling behind his eyes. On days like this, his frustrations and boredom fluttered to the surface, and he would eventually come to act on them.

The soldier, though, seemed perfectly sober. His dark eyes glowed with anticipation, and his fists were clenched.

Orsova looked at Stiles and Zevon. "What are you doing today?"

Fighting his nerves, Stiles fiddled with the spectrometer, making sure not to do anything by mistake that could wipe out their newfound readings. "Just sitting here making up my mind that zebras are white with black stripes instead of the other way around."

"Get up," Orsova ordered.

Suddenly icy, Zevon turned to the clutter of equipment on the lab table. "We have twenty more minutes."

"Not you, ears," Orsova corrected, and looked at Stiles. "Just him."

Stiles chuckled and shook his head. "Orsova, your timing smells to Tarkus. So does your breath, by the way."

"Get up."

"He can't get up," Zevon protested, but too quietly.

Orsova buried his wide hands in Stiles's collar and dragged him to his feet. Holding Stiles with one hand, he held the other hand out to the soldier. "Pay."

Grinding his teeth, the soldier dug into his thigh pouch and came up with several of the thin minted chips the Pojjana used as a medium of exchange and piled them into Orsova's hand.

Without ceremony Orsova handed Stiles over to the soldier, who by now was fairly gasping with the thrill.

Zevon said nothing, did nothing as the soldier hauled Stiles to the middle of the floor, reeled back his muttonlike arm, and backhanded Stiles across the jaw. Lacking the strength to counter the sheer force, Stiles whirled into the far wall. As he slid down, a streak of blood smeared the dirty plaster.

As he landed on his knees, Stiles pressed the back of his hand to his cut lip and hoped the blood would clot. He didn't want to die of a slap. That'd be so stupid.

He turned and slipped farther down, but looked up as Orsova's barn-wide shoulders blocked the bare light from the ceiling. "Picked a weakling this time," he choked. "No loose teeth."

"He'll try again," Orsova said.

"Sure. I can't feel much these days anyway."

Beyond the soldier's balled fists, Stiles could see Zevon seated at the lab table, both hands pressed to the edge of the table. As the soldier's fist plunged into Stiles' gut and the familiar lights of agony flashed, Stiles let his mind go blank. That little trick was getting easier as the months and years drained away the defiance Zevon somehow still saw in him. He was glad he was on his knees already, for he could never have stayed on his feet and he didn't want to be seen falling again. His lungs cried for air. If Orsova's soldier hadn't been holding him by the collar again, he'd be on the deck, shriveled up like a jellyfish.

"You aren't afraid anymore," Orsova commented from over there.

Stiles blinked at him, still seeing only the flash and pop of pain's decorations. "Well, what's another pound to an elephant? So you hire me out again. So what? One of these days you ought to beat me up yourself instead of auctioning me off. Or can't you handle it?"

Furious, the soldier heaved his victim to his feet, then rammed his thick elbow into Stiles' ribs and flung him into the wall again. Stiles tried to go limp, but this particular soldier didn't fall for the trick. Some did, but this guy knew to drive the air out of his plaything's body before flinging him, assuring that Stiles was tense as he struck the wall. Worked.

Shuddering, helpless, Stiles writhed like an unlicked cub on the cold cement. His own moans rattled from his throat, but he had no connection to them nor any control, and was blinded by the lights popping behind his eyes, so familiar he'd started to name them. He was up to Louise when they began finally to fizzle and he blinked back to the apparition of Orsova's left boot near his nose, as the big warden pulled the rabid soldier off and held him to one side.

"Let me finish him!" the soldier bellowed. "He's an alien! There's no other alien anywhere!"

"No," Orsova flatly refused.

"Then let me kill the Romulan!"

"No."

"You dumb drunken mule," Stiles struggled. "You're blowing a—chance to—save half the planet. We've found a way to—predict the Constrictor. Pound me all you want—but get a message to the—authorities. We've finally—done it!"

"Done it," Orsova echoed. "You know we're tired of keeping you. There's talk of just executing you."

"Fine," Stiles grunted. "Execute me. But bury me deep. I don't want to come heaving up when the big one hits."

Orsova's reddened eyes turned hard. "There hasn't been a Constrictor in two years. Maybe it won't come again. Why should we feed and keep aliens here, and give you a lab and let you work, after what you gave to us?"

"It wasn't him," Zevon said without turning. "It was—"

"Shut up, Romulan," Stiles barked from the floor. "I don't need your—pointy help."

"And it will come again," Zevon persisted, looking now at Orsova. "Like seismic activity, it doesn't go away. It builds up to something worse. The two of us have used our time learning to read the spaceborne graviton pulses—"

"You two aren't as much fun as you used to be." Orsova cast a furious glance at Zevon and added, "I know the game. Pretending."

Stiles wiped blood from his mouth with a shaking hand. "Not—pretending. We just don't—give a damn anymore. You've had two—two years of good crops . . . that haven't been squooshed . . . two years of—"

"I paid you!" the soldier roared, shoving at Orsova's arm,

Orsova held him back. "Less and less reason to let enemies work on our equipment," he said to Stiles. "We should put you on trial and execute you now. It isn't enough that we stop taking care of you when you're sick."

Might as well talk to the wall.

"Take the message," Stiles attempted one more time. "There's another Constrictor coming. The planet . . . can get ready. Save the billion—"

The effort of speaking coiled Stiles into a knot and apparently gave Orsova the idea that this was the best satisfaction he would get today.

"I paid!" the soldier shouted.

"You paid to beat an alien," Orsova said, "not to kill one. Go out now. Go."

Orsova yanked the door open and shoved the soldier out, then left the lab and shut the door behind him.

That was the paradigm of their life—Orsova sold opportunities to beat up the human alien, while he got his own jollies from watching the effects on the Romulan alien.

Zevon watched the frosted glass door, saw something that held him in his place—Stiles couldn't see the door from where he lay, but knew to simply lie gasping and wait. Ultimately a shuffle in the corridor spared him, and Zevon broke from the table and rushed to his side.

"Curses," Stiles wheezed, "foiled again."

"Eric . . ." Zevon sorrowfully turned him enough to raise him to a nearly sitting position and held him there. Stiles could never have held himself, but would simply have slumped back into a supine position and probably suffocated on the deck. "Look at you. . . ."

"What a way to—live—aw, God—I hate that son of a bitch. . . ."

"Orsova is a walking symptom. He lost his children in the last Constrictor. Now he tortures us to ease his bitterness. The soldiers he brings here . . . they're the same."

Zevon got to one knee, then hoisted Stiles up and deposited him on the only cot in the lab. The Romulan's face was creased with misery, overlaid by a firm mask of bottled rage.

"Hey," Stiles gasped. "Your emotions are showing."

"I keep telling you—I am *not* Vulcan." Zevon angrily snatched a beaker of purified water from a shelf, soaked a rag, and pressed the cool compress to Stiles' bleeding lip.

"We'll never convince him to let us talk to the chief warden or anybody," Stiles murmured. "How can we convince them that this is their chance?"

"We're not that certain of our readings," Zevon reminded. "The prediction might be off by months. Stop moving."

"I'm not moving . . . I'm writhing in agony."

"Exercise some self-control."

"But *you're* not a Vulcan."

Obviously troubled, Zevon frowned. "All we know is that another Constrictor, a very strong one, has been building for two years and will certainly strike. The phenomenon hasn't gone away at all."

"But we *know*, Zevon, that's something. Help me—"

With Zevon's help, Stiles jerkily shifted onto his side as his aching ribs and stomach muscles cramped again. His eyes clutched shut as he bore through the spasm, feeling worse for Zevon than himself. Zevon could do nothing more than grasp him and wait until the torment worked its way out. Stiles paced himself, breathing chunkily, until he could finally count through ten long breaths and his face and hands stopped involuntarily flinching.

"Orsova and his kind," he began when he could speak again, "they think we're just stalling to avoid execution . . . we've got to convince them somehow. Or go over them to the consul general."

"They will be convinced when the Constrictor comes."

"And we can laugh in their faces, if Orsova or some other anti-alienite doesn't find a way to kill us first."

Zevon sat down on the cot beside him and gazed at the dirty floor. "I can hardly blame them. A billion people dead . . . what would we do to anyone who caused that on our planets?"

"If we can predict the Constrictors," Stiles muttered, "then it's only a matter of time before we can reduce the effects."

"A thousand years of time, perhaps, between those two miracles."

"But if we can just predict them, then planes can be landed, people can put on compression suits, get into reinforced buildings, put the babies and old people in antigrav chambers—you know how to build those. Why won't they listen?"

"I don't know."

Stiles managed a sustaining sigh, let the lungful of oxygen flow through him and clear his head a little more. When he could relax a little more, he gazed at Zevon. "You think I can't feel what's happening to me? I know how sick I am. My muscles are deteriorating. I can feel my innards slowly dissolving.

When Orsova's customers kick me now, it doesn't heal anymore. I won't survive the Constrictor when it comes. You don't have to pretend. Even without the Constrictor I don't have that long. Orsova'll have me beaten up once too often, or I'll fall down and my heart'll collapse . . . I can't have more than a few more weeks."

"If I hadn't caused the Constrictor, you would be somewhere else today. Probably a lieutenant." His sharp features creasing, Zevon pressed the heels of his hands into his thighs as if the mental torture caused him some physical pressure too. Several seconds passed before he could finally say, "Now my great mistake has killed my only friend."

Stiles gazed at him, feeling supremely wise. The inner peace would've knocked him over like phaser stun if he'd been standing. He was completely content, as if lying in a hammock under a bower of autumn leaves. Zevon's grief actually amused him, and he smiled.

"Jesus, do you do Irish tragedies too?" he chided. "Zevon of the Sorrows . . . Listen, clown, you gave me four extra years. My own mistake killed me that night, the night we met. I was in the hole. I died there. You crawled through the wall and gave me four years I wasn't gonna get."

Irritated by the compliment, Zevon shook his head. "You wouldn't have been here at all—"

"Yeah, well, flog yourself again. Gimme that broom over there to hit you with. If I could get up, I'd beat your ass blue."

"It's already green."

Stiles laughed, despite the fact that his midsection had cramped again. He stiffened and moaned, but then he laughed again. Zevon smiled as he stuffed a rolled lab apron under Stile's head. For a moment they retired into peaceable silence. Over the years, they had learned to be silent together. In fact, they seldom talked like this anymore. Seldom needed to. They knew each other so well, and what a great feeling it was to be silent, silent together.

The lab seemed quiet, but now as they sat together Stiles focused on the chitter of the computer as it doggedly worked on the last problem fed into it, the burble of chemical processors trying to separate molecules for identification of spaceborne particles brought to them by the Pojjana Air Patrols, and the plink of the faucet in the sink dripping. Plink . . . plink . . . plink. . . .

Nice sound.

He dared to draw a longer breath, which forced him to cough convulsively. When that cleared, he wiped spittle from his beard and tried to relax.

"I was pointless back in Starfleet," he wandered on. Why did he feel like talking? Oh, well. "There were a thousand of me. Ensigns by the carton. Probably most of 'em officers by now. Wouldn't have happened to me . . . botched the mission like I did . . . might as well be here, distracting somebody like Orsova. I mean, if he wasn't hitting me he'd just be . . . hitting you."

"Quiet."

"After I die, you go on without me. Don't you quit. You don't need me. Don't let Orsova slow you down. If you can predict the Constrictor within days, you can save thousands. Within hours, you can save millions. If you can get the Pojjana to listen, they can save ten million this time, maybe a half billion the next—"

"Without you, I have no wish to keep working."

"You don't *need* me." Stiles raised his head and grasped Zevon's arm with a ferocity of strength he didn't think he still had. "I've never been anything much more than raw material anyway. Starfleet tried to whip me into something worth having, and I thought they'd succeeded, but twenty-one-year-olds never think they're young. They'll go out and hoe a row of stumps before they realize they forgot to bring seed. That was me . . . was it ever me."

"Eric," Zevon pointlessly admonished, but had nothing new to say about that.

"You think you can do it, right? Whether I'm here or not, you *can* do it, right?"

"I can improve the predictions . . . if this first one is accurate within days, I can learn to fine-tune it. Bring it to hours. After the first one, I'll know how. If they let me continue—"

"They'll let you. You'll convince them. Don't you stop trying, right? If you stop trying, I'll be dead for nothing. I don't mind being dead, but dead for nothing stinks."

Inexpressibly disturbed, Zevon nodded. "I promise, Eric."

Scarcely were the prophetic words out than the door suddenly rattled and both men flinched—they hadn't even noticed the sound of footsteps in the hall. Abruptly aware of the great serviceability of silence and how much they sacrificed if they talked too long, Stiles willed himself to a sitting position and shifted until his legs hung over the end of the cot and Zevon was sitting almost beside him. They didn't stand. That would've been taken as threatening. They'd learned that too, a long time ago, the hard way.

Orsova rolled in, a little less drunk than before, his bulky guard uniform somewhat askew and a bundle under his arm.

Desperate at the prospect of two beatings in a single day, Zevon bolted to his feet between the big Pojjana and Stiles, standing out of the way of Stiles's grasping hand. "Leave him alone! If you want me to beg, Orsova, this time I will."

But the big assistant warden skewed a glance at him, then said, "I didn't come to beat him. I came to give him clean clothes."

The astounding claim literally drove Zevon back a step, enough that Stiles could get a grip on his arm.

"Why?" Stiles asked.

Orsova dumped the bundle of clothing onto Stiles's lap. "Because a deal's been made. They're coming to get you. You're going home."

"Starfleet's coming?"

"Somebody is," Orsova confirmed without commitment. "The orders to free you come all the way from Consul Bellinorn, and he hates everybody."

At the name of the chief provincial judiciary consul, Stiles felt the air fly from his lungs. "We're . . . we're going home?"

Orsova shrugged. "Just you."

"What? What about Zevon!"

"He's Romulan."

Stiles used his grip on Zevon to yank himself up despite the protests of his body and rage gave him the strength to be there. "You're kidding! I'm not going without him!"

"Yes."

"No! You're doing this on purpose!"

"Stop, Eric." Zevon pulled him back.

Orsova blinked his reddened eyes, peered with something like sentimental regret at the bundle of clothing, shrugged again, and simply left the room, bothering to clunk the door shut behind him, as if to give them a few final minutes alone. Courtesy? Since when?

Shuddering like an old man, Stiles stood beside Zevon, and the two of them stared at the door. They couldn't look at each other. Not yet.

"He's lying," Stiles rasped. "He's tricking us for some reason . . . he wants something. That's got to be it, Zevon. He's telling lies. This is Red Sector. Starfleet wouldn't come in here. It's a lie."

"Perhaps something has changed," Zevon suggested reasonably. "If the sector has been declared green, how would we know it, here in prison?"

"We'd hear about it . . . somebody would say something. We'd hear rumors."

Slowly shaking his head, Zevon stood with his arms at his sides and common sense on him like a cloak. "No, Eric. No."

"We'd hear about it. . . ."

"No."

Barely aware of where his legs were, Stiles sank back onto the cot. The metal frame squawked under his weight and the sound nearly knocked him unconscious. His head drummed, hearing the squawk again and again. Before him, Zevon's legs seemed to be surrounded by a slowly closing tunnel.

After a moment, Zevon came to sit beside him. Together they stared at the lab, still not looking at each other. Their world, this lab, this prison, this planet, turned inside out for them both in the next ten seconds. Suddenly everything was changed, heaving as if in some kind of earthquake, and for a ridiculous moment there seemed to be a Constrictor holding them both to this cot, to this floor, to the bedrock beneath the building.

Who was coming? If the Sector had turned green, they probably would've heard about it, and there hadn't been a whisper. Not a thing had changed, not a flicker of instability—nothing.

Who was strong enough to come through Red Sector after Eric Stiles?

"It must be the ambassador," Zevon said, as if reading Stiles's mind. "He must finally have found a way to bring you out."

"I don't care if God Himself is coming," Stiles uttered. The words gagged in his throat. "I don't want to go."

"You must go," Zevon told him firmly.

"I don't *have* to go. Nobody can make me . . . I won't go. Not even for Ambassador Spock . . . no, not even for him. Everything I've done, I did so he'd be proud of me. If I go back, everything'll fall apart. If I die here, he can be proud of me. I'll be lost in the line of duty. If I'm alive, I'm headed back to disgrace. Court-martial. Home to humiliation. Zero purpose . . . complete uselessness. I cheated my dopey destiny for four years. Now I'm twenty-five and dying, about to be crushed in name as well as in body . . . and you and I . . . Zevon . . . we'll never see each other again. I don't want to go. I'm not going."

Without really turning to face him, Zevon glanced down at his side, at his own arm pressing against Stiles's, and he moved enough to clasp Stiles's hand. Still, they did not look at each other.

"You must go," Zevon told him firmly. "They can save you. The Federation will cure you. You will go."

Despite the physical abuse, the sickness, the deterioration, the pain, Stiles found himself looking fondly back upon the years of working side by side with Zevon, at first concentrating on keeping each other alive, later on the goal of deciphering the erratic Constrictor pattern. Their discoveries—that there was no pattern, but that waves did build before a Constrictor and could be measured . . . the possibility of predicting the disasters before they hit . . .

"Y'know, I didn't mind the pain or the beatings, or anything," he said. "I didn't mind the chance to stay here and do what I perceived as my duty. It's better for me to die here than go back and die humiliated. You understand, you're Romulan—it's better for my family to believe that I died in battle."

"That is often best," Zevon conditionally agreed, "but not always. Not this time."

He squeezed Stiles's hand, careful of his own strength and the possibility of actually crushing the weakened muscles and the thready bones.

Stiles gazed at their clasped hands, and sucked each breath as if it were his last.

"You're the only friend I've got," he uttered. "I'm dying and they're taking me away from my only friend."

"They'll cure you. You'll live."

"I don't want to live humiliated. I want to die here. At least I died trying, instead of going back disgraced and a failure, court-martialed—"

"No, Eric. You must go."

"Why? Why do I have to go? I'd rather die here."

"You must go for the billion."

"Huh?"

"You forget, as usual, that others are involved who are not looking at you or judging you."

"Who?"

"The billion we can save."

"You son of a bitch . . . don't do this to me."

"And me, Eric. You'll save me too."

For the first time, the idea of going home seemed less prickly. "How?" he demanded.

In a measured tone, Zevon explained, "If you go back and they cure you, you can get word to the Romulan Empire that I am here, that I'm alive. The royal family will have no choice but to breach Red Sector and get me out. My people don't think I'm alive, or they would have come already. They can find resources to make a deflection system. Look what I'm working with—ancient trash, chips and coils and conductors, a spectrograph the age of my mother, and still we've found a way to predict. Look at those copper wires! On my ship, I had more facilities in my cabin than we have here. Mathematics based on assumptions of certain things happening at the same time—think what I could do with real technology!"

Zevon paused, seemed to dream briefly, then leaned back until he could rest against the wall. He had to tip his head forward a little to avoid scuffing the points of his ears against the wall when he turned his head to glance at Stiles.

"I am still royal family, Eric. If they know I'm here, they'll get me out. They'll negotiate, they'll threaten, but they'll gain my freedom. And I will come back—I'll wring cooperation out of my people for what we've done here. The Pojjana will finally believe, when I come back with resources. I know what can be done. You must go out of Red Sector, Eric. Go out and get cured, and tell my people. And they will come. This is the greatest favor you can do, of all the good you have done here."

Stiles blinked, surprised. "Me? What'd I do? I'm barely an assistant. Don't treat me like that."

"I would never bother to patronize you," Zevon said, giving him a glare of inarguable clarity and conviction. "You are nothing like the young man in the pit. That boy, yes, he died there. But the boy in us always fades, Eric, if we're fortunate. Now you're a different man, a better man. Look at what you've learned in four years. I know technical things, but you're the one who had the breakthrough with the flux meter. You're the one who told me to check for invisible phase shifts in the infrared. I told you how ridiculous that was, but you insisted I check, and you were right. Look what you and I have done here, with tricks and dirt and screwdrivers. I explain what I'm doing, and you provide the leap of imagination that sends us to the next step. We . . . Romulans and Vulcans, even Klingons, we were all in space before Terrans, but look at you. Look how fast your progress has been . . . You've caught up in a century and charged beyond us. You are the people who see things the rest of us miss. One day together, with real facilities . . . your people and mine, working together . . . some day we'll stop shooting at each other, and think what we can do then!"

Now Stiles did look at him, and did not look away. Zevon's dark umber hair had long ago lost its polished-wood gloss, his complexion its glow of youth, and his face was creased now with weariness, starvation, physical stress, and the unending worry that their time would run out, yet still his brown eyes held a glimmer of purpose and hope that had never once flagged in all these years. Zevon had been in the pit with Stiles. Together they had crawled from the lowest place a man can go, the place of worthlessness and damage, and they had made something of it. They had made a bond with each other, and they had achieved a breakthrough that could save a billion people.

If things went right . . . just a little more right.

"If I go," Stiles murmured, "we'll never see each other again."

The words struck them both with the force of a physical blow. It was the one thing they'd never mentioned. Excuses, platitudes, hollow reassurances dodged through his head. The Federation would make peace with the Romulans. There'd be a treaty. Most Favored Systems status. Mail. Visits. The curtain rising so the two of them would be able to . . . see each other.

No matter how the story played in his mind, the final scene was the same. None of that would happen. He and Zevon would never see each other again.

He held on to Zevon in mute torment, the light touch becoming a sustaining grip, and he didn't know what in the universe to say.

"You must go," Zevon quietly insisted, "because you must live. You must live because I have to get off this planet so I can save these people even against their will. If I leave, I will come back. If you leave . . . you must *never* come back."

The faucet dripped, the computer clicked, and with a palpable crack Eric Stiles's heart broke in half for the second time in his life. In Zevon's angular features he saw the blurred echo of the face of Ambassador Spock, calling him from the distant past, beckoning one more act of Starfleet honor from the carved-out gourd of failure.

Zevon squeezed Stiles' hand again and thumped it placidly against the edge of the cot in punctuation, as if instructing a child about something which must, absolutely must, be the choice of the day.

"Go home, Eric," he summoned. "Go home, and live."

Chapter Eight

"THAT'S NOT A STARFLEET SHIP. What is this? Who in hell's coming for me?"

Stiles wrestled back against the grip of Orsova and one of the prison guards. They had him by the elbows, and there was no breaking away. He was too weak to do more than protest with anger and suspicion in his voice.

Orsova clapped a wide hand to Stiles's chest and said, "Stand still or I'll be happy to take you back to your cell."

"Take me back, then! Fine!"

"Stand still."

There was no chance to run, even if he could. The landing field was dotted with Pojjana soldiers, their red-and-brown jackets flashing in the landing lights, their coppery faces flinching at the approach of the unwelcome craft. Alien space-craft hardly ever landed on the planet anymore. They just weren't welcome. This was a bizarre occasion and Stiles still didn't know what he was watching.

His head swimming with regrets, fears, and rough-edged anguish, Stiles begged the stars to put things back the way they'd been this morning, but no miracle came his way. The clanky-looking merchant trader, bulbous and utilitarian, with its exhaust hatches flapping and its hull plates chattering, continued its inartistic approach.

"If that's a Federation ship, it's second-hand," he commented. "No Federation spaceport ever built anything like that."

Unable to wrestle Orsova or the other guard, Stiles condemned himself to watch the landing. Port fin was high . . . too much pitch . . . not squared on the strip markings . . . lateral thrusters going too long.

Ah, the echoes almost hurt, echoes of another landing, not so far from here. He'd come to this planet an outclassed hotfoot who let haste get the better of him, overwhelmed by proximity to greatness, the approval of his hero, whose face he'd seen in the back of his mind all these many, many months, urging him to rise above the mangled messes he'd made. His life had imploded, his preconceptions defoliated, his internal fortitude hammered to a fine edge by circumstances he'd never anticipated, and he'd been preparing himself for a long time to die. Now living was a lot more scary than dying of whatever was eating his muscles. Strange . . . he and Zevon didn't really even know what illness Stiles had. The Pojjana doctors hadn't been able to identify it. Of course, since the patient was a prisoner and an alien, they hadn't tried all that hard.

So Stiles had gotten ready, over the months, to pass away. Now he was suddenly afraid not to go. Today, once again, the universe turned on its edge for him. He stood now at the municipal landing field, barely an echo of that feckless and slapdash boy, but he was still trembling like a kid, so fiercely that Orsova and the other guard had to hold him up. Would Ambassador Spock himself step down the black ramp of the unfamiliar vessel landing out there?

"I don't want to go," he muttered in his throat.

Beside him, Orsova watched the ship settle. "I'll miss you, too."

This time there was no Zevon to talk sense into him. Zevon was back in the prison. For him, nothing had changed. Except, now, he would be alone.

Terrible guilt racked Stiles's chest. All the words of sense and reason from the lab suddenly seemed to leak like cheesecloth. How could he leave Zevon like this? Here in this dump, alien and hated, alone, powerless, with another Constrictor coming and nobody to believe him about it? Before this, they'd at least always had each other.

"Who's doing this?" he demanded as the ship settled and its thrusters shut down with a wheeze. "Who're you giving me to, Orsova? This is your doing, isn't it? You weren't getting anything out of watching Zevon while you tortured me anymore, so now you're up to something else, aren't you?"

"You're going home," Orsova drably said. "I would enjoy keeping you, but you're going."

"Why?" Stiles glared at him. "Why would you let anybody shove you around? Who are you afraid of?"

"You're an alien. Your own filthy kind have come to get you. Shut your mouth and go with them."

"What about Zevon?"

"He's mine from now on."

Summoning his last threads of energy, Stiles raised his elbow and rammed it laterally into Orsova's round face. The big guard staggered, but never let go of Stiles' arm. Before even regaining his balance, Orsova shoved Stiles viciously sideways, into the rocky substance of the other guard, who pivoted to provide a backboard for whatever Orsova wanted to do.

Stiles tried to brace himself, but he might as well be skinned alive as drum up a vestige of physical superiority—hell, he could barely keep standing. Orsova reeled back a thick arm like a cannon, poised to turn Stiles into mashed oats.

Refusing to close his eyes, Stiles winced and prepared for pain and flash.

"Stop!"

Though he attempted to turn toward the sound, Stiles found his head reeling and comprehended that somehow Orsova had gotten a lick in there someplace. He shook his head, squeezed his eyes shut briefly, and fought to focus.

When he could see again, he frowned at a clutch of odd-looking aliens he didn't recognize, yellow in the face with some kind of green growth on their heads that might be their idea of hair. Their cheeks were smooth as babies' butts, they had no recognizable nose, and two eyes pretty far apart. Their

Diane Carey

clothing was a mishmash, obviously not uniform in any way, so this wasn't anybody's military unit, just a ship's crew from some ungodly where. Sure wasn't Starfleet. Why were yellow aliens coming for him?

From the middle of the clutch came the sharp voice again. "Stop that. Get away from that man."

Abruptly—and that was the shock—Orsova flinched back, and *so did the other guard.*

And so did about a dozen other Pojjana soldiers who were standing within flinching distance.

What?

Stiles found himself struggling to stand up all alone, without even the assistance of his daily tormenter to help.

An old man strode bonily up to him, right up until there wasn't even a foot between them. Human. Old, darn old. Over a hundred, maybe, with a full head of frost-white hair, a simple flight suit framing his narrow body. The old man flicked a medical scanner between them. Piercing blue eyes watched the instrument's indicator lights.

"You Eric Stiles?"

"Who wants to know?"

"I'm your new grandad, son. Grew a beard, huh? I had one of those once. Itched." The ancient man turned to the yellow aliens who flanked him and said, "Get him aboard, boys."

Stiles backed up a clumsy step as two of the yellow aliens stepped toward him. "Who are you? Where are you taking me? You're not Starfleet. There's nobody like them in the Federation—what do you want?"

From behind, Orsova and two other Pojjana guards shoved him forward again roughly, but the narrow old man snapped his fingers and his blue eyes flashed with confidence and barked, "Hands off him!"

So abruptly that Stiles almost collapsed between them, the guards—even Orsova—relaxed their threat.

The old man approached and leered at Orsova. "Don't get any ideas, butch. I'm old, but I'm ornery."

Amazing! The burly Pojjana all backed away again, so fast that the suction almost dragged Stiles off his feet.

"What the hell—" Stiles glanced at them, then glared at the

96

frail white-haired codger. "Who are you that you can make them flinch like quail?"

The old man was completely unimpressed by the lines of Pojjana soldiers, and indeed they shied away from him. "Let's just say that once upon a time I removed a thorn from the lion's paw. Now the lion thinks I'm powerful. Of course, he's right."

Weird—somehow this old man's voice . . . it sounded familiar. The way he snapped at those men—

"What's all that mean?" he asked. "What thorn?"

But the codger, without taking his eyes off Stiles, waved at the yellow guys, who moved forward again. "Don't look back, son," he said. "It doesn't pay."

As the yellow aliens pressed toward him, Stiles stumbled back. "You keep your alien paws off me!" He slapped at them as they attempted to get a grip on him. "I don't want to go without Zevon! Orsova, I'll get you for this someday! All of you get away from me!"

"Hypo."

"I don't want to go! I don't want to go . . . I don't . . . want. . . ."

Familiar voices. How secure they sounded, how wondrous! The anchorage of life, those voices. All the hours upon hours, watching historic mission tapes, memorizing the fiery defiance of Captain James Kirk during the M5 experiments, the Nomad occurrence, the incident at Memory Alpha, sinking into Mr. Spock's baritone warble explaining where the probe came from, listening to the counterpoint of Dr. McCoy's perplexed and concerned protests, the voice less of an officer than a humanitarian trying to expand his humanity beyond natural limits . . . those men, they always pushed themselves, teased every limit, never backed away. . . .

Wish I'd been there, with those men in those times, taking those orders. I could've followed those orders and given them ten cents change! Just imagine—First Officer Spock saying, "These are your orders, Ensign Stiles." Imagine. . . .

Their voices were more familiar than his own family's, more familiar than Travis Perraton's calming tone behind him making sure he didn't make quite as much a fool of himself as he otherwise might, or Jeremy White taunting him while the others laughed. But it had been a good laugh . . . he hadn't appreciated it back then. They were having fun, enjoying themselves all because he was with them. That was worth being laughed at. It never hurt so much, except that he let it hurt. If they were enjoying themselves, then the existence of Eric Stiles was doing some good.

He wanted to wake up. Usually he could will himself out of unconsciousness after a short struggle. Orsova commonly knocked him into a dither, and he had learned to claw his way out of the tunnel to the light place where Zevon would be waiting for him, usually stitching a cut or stanching a nosebleed. Wounds could actually heal without a tissue-bonding beam.

That medical scanner, it looked like a super satellite to him after four years in a culture backed off a hundred fifty years from what he'd grown up with. Funny how quickly he'd gotten used to the downteching. Before, he'd never thought a person could get through a day without Federation flash and spark. He'd gotten through a day.

"At a time."

Oh—his own voice this time. Didn't sound so bad. Come on, fight out of the hole. Zevon would be at the top of the tunnel, pressing a wet cloth to Stiles's head.

"Mmmm . . ."

"That's it, son, wake up. You're bound to have a headache, Don't fight it."

Stiles fought anyway. He defied the thrum in his skull and finally found the power to force his eyes open when he sensed there was some kind of light on the other side of the lids. Zevon would be there when he got them open.

Red lights? Familiar too . . . shipboard lights in an alert situation. Red, so the eyes could still adjust. Most eyes, anyway. Human eyes . . .

"Let me get the lights."

That gravelly, homespun voice again. The codger.

"Where's Zevon?"

Stiles registered his own voice and clung to the sound,

which brought him all the way up to consciousness. When he could see, he realized the lights weren't red anymore, but were a soft golden light, shining in small, obviously ship-built quarters rigged as some kind of sickbay. He saw a shelf with rows of bottles, piles of folded cloth, several pieces of medical scanning equipment, hyposprays, and a dozen other recognizable and somehow foreign contraptions. He knew what they all were, yet they were foreign to him, and unwelcome.

"So I'm out," he managed.

"You are," the old man said.

Forgetting himself for just a moment, Stiles fixed upon the old man's face and tried to register that voice. He felt like a computer with a new search order—*identify, identify*.

"Who are these people running this ship?"

"Smugglers."

"Why would a human ride with them? And why'd you come into Red Sector? Are you an expatriate or something?"

The old man's icy blue eyes flickered and one brow arched. "I came because of typical pointed-eared hardheadedness, that's why."

"Huh?"

"And once in a while a man's got to slip into forbidden territory. Inoculations, contraband chemicals, antitoxins . . . makes the stars spin."

"But . . . if you . . . why would they. . . ."

"Why don't you just relax, Ensign?"

"Ensign . . . haven't heard that in a while. You better call me something else."

The doctor tilted his snowy head. "Why should I? You haven't surrendered your commission, have you?"

"It got surrendered for me. I'm not that kid anymore. Starfleet gave up on me. I gave up on them."

"You're here, aren't you?"

"Look, don't you think I know pity when I see it? Guilt? It's not Eric Stiles they came after. It's their own reputation for not leaving a man behind." Stiles huffed. "I grew up back there. I *did* leave Starfleet behind. I could handle myself. I didn't want to be rescued. Starfleet can't just fly in and order me to leave when I don't want to go."

"Well, actually, Ensign, they can. You're still on the duty roster."

"What do I care? And I told you not to call me ensign. All this is just a joke on you anyway. I don't care how many famous people they send after me, Starfleet's not getting its pound of flesh out of Eric Stiles. I'll never make it home."

"Oh? Why not?

"Because I'm dying. There's hardly a pound of flesh left. Can this boat turn around? Do these yellow guys have a reverse button?"

The old man wiped his pale, gnarled hands on a blue towel. "You're not dying, boy. I just cured you."

Stiles rolled his head on the pillow and challenged the codger with a glower. "I'm too far gone for that."

"Not too far for me. You had a viral infection of operational tissue. Your heart, your muscles, intestinal walls, a few internal organs . . . it's just something that hits humans on that planet. We had to watch out for it back when we maintained an embassy. To the Pojjana, it's barely a common cold, but to humans, it eats muscle. In five or six months, with some physical therapy, your tissues will be rebuild. You'll be young again, kid. Just call me the fountain of youth."

"Starfleet sent us on a mission to a planet with a human-killer virus?"

"They had a vaccine, but didn't bother to vaccinate the evacuation team. You boys weren't supposed to come in contact with any native Pojjana during the evac mission, and that virus requires twelve weeks of repeated exposure. Nobody expected any of Oak Squad to stay there for four years. You probably got it from the food supply at the prison."

Stiles stared at him. "How do you know so much about me?"

"Ambassador Spock sent me. Ring a bell?"

Taken unaware by the dropping of that name, Stiles heaved up on his elbows—and then the second shock came. He was up on his own elbows!

"What's wrong?" the old man asked.

"I haven't been able to sit up by myself for . . ." All at once Stiles dropped back on his pillow, but not from weakness. He stared at the old man and watched decades peel away before his eyes as he suddenly realized—

"Ambassador Spock sent you . . . of course! You're— you're—my God, you're—"

"Yes, that's who I am. The Supreme Surgeon. The Mighty Medicine Man. The Hypo-Hero. The Real—"

"McCoy! Doctor McCoy!"

"You can have an autograph later." The elderly man snapped the top back onto a bottle and placed it back on the nearest shelf. "Now relax before you have a bacterial flareup. Where'd I put that sedative?"

"Are you Doctor Leonard McCoy? *The* Doctor McCoy?"

"Betcha."

"Then it *is* an official rescue?"

"No. I convinced the consul general to remand you into my custody. When we cross into Federation territory, you'll be officially handed over to Starfleet."

"You gave the Pojjana some kind of medical help?"

"That's the short version, yes."

"Then you broke the Prime Directive?"

"Sure did," the esteemed elder proudly confirmed. "You would've too. The P.D.'s been through so many incarnations and reinterpretations in my lifetime you'd think the thing was written on rubber. In a changing galaxy, you've got to have that."

"But you're a Starfleet surgeon—"

"Retired. If I come into Red Sector, it's my own affair. I'm a free agent. Took me a year and a half to get the Pojjana to owe me enough to get you out. It's a damned shame what happens to you kids who get caught in the crossfire—"

"I'm not that kid anymore," Stiles bristled. "I'm an old man now. I can stick up for myself."

Leonard McCoy lasered him a scolding glower that cut him off in mid-thought. "Boy," the doctor said, "I got socks older than you."

Perfectly intimidated, Stiles settled back and shut his mouth. He'd have to keep it shut until he figured things out. How much had changed out there? Four years in prison was an eternity. Stiles knew he'd broken Federation rules by helping

Zevon try to learn how to predict the Constrictor. And he'd have done more to help those people, done anything he could to curb the results of all-encompassing natural disaster. Plain decency didn't allow a man to sit by and watch. What other rules had he broken in his distance and ignorance?

He didn't care. Even after a lifetime of family conditioning, Starfleet had been surprisingly easy to leave behind. Now, this force in his life that had faded to an echo, something he could ignore and forget, now it held ultimate sway over him. Four years ago, though restricted in a jail, Stiles had taken control over his own life. That control was about to be wrested from him again. He was an ensign again, a man in uniform. Today he was free—but more imprisoned than ever.

Then he thought of something else and pushed himself up again. "Can you get Zevon out?"

"Who?"

"Another prisoner. We were together the whole time. We kept each other alive."

"Not another Starfleet man. I'd have known about that."

"No, he's . . . he. . . ."

As the doctor waited for the word Stiles was about to unthinkingly spit, Stiles held himself back. For four years he'd said whatever popped into his mind, careless of consequences because there weren't any consequences, heedless of hurt feelings because he and Zevon endured so much hurt that feelings stopped making any difference a long time ago.

He'd made a promise to Zevon to inform the Romulan Empire that their prince was a captive, not dead as they probably suspected. Was it a good idea to tell anybody else Zevon was Romulan?

I'll get the message to them myself, somehow. I'll figure out a way.

"One miracle at a time," McCoy told him. "We can make a report on your friend, see if Command has a process—"

"I'll take care of it." Stiles lay back again, enjoying the sensation of getting a lungful of air without pain, entertaining thoughts of breaking away and running back to the Pojjana and continuing his work with Zevon now that he was cured. Cured . . . the idea of dying was easier to grasp.

But how would that be? The sector was still red. Zevon was right—he'd be better served to tell the Romulans and let them get Zevon out, then let Zevon pressure his own people into helping the Pojjana. It's the least they owed . . . and the Pojjana still saw both Stiles and Zevon as evil aliens. They might have to be forced to accept help.

The Constrictor was coming, he was sure of it. Zevon would be caught in the middle of it, maybe even killed if the Pojjana wouldn't listen to him.

"I've got to fight my way to somebody with influence," Stiles grumbled aloud, gazing at the scratched brown wall of the small quarters. When he realized he'd spoken aloud, he turned to the elderly surgeon, but the famous old man was busy with something medical and apparently hadn't heard him or didn't care.

"They're going to court-martial me, aren't they?"

"Hmm?" McCoy glanced at him. "I wouldn't know. Why would they?"

"I botched a critical mission."

"Did you?"

"I thought I knew everything."

"Show me a twenty-one-year-old who doesn't." McCoy pulled a hypo off his shelf and fitted it with a newly loaded—whatever that thing was called that held the medicine. "I'll give you something to make you sleep. Tomorrow we'll start your physical therapy. You might as well relax for a while. It's a long ride back from Red Sector to whatever Starfleet's got waiting for you."

Chapter Nine

"ORSOVA."

"Mffbuh . . . muh?"

"You're not unconscious. Stand up."

"Huh? Stand up?"

"You're not dead. Stand up and shake off the daze. Find your feet."

"Who . . . who . . . r'you?"

"This mechanism distorts my voice. Forget trying to recognize me. You will never know me."

"Where is this? Where have you brought me to?"

"You're on a space vessel."

"Space? Space! . . . Prove it."

"Look out that portal. See your planet, your moons."

Disoriented, nauseated, Orsova tripped over his bootlace and stumbled from the cool floorspace to a carpeted area where there was a hole in the wall. There he fingered the porthole ledge and peered out three layers of thick window.

Breath stuck in his throat. He choked and wobbled. There, before him, near enough to touch, hung planetary bodies he had seen hanging in the distant night since he was a child. He had seen them as egg-sized eternalities, and today they were in his lap. Crisp sunlight and shadows like hats rode the bold sandy satellites.

"Oh!" he gasped. "Oh—moons! Too close! How did you make me come here! How did I come here! Oh . . . those moons are close. . . ."

"Beautiful, aren't they? You were transported here with an energy beam."

"A beam . . . through space . . ."

He tried to remember, but there was only the hazy idea of being trapped in his tracks, of looking down to see his knees dissolving and his boots disappearing. He had heard of those transport beams, but thought they might be myths.

But he was here, and he had not walked or flown here. Something had flickered and brought him here. He accepted that.

The buzzing mechanical voice spoke again.

"Now you know you are really in space."

Where was the buzzing voice coming from? It was speaking fluent enough Pojjana, but with an accent. Machines didn't have accents. Somewhere, there was a person talking.

Nothing familiar in the voice. No accent he'd heard before.

"Who are you?"

"These are the conditions. You will not try to look at me. We will speak through this device."

"Where are you? Are you in this ship with me?"

"Nearby. Stop trying to find me. Take your hand from that latch or you die here! . . . Yes, back away. Remain in that chamber."

Orsova chose silence for a moment, to think. Failing that, he asked, "Why do you come here? And why now?"

"The Federation has come here," it went on. *"Why did they come?"*

"To get their man," Orsova told it. "How did you know they came?"

"I follow the medical trail," the voice said. *'The old doctor came here. I kept watch."*

"Why would you keep watch on doctors?"

Stepping foot by foot, toe by toe around the dim cabin, Orsova looked at every panel of the glossy interior plating.

Was the metallic surface thin? Was he seeing shadows of a living form? Just a haze? Or were these echoes of his own reflection deep in the polished surface?

As he moved around, pressing his fingers to each panel, leaving prints on the sheen, he asked, "What do you want?"

"I want to help you."

"We accept no help from aliens. How did you get past our mountain defense?"

"We are nowhere near your defenses. We have beamed you far out. You can see how far."

The strange mechanically disguised voice reminded Orsova of the growling of awakened rezzimults in the swamps near the capitol city.

"What do you want?" he asked, abruptly nervous, as if someone had turned off the heat. "Why did you bring me to space? What do you need me for?"

"Tell no one that I spoke to you, and you will have greatness beyond your dreams. I will help you gain influence, become powerful. You will find my friendship wondrous. When I need you, you will be here."

"I don't even know who you are."

"You will never know me. I must not be known. You are one of many pawns throughout the galaxy. I tend many fronts, light many candles. Do as I say, and we will see what the years may bring."

Chapter Ten

SEVENTEEN WEEKS LATER, after a blur of physical therapy, drug treatments, rebreaking and re-fusion of his old fractures—so they'd be somewhat recognizable as human bones to the archaeologists of the distant future—and a flurry of puzzling comments from Dr. McCoy, Eric Stiles stood in the loading area of a smelly livestock transport ship that stocked colonies with cows or sheep or something. After weeks of treatment, a trim of the beard he couldn't quite yet bear to shave off, and fresh clothing—blessedly not a uniform—he felt as if someone had cut off his head and spliced it onto a new body. He could stand here by himself for a long time before even feeling the first shivers of weakness. He was far from rosy health yet, but a lot farther from the death he'd been passively anticipating.

He and McCoy had transferred nine times in the past seventeen weeks, in a flurry of passage notices, manifests, bribes, seamy personages, and shady deals. Stiles scarcely had an idea of what ship he was on, except that this one had obvious Federation markings–and stank. Generally the ships were hardly distinguishable one from the other, and he and the doctor had remained relatively confined, to keep from "seeing" anything, whatever that meant.

Seventeen weeks of physical therapy and quaint tales. No matter how many times Stiles asked what was going to happen to him, Dr. McCoy always played old and swerved into some tall story about the glorious past, or the irritating past, or the past that could've been done better if only so-and-so had listened to him. Stiles got the idea. The doctor didn't want to be the one to tell him what was coming.

Now they were about to rendezvous with the first Starfleet ship Stiles had seen since he'd been dragged out of his fighter. On one of the courtesy screens, he and Dr. McCoy watched the brand new Galaxy-class *Starship Lexington* pull up to docking range. Then a transport pod came out of the starship and made its way toward the livestock transport.

"Why don't they just get it over with and beam us over?" Stiles complained. "The sooner this is done, the better for me. I can take my dishonorable discharge and vanish."

"Discharge?" McCoy didn't look at him. The lights of the airlock flashed on his papery face.

"It's the only way to get out of a long, drawn-out court-martial. I don't care if they put me on trial, but I don't have the time to waste. I've got a message to deliver. They'll offer me a deal. Dishonorable discharge. And I'll take it."

"Don't blame you."

The vessel around them endured a slight physical bump, and a moment later the nearest airlock clacked and rolled open. Two Starfleet security men stepped out, with holstered phasers and full helmets. One of them stepped forward.

"Dr. Leonard McCoy and Ensign Eric Stiles?"

McCoy stepped forward. "That's us, son."

"Ensign Pridemore, sir, and Ensign Moytulix, here to escort you to the starship. If you don't mind my saying so, sir, I'm honored to have this duty."

"Thank you, Ensign," McCoy allowed with a practiced nod. "Carry on."

"Yes, sir. If you'll both follow me—"

The security officers parted, and Pridemore led the way back into the pod. Stiles let McCoy go first, though he was feeling the bristling power of strong legs again and nearly plowed into the pod just on the hope of getting this misery over with sooner. There was no getting around the next few days. He'd have to face the music, take the stain on his record, plead guilty to whatever they threw at him, and get out so he could find a way to notify the empire about Zevon. That was everything, Zevon was everything, and Stiles was in a perfect panic of worry for him.

His head was swimming. Yes sir, no sir, carry on . . . all the common phrases he'd abandoned so easily . . . they spun him like coins on a table. He felt as if he were reliving somebody else's life, detached from any real involvement of his own.

"Right over here, sir." Ensign Pridemore gestured Stiles to a seat in the cramped back of the transport pod.

"I'd rather stand and look out the viewport."

"Sorry, sir. Regulations."

Stiles stepped to the seat. "You don't have to 'sir' me. I don't outrank you."

"It's my honor, sir." Pridemore took off his helmet, hung it on the bulkhead hook, and turned toward the piloting console.

"Yeah, yeah." Stiles dropped into his seat and slumped into the cushions.

McCoy sat across from him. The other security ensign, his helmet obscuring his face, stood at the airlock hatch at full attention. Seemed kind of silly.

Within twelve minutes, they were landing in the bay of the starship. The pattern of approach and responses from the bay-master seemed like echoes of his past, as Stiles eavesdropped on the cockpit action and imagined himself in the pilot's seat.

As the interior lights of the starship's hangar bay flooded the pod, Dr. McCoy clapped his knees with those gnarled white hands and said, "Ready to get this over with?"

Stiles sighed. "Do elephants have four knees?"

McCoy stepped over and helped Stiles to his feet, which seemed bizarre and distorted. Being helped by a man well over a hundred—and needing it—reminded Stiles that he had a few months of recovery yet to go.

Ensign Pridemore got up and stepped to the hatch. "This way, gentlemen," the young man said.

Young . . . yes, Pridemore seemed young to Stiles. A long time since he'd seen a person younger than himself in any authority. He felt a sudden pang of sympathy for the two ensigns here with him today. So much was expected of them—

"If you'll stand here, Mr. Stiles," Pridemore said, motioning him to the middle of the hatch entrance, only then motioning to McCoy. "Doctor? Here, sir."

Without comment the old surgeon came to stand beside Stiles. The staging was mysterious, but Stiles assumed a security team was stationed outside the door and would be escorting him to quarters under guard. The brig? Probably not. He wasn't a criminal, after all. Just a turkey being led to the slaughter.

"Ready, sir?" Pridemore asked.

"We're ready," the doctor confirmed. "Open'er up."

Pridemore, curiously, stepped aside then instead of leading them down the ramp that must be out there, and punched the hatch controls.

The hatch swung open and for a moment Stiles was blinded, after weeks of dim smugglers and tramp ships, by an unfortunately placed spotlight somewhere in the hangar bay that plunged instantly into his eyes and made him blink.

Then a sound rushed up the ramp and engulfed him. Was something exploding?

He moved slightly to one side, enough to get out of the direct beam of that one culprit light, and let his eyes adjust. As he blinked, he identified that unfamiliar sound. Applause.

He stepped forward to see what was happening, and saw sprawled out before him a field of Starfleet crewmen, officers, civilian guests and dignitaries, all knocking their hands together and looking up the ramp at him and McCoy.

"Sorry!" Stiles gasped. He was standing right in the way. Careful of his new physical coordination, he stepped quickly to one side, faced the famous Leonard McCoy, and began to politely applaud also.

"What're you doing?" Dr. McCoy asked.

Stiles kept applauding. "I was in the way."

The doctor's leathery face crumpled in disapproval and he grasped Stiles by the arm and pulled him back to the middle of the ramp. "They're not applauding *me*, hammerhead!"

"Honor Guard! Atten-HUT!"

The sharp disembodied order echoed in the huge hangar bay, answered by the crack of heels on the deck as a tunnel of uniformed men and women came abruptly to attention, flanking the red carpet which stretched out from the end of the ramp to the edge of the crowd.

"What?" Stiles stumbled a few steps down the ramp, baubling drunkenly as he realized Dr. McCoy wasn't following him down the ramp. He stopped in the middle of the slope and stared at the throng of people applauding before him.

And there was music—trumpet fanfare in vaulting military tradition. He hadn't heard music in years.

A stimulating cheer rose now above the continuing applause, and some of the people in the crowd were jumping and waving, calling, "Eric! Eric! Eric!"

Stiles turned halfway around and looked back up the ramp at Leonard McCoy. The doctor wagged a scolding hand at him, waving him the rest of the way down the ramp.

Spreading his hands perplexedly, Stiles complained, "I don't get this. . . ."

But he barely heard his own voice over the cheering. As he turned back to the crowd, confused and overwhelmed, a flicker of sense came into the picture—Ambassador Spock now stood at the end of the tunnel of uniforms. The senior Vulcan now looked more ambassadorial than the one time Stiles had met him. That day four years ago, the ambassador had been wearing a jacket and slacks. Today he wore a ceremonial robe of glossy purple quilted fabric and a royal blue velvet cowl. Apparently this was some kind of ceremony. With him stood a captain and some officers and a couple of dignitaries. They continued applauding as Stiles meandered down the red carpet, entertaining ideas of slipping between a couple of these guards at attention and maybe getting out of here somehow without anybody noticing.

He stopped five feet short of the end of the runway, staring like a jerk at the ambassador and the captain and all those other spiffy dressers.

The ambassador waited a few seconds, then came forward into the honor guard tunnel. The other dignitaries just followed him in there.

Ambassador Spock's weathered face shone every crease in the harsh hangar bay lights, but under the Vulcan reserve there was an unmistakable sheen of pride and delight. In fact, a hint of a grin tugged at his bracketed mouth and his slashed brows were slightly raised. As he stood flanked by the captain and the dignitaries, all facing Stiles like a vast wall of phaser stun, the applause tapered off and then suddenly stopped in deference and respect.

"Welcome home, ensign," the ambassador said warmly. The soft knell of victory rang in his words and triggered a whole new wave of applause and cheering. As he turned toward the captain beside him, the applause almost instantly fell off again. "I am honored to present Captain James Turner of the *U.S.S. Lexington*."

"Ensign Stiles, I'm pleased to finally meet you in person," the thin officer said, smiling broadly and pumping Stiles's hand. "I first heard about you when I was in command of the *Whisperwood*. Your story was very compelling to me, and I used it to train my fighter squadrons. I admit to pulling some strings so the *Lexington* could be the ship to meet you today."

"Oh . . . I . . . thanks." Stiles leaned closer and urgently told him, "This is some kind of mistake!"

The captain grinned again and took Stiles's elbow and turned him slightly. "My first officer, Commander Audrey."

"Welcome aboard, Ensign," the smiling woman said, "and welcome home."

The captain turned him a little more, while Ambassador Spock watched in passive approval despite the desperate glance Stiles tossed him. In a whirl he was introduced to a half dozen other people.

"Federation Ambassador Whitehead . . . Provincial Ambassador Oleneva . . . Chief Adjutant Kuy, representing Admiral Ulvit . . . Governor Ned Clory from your home state of Florida . . . Port Canaveral's Mayor Tino Griffith, Princess Marina from the Kingdom of Palms on our host planet here in this star system. . . ."

They each greeted him and pumped his hand and patted his arms, some even hugged him, but he scarcely caught a syllable, registering only the mention of an honors breakfast in the ward room.

"You've—got the wrong guy," he protested again as Captain Turner steered him back to Ambassador Spock. By now, Dr. McCoy had shuttled down the ramp and was standing beside Spock, and for an instant as Stiles turned the years peeled back and he saw them as they had been so many decades ago. Spock, streamlined and subdued in his blue Science Division tunic, his black hair glossily reflecting a single horizontal band of light from the hangar ceiling. Leonard McCoy, in a short-sleeved medical smock, strong arms casually folded, his thick brown hair glistening in a much more raucous way, his supremely human expression enjoying a proud and friendly grin, cirrus-blue eyes set in a square face now famous through-out the settled galaxy. Two legends, standing together, for Eric Stiles.

This couldn't be happening. They had something *so* wrong.

He was whisked to a podium mounted at the far end of the hangar bay while a team taxied the pod into its cubicle and the crowd closed in on the hole it made. Somebody ushered him to a row of chairs and put him between Ambassador Spock and Dr. McCoy—good thing, too, because then he had a buffer from those adoring grins. As Captain Turner and those other ambassadors stood up to make speeches—heroism, selfless-ness, sacrifice, fortitude, survival, strength, pride of Starfleet, son of Federation dynamism—Stiles caught only the odd word or phrase, none of which struck him as applying to himself, and he leaned slightly toward Dr. McCoy. Through his teeth he implored, "Will you please *tell* them?"

"Just smile and nod a lot," McCoy wryly advised. "Let 'em have their ceremony. Next week the president's giving you the Federation Medal of Valor."

Stiles stared at him briefly. How could anybody be so casual with a sentence like that coming out of his mouth?

"The m—" Nope, couldn't get it out of his own. "God . . . I don't get it . . . I just don't get this at all. . . ."

"Indeed?" Ambassador Spock offered a solemn gaze. He *did* look amused! "A hero's welcome is a mystery to you after your great sacrifice, Ensign?"

"I didn't sacrifice anything," Stiles argued, keeping his voice way down while the speaker's boomed over the P.A. system. "I crashed into a mountain, and sat there about to wet my pants because I was afraid of the big bad aliens. I must've looked like a kid to you!"

"You *were* a kid," the ambassador blithely told him, startlingly familiar with the vernacular.

Dr. McCoy leaned forward a little. "My eighth psychology textbook, Spock," he explained, speaking from the corner of his mouth. "Chapter Four."

The ambassador looked past Stiles to the doctor, and they communicated with a few eye movements.

After a moment of this, Spock leaned back. "I see."

They were both silent for several minutes while listening— or pretending to listen—to the princess of somewhere happily welcoming the famous survivor Ensign Stiles and all the various dignitaries to her star system. Stiles heard part of her words as if listening to a training tape. The words bore no attachment to himself, except that he had the feeling he was getting into deeper and deeper trouble. When they found out what really happened—

"Stiles."

Maybe he should stand up and just explain what occurred and the mistakes he made and then offer to quietly retreat while they went on with their party. Would it be a good idea to compromise Starfleet's perception, point out this big mistake, right here in front of all these people? He'd hardly spoken to anybody but Zevon for so long . . . get up and talk to this crowd? His knees started shaking.

"Kid. Psst."

"Huh?"

McCoy still didn't turn to speak to him, and kept his voice barely above a whisper. "Now, listen and listen good. You did all right four years ago. Some deskbound paperpusher sent a bunch of kids into a tricky, dangerous political powderkeg without an experienced senior officer—"

"Without briefing them about what they could be facing," Spock took over, very quietly, "to rescue some very important personnel—"

"With Romulans all over the place and riots going on," McCoy interrupted. "They took a pack of untried kids barely out of officer school, with no black space experience at all, and sent you into a civil war and said, 'Go, do.' "

"Without a second thought," Spock added, "you took the initiative, sacrificed yourself, and allowed everyone else to get out alive. Then you kept yourself alive in an untenable situation long enough to be rescued. You are a hero, young man, by any measure."

Stiles felt his legs quiver, his hands grow cold as they spoke to him of these indigestibles as if telling tales of some unconfirmed legend. The crowd of dress uniforms, court gowns, and Sunday best shifted before his eyes and swam with applause as the speaker handed over the podium to the next one.

"Twenty-one-year-olds fail to see themselves as young," the ambassador explained, able to speak up now in the cover of the applause. "They lack the perspective of experience. In Starfleet, they are frequently older than everyone else around them. That is the curse of being a 'senior in high school,' if you will."

"You're one of the older kids," Dr. McCoy said, "so you figure you're not a kid at all. I'm bigger than everybody, so I'm big. Kids feel as if they should know everything. Starfleet handed you a situation that should've gone to a lieutenant. You improvised. You did what you thought was right. We don't damn people for inexperience."

"To you," Spock added, "your mistakes looked like crashing failures. To me, they simply looked like inexperience."

Now the ambassador did turn and fix him with those eyes nobody could look away from. "All these people are proud of you."

"And you deserve it," the doctor finished. "So shut up."

Another round of applause. Another speech, more appreciation, more applause, cheering. They were as insubstantial as dust. All he heard was the ambassador's words and the doctor's over and over in his head, like some musical echo or siren song drawing him along. His memories were of a butter-fingered ensign crowing his own authority and trying to win his spurs, fumbling every ball and landing ass-backward in a flat failure. He balked at any other explanation. They were being kind to him, he knew, and to themselves for their part of the mistake. Starfleet was better at admitting its errors than Eric Stiles ever had been.

He *had* been young then, too young to know it was okay not to already have all the experience of life. It was all right not to know everything. Or much of anything. It was okay . . . it was okay.

I'm okay, Zevon. Don't worry.

In a flush of emotion and self-examination he endured the next half hour of applause and honors without really registering much of it. By the time Spock took his arm and drew him to his feet, Stiles was humbled beyond description. He collected his only pleasure from knowing his survival was making so many people feel good about themselves. That was pretty good, really. When they teased him and spoke poorly, he'd at least been giving them something to converse about. Today he was doing the same sort of thing, deserve it or not. He shook hands and denied his way across the platform, then down to the crowd as the people smiled and then left him alone. They seemed to understand that he was overwhelmed, and the crowd funneled politely to the exits, heading for the ship's mess and ward rooms where the banquets were waiting. Music played again over the PA, and everyone was laughing and cheery, all because of him. On this astonishing day, he had everything he'd once thought he ever wanted.

And now he didn't want it.

"If you'll come this way," Ambassador Spock was saying, "there are some other people who've been waiting a long time to meet you."

"Not more," Stiles moaned. He lowered his eyes. Maybe whoever it was would just get the idea he'd had too much and leave him alone. The ship's captain had gotten the message and corralled the princess and the mayor and governor and were waiting with them about halfway to the exit, giving Stiles a few minutes to breathe. They were conversing with each other, obviously waiting for him, but also deliberately not looking at him.

He needed the time too. He stood at the side of the slowly

emptying hangar bay, with Spock and McCoy providing a welcome buffer between himself and the throng.

"Eric!"

"Hey, Eric!"

With a notable wince, he turned away from the sound. If he kept his back to the masses, maybe they'd think he just didn't hear.

"Lightfoot!"

Something sparked in his head. Now he turned toward the calls. Not twenty steps away, held back by a couple pillars of meat in security uniforms, were the last people in the universe he had expected to see alive, never mind here.

"Travis?" Stiles's voice caught in his throat.

At his side, McCoy gave him a little push. "Go ahead, son. Go see 'em."

Behind Travis Perraton, also crowding the guards, were Jeremy White, Matt Girvan, Greg Blake, Dan Moose, and both the Bolt twins. At the front of the group, Travis Perraton's dark hair was grown out from the Starfleet junior-officer close-clip, and his blue eyes gleamed and bright smile flashed like a star as he reached between the guards and said, "They won't let us through!"

"Security guard," Ambassador Spock smartly ordered, "stand down."

In unison the four guards snapped, "Aye, sir!" and came to at-ease, allowing Perraton, White, Blake, Girvan, Moose, and the Bolts to flood into the reception area. All at once Stiles was engulfed in a coil of embraces, until finally he was clinging to Travis Perraton and getting his back slapped by everybody else.

Spock and McCoy graciously moved away, leaving the young men together without interference. The row of guards between them and everyone else would assure that the former evac team would have a few private moments before all the ringing and tickertaping started again.

Stiles shook like a scarecrow as he clutched at the physical reality of Travis and Jeremy and the Bolts.

"Thought you were all dead!" he gasped, tears flowing freely down his balanced face.

"Dead?" Jeremy White repeated. "Where'd you get that idea?"

"You showed up in the . . . I heard you . . . you said . . . the anti-aircraft guns—"

"We got clear, Eric," Travis said. "You gave us the extra seconds we needed to get away."

"You gotta be kidding," Matt Girvan protested. "He knows. He's just making us say it over and over."

Zack Bolt laughed. "And he'll never let us forget it. Wait and see."

"What is this?" Jason Bolt reached out and grasped Stiles' beard and shook it warmly. "Nonregulation Stiles! Since when!"

Dan Moose poked at Stiles's ribs. "And he's skinnier than Jeremy!"

His eyes blurring as he shuddered under the coil of Travis's arm, Stiles blinked from one face to the other, then ran the route again. Without a bit of the shame he would've once felt, he wiped tears from his cheeks. "Where . . . where are . . ."

Typically, Jeremy took over with a clinical explanation. "Well, Bernt and Andrea left Starfleet and went back to Holland, but they send their good wishes and demand a crew reunion as soon as you feel up to it. Bill Foster got promoted, and he's stationed on Alpha Zebra Outpost. Brad Carter's a civilian now too, and he's coming in tomorrow. He's just finishing exam week at college, so he couldn't be here today."

Only now did Stiles register that Travis, Greg, and Matt were not wearing Starfleet uniforms.

Civilians?

Jason held up a stern finger. "But they're all waiting for a communique on when and where we're having a crew reunion. Those of us still in the service have been given special dispensation from our current duties just so we can attend. The dope civvies among us, who shall remain rankless, are being offered free transportation and hotel, as *if* they deserve it."

"Troublemaker," Travis said with a laugh.

Greg Blake shrugged. "So I'll re-enlist," he tossed off. "Eric's bound to need a new wing leader. Can't do without me, can you?"

"He can't do without any of us," Zack said. "Who'd pick him up when he trips?"

Matt laughed. "Who'd stop him from putting his hand in front of a phaser?"

"Who'd he have to shout at when things didn't happen fast enough?"

"You need us, Lightfoot," Jeremy punctuated.

"Not so fast." Travis protected Stiles from them and held up his free hand judiciously. "Don't be a tidal wave. Eric made it through four years in prison on a hostile planet without anybody to help him keep from making a jerk of himself. Maybe he doesn't need our help for that anymore."

Stiles laughed with them. The ribbing that would've unsettled him once today felt like cool pond water.

Travis gave him a comradely squeeze. "Maybe he doesn't even want to stay in Starfleet."

"I sure wouldn't," Jason commented.

The other twin added, "He's done his duty."

"Twice over," Matt agreed. "They owe *him* now."

"What a life," Travis went on. "Speaking engagements all over the Federation—"

"Scholarships," Dan Moose said.

Blake made an exaggerated bow. "Honorary degrees—"

"Ceremonial dinners," Matt fed in.

"Starring in training films, have books written about you— hell, write your own book! Any idiot with a pen can do that!" Perraton looked at him admiringly. "You're gonna get rich and fat, Eric. Wish to the devil it could've been me!"

Until this moment Stiles had been lost in a daze, but Travis's latest sentence snapped him into biting clarity. He straightened his shoulders—a miracle in itself—and slipped abruptly back in command. Escaping from Travis's cordial embrace, he took hold of his friend's arm and control over the moment.

"No, you don't," he said. "I'm glad it wasn't you and you're glad too, and don't forget it, Travis. I'm so happy I could cry to see all of you, but I'm not the kid you knew."

Their faces changed, subtly, though even after all this time he could still read them. Perhaps even better than before. Some were arguing with him in their minds. Others were realizing they may have made a mistake to say what they'd been saying, perhaps even to be here today.

From the captain's group nearby, Ambassador Spock and Dr. McCoy finally breached the bubble of intimacy encircling Stiles and his crewmates.

"Mr. Stiles," the ambassador began, "excuse me. As soon as you're ready, the captain and dignitaries are ready to go to the wardroom for the honors banquet. We have a table set aside for you and your friends."

"Yes!" Travis beamed, and shook hands victoriously with one of the Bolts.

"You're most welcome, gentlemen," Spock allowed. "And Dr. McCoy has something for Mr. Stiles."

"Me?" Stiles rubbed his clammy hands on his thighs as Dr. McCoy stepped past Spock.

"Here you go, son." The doctor handed him a leatherbound packet with a Starfleet seal.

"What is it?" Stiles asked, as he took the plush folder with its satin ribbon and official wax seal.

"It's your way out," the doctor said. "Clean and legal. A medical discharge, issued directly from the surgeon general, with a retroactive field promotion. You'll go out as a full lieutenant, with commensurate pension."

Stiles looked up. "But you cured me. I don't have a legitimate medical claim."

"I cured your body," McCoy told him. Those active and ancient blue eyes flared. "Your soul is still scarred."

As the moment turned suddenly solemn beneath the doctor's prophetic words, the men around Stiles fell silent and stopped shifting. Their hands fell away from him and they made clear by their demeanor that he was once again in charge, once more the man who would make the important decision of the moment for them all.

A man, making decisions . . .

He glanced at them, saw the civilian clothes on some of them, Starfleet uniforms on others, and his two worlds suddenly collided. They looked young to him, young and unscarred and inexperienced.

"Thank you, sir." He handed the pouch back to Dr. McCoy

and straightened his shoulders. "But I've got too much to do. My soul's just gonna have to heal."

His friends erupted into silly cheers around him, as if they understood something he wasn't registering at all. Over there Captain Turner, the princess, the governor and mayor were all looking at him, and now they had started applauding politely. Not the cheers of the huge crowd this time, but something much more substantial and wise.

How come everybody knew what he had just thought of?

Ambassador Spock reached out and took Stiles's hand. "Congratulations, Lieutenant. And welcome back to Starfleet."

Chapter Eleven

Eleven Years Later . . .

U.S.S. Enterprise, Starfleet Registry NCC1701-D

"THERE HAVE BEEN over fifty major outbreaks of raids or attacks on the Neutral Zone by angry Romulan commanders who before this made no violent overtures at all—and with no apparent reason. We've got to get some better intelligence."

Captain Jean-Luc Picard's comment would generally not have traveled beyond the ears of his first officer and the physician who stood at his side on the command deck, but Ambassador Spock's Vulcan hearing brought the private conversation to him as he stepped from the turbolift. These were troubled times. Despite them, reverie clouded his thoughts.

To step from a turbolift, to hear the sibilance of the door and sense anticipation, the murmur of a starship's bridge electrical systems softly working—these were mighty memories.

For a brief moment in a frozen pocket of his mind, the carpet changed texture, the bulkheads drained from tan to blue-gray, the rail turned glossy red, lights dimmed, and there were crisp shadows over his head. More blue, more black, and at the center that oasis of mesa-gold. The center of his universe, that dot of gold.

Memories only. He dismissed them, but they pursued.

He failed to escape them, as he stepped down to the command deck, also failing to understand—until his foot struck the lower carpet—that he was treading the sacred ground of officers aboard a starship, of the captain and his chosen few: and that he was no longer among them. For decades he had not been among them. How swiftly these automatic impulses flooded back! Perhaps this was why he spent so little time aboard ships anymore.

He nearly stepped back and waited to be invited, but by now Captain Picard had risen and turned to greet him.

"Ambassador, welcome aboard," the captain began, his deep theatrical voice communicating undisguised delight, and he even smiled.

Spock took his hand, a gesture he had come over the years to find suspiciously comforting, and thus held it longer than necessary for courtesy. When embarking on difficult missions, especially those couched in mystery, he had come to depend upon the sustenance of the human tendency to get to know one another quickly and with a speck of intimacy. Few races in the galaxy had that talent. He had come to cherish it.

"You know Mr. Riker," the captain invited pleasantly.

"Ambassador, hello!" William Riker, yes—the ship's first officer. A bright smile, and no attempt to subdue his pride that a distinguished Federation identity had come aboard his starship.

"Good evening, Mr. Riker," Spock offered, and also took Riker's hand.

"And Dr. Crusher, of course," the captain added, turning.

Only the ship's doctor, Beverly Crusher (in fact the person he had come here to meet), restrained herself from offering to shake a Vulcan's hand.

She was a stately woman, tall, reedy, and red-haired, with a sculpted face that echoed a Renaissance painting Spock had once seen in the Manhattan Museum of Art. He found it a credit to Dr. Crusher that he remembered the painting now for the first time in nearly nine decades, but recalled also his thoughts at the time that the woman in the picture was pale and too thin. Understanding that humans' emotional condition frequently communicated itself to their physical appearance, he surmised that the doctor was strained and troubled. She did not smile as did her captain and first officer, and that he also found suggestive.

"Good evening, Doctor. I'm gratified to have you involved."

"Now you'll get some answers, Beverly," Captain Picard told her with a placating smile.

She glanced at him, then stepped closer to Spock.

"I'd like to say it's my pleasure, Ambassador," the woman said, "but unfortunately I doubt any of us will enjoy the next few weeks."

"That will depend upon the outcome, as always."

Spock slipped his traveling cloak from his shoulders and let his attending yeoman take it from him, leaving his arms a little cool with unencumberment. Though he felt obliged by tradition to wear the Vulcan robes and plastiformed emblems when moving among the public or visiting Starfleet localities, such dress aboard a ship seemed provincial. Among these men and women, he could feel comfortable in simple black slacks and his cowlnecked daywear tunic. The cobalt-and-purple quilted strips running from his shoulders to his thighs were the only jewel-tones on the bright tan bridge, excepting only the shoulder yoke of medical blue on Beverly Crusher's uniform.

Again, he found himself wading in memories unbidden.

And a few he had dismissed freely—the officers here on this bridge were people he knew, had encountered in a previous mission, and since allowed to fade from his mind. He had learned long ago to remember the names of ships, captains, and some officers—but that cluttering one's mind with lieutenants, yeomen, and others tended only to inaccuracy. Eventually those crewmen and officers either disappeared into the mists of service or civilian life, or became commanders and captains themselves, in which case their names and ranks and ships turned into a long roster he would just have to amend later.

He remembered Captain Picard's senior security officer, the noted Klingon who defied so much to be here, but he could not summon the name. The android at the science station, however, had a name that no mathematician could forget—Data.

"There've been two more skirmishes this morning, Ambassador," Captain Picard reported. "The Starfleet ships *Ranger* and *Griffith* were set upon just outside the Crystal Ball Nebula, and the *Ranger* was actually boarded."

"Is everyone all right?" Spock asked.

"No fatalities, sixteen casualties, and apparently one of their passengers was kidnapped. The details are hazy so far."

Troubled by these unpredictable rashes, so obviously driven by emotion rather than by tactical plans, Spock paused a moment to gather his thoughts.

"Unfortunately, events are moving forward with the rapidity typical of a national crisis. We can now officially call the disease an epidemic." Spock lowered his voice and significantly added, "Captain, the proconsul of the Senate died yesterday."

"Uh—oh," Riker opined.

Picard grimaced. "That means instability at the top of the empire."

"Dr. McCoy should be arriving soon," Spock told them, "with current information about the medical aspects of the Romulan crisis. You should shortly be receiving a signal from a Tellarite grain ship upon which he's traveling at the moment."

"Leonard McCoy," Dr. Crusher observed, "is the only man I've ever known who can shuttle in and out of nontreaty cultures as easily as the rest of us visit the stores in a shopping promenade. He can charm his way past border guards and squirm past warrants like some kind of spirit."

"Hardly charm," Spock commented. "In any case, we should shortly have fresh information. The massive sickness is causing havoc throughout the empire."

"We've been feeling the effect," Captain Picard validated. "These border eruptions are like wildcat strikes. Isolated leaders are finding excuses to attack Federation outposts and ships, staging incidents on purpose, hoping one of them will flame into all-out conflict. Nothing that smacks of coordination, however, not so far."

"They are not coordinated attacks at all," Spock concurred. "As certain members of the royal family die, their followers— and sometimes the family members themselves—are flaring up in frustration and anger."

"And fear," Crusher added. "The royal family is spread all over, and they're all in charge. And they're all terrified. They're not only dying themselves, but also watching their children die. It's not a gentle disease, Ambassador . . . it attacks quickly, painfully, then inflicts a slow death. It behaves like a curse. Some people think that's what it is. Terrified people do terrible things."

"We've got a reason to be terrified too," her captain said. "As more and more of the royal family die, others who have had no chance for power are seeing an opportunity for upheaval. The Federation's managing to handle these spurts without considering any one of them an act of war, but how long can we hold out? If the structure breaks down too much—"

"Could that happen?" Dr. Crusher asked. "Could the empress really be deposed because she and her whole family are sick?"

Riker looked at Crusher. "If the empress dies, all the hungry near-orbiters who never had a shot at the throne will start smelling velvet."

"With too many decisive defeats of Romulan flare-ups by Starfleet crews," Picard added, "the empress could be deposed very quickly and someone more hungry for war could take over. No matter how you look at it politically, there's every reason to stir up trouble and virtually no reason not to. So our goal in these skirmishes is to prevail, but not so decisively that the Romulan commanders are deeply humiliated or destroyed. We try to push them back without squashing them, stalling for time, seeking a biological solution. If the empress falls and her relatives are all infected too, there could be decades of instability on one of the Federation's longest borders. We have a stake in restoring the status quo."

"True," Spock agreed, relieved that they shared his hopes. "Better to have a stable empire as a neighbor than anarchy at our gates."

"Well, we've done a good job so far," Will Riker injected, "of keeping these flare-up attacks from turning into acts of war."

"As the family breaks down," Spock said, "some dissident

elements are striking out at the Federation, even though the core of the royal family is not yet ready to do that. Some of these elements are in control of ships."

Spock turned a fraction toward him, careful not to turn his back on the captain. "Those closest to power—the empress, her immediate relatives, and *their* immediate relatives—seem more concerned about stopping this biological attack than using it as leverage to foment trouble."

"Wouldn't you, sir? They see a chance that they might not have to die."

"Not everyone craves havoc, Mr. Riker. As Dr. Crusher pointed out, many of these victims wish only to live and see their children live, and to do so in a fairly stable civilization. Unfortunately, the empress must walk a very thin tightrope. For her own survival as a ruler, after nearly two hundred years of anti-Federation propaganda, she must not be seen as cowardly or complacent toward the Federation. The Romulan people on the outskirts, including those in command of ships, have been told all their lives to distrust the Federation. Now all the Romulan leadership is suddenly dying. What would you expect them to think?"

"Yes . . ." Riker's eyes widened. "How much of a leap would it be to assume the Federation is doing this?"

Spock rewarded him with a nod. "The propaganda is turning on them."

"And now they need our help," Dr. Crusher folded her long arms. "It figures. Has it occurred to anyone that this may be a genetic anomaly?"

"Isolated to the royal family?" Picard protested. "How likely is that?"

"Pretty damned likely, Jean-Luc." Crusher held out a hand. "The Romulans used to do genetic experiments—about a century ago, a little more. Those experiments could just now have incubated to mutancy and be coming back to bite them. It could be completely incurable. In that case, are we getting involved just to prove we *didn't* do it? I'm not sure I can prove a negative that big. If that's what the Federation expects, I've got an impossible mission here."

Wondering if indeed all physicians were necessarily cantankerous, Spock found himself sympathetic to her dilemma. The ball she had been cast was a familiar one to medical specialists with deep-space exploration, for they had the most experience dealing with the unknown, the foreign, and the unheard-of as commonplace. He had in his long life seen this first-hand, seen that expression in the eyes of many doctors into whose hands a monumental task had been shoved.

"Like myself, Doctor," he placated, "I know you prefer clarity to choices. However, choices are the more frequent curse of authority. The Romulans are advanced, but the Federation is much more advanced in the medical field. We've had to deal with so wide an array of alien members."

Will Riker cocked a hip and leaned against the navigation station, drawing a glance from the crewman manning the helm. "They might as well accept our help. They can always kill us tomorrow."

"Whatever the sociopolitical ramifications," Spock added, "they simply need our help."

"Captain, short-range emergency sensors," the fierce voice of Picard's Klingon officer erupted suddenly. As they all turned to look up at him, towering there over the tactical station at the back of the wide bridge, the surly lieutenant raised his eyes from the board and glared at the forward screen. "A Romulan Scoutship just decloaked off our bow!"

"Shields up, Mr. Worf. Red alert. Battle stations. Helm, hold position."

Lieutenant Worf watched the incoming angular feather-painted Romulan wing on the wide forward screen. "Should I arm photon torpedoes also, sir, considering their duophasic shields?"

"Ah, certainly."

Spock turned. "Captain, may I suggest—"

"I understand, Ambassador, but no Romulan commander expects less and I don't intend to show squeamishness."

Retreating, and somewhat embarrassed at this change in himself, Spock instantly acceded, "Forgive me."

"Captain, they are hailing," Data reported.

"Ship to ship, Mr. Data."

"Frequencies open, sir."

"This is Captain Jean-Luc Picard, *U.S.S. Enterprise,* Starfleet. Identify yourself, please."

"Subcommander Cul, Captain, Imperial Reconnaissance Scout Tdal."

"You're in violation of the Neutral Zone treaty by several light-years, Subcommander. Explain your presence here."

"Our weapons are cold, Captain. We have a passenger."

Picard paused, then glanced at Spock.

Spock was careful to keep his expression subdued, although this was probably a fruitless attempt, for even that subtle effort belied involvement.

"Yes," Picard drawled. "Mr. Worf, shields down. Subcomander, prepare for beaming."

"We are prepared."

Impressed, Spock once again looked at Picard. "How did you know, Captain? Even I was not sure."

"Because it's logical, Ambassador," the captain responded, his dark eyes glinting. "Mr. Data, please scan for human physiology and beam their passenger directly to the bridge."

"Understood, captain. Transporter room, this is the bridge."

The android relayed the captain's orders, and in 4.9 seconds the shaft of glittering energy appeared as expected on the portside deck ramp leading to the captain's ready room. Spock noted the angle of the ramp and hoped it would cause no trouble or surprise.

As the column of lights coagulated into familiar form, he stepped toward it, then again restrained himself, not wishing to appear too custodial. He was relieved when Mr. Riker stepped to the ramp and put out an assisting hand in anticipation. Another two seconds brought the white-haired, pin-thin form of Leonard McCoy fully onto the bridge, shouldering a simple canvas satchel. The work of the Romulan wing was done.

"Sir, the *Tdal* is bearing off," Worf reported immediately. "They are vectoring back toward Romulan space at emergency high warp."

"Very good—and I don't blame them," Picard said. "Stand down from general quarters. Welcome to the *Enterprise,* Dr. McCoy."

"Captain Picard, nice to be aboard," the doctor's elderly voice scratched. "Can you turn the heat up in here? That Romulan shoebox was cold as a coffin nail. Hi, Spock."

"Doctor."

"You're looking stiff."

"Thank you."

"Back trouble?"

"If you like."

"I brought a big hypodermic needle from my medical antiques collection."

"A display which ideally fits your personality, I have always reflected."

"I . . . ah . . . all right, I owe you one. Morning, Beverly."

"Leonard," the other physician chuckled. "And it's evening here."

"Dammit. Why can't the galaxy just go to Federation Standard Time?"

William Riker smiled again and took McCoy's sticklike arm in his to escort him down the ramp. Spock resisted the urge to reach out and stop Riker's robust grip—McCoy's spidery limbs seemed so frail—then chided himself for his absurdity.

"That was hardly a Tellarite grain ship, Doctor," he commented instead.

"So I lied. It was the only way I could get a ship with high warp to bring me all the way back. Anything else would've taken ten weeks. We don't have ten weeks."

"No, we don't," Crusher endorsed. "The Romulan royal family is not a dozen people. It's over a thousand, installed in positions of power all over the empire. How close you are to the current ruler causes a lot of jockeying and marrying and even assassinations, but there's never been anything like this. This certainly isn't just some jealous cousin maneuvering for the crown." She turned specifically to McCoy. "What have you concluded?"

"Concluded? Oh, I did say that in my message yesterday, didn't I? What I came up with is that the Romulans are right. The infection is definitely man-made. Not an accident."

"How did you come to this?" Spock asked, careful to phrase

the question in a way that would dodge McCoy's still-youthful barbed humor.

"I've made some progress. What else do you expect from a man old enough to call Moses by his first name? Anyway, that's why I need Beverly's help."

"You need *my* help?" Dr. Crusher asked.

"Hell, yes, I need help. I'm old, all right? Besides, you're the one who worked on this mess before."

She regarded him with a gaze startlingly similar to the way Captain Kirk used to regard McCoy. "You mean this Romulan disease is the same multiprion nightmare—?"

"That's right. The same thing you and Dr. Spencer of the *Constitution* encountered back on Archaria III. It's mutated or been artificially mutated. That's why you haven't recognized it. It's been targeted to the genetics of the Romulan royal family."

Clearly irritated that her victory was being compromised, Crusher scowled. "How did you recognize it if it's mutated?"

McCoy's white head bobbed in a nod. "My dear, you remember the line 'Methinks he doth protest too much'? Well, me have begun to think this infection doth show up too much. Prion-based infections just don't appear randomly this often, and certainly not in a pattern that leaps from one planet to another, infecting a vastly different DNA makeup. Somebody's forcing mutations, combining prions that would never hook up naturally, then targeting whole races for infection. This biological terrorism smacks to me of experimentation."

"My God!" Riker blurted.

Spock heard the exclamation, but was himself focused on the doctor's unexpected declaration. "Someone is working toward a larger goal? The Romulan royal family is not the target?"

"I don't think so," McCoy said. "I don't think the goal is to kill off the royal family at all. I think they're being used as an incubation test site. I think the goal is to develop a bioagent that can be neither cured nor treated."

"Upon what do you base this?"

The doctor's gravelly voice took on a surge of confidence. "On the same multiprion sickness popping up all over the place, sometimes in isolation, other times in populated areas, but each time with some new aberration. A plague here, a flu there, an infection yonder, a couple of them leaping racial boundaries . . . until now, nobody's tied the incidents together; but I've seen this kind of thing before on a smaller scale, and I got suspicious. So I started ordering some quiet information gathering about three years ago. And, folks, this isn't just an epidemic. It's a *pan*demic."

The word sent a chill through the bridge that Spock found nearly palpable. Even he discovered his hands suddenly clenched and forced himself to control his reaction. Ever since the first armies began forming and moving in the first civilizations on the earliest planets, pandemics had been a far more insidious scourge than any war.

Dr. McCoy paused long enough to see his revelation run its course of shock and nervousness, then enjoyed center stage again.

"When the Romulan royal family popped up with this deadly strain," he went on, "I started gathering the results of tests all over the quadrant, and sure enough they've got enough common characteristics to eliminate either the idea of coincidence or the idea of any other cause. These aren't dozens of isolated biological occurrences—they're all mutations of a single strain."

"So it couldn't be remnants of genetic testing?" Riker jabbed, leaning a little toward Dr. Crusher.

McCoy swiveled to him. "Genetics? Whoever said that?"

"Nobody said that," Crusher injected quickly. Her face masked a cold and bottled fury, as a knight's who had just been told the dragon is still alive. "Did you bring the results of all these tests? I'd like to examine them."

He patted his satchel. "Along with a cache of Scaffold Mints for the wardroom."

"As ever," Spock commented, "you keep your eye on the future."

"Watch it, pal, or I'll sit on you and give you a lecture on how long two cockroaches can live off the glue on the back of a postage stamp."

Dr. Crusher clasped her hands in a manner of controlled

anxiety. "Who ever heard of 'two cockroaches'? Doctor, have you isolated the matrix on this Romulan mutation?"

McCoy's ancient blue eyes fixed on hers with the zeal of youth. "First thing. And, bless us all, it's a DNA strain, not RNA, which mans we can beat it with one medication if we can come up with the right one. Healthy blood cells can replace the atrophied cells. All I need is a continuing source of uninfected royal blood for about a week to generate healthy plasma. But first, we've got to keep the members of the royal family who're still alive from dying. That's going to be your job. Keep them alive long enough to throw the infection off or for me to synthesize a cure."

"Treat the symptoms."

"But treat them in the right order. It might not be the right thing to do to lower a fever. The fever's something that I think helps. You're going to be treating the empress herself and over twenty of her family members on the home planet. You'll be communicating with physicians all over the empire, telling them how to treat the family members they've got. Meanwhile, I'll be trying to find a cure for the mutation. I've had my network of spies quietly sifting through information on the whole empire and the Federation—even through the Klingon Empire—for weeks now. So far, we haven't found a single family member who's not infected."

"Ripple-effect contamination," Crusher breathed. "God, that's a new twist. . . ."

"What's that mean?" Riker asked.

Spock almost answered, but restrained himself. He was curious to hear Dr. McCoy's analysis of what was happening to the Romulans, and forced himself to remember that his role on a starship was no longer to provide information and move events along.

"Means we can't synthesize a cure without an uncontaminated family member. I need clear blood, and I can't find anybody. Also means this is no accident. Somebody's doing this on purpose. Somebody planned this plague in such a way as to make sure it can't be cured. That's why," McCoy added, now turning to Picard, "I arranged to have this rendezvous on board the *Enterprise*."

"I beg your pardon?" Picard asked.

"Three years ago, Captain, you picked up a Romulan defector. He left the empire in disgrace after leading a coup against the empress. When that failed, he fled to the Federation and you offered sanctuary. Correct?"

"Oh . . . yes, a minor incident for us. We gave him sanctuary and resisted the extradition police on the planet where we found him. What was his name, Mr. Riker, do you remember?"

"Uh . . . believe it was Renn something, wasn't it, sir?"

"Check on the man, would you, please?"

"Aye, sir." Riker moved to the science station and looked over the android's shoulder. "Check ship's log and all ancillary documentations for Stardates 41099.1 through the ensuing six months. It's in there somewhere."

"Checking, sir."

"Then link into the archivist's computer at Starbase Ten. We're still in range, aren't we?"

While they worked, McCoy said, "Disgraced blood's as good as any. This defector's the third cousin to the empress on her mother's side, so it'll be undiluted blood and give us a strong base for immunological work."

"That must be what the message means," Picard said, glancing at Spock. "The admiralty gave me orders to cooperate with you both and transport you to any location in Federation space that you specified. They must mean for us to take you to this Rekk person, once we find where he is."

Spock nodded. "Rather than risk transporting him from station to station, we hoped to use the starship, for safety and security reasons."

"We're at your disposal, of course," Picard assured.

"If I can't find any uncontaminated plasma," McCoy contemplated, "then it's all over. Ninety-five percent of the infected people are going to die and there's no way to stop it. You get this thing, you are dead."

His flat statement had a chilling effect.

"The next trick," McCoy added, "is getting us in there."

"What?" Crusher asked. "Why don't we just go in? They know why we're coming, right?"

"They'll give special access to Dr. McCoy and to you,"

Riker told her, "but not to the starship. Medical access is a little different from military access."

"Correct," Spock said. "If any starship moves through the Neutral Zone and into Romulan space, the imperial leadership will be forced to act against us. Their own people will stand for nothing less. The empress knows Federation medical science may be their only chance, no matter who concocted this attack, but she would be forced to respond against a ship of the line or she could lose power before she loses her life."

"That's why we're not going," Picard explained. "At least, *we* are not." And he looked worriedly at Beverly Crusher.

"Arrangements will be made," Spock assured her, and felt suddenly remiss in having delayed securing passage. In fact, permission for passage into Romulan space had been secured, but not the method of passage.

"It's a problem," Captain Picard said. From the captain's expression, Spock could tell that the blueblooded commander of this *Enterprise* thoroughly understood the ramifications of secured space, and when a starship could and could not be of service.

"Yes," Spock reluctantly admitted. "Even the UFP diplomatic corp cannot breach imperial space. This time, the royal family wants us in, but no one else does. Perhaps . . . secrecy required concessions I should not have made this time."

"Sir?" Riker straightened at Data's side. "We've got something here."

The android touched his controls and read off, "The Romulan defector Rekk Devra Kilrune is no longer living in the Federation."

"Where is he, then?" Picard asked. "We'll go get him."

Data swiveled around in his chair, his expression particularly childlike. "No, sir . . . he is no longer *living* in the Federation."

Riker held out a hand that stopped what seemed to be turning into a debate of unclarity, and looked at his captain. "Rekk Devra was murdered, Captain . . . fifteen months ago, during a visit to Deep Space Nine."

A mantle of chill descended upon the bridge, as winter

cloaks northern hills. Spock felt it, and saw that all the others also felt it. Shoulders tightened, pensive glances traveled, fists clenched, lips pressed. Strange how a revelation could be so tangible, so very present.

The last living uncontaminated royal family member, dead. Whoever was driving the force of this plague was a critical step ahead.

And now . . . what?

Chapter Twelve

Combat Support Tender Saskatoon,
Starfleet Registry CST 2601

"DAMAGE CONTROL, TOP DECK!"

"Take some of the new midshipmen up there with you."

"Right. You and you, and your friend over there, come with me."

"And this one."

On the severely angled bridge deck of the *Saskatoon,* Eric Stiles hooked the nearest midshipman and handed him to Jeremy White as Jeremy rushed past him, dragging the other three kids.

"Did it hit us or just skin us?" Stiles tossed as an afterthought as he brushed hot bits of plastic from his shoulders. "Mr. Perraton, have somebody trim the deck gravitational compensators, please. Rafting hands, man umbilicals one, two, and four."

"Direct hit, midships upper quadrant, lateral shield, port side."

"Did you say upper quadrant?"

"Upper. At least I think it's there—" Jeremy's words became garbled as he disappeared into the bulky body of the CST, jumping through hatch after hatch until he got to the tubular companionway that would take him to the operational deck

137

above the middle of the ship. Smoke rolled freely from chamber to chamber through the body of the CST, a ship built on lateral lines to avoid transfer of equipment up and down ladder wells. Despite its 200-meter LOA, the tender only had three decks. Factories didn't need stairways.

"Rats," Stiles muttered, surveying the shattered trunk housing that had just been blown all over the deck. "Ship to ship."

To his right, at the comm station, Midshipman Zelasko controlled a cough and squeaked, "Ship to ship, sir."

Nearly choking on the acrid smoke from fried circuits in the deck and sparks on the smoldering carpet, Stiles held onto the helm stanchion as the CST rolled noticeably under him. "Captain Sattler, I've got to be able to get closer than this. If both our ships can't move off as a unit, you've got to kick those fighters off harder when they come into range. I know you've never done this before, but—"

"Sorry, Commander—Fire!" The captain's voice from the Destroyer *Lafayette* crackled back at him through the electrical charges of phaser and disruptor fire in open space. *"Sorry again. Two units got past us. I can't move off with a kinked nacelle, not even on impulse, without knowing what else is damaged up there."*

"The arbitrariness of battle is for you to worry about, Captain, thank the god of problems."

"He said cheerily," Travis Perraton edited from the other side of the narrow horseshoe-shaped bridge, where he was dodging from station to station coordinating the next few moves. To somebody on the upper deck, he spoke into a comm unit. "Just control the damage, Adams, don't repair it yet. We don't come first out here, remember?"

Spitting dust from his neatly trimmed moustache, Stiles turned forward again and wrapped up his communication with the destroyer. "We'll have your external diagnostic in a minute, Captain."

"Are you damaged? You're venting something off your upper hull."

"Yes, we've got some damage, but we'll repair it later. Your ship comes first. Keep the comm lines open if possible. You'll have to drop your shields while we raft up and do the work.

That'll be the tricky part. You'll want to have one of the other Starfleet ships run a cover grid."

"I'll contact the Majestic *and—tactical, broad on the bow— fire! Deflectors, shift double starboard! Hail the* Majestic— *fire at will, Samuels!* Majestic, *Sattler here—"*

"She's got her hands full." Stiles turned and called back into the scoped hatchways, not bothering with the comm. "Tell me when you know something, Jeremy! Those Romulans can see we're vulnerable, so work faster."

Jeremy's disembodied voice trailed back through three sections. *"Scanning . . . nacelle hasn't been breached . . . not on the outside, anyway . . . could be internal feedback from a hit someplace else, though. The main injector's secure . . . there's a crack in the sliding bulkhead. Let me follow it down . . . I got it, Eric, I see a fractured buckler. It's not the nacelle. It's the strut."*

"Great!" Stiles clapped his hands once, and startled the socks off his new helmsman. "That's a relief. Ship to ship— Captain Sattler, good news. It's not the nacelle that's kinked. It's only the strut. We'll raft up right here and square it, but you've got to keep those stingers off us for a solid fifteen minutes. I have to put extravehicular crew on the skin of your ship and I don't want anybody barbecued on your hull."

"Commander, you fix my nacelle in fifteen minutes in the middle of this mess and I'll owe you a big soppy kiss and a crystal decanter of your favorite. We'll put out the warning pennant and anybody who comes near your workers will feel the heat. There's nothing like a movable starbase when we need one!"

The charming—oh, yes—and sultry voice of the destroyer's captain made Stiles smile again. For a moment, he had trouble imagining her in a uniform. "I'll take the kiss and send the decanter to my grandfather. Maintain standby communications and let us handle the rafting. Drop your shields on our mark."

"Pennant's flashing. Standing by for rafting approach. Do you intend to use tractors or umbilicals?"

"Both," Stiles told her.

"Aren't tractors faster?"

"Usually, but if we get hit and there's a power failure, our ships would just drift away from each other and we couldn't help each other. With umbilicals, we'll be netted together no matter what happens."

"Good thinking. Ready when you are."

"Three . . . two . . . one . . . mark."

"Affirmative, shields down. Approach when ready."

Glancing at his bridge crew, Stiles said, "Okay, boys, we've got fifteen minutes! That's two to raft up and thirteen to effect repair. Let's clone that destroyer a new nacelle strut. Sound off."

From deep through the body of the combat support tender, team leaders and section masters called off.

"Internal repair squad ready, sir!"

"Rafting hands ready. Umbilicals one, two, and four manned, magnetic tethers hot."

"Rivet squad suited and ready, sir."

"Caissons ready."

"Gun team?"

"Weapons armed and ready!"

"Where are the evil twins?"

"Already in the airlock, Eric."

"Beautiful. Lateral thrusters one half. Let's move in."

"All hands, brace for action rafting! Shields down!"

Ah, the chatter of activity. What a good noise.

Out there, not far away on the cosmic scale, a half dozen Romulan fighters darted around two Starfleet destroyers, one patrol cutter, and three merchant ships caught in the crossfire. Bursts of phaser fire, disruptor streams, glancing hits and direct detonations lit the fabric of black space like flashing jewels. There was a startling beauty about it, stitched firmly into the crazy quilt of hazard and excitement.

"Okay, you lot—tea time! Battle Cook Woody reportin' f'duty, sah!"

Stiles rolled his eyes and groaned. What timing.

At the port entryway, Ship's Mess Officer Alan Wood came rolling in as he always seemed to in moments of critical action, or did critical action always happen at teatime?

Stiles didn't argue, as their in-house real-live London butcher distributed cookies, tea, and coffee to an obviously busy crew.

"There y'go. Two sugars, Trav. Told y'I wouldn't f'get. Eric, sir, no caffeine for you, double cream, honey, and ye olde ginger snaps."

"You always know what calms me down, Alan. And don't call me 'honey.'"

"Aye aye, dear."

"Put the tray down and take over Jason's driver coil balance, Battle Cook."

"You got it."

They were completely vulnerable now. Both the CST and the destroyer were shields down. These were the crucial minutes during which any enemy shot could cut all the way through any bulkhead or hull plate and take out anything inside, man or machine.

He glanced around at the bridge crew, peeked back through the infinity mirror of hatchways leading into the depths of the *Saskatoon* and its work areas, saw the unit leaders looking back at him from their various places, and satisfied himself that all segments were ready to work. He turned now to watch the two main screens, one always viewing forward, one always aft, and the sixteen auxiliary screens around the horseshoe. On the screens, shown from a dozen different angles, there was a hot battle going on at this edge of a small solar system. He stood beside the command chair, so seldom used that it held parts and charts and anything else they needed handy at any given time. He almost never sat in it. Should have it removed altogether.

"Watch your aft swing," he told the helmsman. "There's a solar current here."

"I can do it manually, I think," the helmsman boldly claimed.

"You think, *sir.*" Travis turned at the brash helmsman's statement, reached across the auxiliary board on the upper controls, and tapped one of the pads. "I've got it. Stabilizers on."

The young helmsman fumed, but said nothing.

Stiles glanced at Travis and shrugged. Kids.

He stepped a little closer to the helm, just to intimidate at the right level. If only he could remember the kid's name.

"Okay, junior," he decided, "this is your first battle rafting. Let's do it right."

The midshipman gritted his teeth. "Aye, sir."

"Adjust to starboard on the transverse axis . . . watch your amplitude of pitch . . . not bad. Don't let the roll go . . . quarter reverse on the port lateral. More thrust to port . . . less underthrust . . . never mind the bumpers, don't try to be graceful. . . ."

On the starboard deck, Travis clamped his lips to keep from laughing at the helmsman's obvious annoyance with help he clearly needed. Stiles saw the effort, but any possibility of amusement for himself was lost in the sheer danger of what they were about to do. An action rafting was never routine, no matter how well-drilled the crew could possibly become.

When the CST and the destroyer were snugged up beam-to-beam and in line, and the CST had been raised to near-touching level with the *Lafayette*'s starboard nacelle, Stiles called, "Pass line two."

"Pass two!" the response came from amidships.

On one of the small monitors, umbilical number two snaked out and grappled the attraction bracket on the high side of the destroyer.

"Capture two!" the line handler called.

Suddenly the destroyer heaved up on its port nacelle as a Romulan fighter veered in too close and opened fire. Bright light washed Stiles and everyone around him from all the starboard screens, a fierce shining glitter of destruction and raw heat.

"Whoa," Stiles murmured, shielding his eyes. "Close one."

Travis flinched at the proximity of death. *"Lafayette,* steady your position, can you?"

"We're attempting to hold as steady as possible, Saskatoon," the other commanding officer responded. *"That current came up under us just as that Romulan fired on us. Double whammy."*

"I know you're taking fire," Stiles interrupted, "but we only need thirty seconds to finish this. Hold still that long."

"Understood."

"Spring in closer now," he said to the helm trainee. "Keep us trim. Work a little faster. Don't overcompensate. Let the gravitational umbilicals do the heavy lifting."

"Closing," the kid said. "Twenty meters . . . fifteen meters . . ."

"Pass one."

"Passing one!"

"Hold two."

"Two holding."

"Capture one!"

"Forward starboard thruster one quarter and shift down port bow 10 degrees."

"Forward one quarter, port bow down ten, aye."

"Pass four, hold one."

"Passing four!"

"Hold one, aye."

"Two and four, haul away."

"Haul away two!"

"Haul away four!"

Music, music. the church chimes of efficient rafting. Thirty seconds to spare. Snuggling his CST up to a big, powerful, scarred, smoldering battleship in the middle of a flashing firefight—ah! The chunky hull of the CST didn't fit well against the streamlined multihulled destroyer, so he had to pick and choose which umbilicals would line up best, then cast one and pivot in on it. What a gorgeous process.

"I love skirmishes," he effused happily. "That's good! Cut thrust. Engine crew, stand by. Mr. Blake! Scan for stress."

"Scanning, sir."

As disruptor fire flashed on some of the smaller monitors, showing the ongoing space battle between another destroyer and those Romulan buzzsaws, Stiles nodded in satisfaction, even though Blake couldn't see him. Greg Blake had known him since they were both fifteen years old. The "sir" was almost silly in that regard, but he knew his long-time crew threw it in for effect at moments like this. There were always impressionable midshipmen and junior officers serving on the CST, most of whom would move on after the grueling training they would receive here.

On the screen to his left, the streamlined body of the Destroyer *Lafayette* drew close to the lumbering CST, in fact close enough to touch if that viewport had been a window they could open. He saw the gleaming hull plates and the button-head rivets as clearly as his own fingernails.

"What a great way to live," he muttered. "She gets all the glory and the headaches, she has to guess what the enemy's doing—and on top of that she has to protect us in the middle of a battle. This is the best damn duty around."

"You could ask for a date," Travis suggested. "I bet she'd go, the way she sounds when she talks to you. Maybe if you grow your beard back—"

"I'm not dating anybody who outranks me," Stiles commented, aware of the glances from Midshipman Zelasko at the comm station and the two little ensigns over at the engineering board. "Bad enough having a cocky Canadian first officer around. And the beard itched."

Outside, close enough to smell the gunpowder, seven other ships were engaged in a spark battle, a border skirmish with hotheaded Romulans. These eruptions had been going on for months now, sparks of aggression that seemed like temper tantrums from isolated Romulan units. The empire kept claiming nothing was wrong, that these were just dissatisfied commanders venting their frustration, but Stiles didn't believe it. Something was going on in the Romulan Empire that was causing rogue attacks. The Federation wanted to be prudent. Ignore acts of war. Avoid any one of these bursts turning into a lit fuse that couldn't be put out by anything other than full-out conflict.

"Okay, Travis," Stiles said when he was satisfied that the ships were as close as possible and the umbilicals were taut. "Go do that voodoo that you do so well."

"Ten seconds and counting," Travis responded, and hit a comm button. "Rivet team, hit open space. Signal when you're on the davit boom."

"Acknowledged," one of the Bolt brothers responded. *"Ready."*

"Launching." Travis hit his controls.

The hiss of the airlock shot through the whole ship. There

was no place on the CST to get away from that big sound as the lock depressurized and the repair crew sprayed out from the tender on a spider web of cables from the swinging davit, two men to a cable, a total of twelve men in spaceworthy suits, each fully armed with a trapeze harness and a tool vest. Their job wasn't to fight the enemy—it was to fight the enemy's results.

The interior of the CST fell oddly silent, giving way to the bleeps and whirs of shipboard mechanical redundancy, and a symphony of eyes swept the wall-wide grid of screens. Dozens of angles, each fixed on some aspect of the repair job—only a few were dedicated to the fight that was still going on within phaser-striking distance of this oddly protectionless refuge.

Stiles settled back on his heels and listened to the critical exchange between Jeremy White, back in the engineering control room, and Travis here on the bridge, whose job it was to manage the rivet squad. In less than a minute, the two men had the rivet squad swung over on the external davits to the nacelle of the *Lafayette,* crawling all over it with their magnetic boots like a tidy infestation.

The open comm lines brought in the work as if it were happening right at his feet, bits of dialogue overlapping others as the squad split up to do a half dozen jobs in a matter of minutes.

"Got some burnoff plating infecting this binding strake."

"I'll help you."

"Stand clear."

"Two more centimeters."

Travis talking at the same time: "Don't crowd him, Zack. You're too close to the welding stream."

"I'm Jason."

"Clone."

"I need the spreader over here."

"—swing that caisson under me, will you?"

"—and engage the thrusters so you've got balance—"

Then Jeremy's voice from two sections back: "Mr. Evans, countersink those outer rivets before you caulk them in."

"You sure, sir?"

"We always countersink. Maintains a flush surface."

"What difference—"

"A big one at hyperlight. Morton, what are you doing? Move your arm so I can see."

"Chocking the vertical bracket stringers?"

Stiles touched his comm button and interrupted. "Chock 'em in under the shell plating, Mr. Morton. Then caulk it with foam."

"Won't hold more than a week."

"It only has to hold a day. Just double-secure the center of effort and wrap it up. You got nine minutes left."

"Thank you."

"Welcome."

"Mr. Lightcudder?"

Startled by a completely unfamiliar voice only inches from his shoulder, Stiles cranked around and found himself face to face with a total stranger. Total! Never seen the guy before. Right here on the working deck!

Civilian. No uniform, no identifying patches or badges. Work clothes.

How could this happen?

It couldn't, but here he was, grinning like a Halloween pumpkin. No escort, no nothing.

Oh—actually there was a nervous ensign standing at the bridge hatchway, evidently having just brought the man in. Why hadn't the ensign done the officer approach? The ensign shrugged as Stiles raked him with a glare.

The civilian was stocky, wearing a bulky tan jacket with big round buttons and a heavy neck scarf, which gave the man an illusion of being short. Actually Stiles looked him nearly in the eye, so he was at least five feet nine. He had a round face with flush-dots on the puffy cheeks, a halo of metal-shaving hair mounted behind his balding forehead, round brown eyes, round shoulders—the guy was round.

"Are you Mr. Lightcudder?" the round guy asked.

"What?" Stiles stepped back and got a better look. "Who are you? How'd you get on my bridge?"

The odd newcomer kept his eyes fixed on Stiles. "They just put me on board from the *Lafayette*. I was told to report to Mr.

146

Lightcudder. My name's Ansue Hashley and I'm *so* grateful for—"

"A civilian is transferred to my CST and this is the first I hear of it?"

Greg Blake strode by and handed him a padd on the way past. "Nobody likes to talk to you."

"We avoid it," Matt Girvan said from the engineering support station.

"Any of you know about this?" Stiles asked, swiveling a glance around the bridge.

Nobody did.

"Well, Mister—"

"Hashley. Ansue Hashley. I'm—"

"You'll have to stand by a few minutes. We're in the middle of an operation. Just park right there and don't do anything and don't touch anything."

"I will, Mr. Lightcudder, I mean I won't, and I'll stand right here." Hashley planted both feet and pointed a sausage finger at his boots.

Stiles glanced at Travis, who frowned and muttered, "Lightcudder . . ."

"Stiles, Jason. There's some kind of Charlie Noble sticking up here and it's actually hot."

Turning back to his job, Stiles twitched at the proximity of the stranger. "Hot? Electrically?"

"No, it's actually radiating heat. In fact, it's glowing."

"That can't be right. . . ."

"No kidding. I don't want to touch it."

"No, don't touch it. Jeremy!"

"Copy that," Jeremy called from two hatches back. "Pretty weird, Eric. You want me to suit up?"

"Talk to the destroyer's CE first. Have him tell you what that thing is and turn it off if he can. I don't want a hole burned in somebody's EVS."

"Closing the breach now . . . two more centimeters . . . one more . . . hold!"

"Hold the crane!"

"Holding."

"What's all that they're talking about?" Hashley asked.

Annoyed, Stiles quickly said, "Just shortcuts we take, Mr. Hashley. We have to get the *Lafayette* back into action so they can press the Romulans back."

"Are they going to kill the Romulans?"

"Not if they can avoid it."

"Isn't this a battle?"

"No, it's just a commercial blockade. Some hothead venting off at us."

"But the Romulans attacked your patrols, didn't they? Isn't that an act of war?"

"It's more complicated than that."

"I thought we were having a war and that's why they wanted me."

"No war yet." With his demeanor Stiles did his best to communicate that he was preoccupied.

"Rig a gantline over here. We'll just horse the strut with brute force and tribolt it."

"I love brute force. Gives me a sense of superiority."

"—the magnetic coupling?"

"No, the spreader. I'll hand it—"

"—the only way you'll ever get any respect."

"What kind of a ship is this?" Ansue Hashley looked all around. "It's not a starship—"

Stiles watched the screens, told himself that he should ignore the man, then decided he would enjoy showing off a little. "No, not a starship."

"Cruiser?"

"No."

"Battleship."

"Hardly. Jason, Stiles. Pull that spreader all the way out of the bridle and discard it. Don't be tidy. Six minutes."

"Six, aye."

"What kind of ship are you, then?" Hashley asked again.

"We're a combat support tender. Some people call us a 'floating starbase.' We're a heavy-laden, multipurpose vessel made to support more specialized Starfleet vessels. We carry structural and weapons-repair specialists, materiel, fuel, ammunition and dry stores. We can resupply a ship on the fly or right in the middle of active engagement, like we're doing now. One of our jobs is to quickly make operational any ready-reserve ships on standby. We did that to *Lafayette* last week."

"And now she needs you again!" Hashley's eyes flew wide. "Right in the middle of a fight! How do you do something like that!"

"With step-by-step processes. Being fast is a matter of survival, not just success."

"You must've been busy lately, with all the trouble that's been erupting."

"We've been nonstop for months," Stiles agreed. "Wish we knew why all these skirmishes were erupting—"

"I know why! Do you want me to tell you? I know all about it!"

Stiles leered briefly at the man, sure he didn't actually know more than Starfleet frontliners, but disturbed by Hashley's confident claim.

"Crossfire! Incoming!" Ensign Ashikaga shouted from the tactical sensors.

"Detonate!" Stiles authorized, and the shots lanced out before the sound his words had died.

At the weapons console, Matt Girvan fell on his controls instantly, obviously expecting the authorization to fire while there were extravehicular crew out there. He'd been ready to defend the CST, despite the attempts by *Lafayette* and *Majestic* to protect the wounded destroyer and her rafted repair ship. Phaser fire blew from the *Saskatoon,* cutting across the paths of two streams of disruptor fire that actually were meant to hit the *Majestic* but had missed. The shots detonated in midspace—good work, though the power wash and the stress of opening fire rocked the CST and caused the umbilicals to sing through their hull mounts. The inside of the ship whined freakishly, buffeted by the power wash.

"Oh, what happened?" Ansue Hashley's arms flew wide as the deck rocked. "Did we get shot?"

Not a direct hit, but the wash did enough damage to fritz several of the monitors. Two went completely dark, and a half dozen flashed and became garbled, losing the view of the rivet team on the destroyer's nacelle strut.

His ears aching, Stiles crossed to the portside monitors and called over the whine. "Check the men!"

Horrified by the shouts and calls rattling over the comm from the repair team, he fixed on the nearest monitor, which showed a closeup flurry of elbows and parts of suits, but didn't give a clear view of any one person.

Frantic for a wide view, Stiles muttered, "I'd really like a look."

"I'm getting green on all the life-support signals," Travis said with undisguised relief. "The body of the ship deflected the wash."

"Lucky angle. I hate to fire when I've got men out." No one paid any attention except Ansue Hashley, whose eyes somehow got even wider at the declaration. Stiles punched the nearest comm link. "Rivet squad, running out of time. Minute and thirty left."

"Shouldn't you be out there, Mr. Lightcudder?" Hashley asked. "If you're in command?"

"No, they don't need me out there."

"Maybe there's something I can do. . . ."

"Not right now, thanks."

"Stiles, Bolt. Strut cradle's secure, riveted, and caulked. Main injector's flowing and the sliding bulkhead is jury-rigged over the cofferdam and—Monks, is it glazed? Yes, it's glazed and chemical-bonded. Ready to retract the caissons and the davit."

"A whole minute early!" Stiles whooped. "You guys are singing! Back inside before we get another visitation."

He stood back to listen to the tumble of orders as the rivet team handled their own reshipping. This was when all the hours of brain-frying drills paid off.

"Mr. Stiles, this is Sattler. We saw the crossfire. Do you need assistance?"

"Don't worry about us, Captain. Your ship's the important one here, not ours. Soon as I get my men aboard, we'll shove off and you can do your job with those Romulans. Congratulations on your first combat rafting."

"You're a piece of work, Mr. Stiles. Now I know where you get your reputation."

"All lies. Stand by, please."

Travis met his questioning gaze as if cued in psychically. "The caissons are boarded, davits coming back in, and all hands will be aboard in another few seconds."

"Ready on the umbilicals. Prepare to shove off," he called through the ship, not bothering with the comm.

"Ready one!"

"Ready on two!"

"Ready four!"

"Release four."

"Release four, aye!"

"Slack one. Helm, swing out on number two." Yikes, he sure had to find out that kid's name soon. Always happened when they got a new batch of trainees. "Hey, I said slack one!"

"Slacking one!"

"Haul away, four."

"Hold it!" Jeremy suddenly called from three compartments back. "Four's fouled."

"Hold all lines!" Stiles poked his head through the hatch, but didn't actually leave the bridge. "What's the story?"

"Looks like the retractor's jammed. Must've taken a hit we didn't notice."

"Disengage the line."

"Cut and run from our end?"

"Right, let it float. We'll pick it up later if we can. It's not fouled onto *Lafayette,* is it? Because we'll have to go out again if it is. They can't trail a line into battle."

"No, line's free. It's our retractor housing."

"Cut it."

"Aye aye . . ." They all waited until a loud *chunk* boomed through the ship's body. Then Jeremy spoke again. "Line's detached. We're clear, Eric."

"Ship to ship." He watched while the communications kid tapped in, then looked at the screen displaying the nearby plates of the destroyer. "We're clear of rafting, *Lafayette.* Bear off laterally. When you've cleaned up the mess out there, we'll reprovision you and the *Majestic.*"

"*Excellent job,* Saskatoon. *Bearing off. Shields up. And thanks again, double trouble.*"

"No problem. Good work, Mr. Perraton, Mr. White, everybody."

He turned to the main screen as, with nothing less than heart-stirring dynamism, the great shining gray form of the destroyer peeled off at quarter impulse and drove into the swarm of Romulans.

"This is wondrous!" Ansue Hashley hopped on his toes and spread his hands wide. "You should be in the headlines!"

"Nah, no headlines. This is nuts-and-bolts duty."

"But you should get recognition for this kind of wonderful thing!"

"Do without food and bandages for a while. Helm, hard over. Come full about and give them room to fight. I don't want the destroyers to have to protect us."

"Hard over, sir."

"I could write an article!" Ansue Hashley insisted. "I know some people where I could send it! You do such a vital, glorious thing!

Stiles watched the screens, deliberately not looking at him. "It's vital, not glorious. Headlines are for the *Lafayette* and the *Majestic*."

Shuddering as its great engines vibrated, the muscular combat tender turned on an axis and hummed away from the center of the dispute, leaving the cloud of Romulans and the two Federation ships behind in a sparkle of weapons fire.

"Secure the ship, Travis," he said casually, knowing that the actual activities were hardly casual. Punching the comm, he added, "Clones, Stiles."

"Bolt and Bolt, Ship Riveters-at-Large. Would you like an appointment, sir?"

"Great work, rivet squad, excellent. You get an 'A' for speed and an extra minute to sleep tonight."

"Wow."

"Bailiff, shoot that man."

As the laughter of relief and satisfaction rippled through the CST, Stiles turned like an old-time gunfighter and hooked his thumbs in an imaginary holster belt.

"Okay, Mr. Hashley . . . what's your story?"

"Oh! Me—yes!" Ansue Hashley stuck out a computer cartridge. "I watched while they composed this. It says right on here to report to Mr. Lightcudder and give this to you. Is it all right to?"

Stiles pushed the card into the nearest terminal, which clicked, and flipped, but nothing came up on the monitor above it.

"Where is it?" he wondered.

From the tool alley, Greg Blake called, "It's back here, Mr. Lightcudder."

"Uh . . . yeah, would you pass it back up here, please?"

"Certainly, Mr. Lightcudder."

The screen flickered once, then a message came up on it— printed, not vocal. Obviously somebody didn't want this read aloud by anybody, including the ship's systems.

"Mmm . . . explains . . . almost nothing." Stiles looked at the printed message, sensing Travis and the bridge guys looking from behind him. "You don't deal much with Starfleet, do you, Mr. Hashley?"

ATTENTION MR. LTCDR
EYES ONLY DO NOT BROADCAST
HOLD ITEM TOP SECURITY

"Not even the name of the ship in the message," Travis said as he came up behind Stiles. "What item?"

Stiles cocked a hip and glared at him until Travis uttered, "Oh . . . right."

They both turned to Hashley, who looked back and forth between them again and again.

"Smuggling?" Stiles asked.

"Oh, transporting. I'm an agricultural broker. Usually, anyway. Well, I used to be. Sometimes I take other cargo. Well, most of the time. Well—"

"What other cargo?"

"Anything anybody wants. Mostly stuff the Romulans want. Most of the time I don't even know what's in the crates and casks. I don't ask much. I've been running the same twenty-light-year relay for the past seven years. The Romulans had laws that said I shouldn't be doing it, but they were liking what

I did. They could've stopped me any time, but they bought what I had and paid me to move more. If the patrols stopped me, they usually settled for a quarter of my cargo." Ansue Hashley smiled, and suddenly looked like a carved pumpkin. "I give very generous bribes."

How could you hate a jack-o-lantern?

"First of all, 'Lightcudder' isn't anybody's name. Those letters mean 'Lieutenant Commander.' "

Hashley blinked as if he'd been slapped. "But aren't you . . . the captain? Oh, no, did I make a terrible mistake?"

"No, you didn't make a mistake. Combat support tenders are piloted by lieutenant commanders, officered by lieutenants, and crewed by chief, ensigns, midshipmen, and able crewmen. Most of these young people are here for experience and training. CST duty is considered good experience because of the active labor, tactical judgment, and hands-on ship handling. You also get a taste of battle situations without actually having to fight. Not usually, anyway. So I'm not 'Captain Lightcudder.' I'm Lieutenant Commander Stiles."

"Oh . . . oh, goodness, oh, my goodness, I made such a big mistake. . . . Stiles, Stiles, I won't forget again. Oh, I'm so sorry. . . ."

"No, no."

"But I feel just awful, horrible—"

"It's not important. What *is* important is how you got transferred here without my knowing about it, and why the *Lafayette* would do that."

"Oh, I'm top secret! At least, my location is."

"Why?"

"Because the Romulans are trying to kidnap me."

As Travis finished his immediate duties and came down to the center of the squatty bridge to stand behind him, Stiles folded his arms and insisted again, *"Why?"*

"Because I know too much. I'm the one who knows why the Romulans have been skirmishing with the Federation on all the border fronts. You said you didn't know, remember? But I do."

Stiles glanced at Travis, who made a subtle shrug with just his eyes.

"The *Lafayette* slipped you on board here to sort of shuffle the cards so the Romulans wouldn't know which ship you're on?"

"Yes! Also to get me out of the line of fire. The Federation doesn't want me to be a scraping goat."

"Well, how do you feel about telling me this big secret that suddenly makes my ship a target?"

"Oh, I feel fine about it! I know everything. I know why the Romulans are panicking."

Hashley stepped closer and poked Stiles in the folded forearm, and his eyes got big as golf balls.

"Poison! The whole Romulan royal family! Every single member of the emperor's bloodline, no matter where they are, all over the empire. They're all dying!"

"What?"

Astonished, Eric Stiles sank back on the edge of the helm. His feet felt molded to the deck. His arms wouldn't unfold.

"We haven't heard anything about that!" Travis blurted, glancing custodially at Stiles, then back at the funny agricultural broker who had been dropped on them.

"It's a big, huge secret," Hashley went on. "The Romulan royal family is trying to keep it secret. They don't want anybody to know their empire's leadership could all be dying, one by one. It'll be just a mess if such a big weakness gets discovered, even if only by people inside the empire."

Behind Stiles' shoulder, Travis asked, "And they think the Federation's behind the . . . the whatever's killing them?"

"Poisoning," Hashley said. "Or maybe an engineered virus—anyway, it's something definitely artificially constructed. A hundred and ten members of the royal family have died already, and all the others are infected. I'm the only Federation citizen running the Neutral Zone, so they know I'm smart and I know why they're attacking Federation ships."

Stiles swallowed a hard lump and registered that his feet were suddenly blocks of ice. That didn't sound right. Nobody cared that much about one Federation guy running cargo, and Hashley sure wasn't the only one.

"What's this thing they've got?" he asked. "How does it manifest itself?"

"They've got a blood disease. First they get real weak, real suddenly. Then their arms and legs start hurting. Pretty soon they can hardly walk and breathe. It's infected every single member of the emperor's bloodline. It's specialized to the blood of the royal family, so they know this is a mass-assassination attempt. It's supposed to be a secret, but I found out about it, so they tried to kidnap me."

"The Romulans?"

"That's right. And the *Majestic* came in and rescued me, and they were trying to get back to Federation space with me when the Romulans attacked them. They beamed me to the *Lafayette* to confuse the Romulans, and now the *Lafayette* beamed me to you, to keep confusing them. Now they don't know where I am."

The bridge fell to an uneasy silence.

"Aren't you kind of . . . blabbing a lot, Mr. Hashley?"

"Oh, yes! That way I'm never the only one to know anything!"

"Pretty cavalier about it, aren't you?" Travis commented.

Hashley shrugged his round shoulders and showed the palms of his hands, then abruptly clapped them together and drew a sharp breath. "Stiles! Are you Eric John Stiles?"

"Well—"

"I remember you! You're Eric John Stiles the Hero! You got the Medal of Valor eight years ago!"

"Ten," Stiles mumbled.

"Eleven," Travis corrected, and he took Hashley by the arm in a stern manner. "We don't talk about that around here very much, Mr. Hashley. He's just our lightcudder and that's how we keep it."

"Oh, I'm so happy to be here and meet him, though!"

"Mr. Hashley," Stiles interrupted, "is there anything you're not telling us?"

"Me? No! I'd tell you anything I knew. I don't want to know any secrets, not ever. Secrets can get you killed. I never want to be the only one—"

"Okay, okay." Stiles pushed himself off the helm and

uncracked his tingling arms from around his ribs. "I'll keep you in protective custody until I can communicate with somebody about you . . . if you'll just . . . quiet down a little. We'll assign you a bunk . . . Travis, uh . . . get some crew up here to clean up all this broken plastic and chips."

"Oh, I'll do it!" Hashley dropped to his knees right where he was standing and began swiftly plucking the residue of damage off the deck and stuffing it into his pockets. "I love to help. Sitting in quarters while everybody else is working, that's just not for me. I'm an action kind of man."

"Yeah . . . Travis, take us back over the Neutral Zone border and . . . hold position in case they need us again. I'll be in my quarters."

With icy hands clenched, Stiles paused in the dimness of his quarters and closed his eyes. The computer had clicked and whirred, but it had provided only poor answers. A thousand memories shot back as if rocketing from yesterday instead of—what was it, now, fourteen, almost fifteen years ago? Didn't seem so long.

The door chime sounded.

For a moment, he thought of not answering.

"Yeah."

The panel opened and Travis looked in. "Hey, Lightcudder. Can I interrupt?"

"Sure."

Travis came all the way in, carrying a steaming cup of hot chocolate and a particularly concerned expression he was trying to disguise as something else. He stood at the door for a moment as it closed behind him.

"You all right, Eric?" he asked.

Warmed by the solicitous effort, Stiles tried to appear relaxed by brushing the remains of his breakfast toast off his desk chair. "Eh, I guess so. Sit down, Travis. And I, in my infinite wisdom, shall sit also."

He slumped into the chair, and put one boot up on the edge of a drawer that wasn't quite closed and his elbow up on the desk.

Depositing the hot chocolate on the desk near Stiles' resting hand, Travis sat down on the bunk. The quarters were too small for two chairs, so the bunk was almost constantly rumpled, being used more often as a couch than a place to sleep. "Ship's secure. Jeremy's handling the damage we took—it should be repaired in about twenty minutes. And Ansue Hashley's crawling around the chambers sucking up damage with the shoulderheld vac."

"You guys are getting the process down fast with these new kids."

"That's what we do. The fight's still going on, but the destroyers seem to have it locked up. The Romulan fighters are trickling away one by one. I think they'll leave us alone."

"Good," Stiles muttered. "I need to be left alone." As Travis planted both feet and leaned forward, Stiles quickly amended, "No, no, I don't mean you."

The door chimed and Greg Blake poked in when the panel opened. "Eric, okay if we shut down the warp injection system so we can flush the lines?"

"How many of the Romulan fighters are still in the vicinity?"

"Only about four now."

" 'About' four?"

"Guess I better check."

"Guess you better. But listen, hail Captain Sattler and make sure we're not pressuring her by staying in the vicinity. If she needs us to bear off, we'll move out before we shut anything down. Be nice about it."

"Will do. Sorry to interrupt."

The door panel slid shut again.

"You never try to push, do you?" Travis observed. "That's why all the captains appreciate you so much."

"It's just that I'm sweet and polite and I know my place."

"Know your *place* . . . ?"

"Sure, think about it. CST's are usually commanded by the guys who couldn't qualify to run the glory machines, so they get out among the starshippers and try throwing their weight around. They're impolite. They take it out on the captains, who they think surpassed them. I'm just not like that. I try to be accommodating and patient and helpful without being ub—ob—what's that word you used last week?"

"Obsequious?"

"That's it. I'm satisfied with what I'm doing. Remember when we got assigned the CST duty? The team was depressed and down because they thought we'd get something fancier, but they all adjusted, and it's turned out to be great work."

"They adjusted because you packed 'em off to special training for combat-ready missions. You made sure we all had skills in hands-on operations management, not just Academy certificates in theories and simulators. Then you juggled us around until you found our strengths. You even pushed Brad and Bill back out to the private sector."

"I had to push them. We had a good relationship going among all of us, and nobody wanted to be the first to leave. They were ready to go. Starfleet couldn't make as much use of them as free enterprise could. Not everybody flourishes in uniform. CST duty didn't make good use of their natural abilities. For others, this is the best they'll do, or this is where they're most useful. Better this than have them go out and try to be hotshots and wash out. Maybe cost some lives."

Travis grinned coquettishly. "What about me?"

"You? You're a bum. I just keep you here as my first officer out of charity. And me . . . this is perfect for me."

"Eric?" One of the evil twins knocked on the door, not bothering with the chime. "You asleep?"

"No, come on in."

One of the Bolts appeared and stuck his tousled blond head around the doorframe. "Permission to put a team outside and patch the PGV meter?"

"As long as Jeremy says it's safe to go out."

"Right. And do either of you know where the cylinder punch went? As my mother used to say, 'You had it last.' "

Travis spoke up before Stiles could bother saying he didn't know. "It's in the aft locker in the tool alley, Zack, on the inboard side, underneath the conduction paper."

"Thanks. Sorry to interrupt."

When they were alone again, Stiles regarded Travis with

quizzical respect. "How do you tell those two apart so fast? Fifteen years, and it still takes me half a conversation."

"Just doing what any good exo does. So . . . what do you think of Hashley?"

"I think he's into something a lot more complicated than he believes," Stiles said. "I checked the Bureau of Shipping records just before you came in. Ansue Cabela Hashley, human, Federation citizenship, most of the right licenses, skirts the law now and then but not much, originally from Rigel system, nothing much worth putting on record. He's been running the same patch of space back and forth for years like a bug, shuttling minor contraband into Romulan space. The Romulans have pretty much encouraged him by not enforcing their own laws in his case. He probably brings in things they can't get, and they like it. He hasn't been hurting anybody and more people like him than not, so he's been considered small potatoes."

"Till now."

Stiles nodded. "He's a cosmic worker-insect. Now he's stepped in goo and he's stuck. Probably he doesn't even realize that the reason he's been safe is that things haven't been too tense with the Romulans over the past twenty years. Now that they're tensing up, well, he *has* been breaking Romulan law right along. I'm guessing the Federation doesn't have good cause to protest. Then he stumbled on this poison thing and suddenly the small potato is a hot potato."

"What do you think the connection is between the blood thing and Hashley?"

"No idea."

"It's got to be more than he thinks," Travis surmised. "More than just his 'knowing' about the poisoning, or whatever it is. Nobody would try to kidnap him just because he knew about it."

"He said it could be an engineered virus. Some kind of assassination plot. If a hundred or so imperial relatives have died, I can't believe Starfleet's not working on it already. We're a day late and a dollar short to make it our problem."

Stiles sank deeper into his chair, rocked back some, and rested his head on the worn neckrest. As the chair protested with a squawk, the hot chocolate finally drew him with its rich scent, and he scooped up the cup and blew across the milky warmth.

Watching the steam rise, Travis smiled. "You're a contented man, Eric."

"Oh, Travis . . . I lived for four years at the mercy of whim. Would they decide to beat me up? Would they feed us today? Would the Constrictor come? We had no control. After that, even a little control seems terrific to me. I love the day-to-day activities of being alive. Walking freely to and from my cabin, my friends around me, going all over space, meeting alien races, a new batch of trainees every few months . . . I meet all kinds of people and I talk to and like most of them. I kind of enjoy getting through things. People are a lot less prickly when you don't return it."

"You sure don't talk like a man who did the heroic deed and got awarded the Medal of Valor," Travis observed. "What a dismal example for all those punks out there who're shooting for the braids and brass, know that? They want glory."

"Not all it's cracked up to be." Stiles sipped his hot chocolate again and breathed into the steam. "I didn't get the MV for any deeds. I got it for sitting on my bruised ass for four years and not dying quite fast enough."

Leaning sideways, Travis lounged on an elbow and huffed disapprovingly. "What's Romulan for 'crappola'?"

"I think it's 'enushi.' 'Enushmi.' "

"Figures you'd know."

Allowing himself a little smile, Stiles drew a deep breath and sighed also. "I washed my hands of Red Sector nine years ago, Travvy, when I was finally sure the message about Zevon had gotten all the way back to his family. It took me a year to get the message through, and another year to make sure there hadn't been any snags and that his immediate family and the empress definitely knew he was there. He was sure they'd come get him. I made sure he got back home, and now I find out it might have been his death sentence."

"You acted above and beyond the call," Travis tried to confirm, obviously relieved they'd broken through to the real reason he'd come in here. "It's not even in the widest perimeter of imagination your fault, and you flipping well know it."

Stiles nodded. "In my three rational brain cells, I know it. But in the rest of them . . . he's dying because I made sure he got home."

"That's nutty."

Taking a long draw on the hot chocolate, Stiles gazed with growing sentiment into the thick warm drink and saw in there all the wonders of freedom. The foam turned like ebb tide, the swirling dark cream like clouds and wind.

"You ever been a prisoner of war?"

His question moved softly between them as if made of music. Travis had no reason to supply an answer.

Stiles watched the foam bubbles pop in his mug.

"You live together in a way that no two other people ever do. You mop the other guy's blood and bind his wounds, listen to his dreams and watch his hopes decay . . . you can't get away from the smells, the sweat, the fears crawling on you like cancer . . . after a while you run out of words to hold each other's brains inside, so you just stop talking. You start communicating without words. Just a look, or a touch . . . or you just sit there together. The intimacy can't be described. You see each other so raw, so demolished . . . more than you ever wanted anybody to see you. Weak, sick, scared, sobbing . . . crushed by loneliness like a plague, till you finally turn to each other and pray the other guy's lonely too."

He raised his eyes. Deeply moving to the point of sorrow was the expression on Travis's face, a shivering guilt that threaded its way from the distant past and prevented forgetting.

"I survived because of two forces moving in my life," Stiles continued softly. "One was the ghost of Ambassador Spock in my mind, telling me I could survive, I could rise above all this, that he'd be proud of me if I did . . . I heard his voice every night for the whole four years, narrating the plan for how I would behave and what he expected of me. I don't have any idea if it was all in my mind and I was making it up in some kind of hero-worship fantasy, but Travis, I swear to eternity it kept me alive. Just knowing what he expected of me and hearing his voice from the other side of the snow . . . calling me by my first name . . . he kept me alive by making me believe it was my duty and that I could prevail. The other force," he added softly, "was Zevon. Whenever the ambassador's image faded and that leash started to fray, Zevon would be there in the haze, some kind of echo of Spock, holding himself above the trouble we were in, always reminding me without even saying it that something bigger was expected of me. I needed him and he needed me, and together we worked for a common purpose. He gave me a reason to struggle out of my cot morning after morning. If I didn't come, he came to get me and made me get up. If he's out there somewhere, sick, maybe dying . . . I can't let him face it without me."

Travis looked at him and a moment later sat bolt upright. "You mean—you don't mean try to make another contact! The last one took you a year!"

"Zevon might not have a year this time, Travis."

"Oh, my God! This is a little sudden—" Breathing in gulps, Travis glanced around the quarters as if looking for the writing on the wall. "My God . . . I'll contact Starbase Fourteen . . . get another CST out here to cover the precinct . . . I'll have to give them some kind of excuse."

The fact that Travis Perraton so quickly absorbed and didn't question the moral imperative came to Stiles as a compliment, a vote of loyalty, and it bolted into place his flickering plan.

"I'll come up with something," he said.

Travis pressed his hands to his face, shook his head, then let his hands fall to his lap and sighed. "You and your causes. Just when I think you're settling down, you come up with some lofty goal."

"I don't have any lofty goals," Stiles told him. "I've got my goal. Save Zevon if I can, and if I can't, be with him when he dies. That's my goal."

"What about averting an interstellar conflict? If we can make a solid contact in the royal family, somebody inclined to trust us the way Zevon and you trust each other, maybe Starfleet can help the Romulans with this poison thing they've got going."

"That's not my problem. If it's in the cards, great. We're one ship with limited influence and we're better off keeping a leash on our aspirations. If there's a conflict, somebody else'll handle it. If we're there, we'll help. We can only do so much in life. Things change. Then they change again. I've been a hero. Got what I thought I wanted, and it was nice, but how long can you keep that up? Once the handshaking and the medals are done with, the heroness just fades. You can't strut around for the rest of your life being heroic. *I* can't, anyway. I'm not James Kirk. The good thing is that I don't want to be. I'm gonna do *my* part, not his part."

Travis leered at him with narrowed eyes. "That's the most depressing nobility I've ever heard."

"Works, though. You prepared for the hard part?"

"I'm always prepared, Eric."

"That's it then. Ready about."

"Ready about, aye."

Chapter Thirteen

NOW WHAT?

The last living Romulan royal family member, the last chance at uncontaminated blood, was no longer living.

Riker's profound words tolled through the silence on the bridge.

Spock was particularly aware of Dr. McCoy's expression and longed to have a few private moments, but that would not come today. Decades ago, Leonard McCoy had lost his ability—or even desire—to hide his feelings. Now his bent shoulders further sagged, his wrinkled eyes crimped, his dry lips pursed, and he seemed to weaken. This news portended a grueling struggle for the physicians, with no possible short cuts. Spock knew McCoy had seen many failures in his long life, and together they had fielded many fears and changes, and yet somehow McCoy had never lost his hope to alter one more arrow of fate before the years finally caught up to him. Failure this time might mean failure in his last attempt to make the galaxy better.

"Captain," Mr. Worf interrupted, "another ship on long-range, sir."

Picard looked up at him. "The *Tdal* returning for some reason?"

"No, sir. Starfleet encryption."

"Identify her as soon as you can, Mr. Worf."

"Sensors are reading the vessel now, sir," the Klingon obliged. "Heavy keel . . . double hull . . . multipurpose configuration . . . It's a tender, sir, combat support. The . . . *Saskatoon.*"

Picard turned to the forward screen, but nothing was visible yet. "Signal recognition and render salute pennants as we pass."

"Aye, sir."

Instantly shedding despair of Riker's news, McCoy came to life and found the nimbleness in his ancient fingers to poke Spock in the arm. "A CST! Give you any ideas, Spock, ol' man?"

"I beg your pardon?"

"Double-hulled, industrial, strong enough to defend herself, but doesn't attract much attention? Get it?"

"Ah—" Spock felt his brows flare. Decades ago he may have been embarrassed, but such social pressures were long withered from disuse. "Yes . . . conveniently unprovoking, yet combat-ready . . . possibly, Doctor!"

McCoy turned gingerly to Picard. "See if you can get 'em to stop! Pull 'em over on a traffic violation or something!"

"I don't think that'll be necessary, Doctor," the captain said as he watched the helm console from where he stood. "The CST is on an approach vector. They're reducing speed."

"Captain," Data reported, *"Saskatoon* is hailing us."

"Mr. Data, go ahead and give us ship to ship," Picard ordered.

"Aye, sir. Frequencies open."

"This is Captain Picard, *Saskatoon.* Do you have a problem?"

"What a relief that we found you before you moved on! I've got to speak to Ambassador Spock."

Spock wondered if he had heard incorrectly, though he knew that was unlikely. He had been cautious to keep his whereabouts private. Who was this CST commander that he could pierce top security?

Glancing at Spock, obviously surprised that anyone else knew, Picard sedately required, "Identify yourself, please."

"This is Lieutenant Commander Eric Stiles. Is Ambassador Spock there? It's an emergency."

Chapter Fourteen

COMMANDER STILES APPEARED in the turbolift within ten minutes of the first message, instantly flooding Spock with nostalgia for the young man he had once counseled, for today there
appeared on the upper bridge another kind of young man altogether. His blond hair slightly darkened to an ashy shade, and
the beard he had grown while in captivity was missing. His
face had lengthened to a manful form, lacking the baby-fat of
the twenty-one-year-old, and his hairline had changed. He
looked like a wizened echo of the boy who had stormed the
embassy.

Hesitating only an instant, as if unsure whether to come
down the starboard ramp or the port ramp, Eric Stiles virtually
ran to the command deck.

"Commander Stiles," Captain Picard greeted. "It's a pleasure."

Stiles said. "Sorry, Captain. I'm sorry to barge in. . . ."

Riker reached for Stiles' hand and shook it. "I remember
your return from captivity, Mr. Stiles. I was in the audience on
board the *Lexington*. It's a privilege to have a Medal of Valor
winner visit us—"

"Thanks." Stiles turned instantly to Spock, and it was as if

168

they had spoken only yesterday. "I've got a problem. And I think I can help you with yours. Can we talk alone?"

How odd.

Stiles's eyes were filled with complexity. The years sheared away between them and once again Spock was speaking candidly with the frightened boy who so needed the lifeline of an experienced voice sounding around him. Yet there was more.

Captain Picard gestured to the port side. "My ready room, Ambassador. Help yourselves."

"Manna from heaven," McCoy uttered, staring. "Spock! A Romulan royal nowhere near any other Romulans! And you don't believe in luck!"

"Yes, I do," Spock fluidly contradicted. "This is most startling. You remain certain that your cellmate was a member of the Romulan royal family?"

"Absolutely. And if he's still alive and you help me go get him, you'll have an uncontaminated member of the royal family."

"How the devil do you know about *that?*" McCoy raved.

Stiles blinked. "Well . . . you've had your contacts searching all over the Romulan Empire for an isolated member of the family . . . I've got a few contacts too . . . y'know, Medal of Valor and all . . . you get some connections, even if you don't want them. . . ."

McCoy blew a breath out his nostrils. "What's it take to keep a secret in this galaxy!"

Spock turned to him. "This is troubling. It means the news is leaking out."

"This is the part that hasn't leaked out!" Stiles quickly told them. "I haven't told anybody about Zevon. The only people who know are me and my first officer and a couple members of my original evac squad who stayed with me. And now the two of you."

"How is it possible that nobody else knew?" McCoy asked. "Ten years ago when I pulled you out of there, Starfleet debriefed you thoroughly—"

"Eleven years."

169

"Ten, eleven, twenty, what's the difference?"

"I was debriefed for weeks," Stiles agreed. "I told them I had a Romulan cellmate and they notified the Romulans. At the time there weren't any formal relations, no exchange of ambassadors. . . . I made sure the message got through to the precinct governor, who would have to report directly to the Senate, and they'd have to report to the—well, back then it was the emperor. So I thought the royal family would take it from there.

Spock had listened to these words with growing trepidation, but certainly also with a rising sensation of possibility. "This is a profound blessing in disguise, both for Zevon and for the Romulan Empire. If he is indeed still in Red Sector, isolated, still alive, then he presents a distinct ray of hope."

McCoy pointed a crooked finger. "I'll send Dr. Crusher to the Romulan royal family to treat them and try to keep them alive. In the meantime, I need to get to this Zevon and synthesize a vaccine from his blood, *before* anybody else gets to him."

"Who else could get to him?" Stiles asked. "Why would anybody want to?"

"Whoever's inflicted this biological attack, that's who. You don't think this is accidental, do you?"

"I thought it was just a plague! Something natural!"

"Nope."

His face a pattern of fears and troubles, Stiles frowned with consternation. "That's just what Hashley tried to tell us . . . all his talk about viral terrorism and mass-assassination . . . I thought he was exaggerating."

At that name, Spock felt his back muscles tighten. He glanced at McCoy, who, if possible, was more pale than usual at the casual mention of a key figure. Stiles clearly did not understand the full ramifications of how the puzzle pieces fit into place.

"Hashley again," McCoy complained. "He's as bad as the infection."

Stiles squinted. "Huh? What's that mean?"

"Ansue Hashley," Spock said, "is important to maintaining

stable relations between the Federation and the Romulan Empire, Commander. How recently did you speak to him?"

Stiles's eyes widened, and he swiveled his gaze between them. "You mean the same Hashley I'm talking about? An ag broker? That guy?"

"Yes, that guy."

"You've got to be kidding! He didn't seem capable of being part of a mass-assassination scheme. Starfleet captains had been tossing him from ship to ship like a hot potato to keep the Romulans from knowing where he was. I couldn't figure why he'd be so important. I thought they just didn't want to bother with him!"

McCoy explained, "The Romulans tracked the royal infection back to his cargo. That's why they think the Federation started it. The Romulans wanted him so they could have a scapegoat and tell their people they'd caught the culprit, that the Federation was definitely to blame for the deaths of their royal family."

"Where is Hashley now?" Spock asked. "Aboard *Saskatoon?*"

Stiles shrugged hopelessly. "No, I don't have him. I didn't want him. He's safe, though. We remanded him to the custody of the first Starfleet law-enforcement ship we found."

"Which ship?"

"The *Ranger.*"

Spock immediately turned and depressed the keypad of the bridge comm unit. "Captain Picard, do you know the name of the passenger who was kidnapped from the *Ranger* this morning?"

"I'll pull the report, ambassador. One moment."

"I'll put Dr. Crusher on it," McCoy said. "They want her help. They'll treat Hashley well."

"It's my fault," Stiles said. He had left the conversation they were having and was having one with himself. "I never checked . . . never confirmed that Zevon had been rescued. He was so sure his family would get him out—he made me sure too. Until five days ago I was completely convinced that he was back home. Now I find out he never . . . they just didn't bother to go get him. All these years he's been trapped in Pojjana space, by himself, without me . . . because of me. When I found out they'd left him, the only thing I could think to do was try to get your help."

In all his years Spock had witnessed many examples of human fidelity and found he appreciated them all. At first he had looked down his nose at such demonstrations. Later he had learned to accept them with some curiosity, and even to accept that part of himself.

Spock moved to stand near Stiles, to make sure he had all the attention he needed.

"You and Zevon were friends," he began. "I deeply appreciate that. You depended upon each other in the worst of times. Today you still understand what happened to you, the forces that worked upon your lives. Time has not dulled your decency. Today, as I watch you in your effort and your torments, I cross yet another barrier to fondness. I enjoy the humanity I see in you, this childlike sense of justice that defies all forces. Like a whirlpool you draw us all into your devotion. We will go to save the Romulans, yes. But because of you will we go also to save Zevon."

McCoy watched them both with a charming softness. Spock noticed the doctor's gaze, but did not meet it.

Stiles clearly battled the pressure of tears behind his eyes. Solemnly he murmured, "Every time I see you . . . you rescue me in some way."

A swelling sensation of completeness satisfied Spock deeply. While before this there had been only a duty, a mission, now there was a quieter and more profound purpose. Crossing the quadrant to save a nation had its appeal. Crossing to save a friend had even more.

"Well, Spock," McCoy interrupted, "you and I seem to have a mission in Pojjan space."

Stiles came abruptly to life as a balloon suddenly fills with air, apparently afraid that they would make some other choice for some reason he failed to see. "Let me take you! We've got a thick hull, nonaggressive configuration, support registry— completely unprovoking in nature, just a big industrial muscle. We've got full regulation defensive weapons, and we all know what *that* really means. Let me take you through Romulan space in the CST. It's perfect! It's a good option. And I know the way!"

McCoy raised his frosty brows. "Imagine never thinking of that. Silly us."

Stiles took that as a threat. "If you don't clear me to go with you, I'll go anyway."

McCoy looked at Spock. "Remind you of anybody?"

Chapter Fifteen

"ORSOVA."

"What do you want now? Why do you bring me to space
this time? You always call at bad times for me! I was busy!"

*"The Pojjana lion of science. Genius savior of the planet.
Engineer of the Constrictor meter. Conqueror of the Constrictor. Still amazed to see open space. You know nothing about
science."*

"I know everything. I have power now."

"You have Zevon now."

Picking himself up from the strange carpet where he had
fallen after the dizzying effect of a transporter beam, Orsova
bristled and tried to appear confident. "Zevon works for me."

*"Zevon does all the work you take credit for. I know the dif-
ference. I helped make it happen. Now I want something from
you. A Federation ship is coming your way."*

"Federation? Why! This is Red Sector! How can they come
here!"

*"They have new business here. They have visited Romulan
space."*

"Romulan? Why would they go there? They have no treaty!
Have they . . . ?"

As the Voice summoned him again, Orsova felt the sting of being completely out of touch with the space-active civilizations of the quadrant for so many years. All this time Red Sector had been a huge favor for him, a sanctuary where a prison guard could rise to power if he knew how to play on public opinion—and if he had a Voice to tell him each step.

That had been easy. Play to the hatred. The Pojjana had been ready, eager, to despise and distrust. The Voice was right. Orsova had used that. Found it easy. Surrounded himself with those eager to hate most, happy to have their distrust bring them also to power, and learned how to nurture the distrust even when there was no one around to hate anymore.

Making them accept Zevon, an alien . . . that had taken time. But it had been the most important part.

Now this ghost, this Voice, came to him when he no longer needed it. Orsova knew in his gut that this speaking person was an alien.

"Why would the Federation come again after all these years?" he asked. "What do they want here? We have no Federation people in Red Sector."

"They have their reasons. You will have to be prepared to stop them. Crash their ship, destroy it, or drive them off. Kill them if you can."

"But why are they coming?"

"Can your planetary defense destroy a Starfleet ship? This is not a starship, but a utility vessel—"

"You don't know why they're coming, do you?" Suddenly emboldened, Orsova blurted his revelation. "You don't know, do you, Voice?"

"Information is diaphanous. It changes."

"Means, you don't know why they're coming."

"When I need you again, I will beam you to me."

"In space?"

"Wherever I must be."

"Means, you have to hide from them."

"Go back now. Go now, and get ready to face the Federation. Make them go from here, and there will be even bigger rewards for you."

Chapter Sixteen

The Imperial Palace, Romulan Star Empire

"MY NAME IS BEVERLY CRUSHER, Commander, Medical Corps, Starfleet. I'm here to treat the empress."

"Yes, Dr. Crusher, we have agreed to give you cooperation. I am Sentinel Iavo."

"Sentinel? Not Centurion?"

"I am a member of the Royal Civil Attaché to the Imperial Court, not part of the Imperial Space Fleet. We discovered long ago that military titles for our civil officials only caused dangerous confusion. Where is your ship docked? At the municipal spaceport?"

"No. We were dropped off. The ship has left. It's just the two of us now."

"The two of you? No guards? No Starfleet security?"

"I don't need them, do I? We have an agreement . . . don't we?"

Standing before Beverly Crusher, Sentinel Iavo was a very handsome Romulan with typically dark brown hair but remarkably large and pale green eyes. He wore his Imperial Court uniform with a certain casualness, and his clothing indeed was not like that of the military guards stationed in the hallways they'd passed through. She couldn't guess his age—

176

that was tricky with Romulans—though he didn't strike her as particularly young. He stood in the expected Vulcanlike posture, straight and contrived, the only clue to any nervousness his constant rubbing of the fingernails of one hand against the palm of the other hand.

The palace was a four-century-old monolith, its stone walls dressed in tapestries and heavy draperies like any Austrian castle, except the rooms and corridors were lit by modern fixtures—not a torch in sight. Funny—she'd expected torches.

And there was music playing. Harp-like music, backed sometimes by the hollow beat of a tenor drum and a hint of something similar to a cello in the background. No musicians visible—nope, it was a sound system.

She smelled incense, too, faintly. Or dinner.

The Sentinel gave her a moment to look around, then asked, "What would you like first?"

"I want you to close up the palace completely," she began. "Total security. Nobody in or out without high clearance, nobody at all. You're the highest advisor?"

"Correct, Doctor, I am the empress's senior civil authority. I have held this post since before the emperor died, and my brother before me, and our father before him."

"Oh, isn't that nice . . . then you have the authority to enact my terms. No changes of personnel from now on. Whoever's in the kitchen will stay there and keep working. The same maids, the same servants, the same everybody. These same guards will stay on duty here. They can sleep here if they have to, but I don't want to see anybody new. When you have your security in place, I'd like everything and everybody cleared through my lovely assistant here."

Crusher made what she hoped was a graceful half-turn and held out a hand. At her side and a polite couple of steps behind, Data offered her the medical tricorder. He also held their two duffel bags and Crusher's hospital-in-a-bag medical satchel, full of all the instruments, medications, and a computer with both an immunological database and a general medical lexicon. The load was a little cumbersome because she'd packed everything she could think of. There was going to be no calling for supplies.

Data said nothing. The only expression of personality was the poignant lack of it, and perhaps the sheen of soft lightning, reflected off the velvet, casting a glow that turned his metallic complexion herbal.

"You needn't have brought so many medical supplies, Dr. Crusher," Iavo told her as he took one of the duffels from Data. "We have eight major hospital complexes in the city, which will bring anything you require to treat the empress."

"Mr. Iavo, when I say I want security, I mean absolute security. I want nothing delivered from anywhere as of right now. Nothing comes into the palace. Not medicine, not food, not people, not weapons."

"There are no weapons here, madam," the Sentinel assured. "The palace is completely energy-secure. Our security office constantly monitors any active energy, and would instantly identify an armed disruptor or phaser—"

"Hmm. I wondered why all your guards carried daggers," Crusher recalled. "I thought it was just traditional. Where's the empress?"

"This way, please."

Another corridor. An obviously private series of chambers, more guards, one more short corridor . . . finally, Iavo cleared Crusher and Data into the empress's bedchamber.

And what a place it was. Draped in soft green velvet embossed with ancient symbols, softly lit by unseen fixtures, carpeted with something that seemed like rabbit fur, the room was warm and thick with the scent of burning herbs. In the center of the room was a sitting area with a generous couch and an oblong blackwood table with a single chair.

There were two female attendants hovering near the bed, and four imperial guards, each in a uniform and helmet, standing near the bed posts. The bed had six posts, each as thick as a full-grown man's body and carved with angular features of hands and faces, each hand holding one of the faces and pushing it toward the ceiling. Each face grimaced hellishly, and in its teeth held a carved skewer that stuck out from the totem, so that the bedposts bristled like a bottle brush with wooden spikes. Some of the spikes were broken off, yet the blunt ends darkened and showing no wounded wood, hinting that the bed was very old. The wood had never been stained, it had just blackened with sheer age.

And in the bed, bundled in velvet and fur, was the young empress. Her eyes were closed, but not in rest. Her hair was meticulously combed yet lusterless, almost crispy from her long fight to stay alive, as her body sapped whatever healthy cells it could draw back into itself in its last desperations.

All over the empire, members of the royal family looked like that, or had, or soon would.

Crusher approached the bed, aware that Data was right behind her, maintaining a student-like silence. She listened briefly to the empress's respiration, looked at her complexion, noted her skin color, an obscene russet—*very* wrong—but did not touch her.

"Communications relays have been set up all over the empire for you. Attending physicians are standing by for your instructions."

"Are they willing to cooperate with a Federation physician?" she asked.

Iavo seemed embarrassed, or perhaps hopeless. "They have tried everything they know."

Crusher folded her arms. "Yes . . . I suppose they have."

And she simply stood there, a hip cocked, said nothing more, and did nothing, while the harp music plucked the draperies.

Data's amber eyes flicked between her and Iavo, but he also said, as she had instructed, nothing.

Iavo watched as his empress moaned softly, unattended. The two female attendants peered uneasily. The helmeted guards remained at attention, but their eyes shifted.

"Are you going to treat her?" Iavo finally asked.

"Yes, but I'll need something from you," Crusher said.

"What do you want from us?" Iavo asked.

Now he got it.

She took one step toward him, then locked her stance. "I want Ansue Hashley. Bring him here, alive."

"All right, Mr. Hashley, I've heard enough."

"But I want to finish telling you about—"

"No, that's enough talking. Sit still while I finish sealing this."

Crusher stood over Ansue Hashley's ragged bulk and shook her head in disgust. He was bruised, cut, flushed, nicked in a hundred places, and pale from loss of blood, yet somehow that mouth kept running and running.

"You know, Sentinel Iavo," she began as her seamer's beam sketched closed the last cut on Hashley's face, "you people didn't have to torture this man. If you'd open up your borders and deal with humans more, you'd know after talking to this man for ten minutes that he doesn't have it in him to organize a mass-assassination plot. And we would've told you about the prion-based epidemic we've been fighting. Imperial isolationism has hurt you this time."

Near the empress's bed, Iavo rubbed his forefingernail against his other hand's thumb knuckle and protested with his expression. "The infection was imported on his vessel. We tracked it back to a low-level medication in his cargo bound for—"

"He's a busy little gossip, not a biological terrorist," Crusher insisted as Hashley's big sopsy eyes blinked up at her. "That medicine has been coming in here for more than forty years from a pharmaceutical company sympathetic to Romulans. All Mr. Hashley did was bring it in. Somebody else engineered the tainting of the shipment and then the delivery of the tainted stuff to all the royal family members. Hashley here is just a dupe."

"Whose dupe?"

Crusher shook her head and let herself rattle on, spilling her thoughts. "Nobody clever enough to distribute this infection would run a little trade route for ten years. If you knew more about humans—it's kind of obvious this man's not biding his time to take over the universe. Romulans might be that tenacious, but humans don't have the patience. Or a two-hundred-year lifespan. Why do you think we're always in such a damn hurry? Gotta get things done before we die."

Pacing uneasily nearby, Sentinel Iavo switched fingernails and leered doubtfully at Ansue Hashley, who sat like a bruised puppy. "Whose dupe was he?"

"We're not sure," Crusher admitted. "Dr. McCoy's right, though. It's got all the earmarks of a series of cross-racial multiprion plagues. Until recently, nobody put them together. The first clue was just three years ago at Deep Space Nine. Well— then the station was called Terok Nor."

"I remember that!" Hashley offered. "Cardassians, Bajorans and Ferengi all got the same sickness! They were all accusing—"

"Oh, I missed a scratch right next to your lip," Crusher cut off. "Here—let me seal it up. Don't move, now. . . . The Cardassians suspected a Bajoran rebel group of manufacturing the disease, and they were partly right. The rebels were happy to make sure the Cardassians caught the disease, until they found out that Bajorans could get it too. And there was no way the Bajorans at that time had the resources or the science infrastructure to develop something as advanced as cross-species viral infection. They can't even do it now, and back then they were subjugated. Not only the Deep Space Nine infection, but we also found out that two years earlier several human-alien hybrids were infected with an unidentified virus, and that's unheard-of in nature. This thing's being systematically mutated, targeted, and delivered."

Iavo stopped pacing briefly. "I take it those were not all human and the same alien hybrids."

"No, they were all mixed up. People with that kind of genetics just can't 'catch' the same thing naturally. There you go, Mr. Hashley, all patched up. You'll be sore, but you'll live. Now, I want you to just stay right here with me and Data and help us do what we have to do." She straightened, handed Data the sealer to put back in the med-pack, then turned to Iavo. "All right, Sentinel, I'm ready to start treating the empress. Are you ready to help?"

The tall imperial official glanced at the two female servants, then met the gaze of one of the four guards. They seemed to be communicating, but not in the way one would expect of a senior government official and a clutch of underlings from way, way under. Iavo clutched his hands before him, flexed them, stretched his fingers, looked at the furry carpet for a moment then raised his eyes again at the nearest guard.

Such a simple step took a very long time, as choices go. Finally, seeming to make a decision or part of one, Iavo turned his back to the guards as if deeply troubled by their presence. "What do you need from us?"

Crusher watched the guards for a moment. Were they averting their eyes on purpose? "First of all, I want these women out of here. Data and Mr. Hashley can be my assistants. And I'd like you to cool it off by fifteen degrees in here. Clear that incense or whatever's burning out of the chamber and circulate some fresh air."

"But this is how we always—"

"If 'always' was working, you wouldn't need me here, would you? Cool, and air, please."

Iavo paused, seemed to be deciding between being insulted and some other reaction Crusher couldn't make out.

Once again the Sentinel met the eyes of the guard nearest to him.

"We'll do as you instruct, Doctor," he agreed, speaking slowly. Hypnotically he rubbed a single fingernail. "Do you think you can save her?"

Chapter Seventeen

STILES' HANDS SHOOK as he stood beside the *Saskatoon*'s command chair. On the other side of the chair, Ambassador Spock placidly standing, the elderly Leonard McCoy sitting in a console chair—both men watched the approach of a forbidden planet in a forbidden sector. Stiles had offered the doctor the command chair, but McCoy had demurred, saying that only the "golden boy" should sit there. Stiles hadn't been able to sit in their presence, so the chair went empty through the entire voyage. Even when Alan brought tea.

Every regulation in several civilizations prevented their coming here, yet here they flew. The hoops of outposts, stations, guard ships, patrols, and bureaucratic drumbeating they'd had to jump through had left Stiles with a headache that was still here days and days later. The tension of moving into Romulan space to drop off Dr. Crusher and Data had been enough to peel fruit, and now *Saskatoon* was deep inside Red Sector, trailing deals and bribes and threats and name-dropping that had gotten them all the way here.

For Stiles, though, this was the door of purgatory. He couldn't keep his hands warm any more. The self-examination was no fun either. Why was he so nervous? He had these heavy hitters with him, didn't he?

Why was his stomach twisted up into a spiral? The absence of foolish cockiness should've been reassuring and mature, but the fact was he wished he still had it. That zing of thinking he knew everything had protected him from a whole lot of scared. Wishing he could feel his fingers, he wondered if those two men over there had ever preferred to pull their own teeth out than go in someplace they had to go. Duty, cause, purpose, rank, ability—all those things fell short of the driving force he needed to overcome what he felt. There was only one thing drawing him forward, against all the forces pushing him back.

Gripping one hand with the other to hide the trembling, he looked briefly to portside, to Travis and Alan. Alan winked reassuringly, and Travis gave him a thumbs-up. They were willing to go.

Embarrassed, he puckered his shoulders. His friends were reassuring him, supporting him into the unknown. It should be the other way around.

"Hero," he muttered.

No one heard. He barely heard himself.

Spock glanced at him.

The planet of his dread swelled on the main screen and six of the ancillary monitors.

"Approach, Eric?" Travis prodded from the port side.

"Hm? Oh . . . sorry. Helm—let's see . . . come to point nine, equatorial approach vector, angle four one. No—four two. There's a constant thermal over that big canyon."

"May I ask what you're reading on the planet's surface?" Ambassador Spock asked. "Anything unfamiliar? Any sign of destruction by the Constrictor?"

"I'm picking up airstrips," Jeremy reported, "a couple of things that might be missile deployment facilities . . . heli-ports . . . some satellites . . . pretty typical. Maybe mid-or late-twenty-first-century equivalent or so. I could be all wrong, though."

At tactical, Zack Bolt commented, "You get to a certain level of atmospheric aeronautics and yours is as good as any-body's."

Stiles waved an icy hand toward Spock. "Why don't you have a look for yourself, sir? You were here too, and I'm sure you knew the layout a lot better than I ever did. After all . . ."

If Spock's dark eyes saw through the layers of reasons and excuses, he made no hint of that, except perhaps for the hesitation before accepting.

"Very well," he said, and took the place at the science station as Jeremy moved out of his way. He bent over the readout hood, tapped some of the controls, causing monitors to flicker and change, focus or choose new subjects.

Stiles knew what Spock expected—a devastated planet, a civilization crushed nearly out of existence, the people who'd managed to survive suffering in the few remaining caves and wreckage that hadn't been smashed, hardly any old people, hardly any kids. . . .

But that's not what came up.

Maps of the planet's cities, boundaries in some places marked off by electronic border markers readable from space. Stiles recognized some of what he saw from that first approach all those years ago, and he was stirred by new apprehensions. He recognized the mountains showing up on geographical long-range, and flinched. The idea of returning in triumph, healthy, alive, in command of a ship, dissolved and crumbled away. Suddenly he was twenty-one and out of control.

The hum of the ship around him as thrusters moved them toward orbit pounded like blood in his head. He was grateful when Travis quietly took over the approach orders, doing so smoothly enough that nobody seemed to notice. Or at least they pretended they didn't.

Stiles wasn't much for putting on airs, but he'd have liked to give them a little command puff-up right about now, just for Christmas. Couldn't find it, though. Just couldn't find it.

"Cities seem intact. No signs of catastrophic damage," Spock commented as he clicked his way through the scanner's offerings. "I recognize several of the buildings at the main city complexes on the primary continent. . . ." Now he leaned closer and seemed almost to frown. "Although . . . the architectural style has changed significantly. Many of the old constructions are missing, replaced by complexes with only one or two stories." He turned his head, without straightening up, to look at Stiles. "During your incarceration, did you hear any word of so broad a cultural change?"

"Me? Zevon and I used to talk about what could be done to help buildings survive the Constrictor . . . elastic brackets and joints, different construction materials—either much heavier so they could withstand the pressure, or much lighter so they wouldn't be crushed . . . but nobody ever paid attention to us. That was just us, just talking."

"They seem to have implemented many changes," Spock commented, looked at what he saw on the screens. "Even the colors of the cities are different now. I believe they may have changed materials significantly. They seem to be primarily using quarried granite rather than timber and brick. And I'm reading quintotitantium and dutronium reenforcement members rather than conventional steel and iron. When I evacuated, they were incapable of such a development at their industrial level."

"Granite . . ." Stiles sifted his memory. "Dutronium . . . Zevon and I used to design—we used to think up all kinds of things. Maybe the Pojjana just figured out some of them on their own. It doesn't take that much to figure out how to build a spandex house, y'know . . . most of our ideas just made basic sense. It's not like we had much to work with or anything. . . ."

McCoy watched the continent slowly turn on the large forward screen. "Do you think he's still alive and influencing their development?"

"I hope so, I sure hope so," Stiles said with his heart squeezing fearfully. "Zevon doesn't have a prime directive. But I don't know how he could get anybody to listen to him. We could never get past the assistant warden. And I don't know if . . . they turned on him after I got pulled out or . . . maybe they just . . ."

No one said anything to comfort or refute his tortured suppositions or stem the racing of his imagination.

"There's only so much he could do," Stiles grumbled, his thoughts taking on a life of their own. "After all, the sector's been red for years. Nobody's been in or out, right?"

"We watch the sector constantly," Spock undergirded.

"There has been extremely little breaching, give or take the odd delinquent shaman."

Dr. McCoy's white brows danced. "Or the occasional sublime wise-ass. Other than that, a skinny bird couldn't slip in and out of Red Sector without somebody's noticing. Mr. Stiles, you think your friend could be somewhere other than the capital city? Running some process that engineers those new buildings?"

"Even Zevon couldn't make industries all by himself, even if he were in charge of the whole planet, never mind a prisoner. Besides, he wasn't an architect. Is eleven years long enough to make sweeping changes on a whole planet? Nah . . . probably not. He'd have to get all the way up to somebody trusting him first, and, believe me, on a planet of people who *really* don't like aliens, that could take . . . well, more doing than either of us could manage from a prison cell or our lab. Travis, adjust the trim, will you?"

"Trim, aye. Give it another three degrees level, Stinson."

"Aye aye, sir, three degrees starboard."

"We must not assume," Spock mentioned, "that anything is the same after eleven years."

Stiles strode around to the other side of the bridge, where Spock was still scanning the readouts of the planet below. "Are you saying you think he's dead?"

Spock glanced at him. "You spare yourself by accepting the likelihood. You nearly died yourself."

"I was sick."

"And ill-treated, poorly fed, ignored, imprisoned—"

"Zevon's Romulan. He's stronger than—"

"Not stronger enough," the ambassador cautioned, now standing straight and looking right at him. "The odds . . . are troubling."

McCoy was watching him. Stiles could sense it.

He could sense—and see—the fretful averted attention of everybody around him. They all knew his past. He was too close to this. Maybe it was a mistake not sending somebody completely impassive. There was more at stake than just Zevon. Was he thinking clearly enough?

"What do we do?" Stiles wondered. "Just . . . approach?"

"Almost to the atmosphere, Eric," Travis reported. "What do you want to do?"

"I don't know yet."

"We've got to have an order either to enter or veer off. At this point we can't hover."

"No doubt the planetary monitoring system has already noticed us," Spock told him. "Although they had no space-borne fleet, they were perfectly able to effect short-range scans of the immediate area, for defensive purpose. I'm sure they have identified your ship as a Starfleet unit. If you don't mind my suggesting we broadcast a——"

A shriek cut him off as the CST bellowed around them and the whole ship was jaw-kicked. The deck canted to an instant 30-degree list, as if they'd struck something out in the middle of space. Were they too low? Had they hit a mountain?

Pinned to the side of the helm for a terrible few seconds, Stiles gritted his teeth and fought against the thrust. He heard the cries of his crew as they were thrown violently against the side of the tender, crammed into bulkheads and equipment and each other in a tangle of pressure and shock.

"What is it!" he called. "Did we hit a satellite?"

Jeremy clung to the console one chair down from where Spock was pressed to the science ledge. "Energy funnel! It's pulling us down!"

Dr. McCoy clasped his chair and grimaced. "I *hate* this kind of thing——"

"Is it coming from the planet?" Twisting, Stiles jabbed at the helm over the shoulder of the flabbergasted trainee pilot. "Oh, no, I *know* they shouldn't have this! They didn't have anything like this! Not that could pull in a CST! We can tow a starship!"

Travis scrambled for the engineering mainframe to see if there was an answer there, but when he turned again his face was a mask of bafflement.

"It's as if the planet itself has grabbed us!"

The Imperial Palace

Cool air, finally, moved through the ancient halls of the crown family's traditional home. The soft harp music played eternally over the sound system, just sweet enough to drive anybody crazy after the first twenty hours. The tape had looped a few times, and by now Ansue Hashley had taken to humming harmony to the tunes he recognized.

This, in bitter contrast to the suffering empress, who was roused now and then by Crusher's ministrations and wakened to relentless agony because from time to time medical tests required her cooperation. Even when the young woman was allowed to sink back into unconsciousness, her struggle just to breathe provided a pathetic percussion to the damned harp music. It had been a difficult two days.

"Mr. Hashley, please take these two instruments and clean them thoroughly, the way I showed you yesterday, and then bring them back," Crusher instructed. She'd only caught a few catnaps and was feeling the stress of fatigue. This was like being a resident again.

"I just love helping you," Hashley said. "Maybe when we get out of this, I can join Starfleet and come to the *Enterprise* and be your assistant."

"You could certainly do something like that," she said. "No reason you couldn't take a few paramedical courses and start a new career. I'm thinking of switching to professional wrestler, myself. Whew . . . could you bring me that pillow and put it behind my back? I can't let go of this IV pump right now. I've almost got a result . . . stand by, Data."

In her periphery, Crusher saw Data look up from his communications center, formerly the empress's dressing-room vanity. "Standing by, Doctor."

The imperial communications relays were tied in to over six hundred stations throughout the empire. Data had taken nearly three hours to confirm, through codes, geological information, and star-mapping devices, that the relays were actually working and in contact with a spiderweb of stations on several planets. After all, what good would it be if they were just talking to a con artist next door?

Her head swam as she took a moment to relax her brain, while her hands worked under the blue light of the portable sterile field she'd set up. She even indulged in closing her eyes for a few moments, until the field readings bleeped. Sounded like a cannon going off.

Crusher forced her eyes open and blinked a couple of times, focusing on the readings rushing across the miniature monitor screen. "Good, very good . . . I was right. Data, confirm that the physicians should stop fighting the fever. Let it run its course—it stresses the attacking prions."

"Relaying that, doctor. Your progress is remarkable for only two days."

"That's me—Remarkable Bev. Look at that! I knew it was there . . . add that they shouldn't inject supplements of kelassium, no matter how low the levels get."

Data stopped working the console and looked at her. "Doctor, is it not true that Vulcanoids can suffer irreparable intestinal scarring from lack of kelassium?"

"Absolutely, but this test is hinting to me that the kelassium's not leaving the body at all. Look . . . see these protovilium levels? Those only show up when there's a repository of kelassium. They shouldn't be reading this way if she is really K-deficient."

Hashley looked up from organizing the medical instruments. "I've heard of that kind of thing! When I was delivering industrial incendiaries to Carolus, one of the company medics told me about how the body defends itself with some really weird stuff."

Crusher only half-registered what he said. She had learned over the past hours to pick on a word or two without really committing herself to listening. "Mmm, this is weird, all right . . . if these chemical bonds are leading me down the right track, the kelassium's being stored in the second liver. That tells me the attacking prions feed on kelassium. At least partially—Data, are you getting this?"

"Yes, Doctor."

"Storing kelassium deprives the infection of an energy source. I think low kelassium's part of the body's natural fortification. Let's take a chance."

"Is that wise?" the android asked. "Some of these patients are dangerously ill already."

Crusher leaned closer to her patient and checked the moaning young woman's temperature in a particularly unscientific yet somehow instinctive way—with the back of her hand.

"Mmm . . . brink of death's a prickly place, Data. Sometimes you gotta dance to keep standing there."

Even though she wasn't looking at him, she could still somehow see, perhaps only in her mind, the android's perplexed expression. He didn't counter her comment, though, or question the risk she was taking. Instead he turned back to the portable comm console and relayed the latest thread of hope.

She wished she could speak more freely, venture some opinions about the crassness of hereditary rulership, mutter a few truths about how it always compromised freedom somewhere down the line—and not usually that far down either—but the four guards were always there, and one of the two women. The guards took turns standing watch every six hours, never leaving the immediate chambers or sitting rooms. And Sentinel Iavo floated in and out . . . at the moment he was floating back in.

"Any success, Doctor?"

Crusher looked up and took the moment to stretch her back and shoulders. "A little. Nominal. Enough to give us an idea that we might eventually beat some of this."

Iavo went to the fireplace, which until now had been stone cold, and turned the head of an unrecognizable carved creature on the mantel; a hissing sound was heard, as flames jumped up in the fake logs, rose to a certain height, adjusted themselves, and settled as if they'd been burning all night. The royal chamber was instantly haunted, medieval.

"The empress may live because of your ministrations," Iavo gauged. All across the empire, the royal family members are beginning to slowly outlive their symptoms."

"So," Crusher said, "you've been listening in on our relays, Sentinel?"

He paused. After a moment, he admitted, "Yes, of course."

Still he did not turn from the fire. Turning in her chair, Crusher surveyed his tall form, narrow and dark against the flickering golden glow from beyond it, and marveled—not for the first time—that no matter where she traveled in the stars, no matter what strange forces she witnessed or what bizarre life forms she encountered, what twisted trees grew or weeds crawled, all over the galaxy fire was always the same color.

And also the same was the smell from the cauldron of ambition.

Sentinel Iavo held his hands toward the fire. Crusher saw them spread before him and slightly to the side, framed in paint-by-number fireglow.

Stretching one arm out, Crusher snapped her fingers once, quietly, toward Data. Flinching as if awakened, the android swiveled away from his console and sat watching. With her other hand, she waved Ansue Hashley into the corner behind her, then put a finger to her lips and gave him the evil eye. The man paled, his eyes widened, and with some wisdom garnered from years running an illegal route, he measured the sense of not arguing or even speaking.

Crusher leaned over the empress and touched the pallid cheek whose changes of color and heat had been the cusp of the doctor's life for many hours. The empress moaned softly. A tear appeared in the corner of the quiet girl's eye. Perhaps she knew.

The two standing guards moved away from the end of the bed. The two who had been resting now stood up.

"I suppose," Crusher began quietly, "you've never had a problem like this come your way, Sentinel."

Iavo gazed into the fire. "Nothing like this."

"How does temptation taste to someone who has been loyal all his life?"

For a moment he was silent. He sighed. "It has a certain bitter spice."

"Are you enjoying the chance?" she asked him. "Or are you cornered by other pressures?"

This time Iavo did not answer. The guards stood now in a line, three on one side of him, one on the other, all four facing Crusher, Data, Ansue Hashley, and the dying empress in her bed.

"It must be frustrating," Crusher said, "always to be on the periphery of glory, nearly able to touch it, always condemned to taste but never swallow . . . and now to see yourself within a step of supreme power . . . and your followers to see themselves jumping all the obstacles in one leap—advisors, attendants . . . Sentinels . . . they all see an opportunity that otherwise would never have occurred. The murder of the empress would be hard for the people to accept, I'm sure, but no one here will care if a Federation doctor and her party suddenly turn up missing. *Enterprise* officers aren't exactly on the empire's favorite-people list, are we? Therefore, the empress and her family will die without continued treatment."

Despite the fact that there was no real wood, the fire was engineered to crackle and snap—even to put forth the scent of burning autumn leaves. Still with his back to her, Sentinel Iavo lowered his head as if watching her words spin inside some kind of crystal ball in his mind.

Barely above a whisper, he told her, "You came here with no guards, madam."

Crusher turned fully in her seat and rubbed her hands on her knees. "Now that you know I might save her, you have to go through with it, don't you?"

The guard at Iavo's right drew his ceremonial dagger. A second guard did the same while the others watched and gripped the handles of their own weapons.

Crusher stood up.

Sensing the change, Iavo now turned around to face her. Now the line of Romulans and the threat they posed clicked gracefully into place. For a brief moment Beverly Crusher stood in awe of this elegant race, so Vulcan in their stature, so human in their passion.

The last two guards pulled their knives. Firelight played upon the blades. And Iavo himself touched the still-sheathed ceremonial dirk that was the symbol of the highest nonroyal office in the Romulan Star Empire.

Data came to her side. Ansue Hashley stood behind them.

Crusher pressed back her shoulder-length hair, steadied herself, lowered her weaponless hands to her sides, and looked directly at Iavo.

"How are we going to do this?"

Chapter Eighteen

"WHAT'VE WE GOT?"

Jeremy White responded with typically terse calm. "We've got thirteen minutes before we crash."

"Yellow alert, everybody," Stiles ordered.

"Yellow, aye!"

The CST shifted its manner substantially, as certain lights and meters went dark and others popped on, systems deciding which were important and which could wait. The din was maddening—the ship screamed and strained, engines howling right through the bulkheads, setting up harmonic vibrations in every member.

On the main screen and all the other exterior visual monitors, black space and a planet gave way to the filtering gauze of clouds. They were entering the atmosphere!

While he tried to keep control over his voice, to keep from shouting or sounding excited, it was necessary to speak up over the tin bray of the engines fighting to keep them in space.

"Veer out!" he ordered. "Get us some kilometers."

Both hating and loving the fact that Ambassador Spock and the irascible Leonard McCoy were watching him through a dangerous moment, he forced himself to concentrate on any-

194

thing but the two of them. For a second he thought Spock might stay at the science-readout station, where he so obviously and eternally belonged, where he fit so well on a starship or any ship, but the famous officer subtly stepped aside for Jeremy White to take that position.

Stiles hesitated an instant, soon accepting the appropriateness and grandeur of the sacrifice. Spock was letting them handle their own destiny without interference. How did he know to do that? How could he hold himself in check like this?

His stomach turning, Stiles stepped to the starboard side. "Come on, Jeremy, analyze it."

Jeremy's usually sedate expression was screwed into annoyance, possibly because of Spock's presence. "It's some kind of hybrid of a tractor beam and a graviton ray. I've never seen energy combined this way. If a CST can tow a starship, how can they be holding us?"

Travis asked, "Did they have this tech when you were here, Eric?"

"No, hell, no! Matt, can we—"

Realizing he couldn't be heard five sections back over the scream, of the engines, he struck the nearest comm.

"Matt, can we effect any kind of a fair-lead landing?"

From section five, Girvan called over the mechanical scream, *"Not at seven thousand feet per second at this angle we can't!"*

"Okay, let's come up with something else. How long before the beam pulls us into the mountain?"

"Calculating," Jeremy said. "Draw is increasing incrementally with our thrust ratios. They're pouring the coals to it."

"Let's pour our own," Stiles said. "Let's try impulse point zero five, helm."

"Point zero five!"

"Don't shout."

Stiles shrugged at the kid, a simple gesture that had a visible effect on the young terrified teenagers, who were all watching him to measure how many points they should go on the panic meter. Going into a battle situation, with rules to follow and procedures to rely on, had been something they could handle after Starfleet training. Having the ship tilt and scream under them as a planet sucked at it—that was something nobody'd ever trained for. Of course, having it smash into a planet's surface would be hard to come back from, too.

Stiles found orders popping from his lips and responses coming from the crew in a step-by-step manner that had saved thousands of spacefarers in the past, a protocol upon which he now relied.

"Let's have all the rookies to support positions. Primary crew take your emergency stations. Alan, watch the gyro display and tell me personally if it starts jumping. Let's have red alert."

"Red alert!" Travis echoed.

A dozen changes erupted with that order. The lighting all over the CST shifted to muted cherry. The hatches between sections slammed shut and pressure locked—*sssschunk.*

"Keep up the thrust." Stiles knew they were doing that already. Just wanted to make sure nobody pushed the wrong button. The ship's sublight engines whined valiantly. "Let's see what we've got to fight with. Give me some numbers and colors."

Immediately Travis called into the comm. "Engine thrust control, give us numbers and colors."

Almost immediately section leaders' voices from all over the ship started bubbling through the comm system to the bridge, because now all the hatches were closed. Travis, Zack Bolt, and Greg Blake relayed what he needed to know and left out what he didn't.

"Six GCG, sir."

"Red over yellow on the plasma injectors, Eric."

"Green on the pellet initiators."

"We're nine points overbudget on the MHD. They're trying to equalize."

To his shipmates across the bridge Jeremy called, "Just compensate when it spikes!"

"Hear that, Jason? Compensate the spike only! Jason!"

The engine noise swelled to a howl, as if a hurricane were transferring itself from section to section right through the sealed hatches. Beneath the engine noise squealed the grind of real physical stress, as the ship twisted and cranked against the planetary force hauling on them. It was as if they were towing some great body that insisted upon moving in the opposite direction. And they were losing. . . .

"Thrust increasing!" Greg Blake called. "No effect, sir! We're slipping down even faster!"

"Put more power to it, then."

What else could they do?

Stiles glanced sideways at Leonard McCoy, glad the doctor was sitting down. He didn't want to be responsible for the famous elderly physician being scratched, spindled, or mutilated from falling down in the *Saskatoon*. Spock, too, seemed stable enough, despite the ravaged tilt of the deck and the slow spin that tore at the artificial gravity.

Travis punched at the controls with one hand while holding himself in place with the other. "Maybe we can twist out sideways—use the lateral—"

"We'd gulp too much fuel," Jeremy argued. "We're already burning the deuterium at fail-safe rate! It's all we can do to hold position. Ten more minutes and we won't have anything left at all. We've got nothing to twist with."

Pulling himself bodily upward to Jeremy's side, Stiles tried to make sense of what he saw on the maps and visual analyses of the planet below. "What's the source of this beam? Anybody reading the surface?"

Greg Blake was the one to answer. "Reading an energetic pulse station at the northern foot of the valley. It's east of the . . . looks like a swamp. No lifesigns. It must be automated."

"Yes, there's a swamp. Zack, target that facility."

"Targeted," Zack Bolt responded. "Phasers armed."

"Fire phaser one," Stiles ordered.

A single phaser beam broke from the ship's weapon array and bolted down toward the planet, but hadn't made it a half second away before suddenly bending sharply and bouncing like a ricocheted bullet off an invisible field between them and the planet.

Alan Wood covered his head, as hot sparks and bits of melting metal blew into the bridge from section two.

"Insulate!" Stiles yelled at the same time. From where he

stood he could see his experienced shipmates grab the trainees and yank them to the interior areas of the CST.

Sure enough, the phaser beam lanced around, bending every time it hit the egg-shaped energy field and shooting back past the ship, until finally, inevitably, it struck hull.

An explosion ripped through the midsection electronics, blowing sparks, hissing—and somebody cried out in pain. Shouted orders and desperate measures shot forward, audible even through the closed hatches.

"So much for phasers . . ."

"Rupture! Section four, starboard PTC! Automatic sealant nozzle heads are fused—"

"Tell 'em to do it manually," Stiles called. "Is everyone okay?"

Jeremy looked at him grimly. "It's a reflector envelope! Our own phaser hit us! We can't fire out!"

"Pardon me . . . would you take a suggestion?"

Spock!

The voice jolted Stiles. He spun around and looked up to the grand figure on the starboard deck. "Are you *kidding?*"

The stately Vulcan kept a grip on the buffer edge of the science console and somehow made his awkward position look graceful on the wickedly tilted deck. "Quicksand. If we struggle, the beam sucks us down at a commensurate rate, drawing upon our own energy to exert more pull than we can exert thrust. If we hold still, all it may do is hold us in place."

While the engines howled and the hull peeved, Stiles gazed at the ambassador and Spock back at him as if they had all week. Doubt and illogic spun through Stiles's training and experience, then jumped the gully to irrational trust.

He looked at the readouts, at Jeremy's face skewed with doubt, at Travis desperately trying to make sense of what the ultrascience officer had just suggested . . . as precious seconds slipped away, Stiles found himself adding up the crazy numbers.

His eyes flipped again to Spock, and he shook his head and winced. "I was about to fall for something again, wasn't I?"

"Literally."

"Sir . . . I hope you're everything I think you are." Without turning away from Spock's steady eyes, Stiles tossed over his shoulder, "Cut thrust."

"That can't be right!" the panicked trainee at the helm protested, his eyes swiveling wildly. "We'll get pulled into the planet!"

Stiles started to explain, then cut himself off and waved. "Travis!"

Perraton instantly yanked the midshipman from the helm and slid into the seat himself. "Cutting thrust. Sorry, kid. Go sit down till we see how dead we are."

His own order eating at his stomach, Stiles leered at Spock as if to share the burden. His mind raced, as he scoured his memory of all those recorded missions on the first *Starship Enterprise,* when Spock faced the worst mysteries of the cosmos as Captain Kirk's unswerving sidekick.

The whine of the engines depleted noticeably, like howling wolves running over a hill and disappearing into the mist.

"Is it working?" Stiles dared to ask.

Quiet with victory, Travis half-turned to confirm with a good glance. "We're slowing down. . . ."

"We've just bought ourselves about twenty more minutes," Jeremy assessed. "I wouldn't bet on more."

"Keep measuring."

Irritated with the knowledge that he wouldn't have been able to save his ship if Spock hadn't been here, Stiles bristled with selfconsciousness, fighting to think with a divided mind.

"Can't fire out . . . can we beam through the reflector bubble?"

"I don't know that!" Zack Bolt rebelled at the idea. "I know for sure I could never beam you back up through that thing!"

"That doesn't make any—"

"Beam out?" Travis swung around. "Then what? Find the beam housing and kick it down? That thing can take hand phaser fire!"

"We'll use the nacelle charges," Stiles told him.

"Those are only five-minute charges," Travis explained, with sudden fear in his eyes. "They'll take out a mile and a half. You'll never get away in time."

"We'll do something," Stiles shabbily assured. "Let's try it. Ready the transporter."

"Are you nuts?" Jeremy grabbed at Stiles's arm, keeping one hand on his controls. "Give me time to analyze the reflector envelope! Maybe you can't beam through it."

"How long before it pulls us down, did you say?"

His face sheeting to white, Jeremy shook his head. "All right, all right."

Some inner checklist rang in Stiles's head, and he turned to Spock, prepared to use all the resources he had at his disposal—and this was one dynamite resource. "Can we?"

Now that he'd been invited, Spock leaned to look at Jeremy's science monitors that gave them the energy analysis of that beam. Even after several seconds of study and two significant frowns, Spock could only postulate, "Possibly."

Stiles's leg muscles knotted. "Let's try beaming through."

On his other side, Jeremy protested, "Let me beam something solid out first."

"You got thirty seconds. Somebody get me a jacket. I'm going myself."

"*You* are?" McCoy asked. "Damn! Another hotshot!"

The comm button was hot under Stiles's finger. "Jason, bring me two of the shaped charges we use to blow off nacelles. Meet me in the transporter section." He accepted and yanked on a jacket somebody handed him from the aft bridge locker. "I've got to find Zevon. Nobody else knows—"

"Neither do you know the way around the city," Spock pointed out. He stood squarely before Stiles. "You were a prisoner. But I do."

That's what he needed—a super-shadow.

But he couldn't think of any reason that didn't make absolute sense. Pushy, pushy Vulcan . . .

"What about me?" Dr. McCoy made a rickety effort to stand up.

Stiles gaped at him, instantly in a bind. His mouth opened, closed again, opened—what could he say? McCoy couldn't possibly run or fight, but if he stayed here . . . and what about the others? Offer to beam a hundred-and-some-year-old man down to save his life and leave the entire young crew behind with their lives dangling?

McCoy's ice-blue eyes sharpened. "Are you going to refuse one of the greatest explorers and pioneers in Starfleet history?"

Choking on what he hoped was damage smoke and not something else, Stiles uttered, "I . . . I . . . uh. . . ."

"Eric," Jeremy interrupted, "We're slipping. They're not pulling us down with our energy now, but it's still pulling us with whatever energy it can muster itself. We're slipping deeper into the atmosphere. Sixteen minutes till we hit the surface."

Travis looked at him. "Can we turn so we don't hit engines-first?"

"No chance."

Spock stripped out of his ceremonial robe and dumped it on the deck. "We should go, Commander."

But Stiles was still gawking at McCoy without knowing what to say.

The aged physician leered back at him with singular determination.

Spock snapped up the front of his formal jacket—it turned out the big clunky Vulcan molded jewels also had a clasping mechanism—and simply preempted, "Doctor, please."

Leveling a finger at Stiles, McCoy huffed, "If you don't come out of transport with your arms sticking out of your head and you find that Romulan, you bring me the whole package, not just a sample of his blood. I've got to have a constant, warm, living source for several days to do what I need to do. I need him, got it? Not a sample. Him, himself."

"Thank you," Spock said. "We shall do our utmost."

"You'd better."

And McCoy stepped aside, out of the way of everybody who was working to keep the CST in the atmosphere.

"Travis, come here." Stiles grasped his friend's arm and held it fiercely. "Backup plan three, got it?"

"Really?"

"Yes, really. Got it?"

"Got it."

"Travis . . . don't let my ship sink."

Somehow Travis found a smile. "We'll do what we have to, Eric."

Stiles started to respond, but his words stuck in his throat. Travis assured him by returning the grip, and said nothing more.

Drawing a tight breath, Stiles jumped to the hatchway and grasped the hatch handle, then looked back for Spock. "Mr. Ambassador? Let's fly or fry."

"After you, Mr. Stiles."

The Imperial Palace

What had begun as a complex and troubling medical mission had first metamorphosed into the glimmerings of success—a chance to save a thousand royal family members and shore up the stability of the Federation's closest and most dangerous neighbor on this side of the street—and had now once again altered its form and function. Now Crusher, Data, and the hapless merchant named Hashley were about to fight for their own lives. As abruptly as wind shifts, they had become the targets of an assassination plan that had seemed as distant to them as stars were apart.

As her stomach muscles spun into spirals, Beverly Crusher thought fast, conjuring up a half-dozen alternatives before settling on one. She couldn't sedate them all. She couldn't seduce them all . . . there had to be something better.

"Allow me to play to your sense of honor," she began, with a bluntness she hoped Romulans would appreciate. "If your men can take my man, Sentinel, I'll pack up my instruments and leave, and let the empress and her family die. You won't even have to kill me."

Sentinel Iavo tipped his head as if he hadn't quite heard her right. He nodded once at Data after deciding she couldn't possibly be talking about Hashley.

"Him?"

"Yes," Crusher said. "Him."

"A duel?"

"If you have the integrity."

Iavo glanced at the sergeant of his guards. The sergeant frowned in suspicion, but said nothing.

"How is it honorable," Iavo parried, "for five men to do battle with one man?"

Crusher shrugged. "Well, he works out a lot. You know Starfleet."

The five Romulan men, warriors all, looked at Data and saw a lanky, wiry human who carried Crusher's medical bags.

Crusher held her breath. Come on, men, think . . . how do we spell Romulan chivalry?

"He has no weapon," one of the other guards protested as he finally drew his own blade.

"You told us no active phasers or disrupters could get through the palace's security screen," Crusher said, "so you can either give him a dagger, or fight him like he is."

Despite being obviously intrigued by the wager, Iavo's expression hardened. "There is no integrity in sacrificing everything on a game. I refuse, Doctor. I cannot afford to let you leave here now. You will die today."

Crusher shrugged. "Have it your way. You still have to fight him."

Data stood alone in the middle of the carpet, calm and waiting, seeming very small. Perfect—the Romulans didn't like this at all. Whether they won or not, they were petty about fighting and too chicken to bet on themselves. And she'd piqued their sense of fair play. Conscience could be such a burden, couldn't it? She hadn't expected them to take a silly wager, but now they were ashamed to fight Data in what appeared to be a no-win for Starfleet.

The Romulans glanced at each other in waves of hesitation, doubt, suspicion—and a flash of guilt?

Over her shoulder, Crusher heard the faint voice of Ansue Hashley. "I . . . I can fight . . . a little. . . ."

"Shh," the doctor murmured. "Go ahead, Data."

Without verbal acknowledgement, Data moved forward. Crusher pressed Hashley back, and the line of battle drew itself across the fur carpet. There before her, like a museum painting on a wall, stood the stirring vision of four distinguished Romulan charioteers and their Sentinel in rebellion, and thus they descended to the ranks of hatchet men.

Between the two factions in the bedchamber stood the couch and the oblong table and its chair. For a moment these three objects seemed as insurmountable as any moat. The recorded harp lyricals continued mindlessly to play, the fire to skitter and glow, the empress to suffer through her next breaths.

Ultimately the tension in the room became tangible, breakable—or maybe it was just the accursed twangy harp music—and the standoff was shattered by the battle cry of the sergeant of the guard. He flung off his helmet, dashed it to the hearth stones, and charged.

Blocked by the table, the sergeant drove forward anyway and leaped into the air, took two steps across the tabletop, spread his arms, dagger down, and dive-bombed Data where he stood.

Barehanded, Data's arms shot up; he clasped the sergeant's nubby silver uniform with both hands and parried the man over his head. If Data had simply completed the arch, the sergeant would've landed on Crusher, but Data's shock-fast computer brain measured the pivot—angle, force, velocity, energy—and he twisted exactly right. The sergeant bellowed his shock and surprise, slashed downward with his blade—raking Data across the back of the neck—and then flew into the wall as if shot from a cannon. Though it looked as if he had just struck the velvet drapery, his body made a distinct *thok* of bone and armor striking against sheer rock. He crashed onto the corner of the vanity and thence to the floor.

Enraged, the three other guards now charged in unison, vaulting and smashing past the furniture. Data's hands struck out like cobra tongues, skirting the slashing blades of his attackers with such blinding speed that two of the guards cut each other instead of him and stumbled back. The third received a kick in the gut and was thrown off. The first guard now flew from his position on the floor and jumped onto Data's back, clinging and grimacing viciously while trying to position his knife at Data's throat. Data merely turned under them as freely as a weathervane, his expression completely unfazed.

Sentinel Iavo, astounded by what he saw, rushed between

the table and the couch, his ceremonial dirk's long blade golden in the firelight, as he drove it forward into Data's ribcage. There the blade lodged.

Data reached over his head with one hand to clasp the clinging sergeant by the hair and down with the other hand, to grip Sentinel Iavo's dirk hilt as it protruded from his chest. Crusher winced as the three men waltzed together.

Behind her, Ansue Hashley's gasps and gulps narrated every move, and he somehow had the sense to stay back, no matter what he thought he saw.

"He'll be slaughtered!" Hashley empathized. "That knife—it's in him!"

Restraining herself from idle boasting, Crusher said, "Don't worry yet. Data's the best concealed weapon around."

In a spin of color and firelight, the sergeant slammed to the floor at Crusher's feet, dazed, his face bleeding, lungs heaving, weapon completely missing. Crusher stooped and heaved him up onto his knees. "There you go. Keep fighting."

She stepped back, watching tensely to see if the seed of guilt she'd planted would sprout quickly enough to turn the tide. Already she sensed a halfheartedness in the Romulans' effort—or was she imagining it?

With a prideful roar, the Romulans surged back into the fight just as Sentinel Iavo and one of the other guards crashed into the couch and drove the whole thing right over backward, dumping them into a stand of shelves, whose contents came shattering down upon them.

"You're making a mess," Crusher commented.

"I shall be happy to tidy everything later, Doctor," Data responded as he whirled and took a blaze of vicious stabbings to the arms and upper body and blocked hard-driven blows that were meant for his face. In return he drove his fists, knuckles, and the heels of his hands into the soft tissues of his opponents. "By the way, I am expecting a communiqué from the empress's first cousin's physician on Usanor Four. Would you mind activating the channel?"

"Oh, sure."

Completely rattled by the casual conversation going on while they were panting like dogs, the Romulan guards let their anger get the better of them. Data's hand-eye coordination was at computer speed, he had the strength of any ten Romulans all equalized throughout his body, and he wasn't getting tired. When the next one came within grasping range, attempting to body-blow Data to the floor, Data instead grasped the man fully about the chest and heaved him into the air, propelling him up and into the corner.

"Data, it's getting out of hand. Wrap it up as soon as you can."

"Certainly."

Sentinel Iavo was poised ten feet from them in an attack stance, staring at the body of his guard. Summoning the commitment he had made, he forced himself to swing once again at Data with his dirk blade slashing. The blade fell on Data's shoulder and glanced off. Iavo stumbled.

In that instant, Data managed to drive off all three remaining attackers at once, just long enough to grasp the dagger hilt that was still sticking out of him. With a firm yank, he drew it from his body. The blade dripped with colored fluid as he turned it toward the charging guards and the Sentinel. He was armed.

His eyes narrowed and his teeth gritted, Data's jaw locked, and there was a flush of effort in his complexion. The Sentinel and two of the guards attacked him as a unit with their blades, met with driving force by Data's weapon. The clang and shriek of metal against metal erupted over the harpsong.

"Uh-oh, he's getting mad," Crusher observed. "And they say he doesn't have those emotions . . . apparently he's got something like adrenaline on his side."

"How can he do this?" Hashley asked. "How can he throw those big guards around!"

"He eats his broccoli. This is what happens to all conspirators, Mr. Hashley. Sooner or later they have to show themselves."

Iavo spun around and glared at her while two of his men lunged at Data and were thrown off. "Conspirators?"

"The Sentinel did it, didn't he?" Ansue Hashley reckoned, taking the topic and running with it while the other men fought their way around the arena. "He poisoned the royal family! He wanted power all the time. He's been close to it all his life, like the prime minister waiting for the queen to die, but he gets impatient. I've heard of that."

Crusher rewarded him with a nod, then accused Iavo with a glare. "I guess he thought he could get away with killing the entire royal family."

In the middle of a dagger-swipe, Iavo let his move be parried without challenge as he sang out, "I did nothing to make this happen! I have no idea why they turned ill at the same time! I thought it was their blood!"

Wondering how good an actor he was, Crusher moved sideways, keeping behind the periphery of Data's slashing weapon. "Who helped you engineer the viral terrorism?"

"I did *not* do it!" Iavo shouted. He actually stopped fighting, backed away from Data, and stood there waving his weapon in a kind of helpless gesture, as one of his guards writhed in pain at his feet and the other braced to charge again. "This was providence working! I had the power to see what could be! I wanted to change the hearts of our people, not this . . . this— stop it!"

He lashed out at the last guard, driving the charging soldier sideways into the table just before the other man would've plowed back into Data's circle of engagement.

"Stop, all of you!" Iavo ordered. "Stop . . . stop. No more . . ."

The other guards—the two conscious ones—clasped at their bleeding and broken limbs and obeyed him. Mindful of Data's dangerous abilities, they shrank back, away, and crouched near the fireplace. Somehow Crusher could tell that they weren't obeying because they were beaten. They were obeying because they knew they were wrong.

Emotionally destroyed, baffled and sickened by the rankness of what he had been tempted toward, Iavo stalked the width of the room, then finally sank into the chair at the center table as if some magical pry bar had opened a valve and let the air out of him. He raised his striking jewel-like eyes to Crusher, and she saw mirrors of anguish.

"A thousand loyalties," he mourned, "a thousand pressures . . . these days have been torment for me . . . I have spent my life in the service of the royal family, never once thinking such thoughts, until along came this miracle, this disease that

207

struck every one of them . . . at first it seemed tragic, soon changing to a glimmer . . . the allure of opportunity . . . to cut away the throne's ancient core . . . change the future of the empire, dilute the power of blood succession that causes these terrible dangers and finally try something new—this might've been the only chance in history to try. But I can't finish it—"

Demolished, Iavo sank back on the vanity, his head hanging, his arm draped across the console.

"I could let them die," he moaned, "but I could never kill them. You must believe me. . . ."

"Data, stand down," Crusher ordered.

The android lowered his weapon, although Crusher was reassured when he did not put it away, and remained poised in the middle of the room, ready to spring in case anybody got any ideas.

"Good work," she said as she came to the android's side. "How badly are you hurt?"

"A little lubricant leakage, Doctor."

"I'll fuse you up in a few minutes."

Emboldened, Crusher crossed the furry carpet in three strides and got the dazed Sentinel by the collar, her hands knotted like cannonballs at his throat. She leered into the crumple of his face.

"All right, Iavo. Look at me. I'm willing to have seen nothing here today, do you understand me? Data's not only the devil with a handweapon, he's also got what you might call a photographic memory. We've got a record of everything that's gone on here, but I'm willing to keep it between us if you do exactly as I order. You get your buddies out of here and don't show me another armed guard for the duration of my visit. You're now the empress's one and only bodyguard. Monarchies are stupid, but that little girl didn't do anything except get born into the royal family. It's like a curse, y'know? It's not her fault."

"You must believe me," he beseeched. "I know nothing of the plot to make them all ill. . . ."

"I believe you." She dropped his collar so abruptly that he flinched. "This biological assault's been going on all over the quadrant and it's never involved the Romulans till now. As much as I'd like to hate you right now, nothing points to you. You're just an opportunist. A clumsy one, at that. You think I can't tell that you've never done anything like this before?"

"I never have . . . please forgive me . . . I never expected you to be so brave. We have always been told that humans whimper and sneak, stab in the night . . . I have served loyally all my life, until this opportunity raised it head—"

"And you can still have your coup d'etat someday, I'm all for revolutions, but not while the opposition is lying helplessly ill and I'm around to make them better. If the empire falls this way, this fast, you'll take all the rest of us down the drain with you. You threatened to kill me, so here's the counter offer. You won't kill me, and Data won't have to kill you. I keep treating her and the rest of the royal family, and you and your men pretend none of this happened and quit thinking that this is a good way to change things. You can all keep your positions and get another chance some day to do it right. I'll send you a biography of Benjamin Franklin and you can get some ideas, but until then be patient and do your jobs with some statesmanship. For now, you'll back off and let me do my job without any more theatrics. Simple enough?"

The fire snapped, and the harp chimed.

Chapter Nineteen

"MR. STILES . . ."

The devil's own carnival ride. Hands still tingling. Hate bad dreams . . . Orsova, looming over him while some creepzilla who'd won an auction flayed the flesh off him with bare fists. Arms throbbed. Legs, back . . . wake the dead with that drum-beat.

Leave me alone. Can't go back, can't go back there. . . .

Lips clamped together and teeth gnashed, coming down on gritty slime. Stiles swam back to consciousness. Threads of grit made way between his teeth, the side of his tongue, the back of his throat—he gagged himself awake.

As if something were crawling across his face, he backhanded himself in the mouth and wiped moist filth from his face, then heaved up spitting, weed pods netted with slime sheeting off the left side of his uniform as he rolled.

Someone groaned—he opened his eyes and seemed to see the sound of his own complaint rush into the sky like a bird. Pressing grit from his watering eyes, he forced himself up on both arms and hovered there on hands and knees, as his head battled to clear.

He was kneeling in shoulder-high ferns. The ground was

soft, sticky, made of pea-like pods in a great carpet, light green like duckweed on an everglade. And stank like a bilge.

"What's that awful smell?" he complained.

A few yards from him, Spock rose to his knees in the ferns, his hands dripping with green stuff. "The great outdoors."

As if afflicted, Stiles stood up on a pair of rattling maracas. "God, we lived . . . that was the longest beaming I've ever been through. My head feels like a stone."

"The restraint shield they put around us is apparently geared toward weapons energy, fortunately. It allowed us to beam in—is your phaser active?" Spock was holding his phaser, looking at it critically.

Stiles pulled his own phaser. "Drained! These were fully charged!"

"The shield sensed the charge," Spock said, "and neutralized them. Useless." Just like that he dismissed their lack of weaponry.

"Where are the grenades?" Spock slashed at the ferns with his hands, looking for the only thing they'd had time to bring with them—a pouch loaded with heavy-duty shaped grenades normally used by CST crews to blow off an irreconcilably leaking nacelle before the nacelle exploded and took a whole ship with it.

All around and above them, black trees spindled high and low, wretched branches dipping low into the marshy weeds and snaking up again with newly absorbed nutrients. Hands shaking, Stiles dug at the thickly shadowed overgrowth and wished there were more sunlight. Those clouds up there, blocking the light, those were the ones he'd seen displayed on the *Saskatoon*'s screens as the energy from the planet drew the ship deeper and deeper into the atmosphere. The clouds seemed so passive and blanketing, he had to struggle to recall that they were as deadly as venom, blinding his crew as they were sucked closer to being milled to dust.

Seemed like the ship was a million miles away, down here with the peace and quiet and ferns . . . be easy to lie down and take a nap.

"Twelve minutes," Spock reminded. "At this rate, the CST will crash at six hundred ten miles per hour."

"And disintegrate—I know." Stiles pawed furiously through the

211

ferns now. "It's got to be here. It came through, didn't it? What if the envelope let us through and stopped the grenades somehow?"

"The pouch would be here empty."

"Oh . . . right. Here it is!" He came up from the ferns with a weed-matted satchel, and half a bush attached to his hair. Through the pouch's mock-leather skin, he felt the presence of two charges in their canisters.

"We must hurry," Spock urged.

After a moment's clumsy hesitation, clarity struck him that Spock's statement was meant to let Stiles lead the way.

"Right—this way."

The transporter had put them down at the edge of the weed forest. As they broke out of the knotty growth, tripping on hidden roots and fingers of dipping branches coming up again as independent plants, Stiles immediately saw the center of his universe—a blocky gray beam housing nestled in a meadow, positioned so that it had almost 170-degree firing clearance in every direction, even over the mountain range to his right— those mountains sent a javelin through him, which seemed to drive him backward . . . moving his feet to go toward the building caused such physical stress that his legs nearly went numb.

The blocky beam housing was nothing more than a platform of granite blocks and a spidery dutronium arrangement that acted as legs for a conical device standing about thirty feet above the ground. From that device at this moment a blinding blue beam was being emitted, that bellowed like a concert band trying to tune up.

Maybe they could've brought it down with hand phasers, but it would have taken a while to melt, Stiles noted with some satisfaction. At least the right choice had been made there. They hadn't taken the time to get hand phasers out of the security lockers and had brought only the canister charges. A dumb mistake. A dumb midshipman's mistake. Why did his mind always turn to taffy when Ambassador Spock was around?

"Both sides of the base?" Stiles asked as he handed one of the charges to the ambassador.

"Yes."

"These are shaped charges, sir, so be sure to point the open end down so the force'll go into the ground and not up to the ship. *Saskatoon*'s not much more than fifteen miles over our heads by now."

"Twelve point two. These are five-minute charges? No more, no less?"

"That's it. When you're blowing off a nacelle, all the alternatives have been exhausted. The decision's already been made. All you need is a small safety margin. Five's usually enough."

"It will not be enough today." Spock glanced around as he positioned the canister between the bolted fingers of a stanchion. "Other than the trees, there is no cover here."

"Most of those 'trees' aren't even trees. They're tendrils of an ancient root system. They just keep going up and down out of the glade like some giant's sewing them all over the countryside. They're hollow with liquid inside. They'll be blown down and act like a big net on us. The bark'll just crumble and turn into shrapnel."

"Perhaps we should head in another direction, in that case."

"We'll head over that way, on the open meadow. How far can we run in five minutes?"

"Hardly matters, Mr. Stiles. We're unlikely to survive the blast wave. If the ship is freed from this beam, Dr. McCoy can lead a landing party to collect your friend and continue with the medical mission."

Stiles peered through the dutronium spiderweb. "Is that why you left him up there? To lead a second landing party if we got killed?"

"Yes. Two fronts are better than one."

"Hmm . . . I left him because I figured he couldn't run." With feelings appropriately scornful to that little step down, Stiles pressed the charged canister into place. "Ready . . . it's set. Now what?"

"Four minutes, fifty-five seconds."

Ambassador Spock set his own canister, then stepped back from the granite block, his black eyes vibrant with the moment's risk. He was actually enjoying himself.

"I believe the operative phrase," he said, "is 'run like hell.' "

"Three minutes."

How long can five minutes be?

As Spock ticked off the time in thirty-second intervals, Stiles's legs pumped in unison with the pounding of his heart.

The longest Constrictor on record (the last time Stiles had experienced one) was three and a half minutes. The last eruption of Mount Vesuvius had lasted nine hours. A two-minute earthquake was really long. A ten-minute tornado. Minutes stretched into drawn-out experiences that seemed never to end, seemed to make the whole universe turn slower and slower, until a heartbeat itself became a sluggish kettledrum with the drummer falling asleep.

Five minutes of running across a swamp meadow, splashing through rancid fluids, anticipating the platform back there to blow sky-high and sweep him off the face of the planet—that five minutes shot by faster than a snapped finger. What happened to all those stories about minutes becoming hours?

As the five-minute mark approached, they were only a third of the way across the meadow, running toward a blister of stony hills. At thirty-six years old, Stiles could devour some ground, and he had been holding back somewhat because he didn't want to outpace the ambassador in case Spock needed help. Soon that showed itself to be unnecessary—Spock was tall, long-legged, and Vulcan.

They ran. Hindered by the knee-high meadowgrass and the uneven ground beneath, the exercise became a venture into hopping, tripping, sprinting, and catching on thorns and tangles. Another ten feet . . . another . . . each step drew him deeper into misery. His brain shut down, he couldn't think of what to do but keep running. In his periphery he saw the flash of purple and black—the ambassador's clothing moving at his side, the flick of Spock's fists and arms pumping as he forcefully kept up with a much younger man.

Stretching out his right leg to pass over a depression that opened before him, Stiles gasped suddenly as a cramp tore through the bottom of his thigh, wrecking his stride. His foot connected with the upward slope of the depression, but his leg instantly folded and he crammed into the compacted dirt knee-first, down onto his side, skidding on his right cheekbone into the grass. Not the kindly patch of green at the end of the block, this Pojjana idea of grass had serrated edges and left his hands and face reddened as if he'd just shaved with a sawblade. He was on the ground, and the last seconds were gobbled up.

"Keep running!" he shouted into the dirt. "I'll catch—"

But then the landscape opened up and reached for the sky. Black noise concussed between the mountains and the swamp forest, a great stick striking a great drum, and Stiles's skull rang and rang. He tried to rise, to run again, but the flash blinded him and the raw force drove him into the depression, not more than eight inches lower than the level of the ground they'd run across.

Suddenly he was lying in a furnace, pressed down by weight he couldn't fight. He turned his head to one side and opened his eyes in time to see the blast wave blow over him in a single, solid white-hot sheet. The side of his face turned hot and he buried his head in his arms and waited to die.

Into the muffling warmth of his sleeve, he murmured, "Go, Sassy, go, go . . . push. . . ."

The carnivorous shock wave sheeted across his body, raising the hairs on his neck and limbs. He couldn't breathe—he sucked at a vacuum—

And just as the compression was about to crush his chest, Stiles took one more desperate attempt to breathe and got a lungful of warm dusty air. His head cleared almost instantly.

As he maneuvered his elbows, pinned under his chest, and tried to shove himself upward, a weight across his shoulderblades pressed him down and held him. A wave of cool air now flooded over him, replacing the rushing scalded air of the blast sheet.

"Stay down." Spock's voice rang in his ear. "Cover your head."

Drowning out Spock's words, a shattering hail of granite bits and shards of metal pulverized them as they lay crushed to the floor of the depression. Stiles shrank into the smallest crushed-up ball he could manage as his back was hammered by his own success. The wreckage of the beam housing had taken a little tour flight and was now coming to visit the two little elves who'd arranged the trip.

His chest heaving, he finally managed to press up onto his elbows, then to his knees.

Crouched at his side, Spock was slapping him on the back over and over.

As Stiles was trying to figure out a way to tell the ambassador that he wasn't choking and didn't need to be patted, Spock simply explained, "Your clothes were burning."

"Oh . . . thanks. Was that . . . one . . . explosion . . . or two?"

"Two. One concussion wave." Spock spoke as if nothing had happened at all, then coughed. The cough made him seem perfectly mortal and gave Stiles a bit of comfort that otherwise might've slipped on past him.

As a shimmering cloud of debris—the last of the pulverized housing—drifted around them as if it were a theatre curtain lowering, he winced his way to a standing position and had to lock both legs to stay up. His whole body trembled and pulsed with aftershock.

Through the drifting dust, he peered at the mass of wreckage, completely flattened, in fact depressed into a crater. The steel structure that had held the beam's emitter lay in mangled messes all over the grass, which had itself been seared brown.

"Think it worked?" Stiles wondered. "Is the CST okay now?"

"If they veered off at the correct tangent, yes." Spock made moves to stand up, but faltered. Instead he looked at his legs, first one, then the other, in a strangely clinical manner.

Stiles turned to him. "Sir?"

Before he could ask the question that came up, he flinched bodily at what he saw—a shard of metal the size of a writing stylus embedded in the side of the ambassador's left thigh, with a good two inches sticking out.

"Oh, sir . . ." Stiles knelt beside him. The cloth of Spock's pantleg was stained with his blood, and the Vulcan was plainly stiff with pain, although he pretended this didn't bother him much. "How deep in do you think it is?"

"No way to tell," Spock said, and looked around at the sky. "The blast was substantial enough to have alerted the authorities. Someone should be arriving soon."

Shaken by that, Stiles also looked around at the gray sky. "And here we are, out on the lone prairie, with no way to defend ourselves—sir, don't!"

He put out a hand, though he didn't really know what to do when the ambassador abruptly grabbed the protruding two inches of the metal shard and simply slid it out of his leg.

"You're not supposed to pull out something that's sticking in you like that!" Stiles protested. "What if it hit an artery? You could bleed to death!"

"I clot well." Spock tossed the shard into the scorched grass and pressed the heel of his hand tightly to the wound. "I must be able to maneuver, and certainly a metal implement in my leg would be troublesome."

Stiles stood up again and looked around. "They'll be here any minute. We can take cover in those hills . . . I've heard of people digging down a few feet and finding the hollows made by ancient root systems that aren't there anymore." In the blast-flattened grass, he found a large piece of a support strut with the bolt still attached in one end. "We can dig with this. I think I can hide you for a while in there, and after nightfall we can make it into the foothills."

"Commander . . . would you consider—"

"No, I will *not* consider leaving you and going off on my own. That's not even in the picture, so don't think about it. If you'll let me help you up. . . ."

Holding his digger in one hand, he slipped the other arm around the ambassador, who allowed himself to be pulled to his feet. Smeared with Vulcan blood, their clothing scorched, hair filthy, they hitched their way out of the almost invisible depression that had saved both their lives by allowing the blast wave to pass over them instead of deep-frying them into the ground. Any minute now a patrol would show up to investigate the blast, which probably showed up on every scanner on this part of the continent. Obviously, too, the Pojjana must've known they'd caught something in that gravity-weird contraption.

"This way, sir." He drew Spock along, dismayed that the Vulcan seemed not to be helping much. "We'll hide until night, then we can make a bivouac in the hills and figure out a way to defend it. There they are! I see a plane! Come on, before they spot us!"

Chapter Twenty

STILES PRESSED FORWARD, aiming for the shadowy protection of the rocklands ahead. He could hear the distant murmur of the plane's engine, recognized the type of aircraft, and made his bets.

"They're still miles away," he gasped, pulling Spock along, "but even if they spot us they can't land on this terrain. They'll have to send a recon hoverscout with a patrol team to flush us out. If we can make it to the hills—"

"Commander?"

"Don't worry, I can take more of your weight. We can't slow down. If we can make it to—"

"Of course, Mr. Stiles, but I do have a question."

"What's that, sir?"

"From whom are we hiding?"

"Watch that rock—don't trip!"

"From whom," Spock repeated, "are we about to hide?"

"The authorities. They'll be here any time—"

"And to whom . . . did we come here to speak?"

Stiles dragged the ambassador along another five or six steps before this sank in.

As the drone of the aircraft drew closer to the bomb site, he felt his face screw up in a frown of confusion and doubt. Something just didn't seem right about this.

The ambassador tentatively put more weight on his injured leg.

Stiles shifted back and forth on his own feet and finally met Spock's eyes. "I'm doing it again, aren't I?"

Spock bobbed an eyebrow, flattened his lips, and charitably avoided nodding.

While digesting that little nugget, Stiles lowered the ambassador onto the first sitting-sized rock they'd come upon, a harbinger of the fact that they could've made it to cover if logic hadn't gotten in the way.

They remained still, unresisting, out in the open, as the Pojjana aircraft buzzed the scene of the explosion and Stiles thought his arms and legs were going to fall off with the urge to run again, hide, defend—

The plane strafed the flattened beam emitter for several seconds before veering abruptly toward them. His spine shriveled. They'd been spotted.

'They've seen us,' Spock said with quiet satisfaction.

"How are we going to explain blowing up their emitter?" Stiles circled behind the ambassador and came around the other side as if stalking the plane on its approach. "We had to do it. I couldn't let it pull my ship down—"

"Of course not."

The plane soared over them, one wing tilted low, and they could clearly see the pilot in his helmet looking down at them. He was contacting the Pojjana security forces.

They'd never get away now. Stiles battled inwardly, wrestling with the idea that getting away wasn't the best idea, wouldn't get them where they needed to be, wouldn't find Zevon.

"You needn't call me 'sir,' " Spock told him, as if they were sitting over a dinner table or playing badminton. "I have no Starfleet rank any longer, and you are the commander of the vessel that matters in our lives today."

"Yeah, well . . . well, it'll be long time before I can think of you as anybody other than Science Officer Spock of the *Enterprise*."

The plane circled the area, keeping them inside its surveillance area while no doubt calling for backup. Stiles never let his back turn to the plane, moving constantly to stay between the aircraft and the ambassador, a shield of vellum against rockets if they decided to open fire. Each step drove him deeper into his troubled thoughts.

"Do you know," he began, "do you realize how many hours on end I rehearsed calling you 'Ambassador' before that evac mission? I just knew I'd get down to that planet and call you 'Mister' or 'Captain' or 'First Officer' or 'Your Honor' or 'Your Highness'—something stupid was waiting to pop out of my mouth and I could just taste it. All the way in Travis and the evil twins kept saying, 'Eric, will you quit mumbling the word *ambassador?*' I'll bet . . . I just bet Captain Kirk never had that kind of problem."

Spock paused a moment. His eyes never flinched nor did his expression change much. He peered solemnly into the past and seemed to enjoy what he saw.

"No," he said. "He had others. Those were excellent days. But they are passed now."

Despite the circumstances, Stiles found himself sighing. "Maybe for you. Not for the rest of us."

Looking up now, Spock said, "Because you feel you must live up to them?"

Somehow there was no right answer to that question. Damned if he did, damned—

Apparently the ambassador didn't expect an answer, because he kept talking himself. "If James Kirk's mission logs are the barometer against which you measure yourself, you set too high a task for yourself. You must temper your awe. You can never attain so high a standard."

Even though a patrol scout craft now appeared over the mountains and streaked toward them across the meadow flats, Stiles turned to Spock and didn't bother to look at the patroller as he heard its humming engines approaching.

"Oh, is that right?" he challenged. "I always admired you for the things you did and the—I guess 'style' is a good way to say it . . . I never got the idea you were filled up with yourself. Till now, anyway. . . . Why are you nodding? I just insulted you."

"Rather, you just complimented yourself," Spock corrected. "And you must not expect me to argue with the ship's commander."

His tone was somehow cagey, manipulative, carrying palpable ulterior messages. And that eyebrow was up again. Stiles scoured him silently, wondering what to make of the ambassador's expression. Was he being teased?

"Are you feeling ill?" Spock asked him then.

Stiles flinched. "What?"

"You're very pale."

"Well . . . it . . . isn't easy getting needled by a . . . by a . . ."

"A super-eminence?" Spock supplied.

Stiles peered at him, able for a moment to ignore the approach of the Pojjana security scout. Was Spock smiling? Was that a little smile? Was it?

As the Pojjana scout came to a hover over them with its warning lights flashing, its containment field snapped on to enshroud them in red spotlight—they could no more walk out of it than through a vault wall.

"Stay quite still," the ambassador warned. "They will assume we're armed."

With the flat of his hand Stiles shielded his eyes from the containment field's glare. "We should've been. I botched it."

His hands were ice. Emblazoned on the flank of the scout, the Pojjana symbol of a gray lightning bolt crossed by a red arrow seemed alive to him, a swollen symbol of his captivity. Those terrors and miseries rushed back at him. His legs trembled so violently that he could barely stand. Only Spock's steadying presence kept him from bolting, a spontaneity which would've fried him to a flake at the edge of the containment field. Strange—he knew that if he were the senior "eminence" here and his crewmates were with him, he wouldn't be so shaky. He would never let them bolt. How there could be two men in one suit—

"HOLD POSITION!" the scout's broadcaster boomed, so loud it knocked Stiles back a step.

Spock held up both hands in a surrendering gesture. Stiles couldn't manage that. His hands were frozen at his sides, his chest heaving, his leg muscles bound up.

"Relax, Mr. Stiles," Spock called over the scout's hum as the craft nestled into the crusty burned stubble, his dark eyes squinted into shafts.

Without looking at him, Stiles gulped, "Remember what happened last time you told me that?"

The Pojjana craft settled completely and gave off a loud hiss as its antigravs equalized. The sight of Pojjana guards lumbering down the hatch ramp as it crashed down gave Stiles a cramp in the middle of his gut. All four guards and a sergeant came thundering out and leveled firearms at them.

"Our sidearms are completely drained," Spock stated in passably fluent Pojjana to the sergeant who came to face them down. "We wish to speak to the planetary authorities."

"You are aliens," the sergeant said with malice, and confiscated their phasers instantly, drained or not. "This is Red Sector. We're supposed to be left alone."

Beside Stiles, the ambassador struggled to stand despite the fact that everyone could see his leg was bleeding. Spock faced the sergeant at eye level.

"Things change, Officer," he said. "I am Ambassador Spock of the United Federation of Planets, former emissary to the Pojjana Assembly. This is—"

"Don't tell them," Stiles whispered.

Spock instantly revised. "This is the commander of the transport ship you nearly brought down. We destroyed the emitter in self-defense. We have no aggressive intentions. We have a proposal for the provincial exarch."

"We have no exarch anymore. That position was eradicated."

"Who is in charge?"

"The provost of the works."

Spock tipped his head. "That is the supreme authority on the planet?"

"That's right."

"Please take us to this person."

The sergeant shook his head. His helmet reflected light from the clearing sky. "You'll be incarcerated in the provincial prison until you come to trial for invasion."

"We must be allowed to see the senior authority. This is a matter of interstellar importance."

"I'll put you where I want to put you," the sergeant said. "Then I'll wait to be asked what happened."

Stiles beat down a shudder. "Nothing really changes."

"We cannot wait," Spock told the sergeant. "If you withhold us, you will be blunting advancement of a critical mission. Do you wish your name to be prominent when the provost discovers that he was not informed?"

The sergeant stood with an unreadable expression for a few silent seconds, then gestured them toward the scout's ramp and the four other guards waiting to funnel them inside.

"Clear them for energy signals," the sergeant ordered to his men, and one of them came forward.

The guard lowered his firearm, whipped out some kind of scanner, and ran it over Stiles from ears to toes, then over Spock, front, back, and both sides.

"No active energy or signals of any kind," the guard confirmed. "No readings."

"He told you we were unarmed," Stiles complained, knowing that he wouldn't have believed it either.

The sergeant stepped aside and leveled his own weapon. "Go in."

Obviously there wasn't much more to be done here. Stiles's jaw ached to speak up, spit who he was and insist on some kind of instant retribution, but a thousand warnings clogged his throat. He was in command of the ship, not the mission. If they found out who he was, would they take offense or insult? Stuff him back in a cell and start auctioning beatings again?

Stiles started toward the scout, pausing only when the ambassador took a step on his injured leg and crumpled to one knee. The sergeant stepped forward to assist. Stiles met the uniformed guard with a fierce shoulder butt to the chest.

"Back off," he snapped, and took the ambassador's arm himself.

None of the other guards made any attempt to touch them further. Stiles escorted the ambassador into the scout and to the first of only three passenger seats. They were in custody.

Stiles straightened and maneuvered to take the next seat. As he raised his eyes to scan the interior of the scout while the guards came aboard, he found himself no longer seated but rather standing ramrod straight and staring at a mounted photograph in a gilded frame on the port bulkhead.

After a wicked choke, he blurted, "Who in salvation is *that!*"

The sergeant, just coming aboard, glared at him as if he and the ambassador were complete idiots. "That's our provost of the works. He saved half the planet from the Constrictor. He developed a way to predict the waves. He sponsored engineering schools and guided architectural renovations all over the planet. Don't you even know who you came to see? We owe him our lives."

The idling engines of the scout roared in his ears as Stiles stood riveted to the carpet. His voice gravelly, he managed, "I owe him a couple things too. . . ."

Spock surveyed the picture briefly, seeing that something more than a portrait of a guy beside a tiger oak desk was going on here. "Mr. Stiles? Do you have something to say?"

Confused, demolished, Stiles blinked at him, at the sergeant and finally again at the picture.

"Yeah. Yeah, I do. I know how we can get in. Tell the 'Provost' . . . that Eric Stiles is back."

Chapter Twenty-one

"STILES. ERIC STILES. You didn't die. They cured you some-how."

"Orsova. Somehow, it figures."

In one withering instant, all of Eric Stiles's fears and visceral reactions bonded into a single living form. There, behind an enormous orange-and-black desk carved out of that wood that reminded Stiles of tiger oak, except even stronger, back-dropped by polished paneling and a dozen plaques and awards, there sat the drunken mess that had represented misery to him for four years.

Orsova was less slovenly than before, indeed had lost weight, though he still carried the wide shoulders and stocky build that came naturally to so many native Pojjana. His black hair was now shot with gold—their idea of getting older—and he no longer wore the uniform of the prison hierarchy but the tweedy suit of a Pojjana planetary official. Stiles had only seen that uniform twice before in person. A long time ago.

Orsova sat behind his huge desk, which had hardly any work upon it, and scoured Stiles with the look of a man who was being shown both the past and the future in one picture.

How could events turn this way? How could a devious slob like that become somebody with a title?

"God in a box," Stiles chafed, "what am I seeing?"

His words barely scratched from his throat. As he stood staring, he thought perhaps that only Ambassador Spock, standing with some effort at his side, had heard him at all.

He felt Spock's peripheral glance. But the ambassador never said a thing to him about his reaction to the person they were both standing before. This was crazy. This was a dream.

Spock stepped forward, favoring his bloody leg, to draw the provost's attention away from Stiles and onto himself.

"Provost, I am Ambassador Spock of the United Federation of Planets. Fifteen years ago I was the emissary to your government. We are here to negotiate the greening of Red Sector. Circumstances have caused the Romulans to need Federation assistance. On an Interstellar Temporary Pass, we have come here to make an offer. The sector can be reopened, allowing for trade, assistance, technological exchange, and limited diplomatic relations without requiring membership. We can help the Pojana in many ways—agricultural efficiency, technological—"

"We don't want help."

Orsova stood up behind his big desk, and there was something prophetic and distant about him. The desk sprawled like an emblem—tiger oak. That was something Zevon had talked about a long time ago. The memory sparked to life.

"What do you want?" Orsova asked.

"We wish to negotiate for custody of the Romulan prisoner named Zevon."

Please let him still be alive, please let him still be alive, please—

Orsova said nothing about Zevon, clearly determined not to give anything away. Instead, he simply asked, "Why do you want one of our prisoners?"

"Damn you," Stiles grumbled.

Spock looked at him.

In frustration and contempt Stiles wagged a hand at Orsova. "What am I—chopped cabbage? He damned well knows Zevon's not just 'one of their prisoners' to me! Is he alive or not, you bastard?"

At Stiles' single step forward, two of the four guards launched forward from the sides of the office, blocking his way to Orsova. The guard closest to him drove the butt of his rifle into Stiles' stomach, and he was driven down.

Spock grasped the guard's arm, avoiding the weapon, and pushed him back in such a way that somehow the movement wasn't threatening. As Stiles gasped at the ambassador's feet, battling crying lungs and a bruised rib, Spock spoke again to Orsova.

"If the Pojjana strike a deal with the Federation, the Bal Quonott and all others in the sector will be pressured to deal with you on favorable terms. That would give the Pojjana substance beyond just your planet. Indeed, you would be a power to be reckoned with in the entire sector. Certainly that offers some value."

Orsova's round bronze face tilted a little like a ball rolling. Maybe he was trying to think. Looked like it hurt.

Stiles's legs were watery as he waited. He had to force himself to stand still, not flinch or shift around, to bury the cloying nervousness, cloak the haunt of old terrors.

"You'll be held," Orsova ultimately decided, "as part of the foreign ship that invaded our planetary space. You'll be held as hostages until the rest of your ship up there surrenders. The ship is mine now, property of the Pojjana people. The crew will be turned over to your government after a healthy fine is paid for destruction of property, violating our space . . . and any other things I think of."

This was Orsova's playing ground. That showed clearly, as he stood up behind his big fancy desk, made of the wood Zevon had long ago discovered did not compress during Constrictors. He came around the bright orange piece of furniture, touching it only lightly along the edge. At the corner of the desk he paused, only steps from Stiles. His eyes burned into Stiles' eyes.

"Except you," he said. "I'll keep you for the memories."

Cued by some secret signal or habit, two of the four armed guards in the room came forward as Orsova moved out from his desk and paused again at Stiles' side. The guards were close enough to threaten against any attempts to attack the provost, so Stiles was careful to remain perfectly still. Being frozen into place by past horrors helped some.

Orsova's eyes drew tight. "It was an insult to me when they took you away. I promised the planet I would get you back. I kept your cell waiting. Didn't even clean it. Part of the promise."

With eyes flat and still as a doll's, Orsova motioned to the guards.

"Take them away."

"Orsova."

"You brought me back already? Why? I stopped the Federation people. Their ship ran away."

"Their ship did not leave the solar system. I have been monitoring. They're hiding somewhere. I have discovered why they came here."

At these words from the Voice, Orsova paused and frowned. He had been sure the Federation ship had run away. He had the Federation's Vulcan ambassador and Eric Stiles where no one would find them, and the Federation ship had run off. But this person, this ghost who spoke to him in unexplained terms, with impossible knowledge, said otherwise.

"I have changed my plans. I must have these people alive. The doctors, and Zevon."

"And Stiles?"

"Do what you wish with him."

"Why do you want doctors? Why don't you just kill them? We've killed plenty of others—"

"The have found a way to do the impossible, cure the incurable. I must know how. You must capture them and bring them to me."

Trying to make sense of a puzzle when he had only half the pieces, Orsova paced the small chamber of the humming craft as the planet of his birth rotated outside one of the little holes.

"I have something here," the Voice began again, *"that will make the Pojjana supreme in Red Sector. Even the Bal Quonott will shrink before you."*

Suspicious of such a brash statement, Orsova narrowed his eyes. "What will make spaceships bow before our planes?"

"You will have more than planes if you do as I tell you. Look in the space chest."

Space chest . . . this brass case? It had a lock, but the lid opened for him anyway. He looked inside. There was only one thing in there.

"A bottle?"

"A medical vial."

"Poison?"

"Something similar."

Orsova straightened sharply. "Is this biological war? You want me to put a plague on my own people? I won't!"

"No."

"I have no one else to poison."

"You have Zevon."

At this, Orsova paused and grimaced. "Why should I poison Zevon? Who are you to want it?"

"You'll never know me. All these years, and I am still a stranger. You were a jail guard. You became assistant warden, but you would never have grown beyond that but for the day I spoke to you and told you to believe that Zevon could predict the Constrictor. Now, Zevon's usefulness is coming to an end here. Give this to Zevon before he is enticed away, and the galaxy moves forward by a leap."

"Away?" Orsova reacted. "Why should he go away? He hates his own people. We're his people now! He says it every day."

"He is royal family. They need him. He may go."

"He'll never leave. No one could get him to leave now."

"The Federation and the Romulans both have reasons to make him want to go. If he leaves, you lose your power and I lose my chance to have what I want. The vial will end the Romulan threat and make the Pojjana strongest, because it will stop Zevon from leaving."

"Because he'll be dead? What . . . what do . . . if I kill Zevon for you, what comes to me?"

"This will force the collapse of the Romulan Empire. When it falls, you will get Romulan ships."

"Warwings? You'll give me those?"

"And birds-of-prey, and at least one full-sized converted

heavy cruiser ... for the sector governor, so he will become accustomed to flying in space."

"Sector governor . . ."

He discovered a series of small cracks—or were they openings? seams?—in the panels. . . .

"You will get a Romulan fleet, enough ships to control the Bal Quonott and make the Pojjana the power in this sector. Rather than cowering before the Federation, the Romulans, or any other aliens, you will be the winner."

"Winner . . ."

"Stop ... trying ... to see me!"

The cabin vibrated with the voice's sudden rage. Whoever this ghostly person was, he would not be discovered.

Orsova felt his curiosity wane and let it go. Some things, he didn't have to know. "Zevon's alien," he protested. "How do you know this will kill him? Are you an alien too? Are you a human?"

"No."

"Are you Romulan, Voice? Is that who you are all these years?"

"No."

"Are you—"

"Zevon will be contaminated. Then the Federation won't have any reason to stay in Red Sector, and Zevon will have no reason to leave. Either way, I will honor my agreement with you."

Standing in the middle of the cabin, Orsova gazed at the reflection of himself. An older man, no longer as fat as the prison guard had been, a glowing copper complexion on his cheekbones and streaks of dignified gold in his black hair. This was the leader of a planet, perhaps the leader of a whole sector of space? Dominion over the Bal Quonott, who had lorded their spacefaring capability over the Pojjana since before he was born?

Liking what he saw, he squared his shoulders and imagined a fur cape. The voice remained silent until he decided to ask a question.

"Every time you speak," he attempted, plumbing for more information, "I still have no reason to believe what you say."

"Believe because you can be in charge of this whole sector instead of just one weak and troubled planet, and I will be in charge of you. You will have more power, more comfort, more stability than ever you dreamed on the day you were happy to become a jail guard, the day you were astonished to be made warden, or the day you realized Zevon was right about predicting the Constrictor and that he would be silent for you. This is easy for me because you have already seized power here. With Zevon dead or ill, you will be my wealthy, powerful little puppet. Number two is still very high. Do this, and you will be sector governor when the Romulan Empire falls. Don't, and I will kill you now and find someone else. I don't care. Is this difficult?"

"No."

"Take the vial. You no longer need Zevon. Killing him is better. I will be happier. If you cannot kill him, infect him."

The small undecorated bottle was slightly warm, as if it had been kept heated. He noted the temperature and planned to keep it insulated. If he was going to do this thing, he would do it right.

"Needle?"

"It must go in the body. Skin contact is not enough. Only Zevon's DNA will absorb the virus. Get it into him any way you can. Report to me on this frequency when you have succeeded. The Romulan family dies, you become sector governor and get more than your dreams. You're a small and greedy man, Orsova. But take no insult . . . I need small and greedy men."

Orsova tucked the vial deep into his jacket, against the warm skin of his chest, and looked up to the faceless persona that promised him glory.

"Small and greedy governors," he corrected.

"Something weird's going on. Why wouldn't they want help? The Constrictor still comes—that's obvious from the architecture. And that pig's no provost or magistrate. I don't know how he got that kind of power, but he's nothing but a glorified jail guard. You saw how he acted! Nobody runs a planet honesty and forthrightly and then turns down help."

"He did seem somewhat cross-purposed."

"He's got some kind of racket going on here. How else in hell could a brutal superficial lout like Orsova end up in control of a whole planet?"

"How could a corporal become Führer?"

Stiles felt his face pinch. "Who? . . . oh. How's your leg? It's still bleeding?"

"Yes, it seems to be." The ambassador turned his leg for a better look at the wound. "You were right. I should have left the projectile embedded."

"Let me wrap it up."

Forcing himself to put Orsova aside in his mind, at least long enough to open the first-aid kit they'd been given, Stiles knelt beside the cot where Spock was sitting. The smell in here was *so* familiar—that combination of dust and moisture that never quite goes away. . . .

Spock pressed his hands back on the cot, tightened up visibly, and endured the stinging pain as Stiles cut the trouserleg away from the wound. The puncture had clotted some, though blood and tissue still leaked from it. Stiles tried to remember how big the projectile had been. Details failed him. All he could do was apply antiseptic, then pressure, both of which caused Spock to stiffen noticeably. Typically Vulcan, Spock was suppressing both the pain and any appearance of it. Stiles wondered if he could do that well if somebody put an arrow through part of him.

"At least they gave us a medical kit," he muttered as he gauzed the leg.

"They may have an ulterior motive," Spock suggested.

"You mean they want us to escape?"

"Possibly. What do you think?"

Confronted with having to cough up an answer, Stiles felt as if he were back in grade school and hadn't done his reading assignment.

"If anything made sense, I'd have something to think. Orsova as a planetary leader, no sign of Zevon . . . all sorts of technology and architecture that wasn't here ten years ago . . . that composite beam reaching out of the atmosphere and grabbing a ship as big and powerful as a CST—even Starfleet can't mix those properties that way. How could the Pojjana do that in just ten years?"

"From what you tell me," Spock contemplated, "Zevon knew what every civilization needs to make its quantum leap. Energy. Yet, to build and use high energy, he would need to influence the use of resources and manpower on the planet. If somehow he obtained influence, gained trust . . . yet how does an alien, particularly a Romulan, come to gain trust in a culture as xenophobic as this?"

"He couldn't. Something else must've happened. Orsova would never let us get past him to talk to anybody else . . . he kept everything to . . ."

Everything he'd seen, the inconsistencies and irritating facts, stewed under his skin. He thought of those last few hours with Zevon, with Orsova, the last beating that had been auctioned to an alien-hating Pojjana. Bruises nearly rose on his skin as if by habit, summoned by the nearness of those old miseries. Suddenly, as if being tapped on the shoulder, he remembered what he had said to Orsova during that last beating.

"That's it! Orsova as planetary leader makes no sense at all *unless* it finally sank through that iron skull that Zevon really could predict the Constrictor! I told him myself! I tried to convince him! If after I left he decided to check it out and Zevon convinced him, Orsova could've taken that message to the government, succeeded in warning the planet, saved a bunch of people and parlayed that into power—" Grasping his head to keep it from blowing off, Stiles raved, "That's got to be it! Orsova's getting credit for Zevon's work!"

Spock stretched his leg, thinking. "Why would Zevon agree to such an arrangement?"

"Oh, he'd agree in a flat minute," Stiles tossed. The familiarity rushed back. "Zevon didn't want power. He was never afraid for his own life. He wanted to redeem himself in his own eyes by saving more people than he killed when his team's experiments started the Constrictor."

"A composite graviton-traction beam with polarity that high, as well as the phaser-resistant envelope the CST encountered, can only be generated with very delicately balanced quantum charge generation. They plainly have warp energy, but it seems to be planet-bound."

"I know why," Stiles said. "Zevon wasn't interested in space. He'd been there. If he'd had influence and resources, he would've turned all the energy he could control to saving the planet from the Constrictor and other outside threats. Looks to me like the Pojjana turned out to be pretty sharp, at least sharp enough to follow instructions, learn physics and engineering . . . even Zevon couldn't do this by himself. They still don't have massive warships or anything, but in spite of that we were in for a real surprise when we got here."

"If Zevon is the real genius behind the planet's sudden advancement," Spock continued, "and I agree that is likely, then Orsova is in constant danger of his secret's being found out."

Stiles looked up. "He sure wouldn't want you and me blabbing it around, would he?"

"No. Nor would he want Zevon taken away. No deal or favor from the Federation could be as beneficial to him as having Zevon here, with a pact to remain behind the scenes."

Coming to his feet, Stiles paced a few steps. "If all this is right, then if Zevon leaves or dies, the jig is up. Orsova couldn't keep up the illusion of being brilliant all by himself."

"Sounds like a threatening symbiotic relationship," the ambassador surmised. "Zevon has managed to bridge the Pojjana through this period of Constrictors which otherwise would have killed vast numbers of them. Instead, they thrive despite the Constrictor."

"They thrive. Orsova thrives. Zevon's here somewhere, alive, working for Orsova. And we're here, locked in a stone crate."

His words fell to the floor. With nothing more to do for the ambassador's leg, Stiles sat on the other cot against the other wall, and descended into captivity as naturally as into a warm tub. Its arms folded around him. They'd been waiting.

The walls around them, stone and mortar, lichen and leakage, uttered their opinion. All the old perceptions came rushing back. Someone was using an autovac on a floor one story up. Water ran through the pipes. Other prisoners, probably, taking showers in the next wing. A flicker of the lights. Circuits needed adjustment.

He stared at the opposite wall.

"Somehow I knew," he murmured. "I knew I'd end up back here. It's been like one of those nightmares that won't quit coming back. Look at me . . . I can't breathe right, there's no blood in my hands . . . I used to get like this before academy exams. Or before meeting you."

Across the cell, the ambassador observed him as if he were watching bread dough rise, which annoyed Stiles right to the hairs on the back of his neck. Kicking at a loose stone that had been loose ten years ago too, Stiles vented, "Did it ever happen to you that you didn't know what to do next?"

Spock did not venture an answer to that. Instead of the ambassador's voice, Stiles heard a thousand voices from the past speaking to him, echoing against the hard-learned lessons of a young officer, the struggles of living with crewmates, and finally learning to live with himself. He seldom looked in this kind of mirror any more. He'd never liked the reflection when he had.

Today, though, he didn't look away.

"Funny," he began aloud, "when we were about to die because something grabbed the ship and we had thirteen minutes to live, I wasn't afraid. Standing up there looking at Orsova over the top of that big desk . . . I about crapped my pants."

"I'm glad you restrained yourself," Spock commented lightly.

"Ship disasters don't scare me," Stiles said, keeping on his track. "Disastrous people scare me."

It seemed there was something just around the corner, just beyond his grasp, a whisper in the fog.

After a few seconds, Stiles found himself asking, "Did people scare . . . him?"

The last word, revered somehow all by itself, came out as a pathetic sigh, a comparison that shouldn't be made if any progress was ever to be accomplished. Instantly Stiles regretted that he'd asked.

Spock's answer took some time coming. "Helplessness scared him."

235

For the first time, Stiles felt a steely connection forged in the cool cell. "Did he ever think of himself the way I think of myself? Like I don't belong where I am?"

Veiled contentment settled over Mr. Spock as the past opened briefly before him for viewing and he enjoyed what he saw. His voice was low, even soft, yet carried a scolding tone.

" 'He' . . . was an exceptional man. He was also my friend. As such, we had our disagreements. We saw each other's uglier moments. The mission logs fail to show those aspects."

Stiles looked up. "Are you saying the logs are inaccurate?"

"Not at all. We simply left things out."

"Like what?"

Spock paused to think a moment. "The logs, the legends, the tall tales, the song and story—these are spirit-charging powers for us all. But legend is selective and usually written by the winners. The legends of the first *Enterprise* . . . they reflect the heroic, not the human aspects, of our life together in those years . . . Jim Kirk, Dr. McCoy, the others, and myself. Legend is a great filter. The traits that shame us most, the ones we leave out of the stories, are often the flaws that give us texture. Without them, we would be only pictures."

Spock leaned back on an elbow, maneuvered his leg to a better position, and considered the past through scopes in his own mind.

"I have come over these many years to understand what it means to be a captain not so much in rank but in manner. There are captains of rank, captains of ships, and captains of crews. A few men are all three. I once commanded the *Enterprise* as her captain. I was capable of giving the proper orders and expecting proper behavior, but I was never captain of the crew's hopes and devotions. That is a different passion. A different manner of man than I."

At first it seemed Spock might be selling himself short, judging the past too harshly—but no. Stiles knew too well the symptoms of that, and didn't see them here. This, instead, was a kind of personal honesty, a stunning depth of self-respect.

He wanted it. He wanted to know how to do that. Spock was so graceful at understanding subtle differences that mattered, and didn't recoil from knowing his talents and limitations.

"Different how?" Stiles asked, somewhat abrasive.

Spock tipped his head in thought. "I see chess," he said. "You see poker."

Broiling with envy and impatience, Stiles rubbed his cracked hands on his trousers. He didn't understand that, exactly, but something about it lit a fire under him.

"We've got to get out of here," he announced. "It's time to go. We've got to do something."

"Then you have decided to act?" Spock asked.

Bitter, humiliated, and angry about it, Stiles held back the answer that bit at his tongue. He looked up, met the ambassador's keen eyes. If only he could slap back the undercurrents of mockery and deserve better!

Spock gazed at him with sharp-eyed significance. "Eric, you underrate yourself and it makes you hesitate."

"I hesitate because I get things wrong so much," Stiles said. "And I don't want to get things so wrong it gets somebody killed. Or a whole lot of somebodies."

"That is what everyone likes about you."

Stiles looked up. "Huh?"

"Your reputation among the captains of front-line ships is well known. Every service commander knows you are a Medal of Valor winner. You could have pushed, jockeyed for position, used your commendation to leap over the heads of everyone on the promotions list. Even in civilian life you might have used your hero status to become a senator or gain other power. You could easily have become one of those people with much rank and little experience, but you chose a wiser and less vainglorious way. You went back out into space for more experience, working your way up rather than forcing your way up. You may not realize it, but you are deeply respected and liked by the people who get all the attention. They speak of you fondly. They hope Eric Stiles is the one who comes to repair their ships."

Astonished to his socks, Stiles gawked in complete stupid amazement. His men had said things like that to him, but he thought that was in-house loyalty and dusted it off with the debris of a day's work.

"Sir," he began, "there's something the history tapes don't show about you."

"What would that be?"

Stiles voice was low and sincere. "You're a nice person."

Though Spock's face remained passive, his eyes dropped their guard. "A supreme compliment," he said. "Thank you. Now I suggest we vacate this cell."

"I'm ready," Stiles said. "How do we do it?"

Offering a moment to absorb what they had said to each other, the ambassador raised a brow in punctuation. Then he brought his right hand to his ear and pressed the skin just behind his earlobe, and said, "Spock to *Saskatoon.*"

For two or three seconds there was nothing. Then, out of nowhere, the very faint buzz of a voice, unmistakably human, spoke up from thin air, sizzling as if on a grill.

"McCoy here. What are you clowns waiting for? We've had you located for a half hour! Why'd you wait so long to signal us? You always did have lousy Vulcan timing."

Touching his ear in a different place, Spock tilted his head to clear the signal a little more. "The comm link has been charging, doctor."

"Have you found that Romulan yet?"

"Not yet. We have been incarcerated, but will be remedying that momentarily and effecting a search. Are you and the ship under cover?"

"You bet we are. You can track us with this signal, can't you?"

"Yes. Stand by. No unnecessary signals."

"Standing by. McCoy out."

Astonished all over again, Stiles squawked, "How'd you do that! How could you contact—"

"A micro-transponder embedded in my cochlear cavity." Spock gestured to his right ear as if to display something that couldn't possibly be seen.

"But the guards scanned us!" Stiles asked, "How'd they miss something with a broadcast range?"

"The mechanism was nonactive. Dr. McCoy was under orders to activate a charge by remote after two hours had passed, with short-range microburst—"

"Remote? From the ship? Wouldn't it get interference?"

"The good doctor has many connections on this planet who

owe him favors. I suspect he had the signal relayed through several private sources."

"You 'suspect'?"

"He delights in not telling me."

"But can't the Pojjana key in on an outside signal like that?"

"Why should they?" Spock pointed out. "Until today, there were no Federation frequency combinations being used on the planet. Why would they militate against it?"

As he spoke, the ambassador firmly gripped one of the symbolic polished stones on his jacket. The large stone unscrewed as if it were the top of a jar and came off in Spock's hand. He turned it bottom up. In the center of what had looked perfectly well like a real stone was instead a molded chamber, and in that chamber was a black mechanical nugget which Spock plucked out and examined.

Overwhelmed, Stiles stared at the black nugget and recognized it, the little green "charged" light glowing against his skin.

"You've got a utility phaser!"

Surveying the little palm-sized weapon with satisfaction, Spock said, "Like the comm link, it needed time to charge. Enough time for us to beam down and clear all the security scans. If we had allowed ourselves to be captured with the link and weapon charged, the Pojjana guards would've detected the active energy. Also, I supposed the shield might neutralize them if they were precharged—"

"So you're saying you knew they probably wouldn't deal with us. And you knew that ahead of time."

Spock eyed him cannily. "Of course, Mr. Stiles. One hopes for the best, but prepares for the worst."

At the sounds of those casual words, put across so matter-of-factly by one of the last living pioneers of space exploration, shock descended upon Eric Stiles as if he were under a collapsing bridge. It pressed the breath from his lungs and displayed a shame within him and a smoldering anger that for much more than a decade he had suppressed. Now, today, finally, it sparked.

Prepare for the worst.

He leaned forward on the rusty cot, gazing downward at the

empty floor. His knees before him might as well have been distant planets. What had he done all his life? Revere the best, expect the worst, and be prepared . . . for neither.

His skin felt tight, preformed. He drew another breath, huffed it out.

Across the cell, Spock pressed against the brick wall, moving slowly from place to place. He seemed to be listening for outside activity. Listening . . . trying to decide where to aim the phaser, how to break them out.

His own breath rumbled in his ears. Just outgoing, in huffs, short and hot. Dry lips.

As if in a dream he watched Spock prime the freshly charged little palm phaser. Green light, blue, yellow . . .

The Vulcan now stood sideways to present a narrow profile to the blast field, and extended his arm to aim at the portion of the wall he had chosen as their best bet to open an escape route without bringing the building or the Pojjana army down upon them. Orange . . . red.

"Sir!" Stiles bolted to his feet.

The ambassador hesitated and held fire. "Something?"

Shadows lay across Spock's Vulcan features, harsh limited light on the other side, a life-size paper doll of ideals Stiles had thought were bigger than life.

"I'm sorry about this," Stiles announced. He met Spock's gaze without flinching. "From now on I'm thinking ahead."

"What does that mean, specifically?" the Vulcan asked.

"It means you don't have permission to open fire."

This time both of Spock's brows went up. "I beg your pardon?"

Putting out a cold hand, Stiles noted that at least now he wasn't trembling.

"So you've got a phaser. So what? Once we get out of the cell, they've got energy detectors, tiers of fences, guards, weapons. We'll never get through."

"You have a suggestion for me?" Spock asked.

"No, sir," Stiles said. "I have an order for you. This is a military mission. I'm the ranking Starfleet officer here. This is probably the most boneheaded thing I've ever done in my life, and I don't know if . . . yes, I do know. I've been deferring to you for half my life whether you were there or not, and it's time for that to stop. They're expecting us to escape but, sir, we're not here to escape."

Another step brought him right up to Mr. Spock, face to face, man to man.

"I've been acting like a kid ever since I first saw your face on a history screen. It's time for me to start acting like the commander of this mission."

He turned his hand palm up and did not lower it.

Standing before him in what appeared to be amazement and a few other emotions Stiles couldn't quite identify, Spock passed the next few moments without moving so much as a facial muscle.

His eyes moved first, shifting down to the phaser in his grip. He gazed at the nugget-shaped weapon for several seconds as if it were the mean center of the universe.

Then, quite accommodatingly, he placed the weapon in Stiles' open hand. "As you wish."

Stiles found himself in the middle of a prison cell, holding the center of the universe.

Limping back a step or two, the ambassador gave Stiles room to use the phaser. There was a particular quality to his voice as he asked, "What is your plan, Commander?"

As he checked the phaser to be sure it was set where he thought it was, Stiles felt suddenly warm all over, and strong.

"Orsova thinks he's being cute putting me back in the same cell. He's an idiot. I spent years here. I helped rebuild this place after my first Constrictor. I know more about it than he does or any guard ever did. It's his big mistake. I'm not a twenty-one-year-old kid anymore."

"And this is an epiphany for you?"

Stiles blinked at him. *That* look was back on the Vulcan's face, that almost-smile, with the sparkle behind the eyes.

Amusement? Or something else?

"Your men knew their lives were in danger," the ambassador said, "yet you gave them confidence without deception. You marched them past the frozen moment that kills so many, and gave them a chance to fight for their ship and their lives. Against the checklist that counts more than legends, with all flaws and hesitations understood as cells of the whole . . . you are a captain."

Had the lights changed in here? Was it warmer?

Both peeved and flattered, Stiles shifted his weight and waved a hand at the cot. "You mean, all this time you believed in me and you let me sit there and snivel?"

"It was never enough for me to believe in you," Spock said handily. "You had to believe—"

"Please!" Stiles laughed. "Don't finish that! I smell a cliché."

Spock rewarded him with that hint of a smile and a very slight bow. "I stand rebuked."

Bewildered and amazed that he was actually smiling, Stiles sighed roughly and looked down at the utility phaser in his hand. He aimed it, but not at the wall. Instead, he pointed its bluntly conical nose in a completely illogical direction.

The ambassador looked at the concrete floor. "Where are we going?"

"Sir, we're going straight down."

And the cell lit up in a million lights, and the floor blew up, and the ceiling shredded. And Eric Stiles was in charge.

Chapter Twenty-two

BLISTERING HEAT SHOT through the cell. Pressure struck Stiles from all sides and spun him silly. The floor tilted, then disappeared under his feet and gravity dragged him down. It almost felt like a Constrictor.

He struck the griddle of hot rock with his right hipbone and scraped down fifteen feet until a carpet of muck received him up to the ankles. Somehow he managed to stay on his feet, leaning sideways on a nubby slab that was suddenly very familiar. Funny how the years rushed up to remind him of things.

Took out too much of the floor—probably shouldn't have used the full-destruct setting. Too late now.

"Where's the phaser? Oh, I still got it. Couldn't feel my hand. . . ."

No wonder. His whole forearm was tingling. Probably bumped the funny bone. His fingers had convulsed around the utility phaser, luckily, and he still had it. He craned his neck to look up at the hole they'd created. Had anybody heard the cracking and crashing of stone? There hadn't been a blast noise, instead just the whine of the phaser before the rock cracked. If there wasn't a guard on the floor, maybe the crash hadn't been noticed. Please, please, please.

Where was the ambassador?

Not waiting for his eyes to adjust, Stiles glanced around in the dimness, then started pawing at the broken flooring. Six feet away, the rocks shifted. Springing over there, Stiles tripped and landed on a knee. Recovering, he dug until a Vulcan ear appeared, luckily still attached to a Vulcan head.

"Sir!" he called.

Now, how would this look! Eric Stiles, the man who let First Officer Spock get buried alive!

The rubble scratched his hands. Some of the stones were hot to the touch as he pushed them off the ambassador.

"Sir? Are you hurt?"

Dust and pebbles sheeted into the muck and Spock sat up. "Quite well, thank you . . . where are we?"

Stretching off to both sides of them, bending into infinity not far away, the octagonal passageway was lit only by mediocre pencils of light through wrist-width drainage holes. Stiles knew that they could only see at all because the sun was almost directly overhead and the sky had cleared. In another couple of hours, the tunnels would be pitch dark.

"It's a network of tunnels. We built them right after my first Constrictor. The civil engineers thought the gravity effect would be lessened by a layer of planet strata and that maybe people could hide below, but it didn't work. They were death-traps. Eventually we just gave up and sealed them. I used to imagine using it to escape."

"Why didn't you?"

"And go where?"

"Mmm . . . pardon me."

"I couldn't get off the planet and nobody would help an alien. And I didn't exactly have a way of cutting through the floor either."

Spock accepted Stiles's support as he got carefully to his feet and tested his injured leg. "How long do you suppose our escape will go undiscovered?"

"Depends on whether Orsova wants to auction off a visit now or later. We'll know, because we'll hear the alarms go off.

Until then, we can just make our way through to the fresh-water ducts and get out. Darker in here than I remembered . . . looks like the roots are getting in too. Watch your step, Ambassador. With that comm link implant, can you tell me the direction the CST is in?"

"Yes." Spock paused a moment, and even though it seemed that he was doing something psychic, Stiles knew there was nothing like that going on. "East northeast . . . by north. Four miles . . . one eighth."

"East by—four miles from here?"

"Yes."

"Are you sure about that?"

"Very."

"Perfect. I know just what they're doing."

"Why do you ask?"

"Because we're splitting up."

"That may not be wise," Spock protested.

"Well, it wouldn't be my first time," Stiles flatly told him, and left no room for alternatives. "Come this way."

Picking through the crushed flooring into the muck-layered tunnel bottom, even with Spock's bad leg they moved along faster than Stiles expected. The stink was incredible. Heavy roots searched their way down from the surface, hairlike ancillary tendrils unbroken until his hand tore them away, proving that no one had come down here in years. He led Spock in a direction he knew the search would never go if they were discovered gone. That was the plan, all part of where he had told Travis to bring the ship down—away from the mountains, which was the natural place to hide. Hmm . . . been thinking ahead all this time and never knew it.

"Up at that intersection there," he said to Spock, "you go left. You'll be able to get out in about a half mile. That's where the municipal slab ends. I'll go to the right and find Zevon and catch up, and I'll be better alone in case it's a trap. All due respect, you'll slow me down and I'm tired of being slow. I'm sorry if this isn't what you had in mind."

"I had nothing in mind."

What'd he say?

Must be clogged ears. Didn't hear right. Stiles looked over

his shoulder, seeing only the gray silhouette of the Vulcan two steps back. As he held aside a thick root for the ambassador to step by, he heard that sentence again in his head and finally just asked.

"You didn't have a plan? I thought the great amazing Mr. Spock always had a plan."

The ambassador tipped his head in a kind of shrug and spoke as they picked their way along.

"You remember what I told you about captains. I know my shortcomings. Discipline can be limiting. This is why Vulcans, with all our stringent codes of behavior, have not generally prevailed as great leaders, and humans, with your elastic spirits, have. I've learned over the years to provide information and opportunity, then step aside and rely upon the more vibrant among us for actual tactics. I hoped you would rise to the occasion."

"Are you saying," Stiles marveled, "you just fake it?"

In a shaft of light from a drain hole, Spock's black eyes flickered smartly. "No. I trusted *you* to fake it."

The ambassador offered that canny look for several seconds without even taking a step. Apparently he wanted a point made.

Overwhelmed, Stiles hovered in the middle of a step. Only a brainless drizzle of water somewhere in the underground system drew him out of his amazement and reminded him of what had to be done, and done soon.

"Said Frankenstein to the monster," he cracked. "Bear left and you'll get out. Once you get outside, keep to the low trail. They'll be looking high first, the way to the mountains. We'll rendezvous east northeast at the lake."

Spock reached out to grasp a root, ready to pull himself forward. "Aye aye, captain."

Flushed with delight and newly emboldened, Stiles looked up and laughed. "Thanks!"

Beverly Crusher took her latest series of biological readings on the shuddering body of the Romulan empress, and compared them with the readings from one hour ago. In the room, only the snap of the fireplace and the bleep of Data's computer, as he processed more information and sent what they had discovered onward to the other physicians across the empire, could be heard. There was not that much more that could be done.

For days now she had kept the empress and dozens of others alive by treating the symptoms. Over the past day, success had noticeably shrunk.

Crusher sat back, exhausted, and pressed her hands to the sides of her head. As she squeezed, her eyes throbbed and her thoughts bundled up into a lump. When she put her hands down, they were holding the only thought left that made sense.

She turned on her chair and sighed. Data noticed the movement and looked around at her. Over on the couch, still battered and bloody from the earlier encounter, Sentinel Iavo sat alone with his own guilts and troubles. He'd hardly moved all day.

"Time for drastic measures," Crusher told him. "She's not making it. She's slipping away. I can't hold on to her life much longer. Are you ready to do what I ask?"

A destroyed man, Iavo's face had paled and his eyes were sunken with weariness. "Anything."

Satisfied, Crusher stood up and strode to him. "This is what I want. You're going to get me a fast ship with an escort battalion. I don't want any trouble at the border. I'm taking the empress into space to hook up with Dr. McCoy and a treatment serum."

"There is no such serum," Iavo protested. "Is there?"

"There may be. If she is to have any chance, we have to go."

"Go where? Who has this serum?"

"I'll give you the course once we're spaceborne. I don't want to take any more chances than that. Once again, Sentinel, you have a choice to make. Who's side are you going to be on for the next few hours?"

Iavo stood up, wavered briefly, and clearly noted that Data also came to his feet behind Crusher.

"Your wisdom and silence have given me a new life," Iavo confirmed. "I will help you save hers. Tell me where you wish to go."

The air seemed a bit too cool in the lab office today. Zevon had thought about turning the heat up several times, but had regularly been distracted by suggestions pouring in from the students at Regional Spectroscopy. He had been reading them all day, between adjustments. The deflectors required almost daily adjustments now. Each adjustment worried him a faction more. The network of deflection stations operated fairly well, though only fairly. He had able technicians working the grid, but not skilled scientists. Several more years would go by before anyone on this planet was skilled enough in quantum physics and space science to replace Zevon's own advanced abilities. He was in a race now, a slow and deliberate race to the next Constrictor.

Some of these students had promise. There were occasional glimmers of hope beyond the daily push and grind. If he had more freedom to move about on the planet—

An old argument. Orsova's reins were tight upon Zevon. Their mutuality was fragile. He dared not jar it.

A long morning. The afternoon stretched before him with a dozen problems. The electrical system in the complex had begun having fits a few minutes ago, and he could do nothing effective with the Constrictor system if the power kept blinking.

Perhaps he could accomplish something by remote while he waited. Yes, that would be better.

His chair rolled slightly under him as he reached to the corner of his desk and keyed the external communications system, touching the autochannel.

"Sykora, are you there?"

"I just arrived. You nearly missed me."

"Did you visit the physician?"

"They can do nothing for me here. I'll tend myself as I always have."

"Sykora . . ."

"I'm much stronger today. The welts are responding a little to the poultice I made yesterday. If only I had—"

"You're not a nurse, you know."

"On this planet, I am all there is for us. Would you like to argue now or later?"

"Later, I suppose. Would it be possible for you to route yesterday's matter-discharge telemetry readings to Light Geologics at Laateh Mountain?"

"Are you certain I have them here?"

"Certain beyond life."

"I suppose that means I have them here. Give me time to arrange the files for relay."

"You'll have it. For some reason, several power centers in the complex have failed. They're tracking the source."

"Why would several fail at once?"

"I hesitated to ask. It's enough that I must handle satellite electrical problems. If I begin solving local ones, I may forget to adjust the deflector grid."

"I would never let you forget."

"I owe you my happiness."

"Yes, you do. Who else would cook you Romulan dinners to keep you from choking on the pathetic Pojjana palate?"

Zevon smiled. "No one on this rock. I shall signal you with the relay channel as soon as the power returns."

"What do they say on a ship?—Affirmative?"

"Affirmative, they say 'affirmative.' Are you—"

He never finished his question. The communications system crackled suddenly as if he'd put his hand into the den of a spitting animal. Almost as abruptly, it went dead.

"Sykora? Do you read?"

Nothing.

He tried a reroute of the local flow.

"Sykora?"

But there was still nothing. The system lay quiet. Someone would get to it.

Ah—there were the alarms from the central bunkers. Would the alarms go off for an electrical power failure? Strange. Power didn't even go off after a Constrictor anymore. He'd made sure of that. Perhaps some work was being done somewhere. He should've been notified.

He thought about calling to ask, but how could he call?

"Possibly the reason for the chill," he murmured to himself, and slipped into the leather-fringed chenille cardigan Sykora had given him at the precinct bazaar last year. The six shades of moss green, brushed soft as moss itself, threaded with dyed leather, comforted him when things went wrong. He liked to see the cardigan hanging on the wall hook next to his desk

even better than wearing it. When he had it on, he couldn't see
it so well.

However, today it would keep him warm. He pulled it over
his shoulders, hitched it into place—awkward, since he was
still sitting down and apparently too lazy to stand—and began
tying the leather lacings over his chest.

A green chenille Pojjana cardigan with dyed leather lacings,
leather lacings threaded through his shoulderlength hair . . .
there was so little left of him from that other life, he could no
longer find hints of the times before. Only speaking to Sykora
occasionally reminded him that he had ever lived anywhere
else.

Through the closed window, he could still hear the alarms
going off. Possibly there was some trouble. A revolt, perhaps.
They still happened sometimes, after a Constrictor, in fear of
the next one. He could hide here, in retreat from such mundane
troubles, and do his science, battling the next Constrictor in his
own way. He hadn't won yet, but the enemy feared him.

Someone was pounding up the stairway down the hall.
Through the old walls of his office he could hear the clop-clop
of boots on the wooden stairs. Good. That meant someone else
was as bothered by the electrical burping as he was. Only
when the footsteps pounded up the corridor toward his office
did he look at the door in wonder. Why would the maintenance
team come to this end of the hall?

The door rattled as if someone had kicked it, but did not
open at first. Then, it did. It blew open as if knocked by a hard
wind.

A thousand times Zevon had seen this instant in his mind,
played out in a dozen ways, and it still surprised him.

"Eric!" he gasped.

The years crumbled and dissolved as they stared at each
other, comparing what they used to look like with what they
looked like now. Zevon knew he must look different. His hair
was longer, thonged with the tiny leather strips many Pojjana
wore . . . but as a Romulan, eleven years meant less to him
than it had to Eric Stiles.

Zevon's long-ago friend looked like neither a rosy-cheeked
boy nor a dying waif, the only two personae Zevon had ever

seen. He was a healthy man now, more slender, less clumsy, his blond hair a shade darker, his face clean-shaven. He still wore a Starfleet uniform, but of a new design. There were unborn weed pods stuck to the side of his trouserleg, and drying muck on his boots.

Scarcely able to breathe, Zevon clasped the arm of his chair with one hand and the side of his desk with the other.

Eric's chest heaved from running, from climbing the stairs, and whatever other trials had brought him here. Behind their communion of astonished gawking, the alarms rang and rang in the main complex.

"So I'm a little late," he flipped. "So what?"

Zevon pushed himself around a little more to face him, but still could not find the power to stand up.

Seeing that, Eric simply stepped to him, took his arm, and drew him to his feet. "Let's go."

Zevon came to his feet and gripped Eric's arms in a waltz of amazement and disbelief. "You look—you look—"

"Yeah, got a shave too." Between his fingers Eric spun a piece of the fringe on Zevon's decorated vest. "You look like one of those goofy dancers at the Spring Cotillion when they used to make us work the kitchen. I know you gotta get along here, but do you gotta wear their clothes?"

"I like these clothes."

"Great. Bring 'em along. We're leaving."

Not really surprised, Zevon did find himself startled by the abruptness of the demand. How could he possibly begin to explain?

"No, I can't go."

"Yes, you can. Come on."

"No—I must not leave the planet." He drew back with some force as he realized the serious intentions of what seemed ridiculous. "Eric, I have plans—get your hands off me, Eric!"

"I haven't got time to argue." Eric let go of him, as requested, but instead raised his other hand and aimed a small black device directly at Zevon.

Zevon threw both hands up. "No, no!"

In the same instant a pop of yellow light blinded him. He felt his head snap back and his body convulse. His senses spun wild. His knees buckled, but he never felt the floor strike him. A jostling sensation—his eyes were still open enough to see the ceiling reel, the light flop about, and deliberate movement at his side. His own moan of protest boomed in his head. Voluntary movement sank away.

Through the thickness of semiconsciousness Zevon heard the voice that had come to him so many times in the broken hours of early morning.

"Plenty of seats down in front. Welcome to the opening night of 'Prepare for the Worst,' starring the always effervescent Eric John Stiles. Reset your phasers and enjoy the show."

"Zevon . . . Zevon. Wake up. It's only light stun. Come out of it. You'll feel better in a few minutes."

Some kind of bird cawed in the high tangled roots overhead. The surroundings were ridiculous, an oasis of picnic quality, trying to tell them nothing was wrong and they could just sit here and maybe take a nap.

In the distance, though, more than two miles away, the alarms of the prison still hooted through the open sky. They'd seen airborne patrols sprint from the city toward the mountains, and at least two spotter planes veer toward the valley. None yet angled toward the swamp. Most escapees had more sense than to come in this direction, at least not first.

Stiles glanced around to make sure there was enough root canopy over them that a spotter couldn't easily see them. He knew that if a plane got close enough the infrared scanners would pick up the heat off the tops of their heads. There was nothing to be done about that if it happened.

Zevon lay in a cradle of velvet-coated roots, the kind that were about to plunge into the nearest puddle and release their spores. Till then they were a bony cushion that offered a few minutes' rest. Stiles sat with him, absorbing the leather threads in his head and the Pojjana cardigan, pleased that at least Zevon didn't seem to be starving anymore. They were at least clothing and feeding him for all he'd done for them.

Still drowsy, Zevon gazed at him warmly, with shieldless affection and relief that they were both alive to have this reunion.

"Eric . . ." He smiled again.

Stiles smiled back, knowing the drug of phaser stun was giving them this uncrystallized and uncluttered moment. His hand closed on Zevon's wrist as it had that last day so long ago. For a moment there was nothing around them, no planet, no problems, no past or future troubles to distract them. Certainly nothing to drive them apart anymore.

Gradually, though, inevitably, Zevon's perceptions cleared and he shifted his shoulders. They held onto each other, absorbing the wondrous confirmation that neither was dead, as each certainly had entertained in the troubling hours before sleep.

"I didn't think you'd even speak to me," Stiles attempted. His voice cracked on the last couple of words.

Zevon rewarded him with a kind of glow in his eyes. "Why would I not?"

"Well, I *am* a little late. . . ."

"Yes, you are."

"I swear, I thought they got you out."

"I know you did. Why did you stun me?"

"Oh, because you resisted my charms."

Taking a better grip on Zevon's arm, Stiles helped him sit up and lean against a particularly large and ancient root. Nauseated, Zevon closed his eyes briefly, fielding a wave of dizziness from the change of position.

"Are you okay?" Stiles asked.

Zevon leered at him with unfocused eyes and finally a clearing head. A perception of irony brought the faintest of smiles.

"Yes, Eric, I'm okay."

The buzz of distant aircraft funneled down to them from the foothills. Stiles didn't look away as the awkward moment passed between them.

"So," he began, "how y'been?"

With a grimace of irony and another smile, Zevon sat up and shook pods from his hair. "I've been busy." His face patterned by the shadows of roots overhead, he blinked into the sinking sun. "Where have you taken me?"

"We're out on the swamp flats. Cuffo Lake's a mile or so that way. I was hoping you'd come around so I didn't have to carry you any more. We're under cover, at least."

Another shadow came over them, this one long, crisp, and near. Stiles didn't look around. He knew.

"This is Ambassador Spock," he said to Zevon.

Zevon peered up at Spock, fitted the puzzle pieces into place, and accepted what he saw. He bowed his head courteously. "Your fame precedes you. I am honored."

Spock returned the gesture. "As am I, your excellency."

"Centurion, please."

"As you wish."

As Spock came to sit beside them on a fat root, Zevon said, "Royalty is the mantle I was born to. Centurion is the rank I earned."

"Then Mr. Stiles's report is correct? You are fourteenth in line for the throne?"

"Thirteenth, now."

Spock paused. "Yes, of course. Pardon my error. If you will indulge me for a few minutes, Centurion, I shall explain our problem."

Zevon glanced at Stiles, then back to Spock. "Explain."

"So they're dying. So what?"

A shaft of guilt ran through Eric Stiles at hearing Zevon using affectations of language he had obviously learned during their incarceration. He felt as if he were looking into a curved mirror. Even after all these years, Zevon sounded like Stiles, and it was both nice and weird.

"I understand," Stiles allowed. "They didn't come for you. But it's important, Zevon. And you're the only one."

"I hardly believe that. I am the convenient one."

Stiles winced inwardly. Better let that go for now. "What happened after I left?"

"Once Orsova came sober again that day, he thought about what you said, that we might be able to predict the Constrictor waves. He came to me and wanted to know how. I told him. He understood none of it, of course, yet I suppose it sounded to him as if I understood something. He went to the authorities and warned that a Constrictor was coming."

"I'll bet they listened hard," Stiles chided.

"They hardly listened," Zevon confirmed, his frustration

long scabbed over. "Then the Constrictor did come. Millions died. And the people thought Orsova was a genius."

"Ugh . . . what people won't swallow. . . ."

"Orsova used his new influence to get me more equipment. He became the 'head' of the Constrictor project."

Spock clarified, "The science of which he knew nothing at all?"

"Are you kidding?" Stiles said. "He doesn't have a clue."

"Nothing," Zevon confirmed. "He manipulates the power, I tell him what the science can and cannot do."

"You've been working at the pharoah's counting house while he gets the glory."

"I could never have had the glory, Eric. Don't mourn it. If the population had ever found out I was the one who started the Constrictor, they would've killed me. I cannot be replaced in Red Sector. If I am not here to do this, all the Pojjana will suffer. I would gladly slit my own throat if I thought that would stop the phenomenon. Orsova is the umbrella shielding me from the limelight. He can have the attention."

Witness to humility and guilt taken to the extreme and somehow transmorphed into a positive, Stiles glanced at Spock and noted the Vulcan's unmistakable respect for a much younger and much less accomplished scientist. That caught Stiles in a grip between Spock's generosity and Zevon's humility.

Damn, was this confusing.

"Also, one must say," Zevon began again, "Orsova was most tricky and skilled at playing the politics, in which I had no interest at all except what he could get for me. The Constrictors were coming every few months and I quickly became very busy. Everything depended upon my predictions becoming more accurate. The more accurate, the more people thought Orsova was a genius. He developed a network, he controls many resources and lives like a king—"

"And how do *you* live?" Stiles asked.

"That matters not at all, not in the least," Zevon warned, hearing a defensiveness that wasn't necessary for him. "He's welcome to it. My purpose is served. The Pojjana would never have accepted a Romulan as the genius of the Constrictor.

Orsova allowed me to succeed much earlier than ever would have been possible. I invented new types of antigravs, compression suits, architectural implements, metallurgy—many things that Orsova has parlayed into a huge Constrictor-survival industry. He has the power to decide where all the resources go, all the revenue, new materials, technology, the buildings—and I tell him what to say. He wields so much power now that he is the de facto head of the government. As he works his plans and I work mine, fewer and fewer people die with each Constrictor. In the last one, only six thousand planetwide. Six thousand, Eric!"

The victory in Zevon's voice and the emotion in his expression cut Stiles to the core. He pressed Zevon's arm in approval, knowing what that meant to him.

"I knew we had to control energy to survive," Zevon went on. "I have an energy division, a school of physics, a school of mechanical science, defense division, deflection-grid network all over the continent. . . ."

"Why a defense system?" Spock asked. "Have you had problems with the Bal Quonott?"

"Not yet. And they've had no interest in us. Yet. We have no spaceborne fleet with which to defend ourselves. I knew I could never develop conventional weapons sitting trapped on a planet. Instead I've used tricks I learned while trying to read or deflect the Constrictor waves. Using the mass of the planet as an anchor for—"

"The composite beam that almost killed us, I bet."

"Killed you . . . ?"

"Well, how do y'think we got here? Magic? We came in a ship that got sucked into that damned thing!"

"Oh—" Zevon moaned as if he'd just remembered, just realized. A sheet of pallor drained across his face. "I never imagined you might come yourself. . . ."

Now that he'd gotten his pound of flesh, Stiles gave him a light punch in the chest. "That's okay, we got out of it. Come on, let's get moving. We've got work to do."

He pulled Zevon to his feet, while at their side Mr. Spock also stood up and scanned the horizon for trouble.

The trouble, though, was right here.

"Eric, I want to go back to my lab." Zevon announced. "I don't want to go with you."

Stiles huffed out his disbelief. "I'm serious, Zevon. Don't kid around. Lives are at stake. The stability of a hundred star systems are at stake, the Romulan Empire's—"

Zevon squared off before him. "I want to go back to my life. This is where I belong now, where I do good work. I refuse to go."

"Sure, refuse. I'll just stun you again and carry you the rest of the way if I have to."

"Commander," Spock began, "perhaps we should—"

Stiles waved his stun-set phaser demostrably. "Sir, I'm sorry, but there's no time. I want my ship away from this planet. We can talk while we move. That's the direction. Go on, Zevon, unless you want another dose."

"Eric, this is not at all like you."

"Too bad. Ambassador, which way?"

Hesitating only a moment, Spock said, "Follow me, please."

The traipse through the root swamp was messy, tedious, and most of all uneasy. Stiles didn't like holding a phaser on Zevon, but he never let it waver. Whenever Zevon looked at him, he brandished the phaser and made sure his thumb was on the fire pad. How many times did he look at the weapon himself, making good and sure it was set on stun and nothing worse. It had been years upon years since he'd been in a position to use a hand weapon against another person. The idea of making a mistake absolutely petrified him to the bone.

Before him, Zevon's moss-green cardigan flickered in the rays of the lowering sun through the huge twisted roots overhead and around them. He endured delirious joy that Zevon was still alive and here with him, tempered by the obvious tension of Zevon's resistance. He'd been brainwashed or something. He'd given up on being rescued and, surviving any way he could, had conditioned himself to live here, convinced himself it was right.

I'll talk him out of it. Now that I'm back, everything can go ahead and change. I'll walk him through it. He'll like it in a week.

"Eric, I don't wish to go," Zevon attempted again after a half mile. "How can you force me?"

"You're a Romulan, you understand force, right?"

"Orsova will do everything he can to keep us from leaving the planet. If you let me go, I can convince him to allow you to leave Red Sector. He wants no outside—"

"What's wrong with you?" Stiles blazed, pulling up almost to Zevon's side so they could look at each other between steps. "Don't you understand? Of course he doesn't want outside interference! I saw the looks in those soldiers' faces. The Pojjana see Orsova as if they wouldn't survive without him, like he's holding up the planet all by himself. If you or the Federation or anybody manages to stop the Constrictor, suddenly he wouldn't be the great savior anymore. That's why he stuck Mr. Spock and me in a cell and wouldn't deal. He doesn't want anybody to stop it!"

"I have to stay here, Eric, I have to be here every day. We have succeeded in reducing the effect of the waves, but my system requires almost daily adjustment and no one else can do that. I have no one thoroughly trained enough yet to take my place. Every day I breathe, I extend to the Pojjana the chance of someday outdoing my expertise. That has been my goal. I have arranged for Orsova to sponsor engineering and science colleges, apprenticeships and clinics so that some day the Pojjana can go on without me. That day has not come."

"You're taking this self-blame too far, Zevon." Stiles tripped on a cracked root and almost fired the phaser by accident. Ahead of them, Spock glanced back while Stiles recovered, then moved on.

Why didn't he come back here and lay some logic on Zevon? Why didn't he talk about the numbers? The rational analysis of what a collapsing Romulan Empire would do to everything around it? Why didn't he talk about the political and military and trade black hole that would suddenly suck the life out of everything that had been so carefully balanced for so long? What good was a genius hero Vulcan monument if he didn't come back here and lay down a case nobody could resist?

"You've been brainwashed," Stiles said with contempt. "It

happens. Prisoners go through it all the time. Sympathizing with their captors' causes, forgetting where they came from, forgetting their native language—"

Zevon grasped a network of root filaments and ripped them from up to down. "I do not wish to leave, Eric! Not for the sake of the royal family or the empire or the Federation. I also do not wish to be exposed. Orsova provides me with cover and lets me work. Every day I can make up a little of what I have done. Do you know I am virtually the only alien this planet trusts?"

Stiles paused as his uniform shirt caught on a thorn and he twisted to disengage it. "Just because you were part of what started all this, you don't owe them your whole life. They can do a few things on their own, can't they? You've become way too custodial about these people. You even dress like a Pojjana!"

Zevon whirled and stopped dead in front of him, enraged and insulted. "I *am* Pojjana!"

They stood in a sluice of muck. Up ahead, Spock stopped and waited, his expression grim, curious.

"And elephants have four knees," Stiles chided. "So what?"

A flurry of anger rose in Zevon's face. "You should know better than anyone! Your own people would never have come for you if not for that elderly physician with so many tricks. Have you forgotten? Since coming here my eyes have been opened. I was stifled in the imperial system. Here, unfettered, unrestricted, with Orsova to field the—"

"I know, I know, you've proven yourself brilliant," Stiles confirmed. "You've kept a lot of people alive. I always knew you could. Even the Federation doesn't have that beam you put on us. If you could be that brilliant and save that many lives and you still have to hide behind Orsova because these idiots are so xenophobic that they won't accept help from an alien, then to hell with 'em. You've done enough. Somebody else needs you more now."

"The royal family? All these years I knew you were not the one who failed. I knew they had simply decided not to bother getting me out. Did you think I had no comprehension of my own blood ties? I have worse than apathy for the Romulans, and their way, and their crown. I have hatred for them. Some day, either the Federation or the Bal Quonott or the Romulans will come and overrun the Pojjana, and when that happens I am determined that my people, these people, will be able to defend themselves, hold their own, and even prevail. I have no prime directive. I am free to help anyone I want to help."

Fired by the depth of Zevon's conviction, Stiles raised the utility phaser. "I won't leave you here a second time. Just turn around and walk. I swear to God I'll stun you."

Zevon did move forward after the ambassador, but continued his point with ferocity. "Even without space infrastructure, we have learned to build and operate survival equipment and refined the barometer so that we not only have warning, but can also predict to some degree the intensity of the waves. My equipment requires almost constant attention. If I leave and intensity is misread, millions could die. Does that mean nothing to you? Have you changed so much?"

"Keep walking. I don't want to hear any more."

He kept it that way. With his manner and his expression he cut off any further discussion, as they made way through the swamp and finally broke out into the open valley beyond. Now they couldn't see the city at all, nor hear the alarms anymore, only hear the occasional drone of a distant search plane. So far, so good.

When Stiles broke out of the ferns and growth, freeing his leg from the last of the grasping roots, Zevon and Spock were already standing on the open meadow, looking out over the elongated expanse of Cuffo Lake. The eternally yellow-green water, rich with biology and nutrients that reflected the sunlight with a nearly neon intensity, was enhanced that much more by the sunset. The sun, resting now on the tips of the far away mountains, illuminated the valley and showed them unequivocally that the valley was empty. Three hills, a rocky ridge, the meadow flats, and Cuffo Lake. Not so much as a tree more than that.

The ambassador strode a few yards out into the meadow and swept his gaze in all directions. "The CST should be here . . . I'm certain of the coordinates . . . The directional signal definitely indicates this location, but I see no sign of them."

Zevon turned to Stiles. "You have to let me go now, Eric. Your ship is not here."

"Yes, it is. Ambassador, can you hail them with that implant?"

Spock touched the pressure point behind his ear where the microcom was either situated or had its subcutaneous controls. "Spock to *Saskatoon*. We are at the rendezvous point. What is your location?"

The soft buzz of the tiny mechanism was hard to understand, but good to hear. *"This is Perraton. Is Commander Stiles with you?"*

"Yes, he is."

Stiles said, "Tell him 'Lightfoot confirms.' "

"Mr. Perraton, 'Lightfoot confirms.' "

"Acknowledged. Here we come."

"This is bewildering." Spock frowned and looked at Stiles. "These are the coordinates. The ship should be virtually on this spot. From where are they broadcasting?"

Stiles didn't bother answering. He didn't need to. The answer shimmered on the lake's surface. The still water began to froth, then to erupt as if it were suddenly the center of a resting volcano. Zevon and Spock both looked up into the darkening sky to see if the power were coming from a descending ship, but the sky was still clear.

They looked now at Stiles and saw him watching the lake's surface. They too turned in time to see sharp nonreflective metal formations break the surface and sheet free of the clinging water and the biorich glaze living there. The disruption got bigger and bigger, destroying the beautiful flat lake water with a violent commotion. In the rattle and swoosh of water and engines, the *Saskatoon*'s industrial nose surged furiously out of the water, and the rest of the ship broke free of the suction.

The ship emerged enormously from the water, like a blue whale breaching and not bothering to dive back in. It hovered over the lake while the last of the water drained from its nacelles and spiraled back into the lake, creating a sheen of droplets that sparkled in the setting sun.

"The bottom of the lake," Spock marveled. "Of course. A scan-proof shelter."

"Just thinking ahead." Stiles grinned proudly and eyed him. "You spent too much time on starships."

"Apparently."

"This is Perraton. We'll set down on the plain directly to your right, on the other side of that ridge."

"What's wrong with the transporters?" Stiles asked.

"Is there something wrong with the transporter?"

"Yup. You broke 'em when you beamed through that reflector envelope. They're under repair."

Politely Spock asked, "Permission to grant them permission to land?"

"Permission granted to grant permission," Stiles responded.

The ambassador seemed impressed, maybe a little embarrassed that he hadn't thought of this, and cued his microlink. "You have permission to set down, Mr. Perraton. We shall stand by."

"Let's go over the ridge," Stiles ordered, "and be there when they maneuver down. It'll take us a few minutes to climb over the ridge."

"I don't want to go, Eric."

"My finger's on the button, Zevon."

The ridge was the only rupture on the otherwise pristine meadow landscape, created over a hundred years ago by ambitious roots from the swamp moving below the surface till they hit rock and tried to find the surface again. The roots had grown and grown beneath the crust, fattening and searching and hitting stone, until the stone began to surge upward eight or ten meters. Sometime along the way, the roots had died off, leaving the rocky ridge as the only scar on the meadowlands.

The ridge wasn't very high, only a couple of stories at most, but footing was treacherous and picky. They could hear the hum of the CST as it maneuvered on the other side of the ridge, but could see nothing but the abutments of stone and hard dirt.

Stiles glanced into the sky behind them, fearful that the CST might be picked up on scanners now that it was out of the protective cover of the deep lake. They were only minutes from safety now. Once inside the *Saskatoon* they could buzz away from this forsaken planet and get out there and do some real good. Then he could talk some sense into Zevon. Once Zevon got back into space, saw how wide the galaxy really was, remembered things that Stiles had also forgotten during his incarceration here—everything would be good again. It would be.

Stiles took the rear, holding the phaser where it would do some good as he picked and climbed his way up the rocky slope behind the ambassador and Zevon. He was watching the rocks, nursing out footholds and handholds and avoiding the dangerous sharp edge of the mica-like slabs, when a hard force caught him across the jawbone.

The mighty blow drove him backward and spun him sideways. He skidded onto his side on a sheet of pebbles. As his head rang, he managed to put out an arm and stop himself from sliding all the way down.

"Stand still or die!"

Stiles blinked up through a wave of dizziness.

There above them, taking an attack stance between them and freedom, stood two armed Pojjana assault troopers and an even more heavily armed woman. A Romulan woman!

"Drop your weapon!" The woman aimed her own rifle ferociously at Stiles' head. "Or I will kill you now!"

Chapter Twenty-three

"SYKORA, DON'T KILL HIM!"

Zevon rushed to Stiles's side and put himself between Stiles and the woman's rifle. Spock, luckily, stood aside and let events play out as he watched with attentive interest. He put his hands up, though, so the guards wouldn't arbitrarily open up on him either. A Romulan woman! Or was she Vulcan? Either way, she shouldn't be here at all.

"How can she be here?" Stiles demanded.

From higher on the rocks, Spock agreed. "This is Red Sector. Did the Romulans violate that without the Federation's—"

"The empire has nothing to do with me. I came on my own to protect Zevon," the woman snarled with a toss of her long braids. She was absolutely fierce in her intent. "Anyone who threatens him, I will mutilate!"

As she brandished her weapon at Stiles, Zevon held up a hand to back the woman off. "Sykora, please. This is Eric."

"Eric—" Her tone changed instantly. Her eyes narrowed. "Eric Stiles?"

"Yes."

"What's going on?" Stiles asked as Zevon pulled him to his feet. "What's she doing here?"

"Drop your weapon!" Sykora demanded.

"No," Spock interrupted. "Dropping a phaser could be deadly. If the trooper would simply take it—"

Sykora snapped her fingers at one of the guards, who snatched the utility phaser out of Stiles' hand. That quickly were the tables turned.

Frustrated, Stiles griped, "How'd she find us out here?"

"He is my husband," Sykora said for herself. "I look after him."

"Husband? Since when!"

Zevon nodded. "Sykora is the reason I knew you got the message through to my family. And why I knew they were never planning to come for me."

"I am a subcommander," Sykora interrupted, "in the Imperial Solar Guard. I could never stomach the royal family's abandonment of their prince. I want nothing to do with those disloyal monsters. I confiscated a three-man ship and came to rescue him myself."

"My own defense systems destroyed her ship," Zevon admitted with some sheepishness. "Her two crewmen fought and were killed by the Pojjana planetary guard, but Sykora succeeded in finding me."

"And I will kill any who threaten him," the determined woman said. "Even Orsova fears and respects me."

Even deprived of his weapon and his moment of success, Stiles leered at Zevon in private admiration. "She's pretty tough."

"Yes . . . she is."

"How'd she find us?"

"I actually don't know." Zevon looked at his wife. "How did you?"

A little more agreeable, though no more mellow, Sykora gestured to Zevon's cardigan. "You're always too careless with your own well-being. I take care of you. The fringe is a homing grid."

Zevon touched his sweater, then gazed at her in what could only be adoration. "How kind . . ."

BZZZZZWAP!

Phaser stun! No mistaking that sound!

The Pojjana troopers sprang like stricken cats and flopped to the ground, only an instant before a third beam struck Sykora and she was pitched into a convulsion that left her unconscious in a crotch of stone.

Zevon gasped in anguish and scrambled to his wife's side, but there was nothing to be done for her but wait for the effect to wear off. The tables had turned again.

Over the crest of the ridge appeared a beautiful sight— Travis Perraton leading a landing party that included the evil twins, a handful of security trainees, and Dr. Leonard McCoy.

"We heard the trouble," Travis said. "Ambassador Spock cued his comm link and we heard everything. You all right, Eric?"

"Why? Am I bleeding?"

"Some blood on your neck there."

"I'm okay, Trav, thanks." Stiles accepted a service phaser and looked at the handiwork. "Round up those three and stuff 'em into the equipment locker."

"Even the lady?"

Stiles met Zevon's hopeful eyes, but he had certain decisions to make and certain dangers to consider. "That's no lady. That's a subcommander."

"Uh-huh. Got it. Lock her up, boys."

The Bolt brothers assisted Dr. McCoy down a fairly stable rock incline, where he stopped before Zevon and gave the Romulan prince a good looking over.

"Good evening," he said. "I'm Count Vladimir McCoy. I vant your blod."

"Orsova."

"Again? What do you want now! I tried to put that poison in Zevon, but he's gone!"

"They have escaped through the root swamp. I will give you the coordinates of their space ship. You still have a chance to bring them to me. The doctors and Zevon. Alive if you can. Dead if you cannot."

"How can I chase them if they go into space? I have no spaceships."

"You ask too many questions. You will have my ship. I will arrange for you to be close to Zevon. Prepare yourself. You are about to become a spaceman."

Chapter Twenty-four

As THE TWO POJJAN guards were heaved off into the waiting CST by the crewmen, Zevon hurried to his wife's side and knelt beside her, touching her face. "I will not even speak to you about this unless you treat her first."

"She'll recover," Stiles complained. "It's just phaser stun."

"No, she's ill. Like you when you were trapped here, we have no way to treat her on this planet. She's not Pojjana. Their medicine has been working only poorly for her since—"

"Uh-oh," McCoy preempted, and immediately came to Sykora's side. "Better check that."

Stiles glanced at Spock. Were they too late? Did Sykora have the royal family thing? He scrubbed the conversation they'd just had to see if there'd been any mention of Sykora's bloodlines. Had he missed something? Did she have this plague that had everybody so worked up?

While McCoy scanned the unconscious woman with some kind of double-built medical scanner, Stiles turned to Travis. "Go back on board. Get ready to lift off."

"Aye aye," Travis said.

"I'll be right there. Go on."

Over the fallen form of the Romulan woman, McCoy let

Jason Bolt pull him back to his feet. "She's not royal family. No trace of their DNA at all. She's got hyperplexic myelitis. I've only seen it twice before in Vulcanoids."

Fearful just at the sound of that, Zevon looked at him beseechingly. "Is it dangerous?"

"Eventually, it would be fatal."

"Can you stop it?"

"I need to get her on a table."

The noncommittal answer clearly frightened Zevon.

Stiles watched him. The whole Romulan royal family was sick and dying, and all that meant anything to Zevon was this one woman. He parted his lips to utter some words of assurance, but never got the chance. As the ship sat ducklike on its landing struts, the skin of the CST crackled with an electrical surge that threw sparks all over the people standing on the ridge. For an instant Stiles thought something in or on the ship had exploded; then the culprit came into view. Over the resting form of the CST rose a hovering craft of unfamiliar design, made of dark blue metal and etched with white bolts in an industrial pattern of hull plates. Against the darkening sky, the blue ship was nearly invisible except for the pinpoint etchings of white dots that appeared almost like free-floating constellations.

Would've been pretty if it hadn't been firing on them.

"On board!" Stiles shouted. "On board! On board!"

As Spock and two CST crewmen hustled McCoy down the other side of the ridge and Zevon hoisted his wife's limp form over his shoulder, Stiles aimed his service phaser at the roaring newcomer and opened fire.

His phaser scored the body of the other ship with a great show of noise and sizzling, but the wounds were only superficial.

The blue ship fired again, but not at him. Instead its weapons scored the body of the CST as it had before, leaving steaming gashes on the nose and side of the big tender. As he skittered down the incline, he heard the CST's impulse engines throb to power. In a few seconds, they'd be ready for escape velocity.

That is, if they weren't fried right here on the ground. Gouts of smoke blew across the bottom of the ridge, blinding him to the people running in front of him toward the tender's ramp.

"Keep going!" he shouted, and fired again.

A third time the lumbering blue ship screamed at them. Once more the deadly energy weapons scratched the body of the CST. If that beam hit the defenseless people running toward the ship—

A hard form—metal—slapped the bottom of his boot and tripped him. He skidded forward, almost dropping his phaser. The ramp! In the smoke he hadn't seen how close he was!

"Travis, get us out of the atmosphere!" he called, scrambling on all fours up the treaded surface. "They can't come after us!"

The ramp whined up behind him. He found himself on the midships deck, with Alan Wood pulling him out of the way of the closing ramp.

"Always an English butcher around when you need one," Stiles choked, gagging the last of the smoke out of his lungs.

"Tea's good for that," Alan offered. "I'll get you some. Want cake?"

"I want red alert!"

"Red alert, aye." Alan swung him to his feet and Stiles raced through the hatches to the cluttered little bridge, where Zevon sat on the deck, holding his groggy but awakening wife. Beside them, Dr. McCoy had been planted firmly in one of the anchored chairs at tactical. Jeremy manned the science station, Travis was just ordering full power to the escape velocity thrusters, and the evil twins were at the helm and navigation. Spock was standing beside the helm.

Stiles skidded into place behind the helm and in front of his command chair, but did not sit. "You look good there," he commented.

Spock seemed surprised that he'd even been noticed. "Comforting to know one is picturesque."

Indulging in a nervous grin, Stiles watched the main screen, which showed the thinning atmosphere as the CST powered toward space, and the side monitors, which showed the blue ship with its constellation of white hull buttons moving deliberately after them.

Quite abruptly, the mist on the main screen parted with a nearly audible swoosh, and they broke out into the blackness of open space. Unlike the darkening evening on the planet's surface, here it was once again day, bright and fierce, as they moved away from the protection of the planet with the sun on their port side.

"They're following us!" Jeremy White gulped. "Coming right into space after us!"

Zevon left his wife's side, bolted to his feet and grasped the edge of the helm and stared at the main screen. "Impossible!"

"Well, here they come anyway!"

The whole CST jolted then with a terrible butt-stroke from the pursuing ship, a blow that peppered the tender with hot energy.

Stiles glanced at Zevon, fielding a bitter distrust. "Shields up. Battle stations."

"I'm not imagining things, am I?" Stiles asked. "That's not a Pojjana ship, is it?"

"No!" Zevon insisted.

"Nor do I recognize it," Ambassador Spock said. "I have never seen that configuration or those markings."

"Neither has the computer," Travis confirmed. "No cataloguing at all."

"Increase speed as soon as you can," Stiles said.

Zack Bolt frowned at his nav controls. "They're hailing us through my nav impulses. Must not be compatible with Federation tech."

"Can you make it so we can hear it?"

"Well . . . attempting." He poked at his controls, and a moment later a completely unexpected sound burbled from the other ship.

"Surrender. You have no chance against this fighting spaceship. Turn back now and you will live."

Rage boiled up in Stiles's head till he thought his hair would blow off. He pounded the right button.

"Orsova! What are you doing in that ship! Where'd you get a thing like that!"

"Surrender now or be killed. We have more speed and more weapons. I will kill you before I let you leave the sector."

"Cut him off!" Stiles roared. "I don't want to hear his voice again! He can't want me back that badly—he can't care about me that much! Travis! What's the gasball got?"

Travis bent again over the tactical scanners. "High shielding . . . full warp capacity . . . strike-force shields . . . weapons are—" He paused and shook his head in worried admiration. "It's a fighting warship, Eric. We're completely outmatched."

"Twins, get us out of this stupid solar system!" Stiles ordered. "Full impulse as soon as you can. Travis, you take weapons yourself. Transfer all the reserve from the cutting phasers and find some distance power. Get ready to use the welding torches if they get too close. I want to skin that bastard!"

At the nav station, Zack Bolt turned to look at him. "We're a combat support tender, not a battleship! We can't beat that thing!"

"We don't have to beat it. He wants us alive for some reason."

Everybody looked at him as if he'd grown feathers.

"You're gonna have to explain that one," Travis said.

"If he wanted to kill us," Stiles told them, "why would he shoot at the CST instead of nice bald helpless people on the ground?"

Unsure of that, Spock tightened his brow and waited for more explanation, so Stiles gave it to him.

"That gives me an advantage. It means I should run harder than I fight. Getting away is more important than beating them. All we have to do is knock 'em down long enough to get away."

The CST hummed and cranked its way toward full speed, chased easily by the constellation ship with Orsova impossibly aboard. Against the pure blackness of night, the enemy ship's blue body nearly disappeared and its hundreds of white plate bolts didn't, so that it looked indeed like a set of stars rushing freely after them in space. But every few moments the other ship made its solid presence known with a full-power blast that shocked the CST to its bones and made everybody grab for something to hold onto.

"How're we doing?" Stiles asked when he thought enough time had gone by.

"Not an inch," Jeremy sourly reported. "In fact, they're closing."

His teeth gnashing, Stiles growled at the side screens. "Maybe if I give myself up, he'll be happy and leave the rest of you alone."

Even in the midst of rocking and rolling, Spock found a way to face him gracefully. "No, Mr. Stiles. That is one decision I will not allow."

"You can't tell me what to do, with all due respect, sir."

"I know. Orsova has no ship like that. Someone is either supporting or manipulating him. That power must have farther-reaching goals than being entertained with your capture. And," he added, rather gently, "once in a lifetime is enough to sacrifice yourself to that man."

In spite of everything, Stiles smiled at the sentimental reminder that Spock knew all the mistakes he'd made, and liked him anyway.

A javelin of weapon power struck the CST and backhanded it across space. The engines screamed. The crew and passengers were throttled, bouncing off the equipment around them. Stiles tried to stay on his feet, but ended up sharing a chair with Jason Bolt at the helm as the ship went howling on its edge through space.

While Jason struggled to recover, Jeremy called, "That was our port engine! We can't make top speed any more, Eric!"

"Can we have emergency warp?"

"If you don't mind a complete meltdown."

"That's it. No more running. Get ready to turn and fight."

From the glances of the crew, he might as well have ordered them to cut off their hands and throw them in a pot. They were brave enough going into battle situations when necessary to repair the important ships, but it wasn't often that they were the center of the battle—the thing actually being shot at on purpose.

He saw it in their faces. Turn and fight? Fight that warship coming at them at flank speed?

"It's me he wants," Zevon spoke up. He came around the helm to face both Stiles and Spock. "I am the key to his control, Eric, not you. Let him take me. Then you and your ship can go."

272

"I can't let you go, you know that," Stiles said. "We need you. Your blood—"

"I hate the Romulan ruling family," Zevon claimed bitterly. "I hate the government that flagrantly caused the Constrictor. I hate the relatives who abandoned me. I deride the stupidity of a system that allows birth connections to command important missions. I hate those of my heritage, and now I am told I *must* go save them? I have no interest in saving my philosophical enemies."

"Travis, keep firing on that ship," Stiles ordered. "Just fire at will, any chance you get to hit 'em." That done, furious and frustrated, he barked at Zevon. "So it would be better to go back there and serve a system that allows a scumsucker like Orsova to end up in control of a whole planet? What's the matter with you?"

"My husband is a genius!" Sykora rose from the deck, still pale from the phaser stun, her face a mask of defiance. She moved forward and steadied herself by gripping the back of the command chair. "He has designed a spaceborne barricade that will funnel the Constrictor waves around the planet. If we help you, will the Federation come and build our barricade in space? No! You will go your way and let the Pojjana planet crumble behind you!"

As enemy fire rocked the CST again, the real challenge was right here, right now.

"Why should I trust the Federation?" Zevon confirmed. "After I save the Romulans, you will leave again as you did before."

"We can help the Pojjana," Spock firmly told them both, "but they must be receptive to our help."

Zevon spun to him. "Why should I trust you? Why were you not more persistent? When you saw your presence was good for them, why did you leave?"

"The Pojjana asked us to leave."

"But you *left!*"

Spock seemed to be searching for a way to explain when Stiles took over. "Never mind, Ambassador. Until today, the only Federation citizen Zevon's ever spoken to in his life was me. He doesn't get it." Fixing his glare on Zevon, he forced himself to ignore the pounding the ship was taking. "You're going. I didn't go through this for nothing! We need you to go. If the Empire falls, the whole sector is going with it. Like it or not, you're the last royal family member with unadulterated blood and you're coming with us."

"No, Mr. Stiles. He is not."

Spock's announcement, without a hint of doubt or question, took Stiles completely by surprise. Everyone else, too, from the looks on their faces.

Digesting the words from his idol as quickly as he could, Stiles jabbed a finger toward Zevon. "But he's wrong!"

"He is wrong according to us," the ambassador contradicted evenhandedly. "He has that right."

"Why did we come all this way! Why didn't you say something down on the planet!"

"I entertained the hope that you might be able to convince him."

Setting aside annoyance at being used, Stiles argued, "The Romulans are attacking the Federation for something we didn't do!"

Spock offered only a nod in limited agreement. "I will not force any individual to act against his will."

"Even if it means a war?"

"If that is the price of freedom . . . so be it."

"They're almost in phaser range," Jeremy White reported, a thread of fright rising in his voice.

Stiles didn't blame him a bit. The sight of that dark ship with the white buttons all over it streaking toward them with the posture of an angry bumblebee—it scared him too.

"Jeremy," he ordered, "tell me the two biggest differences between us and them."

With something specific to do, Jeremy concentrated on his instruments while everyone else waited through the tension.

"Their weapons . . ."

No surprise there.

"And shields. Way better than ours."

Unsatisfied with the lack of specificity, Spock leaned over Jeremy's shoulder at the readouts. "High-intensity plasma-fed shielding with direct warp feed. At least four times the power of ours. I must assume their speed capacity and weapons are comparably advanced."

Stiles leered at him. "Situation hopeless?"

"So it seems," Spock said.

"All the odds against us?"

"Correct."

Stiles eyed him. "This is one of those 'leap of creativity' things, isn't it?"

Spock clasped his hands behind his back in a ridiculously casual posture. "That is my hope."

"You wanna just . . . come over here and give me a shove?"

"If you prefer."

From the port side, McCoy offered, "I'll come and push you if you want."

Stiles gave him a floppy wave with his free hand. "Thanks, Doctor, consider me pushed. We need to even things up. Shields first."

"How?" Spock asked.

At the same time, McCoy beefed, "Rhodinium against tissue paper!"

Stiles glanced at them. "Oh, we're a little tougher than that, Doctor. Jeremy, we've got that warp trigger box with the surger for emergency ignition of cold warp cores, don't we? We replaced the last one, right?"

"Always."

"Go back there and take it off the clamps and put it in the airlock, activated. We're going to dump and detonate."

"It'll short out *our* shields!"

"If we're close enough it'll short out his too. He wants us alive—let's use that and play some chicken."

Flushed, Jeremy raced through the hatch toward the aft section.

"Ambassador," Stiles requested, "I'll bet you can take the science boards, can't you?"

"Most certainly I can." Spock moved with fluidity across the bridge and settled at Jeremy's station as if he'd been painted there. Darned if he didn't look happy.

"Travis, fire up the magnetic grapples. Two and four on the port side."

Travis swung full about and gaped at him with his mouth open and eyes like eggs, but talked himself out of asking. "Aye aye," he responded, and got to work.

Stiles stood beside his command chair and watched the screen that showed the approaching blue fighter. "Ready about!"

"Ready about, aye!"

A flurry of activity blew across the bridge, and everybody was suddenly working. Luckily they'd stopped asking what he was up to. Good thing, because he didn't know.

"Helm, you know what to do. Come about and meet him head on, as if we were rafting for a repair."

"While he's moving?" Jason Bolt confirmed.

"Just as if we had to grapple a damaged ship under power. Do it by the numbers. We'll see what happens. Helm over."

"Coming about."

"Then what?" Travis asked—not in challenge, but because to make it work he had to know the next move.

Stiles shook his head and shrugged. "Oh, I dunno, I'm probably about to get us all killed."

Okay, not the greatest slogan to stitch on a banner of war, but there was something to be said for being honest with them. He drew one long breath and held it, watching the forward screen now as the CST turned on its midships keel and the constellation fighter came around. Broad on the bow . . . three points . . . two points . . . one . . . fine on the port bow . . . dead ahead.

Now the two ships were heading at each other in a game that would destroy one of them if somebody didn't flinch.

"Incoming!" Travis called. "They're shooting at us!"

A bright white blast blew from the other ship, looking as if somebody had fired talcum powder out an exhaust port—but when it hit them it didn't feel like powder. The CST shuddered violently but did not turn off her course. Rather than striking them with a single impact, the powder-beam slathered all over the ship as if they'd plunged into a glass of milk, washing along from the prow to midships before dissipating, snapping systems all the way back.

"Hold course!" Stiles called over the shattering of circuits all around them.

"Intentions?" Spock asked. "Do you mean to ram them?"

"We've got an asteroid-cutter prow," Stiles told him. "If they want to try it, I'm game. We can't outrun them. All we can do is make them flinch."

Spock straightened from watching the science panel. "Do you know this man well enough to predict his response?"

"Orsova? Sir, we're willing to die for a cause. Orsova isn't. All we have to do is stand him down."

"Yes, Mr. Stiles, but remember—Orsova has little or no spacefaring experience. It's unlikely he's piloting that ship."

Stiles looked at him. "Who do you think is?"

"I should say whoever provided him with the fighter."

"Oh, good, I love unknown quantities."

Annoyed with himself for not realizing that Orsova couldn't possibly be driving that ship, that he was in fact fighting somebody he'd never met in a ship he didn't recognize, with weapons he'd never seen before, Stiles dealt with a tumbling stomach and a dry mouth as the ships drew speedily closer.

He struck the nearest comm link. "Jeremy, blow that trigger out the hatch right now."

"Ready . . . it's away!"

They waited as the octagonal warp trigger box drifted out into space, visible on a side monitor at starboard, floating lazily out there, brainless to what else was going on.

"Distance?"

"Eight hundred kilometers," Spock ticked off. "One thousand . . . twelve hundred . . ."

"Ignite it."

Before his words were even out, space at their side blew bright with disruption and the whole ship was swept sideways away from it. Half the crew was thrown down. Stiles kept his feet only by hanging onto the command chair with both hands. He found himself looking at Dr. McCoy and thanking all the lucky stars out there that the old doctor had been sitting down. Travis was also holding McCoy in place with one hand, himself with the other.

Over the crackle and fume of their own damage, Spock reported, "His shields are losing integrity. They're flickering."

"Ours are down completely," Travis announced, taking the

gloss off their victory. "Whatever happens now, we'll feel it hard."

"Enemy vessel is slowing down," Spock announced briskly. There was a clear ring of win in his voice. "You've called their bluff."

"Either that or they're not willing to die for whatever we represent to them," Stiles said. "Doesn't mean they won't keep trying to kill us."

"Incoming!"

Stiles gritted his teeth as they rode out another hit of the powder-beam. Damage reports came chattering in from all sections, none of them good. Stiles ignored them.

"Travis, are the grapples ready?"

"Ready, aye."

"Keep up speed until we're at proximity range. Let me know when we get there—"

"We're there!" Travis said. "We can reach now."

On the main screen, the dark blue enemy ship drew up its braking thrusters and surged upward so they could see its underbelly, just as a rowboat surges up on a swell before settling into the sand. They really didn't want to get hit by the *Saskatoon*'s cutting prow.

Stiles couldn't help a little snicker. "Magnetic grapples two and four—launch!"

wheeeeeeeeeeeeCHUNK—CHUNK

"Got 'em!" Travis yelped. "Both grapples are on their hull. Now what?"

"Let you know soon as I think of it," Stiles muttered. "He can't blow us up if we're riding him. Pull up as close as you can, Travis. Zack, heat up the welding phasers!"

"Where do you want me to cut him?"

"Any place you can reach. I want you to connect those white dots into my initials. Right there where I can see."

The Bolt brothers both laughed in spite of the moment's heat.

Heat—yes, it was getting hotter on the bridge, proof that systems were damaged and the ship's computers were selectively saving what they could and sacrificing what they couldn't while waiting for repair. The CST's welding phasers lit up under the viewscreen and scored the blue body of the other ship, leaving trails of white-hot melted metal and snapping circuits exposed to open space. Still . . . how much of this could they do?

As the two ships danced in their locked-together waltz, Spock peered into his monitor. "Reading a power buildup."

"Weapons?" Stiles asked.

"No, sir. Routing shield power, I believe. . . ." He didn't sound sure at all.

Heavy-legged with damage and with the weight of the other ship pulling on the grapples, the *Saskatoon* lumbered around, pushed by the pointless power of the two ships exerting force on each other while going absolutely nowhere.

"Jeremy, can you still hear me?" Stiles called.

"You're breaking up. Boost your signal."

"Forget it." Stiles stalked to the aft hatch, cranked the handle, yanked the hatch open, and yelled through the body of the ship. "Turn on the external hoses! Seal up their impulse ports! Got it?"

"I like that!"

Stiles turned back to the main action, grumbling. "Yeah, I like it too."

Within seconds, the CST's external hoses clacked on. Clear on the main screen, attached to them so closely that they could've touched it if the screen hadn't been there, the blue enemy ship cranked and yanked against the magnetic grapples, trying to break the hold. Now tons of semiviscous compound spewed from the hose nozzles and splattered all over the aft section of that ship, totally clogging the impulse exhausts as if the gods were spewing milkshakes into goblets.

Except this wonderful composite milkshake stuck like glue and hardened chemically within four seconds of contact.

"What's that stuff?" McCoy asked.

"It's chemical fiber bond," Stiles told him. "We use it to coat repairs before putting the hull plates back on. Nasty stuff."

"Their impulse ports are clogged," Spock noted. "They're attempting to fire impulse engines anyway."

On the screen, in the upper corner, they could just see the impulse ports turning yellow, orange, then red with backed-up energy. Volcanic spurts of power blasted through the fiber bond, only to be almost instantly sealed up again. Another kind of battle was going on—between the power of the engines and the strength of a resealing compound that wouldn't take no for an answer.

Flash . . . flash . . . sizzle . . . flash . . . The constellation ship fought with itself, spitting and surging, taking the CST with it on every blurting ride.

The whole CST then began to shake furiously, as if it would break into a billion pieces around them. The sound was horrible, terrifying, the kind of sound that made Stiles wonder what the hell he was doing here in the first place, why anybody would want to come to space when he could stay on a nice solid planet somewhere. Suddenly all the screens flashed a nasty yellow light. A *snap* of electrical surge flailed through the ship, popping everybody's ears.

"What happened!" Stiles called.

"Feedback along the magnetic lines!" Spock called back. "They've thrown us off—power surge is running up the grapples!"

"Damn!"

"What do we do now?" Travis cried. "Surrender?"

"Not since Gabriel's last tea party in hell! Full about! Make some speed!"

McCoy fingernailed Spock in the arm and pointed at Stiles. "I like the sound of that, don't you?"

Still spitting fire every few seconds as the impulse engines coughed through the clinging fiber bond, the enemy ship wheeled clumsily around to face them with its main weapons ports.

"Uh-oh . . ." Stiles' whole body went cold. "Doesn't look like they want to take us alive anymore. . . ."

Spock straightened and watched the ship out there. "Your logic is impeccable . . . we are in grave danger."

His memory nerve tingling, Stiles looked at him. "What?"

"Just a bit of nostalgia. I suggest we distance ourselves."

"Travis, disengage! Jason, full impulse!"

At point-blank range the other ship opened up on them in what could only be described as a fit of anger. Its weapons cut into the CST's unshielded body, blowing systems all around the bridge and all the way through the ship. Stiles agonized as he heard the screams and shouts of his men and knew they would have to see to themselves for now. He hated that—the urge to go back there nearly crushed his chest.

"Speed, Jason," he implored.

"Doing my best."

"Reading power-up on torpedo launchers," Spock warned. "We cannot possibly gain enough distance."

No distance and no shields. No weapons worth spitting back at that ship. Stiles felt his heart sink. He'd bought time, but there was nothing more to do with it. He'd stopped them from maneuvering in space-normal, but the CST couldn't get away fast enough to take advantage.

"Shoot," he ordered. "Fire at will, whatever we can throw at them. At least we'll go out shooting."

The CST's internal systems crackled and complained. His men fired what little working phasers they had left. But they weren't a starship—what could they do? Go over there and rebuild the enemy to death?

As Stiles watched the enemy ship on the screen, pursuing them in fits and bursts with those clogged impulse tubes, he knew that despite its falling behind they couldn't possibly out-run its firepower.

The whole main screen and two lateral ones—the two still working—blasted bright white with incendiary drama. Stiles crimped his eyes, but refused to close them. He wasn't going to die with his eyes closed.

Then he didn't die—couldn't even do that right.

"Romulan bird-of-prey on our starboard stern!" Travis called, horrified. "It's fired on that blue ship! It's driving them off!"

Spock bent over the science station. "Confirmed. Romulan standard warbird . . . in battle mode."

"Now what?" Zack cranked around. "Fire on that one too?"

"No!" McCoy rasped.

"Don't shoot!" Stiles countered at the same time. "Give me ship to ship!"

"You've got ship to ship."

Stiles leaned over the arm of his command chair's comm. "Dr. Crusher, I assume that's you inside that ugly thing."

"It's me, Commander. Everyone all right? Mission accomplished, I hope?"

"Accomplished so far, Doctor." He blinked at the bronze war wing hovering on their flank. "Ugly or not, I'm glad to see that big-eyed bug!"

"It worked." Spock's announcement was reserved, but victorious. "Enemy is moving off at emergency warp one on a retreat vector."

"They're moving off, Commander Stiles. What do you recommend we do? Chase them down?"

Stiles sucked a long breath and heaved it out with a shudder. "No, no, don't chase them. Let them go, Doctor. And . . . stand by."

"Standing by," Crusher acknowledged.

"Do they show any signs of turning back?" he asked his own crew.

"None," Spock congratulated.

Jason's hands shook on his controls. "Think we beat 'em!"

Looking around the deck, Stiles had a hard time believing they'd beaten anybody at all, considering all the wreckage and mess and sparking components. He hadn't even noticed the parts and pieces blowing around him and now cluttering the deck. But the rush of victory was undeniable on the bruised faces of his crew.

"What's that whine?" somebody asked.

"What whine?" Stiles wasn't even sure who asked, and didn't hear anything at first.

Then he did.

"Transporter!" Spock called over the noise that suddenly filled the bridge.

They pressed back, not knowing what was happening until a band of energy crackled into formation in front of the helm and coalesced into humanoid shape. As they stared in amazement, the sparkling form hardened into Orsova.

Stiles opened his mouth to shout an order, but Orsova was already moving, leaping like an attacking lion at Zevon. Stiles didn't see a weapon until the last second before Orsova and

Zevon's bodies collided. A flash of metal, as if he were watching a scene from a swashbuckling movie—unmistakably a blade.

For just a flash this made no sense—why would Orsova, who had at his disposal every weapon on a whole planet, use a blade?

Sykora cried out some unintelligible protest, but Spock and Travis managed to hold her back. Zack and Jeremy sprang from their posts, dove forward over the helm and snatched at Orsova's clothing. It took both of them to pry him off Zevon. By then, Stiles was there.

"Hold him back!" he shouted. He clutched Orsova's left wrist and the metal weapon in it—some kind of spike, polished to a silk finish, with a wooden handle like an ice pick. It's silver surface was spackled with Zevon's blood.

As Jason Bolt joined the effort to hold Orsova, Stiles handed the weapon to Travis and rushed to Zevon. He grasped Zevon by both arms and held him up. Was he hurt? Was he dying?

"Zevon?" Stiles held him and looked for a wound. He found it under Zevon's right hand, pressed to his left side. Pulling Zevon's hand away, Stiles cajoled, "Let me look, let me look."

As Zevon stiffened in pain against him, he found the entry wound, and blessedly an exit.

"It's just a flesh wound, I think." Weakened by relief, he grinned at Zevon. "You just got a good poke!"

Fighting the shock of having been stabbed, seriously or not, Zevon winced and nodded but couldn't manage to let go of Stiles just yet.

Stiles had other ideas. He twisted around and glared at Orsova. "You missed, you filthy ox!"

Orsova slammed an elbow into Jason Bolt and smacked Zack in the face, driving him back. After that, though, he didn't attack anybody, instead crossing to the port panel where the long-range scanner was showing a clear picture of the constellation ship getting smaller and smaller as it ran.

"Voice! Voice, save me!" he cried. "Beam me away, Voice! I did what you wanted! Where are you! Come for me! Voice!"

But nobody came to rescue him.

"Pathetic," Stiles commented.

Apparently just now realizing he was in deep trouble, Orsova cranked around and glared as if trapped in a box. He could do nothing as Stiles closed on him, pressed his fingers into the flesh at Orsova's throat, backed him tight up against the portside scanner panel. "I was afraid of *you?* You're just a quivering little coward when you're standing alone, aren't you?"

"You better not hurt me!" Orsova pressed backward against the panel. "The Voice is coming back for me!"

"Not soon enough." Letting loose a dozen years of frustration—and even anger at himself, that he'd been haunted for a third of his life by the face now crimping before him—Stiles bent Orsova back over the panel until he could push no more. Orsova choked and gagged as Stiles's knuckles kneaded into his throat.

As Orsova's face flushed from copper to almost beet red with strain, quite abruptly, even absurdly, the satisfaction meter began to fall. Stiles glared into the hated face, saw the panic and desperation, and snarled as if looking into a garbage pit.

But he stopped pushing. He even let go a little.

"Damn," he uttered. "You're just a toothache! You're not even worth hitting!"

To the obvious amazement of everybody around him, he pulled Orsova back to his feet and let him reel.

Stiles found himself strangely amused and pleased at Orsova's pitiful display. Over there, Travis was smiling at him in some kind of ironic pride. That felt good.

Shaking his head, he leaned one hip against the helm and commented, "At least I was worth beating up!"

His crewmen rewarded him with a laugh and a round of applause that made him feel like—well, like royalty.

"Just stay there, you puscup," he said to Orsova. "You're as imprisoned as I was. Dr. McCoy, would you have a look at Zevon, please? Zack, escort the doctor around the other side of the helm, away from this mulchy moron."

Playing out his win, he freely turned his back on Orsova as if his former guard were hardly more than a bug on the wall. For the first time, he turned his back on his greatest fear, the ghost of all his nights, and completely dismissed him.

He turned instead to Zevon, as Dr. McCoy probed the Romulan's wound. "How is he?"

"Superficial," the elderly doctor confirmed. "Hardly raising a welt. Punched through the skin, scored the intestines—no ruptures, though. Let me have a better look. . . ."

He drew around his medical tricorder and a scanner and started taking readings.

"All right, Zevon," Stiles began firmly, "you can have what you want. In fact, you can have *more* than you want. I'm going to take you back to that stupid planet and dump you there with your wife, just like you want. And then I'm coming back into space and demonstrate to you exactly what a Federation promise means." Leaning forward with theatrical flair, he announced, "I'm going to build your barricade."

"You, yourself?" Zevon challenged.

From the other side of the bridge, Sykora gasped, "Zevon, can he do it?"

"No!" Her husband flinched as McCoy scanned him. "He certainly cannot possibly do it. The barricade needs raw materials, infrastructure, parts, support—Federation interest will fade before the barricade is built."

"It's not going to fade," Stiles boasted. "I won't let it."

Zevon gazed at him in something like disappointment. "And you have so much influence, Eric?"

"I don't need influence. I have a CST." Stiles swept his hand wide to illustrate the ship around him, and the suddenly proud crew. "We can build it. A combat support tender is a movable starbase, a flying factory!"

"Of course!" Spock breathed. Even he hadn't thought of it, and that gave Stiles a particular zing of pleasure.

"Impossible," Zevon argued. He pointed at Spock, but spoke to Stiles. "You're saying this to get what he wants, because you worship him!"

A rumble of frustration rose in Stiles throat. Better let that one go. "My crew is packed with trained technicians, mechanics, and engineers. We can build almost anything, darned near anywhere, all by ourselves. And even though you're refusing to help us, we're going to go back there and build it."

Zevon squinted with doubt. "But we have no treaty! Starfleet will not give you permission—"

"I don't need permission," Stiles recklessly sparked. "I'm not even going to ask for it. And on top of that, I'm going to use a few other resources available to me right here and now. For instance, Dr. McCoy over there is going to treat whatever's making your wife sick. I don't have to let him do that, y'see, because I'm in command here and he has to do what I say. But I'm going to tell him to do that anyway, Zevon, because not everything in life is a tradeoff. And then we're going to fly away and leave you alone with your planet and your wife and your barricade, and we'll see if you can forget who did for you what you couldn't do for yourselves." He jabbed Zevon in the arm. "You and everybody on that stupid planet are going to find out what real freedom means."

Across the bridge, Ambassador Spock settled back against the science station and looped his arms into that casual appreciative fold that Stiles had seen so many times on the historical tapes. Stiles got a rush of delight at seeing Spock fold his arms like that, right here on Stiles's bridge, just as if he liked being here.

Astonished, Zevon could do nothing but stare at him with a thousand emotions pushing at him. Stiles did not turn away from that gaze, determined to show that nothing would stop him from doing what he said he could do, exercising both the power of his command and the industrial might of his ship.

Dr. McCoy looked up then, and clicked off his medical tricorder. His face was stiff, his voice rough.

"He's not going to find out any time soon. There must've been something on the spike." He looked first at Stiles, then at Spock. "It's all over, gentlemen. He's infected."

Chapter Twenty-five

MCCOY'S WORDS SHOOK STILES to the bone. Spock too, he could tell, was inexpressibly disturbed. Only seeing the worry on his idol's face caused Stiles to finally absorb just how rare Zevon's uncontaminated blood had been to them all. What would come now? Decades of instability in the galaxy? The suction of a collapsing empire on the Federation's doorstep? Endless struggles and endless repairs, so ships and crews could go back into more endless struggles?

"Call Dr. Crusher to beam over here," McCoy tersely said. "I want a corroborating opinion. Not that it'll change a goddamn thing. . . ."

Wordless, his throat too tight to make a sound, Stiles nodded the order over to Travis, who spoke into his comm. "Dr. Crusher, would you beam over please? Dr. McCoy's request."

"Acknowledged. One moment."

The bridge fell to silence. Except for the snapping of electrical systems that had been violated, there was hardly a sound. The squawk of the transporter beam sent a ripple up every spine. Soon Dr. Beverly Crusher stood right there on the bridge, providing a mere haze of hope. But nobody here doubted Leonard McCoy's diagnosis, not for a moment.

The elegant lady doctor looked around, noted everybody, including the only two Romulans, hesitated briefly over Sykora, then silently concluded that Zevon was the only one who could be the person they'd come here for.

"I think we're too late," McCoy told her in a funereal tone. "Doublecheck me, will you?"

Crusher kept control over her expression, connecting momentarily with Spock as she stepped across the bridge to Zevon and ran her med scanner over him. Then she brought up her own tricorder and compared notes with whatever she had collected while she was gone in Romulan space.

Stiles watched her, worried. Over the doctor's shoulder, Zevon's fearful eyes met his. He stepped to Zevon's side, as if he'd never left, as if his presence alone could protect Zevon from the scourge that was apparently inevitable.

Dr. Crusher shook her head. "It's spreading fast. In forty or fifty seconds, he'll be completely contaminated. How did this happen out here in the middle of nowhere?"

"Hah!" On the other side of the bridge, Orsova bellowed with joy. "You see? You lose! Your civilization will fall apart now! The Voice is coming! You lose now! You can't hurt me now! I'm going to be governor of the sector! I won! I won!"

As retorts reeled in his head, Stiles turned toward his old tormenter. Never got the chance, though.

Sykora, until now still fazed by the effects of the stun, came very sharply and dangerously to life. She shoved Travis harshly off his balance and snatched the bloody spike from his hand. As if shot from a cannon, she streaked to Orsova. Before anyone could think of stopping her, she drove the spike through Orsova's neck with a disgusting pop and a faint crunch of shattered bone.

At Stiles's side, Zevon gasped and jolted with shock, but made no move toward his wife. She was an imperial subcommander, after all.

Orsova gurgled as frothy blood welled up into his mouth and he clasped at his demolished throat with both hands, blinked in surprise, then couldn't suck another breath. No one offered to cushion his collapse onto the deck. There, in a puddle of his own fluids, he died.

Just like that. Over.

And Stiles was glad. And he didn't feel ashamed of it either. He promised himself he never would. There were more appropriate things in the galaxy to feel bad about.

Even the sight of Orsova bleeding on the deck couldn't raise the pall that suddenly descended on the bridge. They'd failed. After all this.

Dr. Crusher huffed in frustration. "He's right. He won. We don't have any more alternatives for this mutant doomsday virus. We can't even get the empress back to her home in time for her to die in her own bed." Angry, she stuffed her med scanner back in its case and looked snappishly at Dr. McCoy. "Unless you've got a rabbit to pull out of your hat, we're skunked."

"What do you take me for?" McCoy spread his arms and crowed, "I'm going to stop this venom campaign if it's the last thing I do—and at the age of a hundred and thirty-odd, everything I do could be the last thing I do."

"You've got something?" Spock stepped to him. "Another uninfected royal family member?"

Invigorated, Stiles pointed at Sykora and blurted, "It's her, isn't it? I should've known! It's got to be her! Did he marry his own cousin or something?"

"No, he didn't," McCoy denied. "I told you the truth. She's got no royal family blood at all. Not even close. She's peasant stock if I ever saw it. Couldn't be infected if she took a bath in that toxin. But I've got something even better." He looked at Crusher with a winning expression. "You know what they say . . . fetal-cord blood is about twenty times more potent than the ordinary vein stuff. I won't even have to wake the little fella up."

Suddenly the center of attention, Sykora eyed the doctors, then her husband, then Stiles. "What does he mean?"

"You're pregnant, that's what!" McCoy announced.

"You knew?" Stiles accused McCoy as both Sykora and Zevon gawked in undeniable surprise. "You knew that and you still let Zevon be a target for assassination? A decoy?"

"Well, of course!" The elderly doctor nodded proudly. "After the first eight or nine decades, you learn to keep your mouth shut. Now, I know what you should name him, y'see. You've got to pick something flashy and unique. Leonard James Eric Spock Beverly Saskatoon the First. He'll be the only one of his kind. You won't regret it. Wanna see it written down? Hey, kid, got a pen?"

Epilogue

THE CRAMPED LITTLE SICKBAY on board the *Saskatoon* had never seen so much fame. Over a matter of a couple of days, the midsection of a combat support tender had become the center of the universe. Starfleet's Lord High Oracle Leonard McCoy and its state-of-the-art shamanness Beverly Crusher were collaborating with every medical facility within comm range. The first several attempts at synthesizing a serum failed, but only by tiny fractions. Gradually the fractions became smaller, and hope swelled.

Busy as he was with construction, Stiles broke away from his crew on the evening of the second day, and with an admitted rush of nerves went to check on Zevon's progress.

Zevon lay on the portable diagnostic couch that McCoy had ordered brought in. He was clearly in some pain from whatever treatments the doctors were giving him. Sykora was at his side. She hadn't been able to leave the chamber all this time. After all, she was the center of the center of the universe.

In the small sickbay, Dr. Crusher was bending over a cache of tubes, vials, beakers, microprocessors, and analytical equipment they'd had shipped in. Engrossed in her work, she didn't even look up when Stiles came in.

McCoy hovered nearby, peering at a colored liquid in a test tube.

Stiles felt he was interrupting something private as he came to Zevon's side, opposite Sykora, and fielded the obstinate woman's glare, still loaded with suspicion. Oh, well, couldn't win everything at once.

Pressing a hand to Zevon's shoulder, he gained his old friend's attention through the blur of pain.

"Hey, lightfoot," he greeted. "You all right?"

"Oh, Eric," Zevon moaned. "I think I would rather get the plague and die than deal with the cure. . . ."

A smile of empathy broke on Stiles's face. "No, no, you've got your orders. Get better or face the consequences. You don't want the vindictive captain to find out."

"If only . . . he were vindictive enough to . . . put me out of this misery. . . ."

"Not much longer," McCoy said. "Don't make me break out my hip-pocket psychiatry, boy. I'm whuppin' a dragon here."

Even through his discomfort, Zevon managed a smile. Stiles tightened his grip in silent reassurance.

He tried to come up with something more to say but was rescued when Ambassador Spock stepped in over the hatch coaming.

"Mr. Stiles, I thought you might be here," Spock said with not particularly well-veiled contentment.

Stiles instantly saw the undercurrent of success and asked, "How does it look, sir?"

His face expressive—in defiance of legend—Spock spoke almost merrily. "Looks quite well. Your defiant declaration has stirred the resting spirits at Starfleet Command."

"They're not going to challenge me or throw me in a brig or anything?"

"Hardly. The admiralty has a longstanding policy, albeit unspoken, of backing up their captains' flares of caprice. Admiral Douglas Prothero has offered the Zebra-Tango Division of the Starfleet Corps of Engineers and the services of the Industrial Trawler *True North* to assist the *Saskatoon* in building the spaceborne Constrictor barricade. Within a matter of months, the waves will go from deadly to harmless." He turned to Zevon and Sykora, amicably adding, "Your planet will finally be safe."

Battling a rush of deep emotion, Zevon gripped Sykora's hand and took a few moments to gather himself. "I will go before the Pojjana people," he offered, "and convince them of the Federation's integrity. I can do that . . . they will believe me."

"Such a collaboration," Spock said, "will give Starfleet the leverage to stabilize the sector and declare it green."

With both admiration and suspicion, Stiles quipped, "But you didn't have anything to do with that, I'll bet."

"Nothing at all," Spock loftily claimed.

Stiles grinned. "Thanks."

"You're very welcome. And how is construction going?"

"Oh, we've had to modify Zevon's diagrams a few times. Luckily, we're an innovative pack of wolves. Sir, might I say a few things? They're kind of . . . personal."

Spock seemed a little surprised. "Would you like to speak in private?"

"No, I'm not embarrassed anymore. I just wanted to thank you, for everything, past and present. You had faith in me that I didn't have in myself. I'll believe in myself as I am, as I can be—not as my father or my grandfather or Starfleet thought I should be. I'll believe in the Federation, as long as people like you are speaking for it. And I'll never forget something else you taught me. Probably the most important thing."

Spock's dark eyes glowed. It seemed he knew. But he asked anyway. "What would that be?"

As he gazed at his friends both new and old, Stiles absorbed the value of this moment and swore to himself that he would never forget.

"Freedom is never free," he said.

**Pocket Books
Proudly Presents**

**STAR TREK
THE NEXT GENERATION®**

Double Helix #4

QUARANTINE

John Vornholt

Available Now from Pocket Books

**Turn the page for a preview of
*Quarantine. . . .***

The *Peregrine*-class scout ship looked much like the falcon that inspired her design, with a beaklike bow and sweeping wings that enabled her to streak through a planet's atmosphere. Her sleek lines were marred by various scorch marks and dents, which left her looking like an old raptor with many scars. Larger than a shuttlecraft yet smaller than a cruiser, she was better armed than most ships her size, with forward and rear torpedoes plus phaser emitters on her wings.

Her bridge was designed to be operated efficiently by three people, allowing her to carry a crew of only fifteen. The engine room took up all three decks of her stern, and most of the crew served there. This proud vessel was state of the art for a scout ship—about forty years ago. Now she was practically the flagship of the Maquis fleet.

"What's the name of our ship?" asked her captain, a man named Chakotay. His black hair was cut short and severe, which suited his angular face and the prominent tattoo that stretched across half his forehead.

Tuvok, the Vulcan who served as first officer, consulted the registry on his computer screen. "She is called the *Spartacus*. The warp signature has already been modified."

Chakotay nodded with satisfaction. "I like that name."

On his right, an attractive woman who looked vaguely Klingon scowled at him. "Let me guess," said B'Elanna Torres. "Spartacus was some ancient human who led a revolution somewhere."

Captain Chakotay smiled. "That's right. He was a slave and a gladiator who led a revolt against Rome, the greatest power of its day. For two years, he held out against every Roman legion thrown against him."

"And how did this grand revolution end?" asked Torres.

When Chakotay didn't answer right away, Tuvok remarked, "He and all of his followers were crucified. Crucifiction is quite possibly the most barbaric form of capital punishment ever invented."

Torres snorted a laugh. "It's always good to know that my human ancestors could match my Klingon ancestors in barbarism. Considering what happened to Spartacus, let's not put him on too high a pedestal."

"It's still a good name," said Chakotay stubbornly. Like many Native Americans, he believed that names were important—that words held power. He didn't like having to change the name and warp signature of his ship all the time, but it was important to make their enemies think that the Maquis had more ships than they actually had.

"We've reached the rendezvous point," announced the captain. "I'm bringing us out of warp." Operating the conn himself, he slowed the craft down to one-third impulse, and they cruised through a deserted solar system sprinkled with occasional fields of planetary debris.

"Captain Rowan is hailing us on a secure frequency," reported Tuvok. "Their ETA is less than one minute."

"Acknowledge," answered the captain. "But no more transmissions until they get here."

While Tuvok sent the message, B'Elanna Torres worked her console. "There are no Cardassian ships in scanner range," she reported.

"Still I don't want to be here more than a couple of minutes." Chakotay's worried gaze traveled from the small viewscreen to the even smaller window below it. There was nothing in sight but the vast starscape and a few jagged clumps of debris. This area appeared deserted, but Chakotay had learned from hard experience that it was wise to keep moving in the Demilitarized Zone.

"They're coming out of warp," said Torres.

Chakotay watched on the viewscreen as a Bajoran assault vessel appeared about a thousand kilometers off the starboard bow. The dagger-shaped spacecraft was slightly larger than the *Spartacus,* but she wasn't as maneuverable or as fast. Like Chakotay's ship, her blue-gray hull was pocked and pitted with the wounds of battle.

"Captain Rowan is hailing us," said Tuvok.

"On screen." Chakotay managed a smile as he greeted his counterpart on the other Maquis ship. Patricia Rowan looked every centimeter a warrior, from her scarred, gaunt face to the red eye patch that covered one eye. Her blond hair was streaked with premature gray, and it was pulled back into a tight bun. Captain Rowan had gotten a well-deserved reputation for ruthlessness, and Chakotay was cordial to her but couldn't quite bring himself to call her a friend.

"Hello, Patricia."

"Hello, Chakotay," she answered. "The *Singha* is reporting for duty under your command. What's our mission?"

"Do you know the planet Helena?"

"Only by reputation. Wasn't it abandoned when the Federation betrayed us?"

"No," answered Chakotay. "The Helenites opted for the same legal status as the residents of Dorvan V. Instead of being relocated, they chose to give up their Federation citizenship and remain on the planet, under Cardassian rule."

"Then to hell with them," said Rowan bluntly.

Chakotay ignored her harsh words. "The Helenites have always marched to their own drum. The planet was settled by mixed-race colonists who were trying to escape discrimination in the rest of the Federation. There are some Maquis sympathizers on Helena, and we've been getting periodic reports from them. Two weeks ago, they sent a message that Cardassian troops had arrived, then we lost all contact. There hasn't been a transmission from the planet since then. It might be a crackdown, maybe even total extermination. For all we know, the Cardassians could be testing planet-killing weapons."

"They're not Maquis," said Rowan stubbornly.

Chakotay's jaw clenched with anger. "We can't just abandon four million people. We have to find out what's happening there, and help them if we can."

"Then it's an intelligence mission," replied Captain Rowan, sounding content with that definition.

Chakotay nodded and slowly relaxed his jaw. One of

the drawbacks of being in a loose-knit organization like the Maquis was that orders were not always followed immediately. Sometimes a commander had to explain the situation in order to convince his subordinates to act. Of course, fighting a guerrilla war against two vastly superior foes would make anyone cautious, and Maquis captains were used to acting on their own discretion. Sometimes the chain of command was as flimsy as a gaseous nebula.

Captain Rowan's scowl softened for an instant. "Chakotay, the people on Dorvan V are from your own culture. Wouldn't it make more sense to find out what happened to *them* instead of racing to help a bunch of mixed-breeds on Helena?"

Chakotay couldn't tell if Rowan was bigoted or just callous. He glanced at Torres and saw her shake her head. "Good thing there are no psychological tests to join the Maquis," she whispered.

"Did you say something?" demanded Captain Rowan.

Chakotay cleared his throat. "She said the Helenites are not really, uh, mixed-breeds—they're hybrids, genetically bred. I've heard their whole social structure is based on genetics, the more unique your genetic heritage, the higher your social status."

"A fascinating culture," added Tuvok without looking up from his console. Rowan grimaced, but remained silent.

Chakotay went on, "As for my people on Dorvan V . . . yes, I'm worried about them. But that's a small village, and they've chosen to live in peace with the land, using minimal technology. They're not much of a threat, and of no strategic value, either—the Cardassians will probably leave them alone. But Helena was a thriving Federation planet with millions of inhabitants and a dozen spaceports. When they go silent, it's suspicious."

"How do we proceed?" asked Captain Rowan.

Chakotay gave her a grim smile. "Have you ever played cowboys and Indians?"

Observing the planet on the viewscreen, Captain Chakotay was struck by how Earth-like it was, with vast aquamarine oceans and wispy cloud cover. Helena had small twin moons that orbited each other as they orbited the planet, and he could see their silhouettes against the sparkling sea. Small green continents were scattered across the great waters, but they seemed insignificant next to all that blue. The lush hues were accentuated by a giant red sun glowing in the distance.

On second glance, Chakotay decided that Helena looked more like Pacifica than Earth. Here was yet another beautiful planet stolen by the Cardassians, while the Federation looked the other way.

"One ship in orbit," reported B'Elanna Torres. "A Cardassian military freighter. They use those for troop transports, too, and they can be heavily armed."

Chakotay nodded and spread his fingers over the helm controls. "Let's keep it to one ship. Tuvok, as soon as we come out of warp, target their communications array with photon torpedoes and fire at will. I don't want them sending for help."

"Yes, sir," answered the Vulcan, who was preternaturally calm, considering they were about to attack a ship that was ten times larger than they were.

"Then hit their sensor arrays, so they have to concentrate on *us*."

"What about their weapons?" snapped Torres. "I hope you aren't planning to take a lot of damage."

"No more than usual." Captain Chakotay smiled confidently and pressed the comm panel. "Seska, report to the bridge for relief."

"Yes, sir," answered the Bajoran. She was only one deck below them, in the forward torpedo bay, and Chakotay heard her footsteps clanging on the ladder behind them. Now if B'Elanna had to go to engineering, they were covered.

The captain hit the comm panel, and his voice echoed throughout the ship. "All hands, Red Alert! Battlestations."

Like the falcon which inspired the Peregrine Class, the *Spartacus* swooped out of warp, her talons bared, spitting photon torpedoes in rapid bursts. Plumes of flame rose along the dorsal fin of the sturgeon-shaped Cardassian freighter, and dishes, deflectors, and antennas snapped like burnt matchsticks. Shields quickly compensated, and the next volley was repelled, as the lumbering, copper-colored vessel turned to defend herself.

Phasers beamed from the wing tips of the *Spartacus,* bathing the freighter in vibrant blue light. Although damage to the hull was minimal, the enemy's sensor arrays crackled like a lightning storm. Despite her damage, the freighter unleashed a barrage of phaser fire, and the *Spartacus* was rocked as she streaked past. With the larger ship on her tail, blasting away, the Maquis ship was forced into a low orbit. A desperate chase ensued, with the blue seas of Helena glimmering peacefully in the background.

"Full power to aft shields!" ordered Chakotay.

"Aye, sir," answered Torres.

They were jolted again by enemy fire, and Chakotay had to grip his chair to keep from falling out. From the corner of his eye, he saw Seska stagger onto the bridge and take a seat at an auxilary console. There was a worried look on her face.

"We can't take much more of this," said Torres.

"Making evasive maneuvers," answered Chakotay.

Zigging and zagging like a pendulum, the Maquis ship avoided most of the Cardassian volleys, but the larger ship bore down on them, cutting the distance with every second. Chakotay knew he would soon be in their sights, but his options were limited this close to the planet. He had a course to keep . . . and a rendezvous.

The two ships—a sardine chased by a barracuda—sped around the gently curved horizon and headed toward the blazing red sun in the distance. On the bridge, Chakotay pounded a button to dampen the light from the viewscreen, the glare was so bright. But if he couldn't see, they couldn't either. He felt the thrill of the hunt as he prepared to use one of the oldest tactics of his ancestors.

A direct hit jarred them, releasing an acrid plume of smoke from somewhere on the bridge. The ship began to vibrate as they started into the atmosphere.

"Shields weakening," reported Tuvok.

"Just a little longer," muttered Chakotay. He made another sharp turn, but quickly veered back toward the sun. The Cardassians increased their fire, as if worried that she would escape into the planet's atmosphere. Since the *Spartacus* wasn't returing fire, they had to to assume she was trying to land on the planet.

"They're powering up a tractor beam," said Torres urgently. "Their shields are . . . down!"

"Now!" barked the captain. Tuvok's hand moved from the weapons console to the comm board, while Chakotay steered his craft vertically into the horizon, trying to present a small target. The Cardassians had swallowed the bait, and now the trap snapped shut.

A Bajoran assault vessel streaked out of warp in the middle of the sun's glare. Chakotay knew the *Singha* was there, but he could barely see her on the viewscreen. The Cardassian vessel didn't see her at all, so intent were they upon capturing their prey.

With her shields down, the freighter's bridge took a direct hit from a brace of torpedoes, and lightning crackled along the length of her golden hull. The freighter went dark, but she lit up again as the *Singha* veered around and raked her hull with phasers, tearing jagged gashes in the gleaming metal. The Cardassians got off a few desperate shots, but the *Singha* raced past them, unharmed.

"Aft torpedoes," ordered Chakotay. "Fire!"

With deadly precision, the Vulcan launched a brace of torpedoes that hit the freighter amidships and nearly broke her in two. Chakotay cringed at the explosions that ripped along her gleaming hull, and he made a silent prayer on behalf of the fallen enemy. They were more arrogant than smart, but they had died bravely. Fortunately, that trick always worked on the arrogant. At a cockeyed angle, spewing smoke and flame, the massive freighter dropped into a decaying orbit.

Chakotay piloted the *Spartacus* into a safe orbit that trailed behind the dying ship. "Hail them."

Tuvok shook his head. "Their communications are out, and life support is failing. They have about six minutes left before they burn up in the atmosphere."

The cheerful voice of Captain Rowan broke in on the comm channel. "That was good hunting, Chakotay, and a good plan. What's next?"

"Enter standard orbit and see if you can raise anyone on the planet. We're going to take a prisoner, if we can."

He tapped the comm panel. "Bridge to transporter room. Scan the bridge of the enemy ship—see if you can find any lifesigns."

"Yes, sir." After a moment's pause, the technician answered, "Most of them are dead. There's one weak lifesign—"

"Lock onto it and wait for me. I'm on my way." The captain jumped to his feet. "Tuvok, grab a medkit—you're with me. B'Elanna, you have the bridge. Keep scanning the planet, and try to raise someone. Seska, you have the conn. Keep us in orbit."

"Aye, sir." The attractive Bajoran slid into the vacated seat and gave him a playful smile. "This looks like a nice place for shore leave. What do you say, Captain?"

"I'll put you on the away team," promised Chakotay. He took another glance at the viewscreen and saw the smoking hulk of the freighter plummeting toward the beautiful blue horizon.

The captain led the way from the clam-shaped bridge to the central corridor, which ran like a backbone down the length of the *Spartacus*. He jogged to the second hatch and dropped onto the ladder with practiced efficiency, while Tuvok stopped at a storage panel to pick up a medkit.

Dropping off the ladder, Chakotay landed in the second largest station on the ship after engineering, the combined transporter room and cargo hold. Not that they had any cargo to speak of—every spare centimeter was filled with weapons, explosives, and photon torpedoes, stacked like cordwood.

He drew his phaser and nodded toward the Bolian on the transporter console. The blue-skinned humanoid manipulated some old trimpot slides, and a prone figure began to materialize on the transporter platform. Chakotay heard Tuvok's footsteps as he landed on the deck, but he never took his eyes, or his phaser, off the wounded figure.

It was a male Cardassian, with singed clothes, a bruised face, and bloodied, crushed legs. With their prominent bone structure and sunken eyes, most Cardassian faces looked like skulls, but this one looked closer to death than usual.

"According to his insignia, he's the first officer," said Tuvok.

The Cardassian blinked his eyes and focused slowly on them. When he realized where he was, he wheezed with laughter. "Are you trying to save us?"

"Lie still," answered Chakotay. He motioned Tuvok forward with the medkit, but the Cardassian waved him off.

"Too late," he said with a cough. The Cardassian lifted his black sleeve to his mouth and bit off a small black button. Before anyone could react, he swallowed it. "I won't be captured . . . by the Maquis."

"What are you doing on this planet?" demanded Chakotay. "Why don't you leave these people alone?"

A rattle issued from the Cardassian's throat, and it was hard to tell whether he was laughing, crying, or dying. "You beat us . . . but all you won was a curse."

The Cardassian's bloodied head dropped onto the platform with a thud, and his previously wheezing chest was now still. Tuvok checked the medical tricorder and reported, "He has expired."

Chakotay nodded. "Beam his body back to his ship. Let him burn with his comrades."

"Yes, sir," answered the Bolian. A second later, every trace of the Cardassian officer was gone.

The captain strode over to the transporter console and tapped the comm panel. "Chakotay to bridge. Have you or the *Singha* raised anyone on the planet?"

"No, sir," answered Torres. "But we detected a strong power source that suddenly went dark. It could be a Cardassian installation."

"Are you picking up lifesigns on the planet?"

"Lots of them," answered Torres.

"Pick a strong concentration of lifesigns and send the coordinates to the transporter room. Tuvok and I are going down."

"Okay," answered Torres. "Did you get a prisoner?"

"For only a few seconds—we didn't learn anything. Chakotay out." The captain reached into a tray on the transporter console and grabbed two Deltan combadges, one of which he tossed to Tuvok. The *Spartacus* was so small that they seldom needed combadges while on the ship; they saved them for away teams.

"I've got the coordinates," said the Bolian technician. "It appears to be the spaceport in the city of Padulla."

"Fine." Captain Chakotay jumped onto the transporter

platform and took his place on the middle pad. Tuvok stepped beside him, slinging the medkit and tricorder over his shoulder.

"Energize."

A familiar tingle gripped Chakotay's spine, as the transporter room faded from view, to be replaced by a cavernous spaceport with high, vaulted ceilings covered with impressive murals. The captain expected to see a crowd of people, but he expected them to be standing on their feet—not lying in haphazard rows stretching the length of the vast terminal. This looked like a field hospital, thrown together to house the wounded from some monstrous battle. Coughs and groans echoed in the rancid air.

His first impression was that the Cardassians had wreaked terrible destruction on the people of Helena, and he started toward the nearest patient.

"Captain!" warned Tuvok. "Keep your distance from them."

He turned to see the Vulcan intently working his medical tricorder. This caused Chakotay to look more closely at the nearest patient, who was swaddled in a soiled blanket, lying on top of a grass mat, surrounded by filth.

The man wasn't wounded—he had oozing pustules and black bruises on his face and limbs, and his yellow hair was plastered to his sweaty forehead. Although his species was unfamiliar to Chakotay, his skin had a deathly pallor, just like the Cardassian's had. Chakotay took a step away from him.

Another patient finally noticed the visitors. She propped herself up with some difficulty and began to crawl toward them, rasping and whimpering. Others noticed the intruders, and a chorus of desperate voices rent the air. Most of their words were incoherent, but Chakotay could hear them begging as they crawled forward: "Help us! Save me! *Kill* me!"

"What's the matter with them?" he whispered to Tuvok.

"A serious illness," answered the Vulcan with tight-lipped understatement. "Clear the transporter room—we should be quarantined before we return to the ship's population. But we must leave immediately."

With reluctance, Chakotay tapped his combadge. "Away team to transporter room. Beam us up, but on a ten-second delay. Get out of the transporter room before we materialize."

"Yes, sir," said the Bolian, not hiding the worry in his voice. "Is everything all right?"

"No," answered Chakotay as he stepped away from the advancing tide of disease and death. "It's not."

Look for
Quarantine
Available Now
Wherever Books Are Sold

STAR TREK®
Strange New Worlds III
Contest Rules

1) ENTRY REQUIREMENTS:

No purchase necessary to enter. Enter by submitting your story as specified below.

2) CONTEST ELIGIBILITY:

This contest is open to nonprofessional writers who are legal residents of the United States and Canada (excluding Quebec) over the age of 18. Entrant must not have published any more than two short stories on a professional basis or in paid professional venues. Employees (or relatives of employees living in the same household) of Pocket Books, VIACOM, or any of its affiliates are not eligible. This contest is void in Puerto Rico and wherever prohibited by law.

3) FORMAT:

Entries should be no more than 7,500 words long and must not have been previously published. They must be typed or printed by word processor, double spaced, on one side of noncorrasable paper. Do not justify right-side margins. The author's name, address, and phone number must appear on the first page of the entry. The author's name, the story title, and the page number should appear on every page. No electronic or disk submissions will be accepted. All entries must be original and the sole work of the Entrant and the sole property of the Entrant.

4) ADDRESS:

Each entry must be mailed to: STRANGE NEW WORLDS, *Star Trek* Department, Pocket Books, 1230 Sixth Avenue, New York, NY 10020.

Each entry must be submitted only once. Please retain a copy of your submission. You may submit more than one story, but each submission must be mailed separately. Enclose a self-addressed, stamped envelope if you wish your entry returned. Entries must be received by October 1st, 1999. Not responsible for lost, late, stolen, postage due, or misdirected mail.

5) PRIZES:

One Grand Prize winner will receive:

Simon and Schuster's *Star Trek: Strange New Worlds III* Publishing Contract for Publication of Winning Entry in our *Strange New Worlds III* Anthology with a bonus advance of One Thousand Dollars ($1,000.00) above the Anthology word rate of 10 cents a word.

One Second Prize winner will receive:

Simon Schuster's *Star Trek: Strange New Worlds III* Publishing Contract for Publication of Winning Entry in our *Strange New Worlds III* Anthology with a bonus advance of Six Hundred Dollars ($600.00) above the Anthology word rate of 10 cents a word.

One Third Prize winner will receive:

Simon and Schuster's *Star Trek: Strange New Worlds III* Publishing Contract for Publication of Winning Entry in our *Strange New Worlds III* Anthology with a bonus advance of Four Hundred Dollars ($400.00) above the Anthology word rate of 10 cents a word.

All Honorable Mention winners will receive:

Simon and Schuster's *Star Trek: Strange New Worlds III* Publishing Contract for Publication of Winning Entry in the *Strange New Worlds III* Anthology and payment at the Anthology word rate of 10 cents a word.

There will be no more than twenty (20) Honorable Mention winners. No contestant can win more than one prize.

Each Prize Winner will also be entitled to a share of royalties on the *Strange New Worlds III* Anthology as specified in Simon and Schuster's *Star Trek: Strange New Worlds III* Publishing Contract.

6) JUDGING:

Submissions will be judged on the basis of writing ability and the originality of the story, which can be set in any of the *Star Trek* time frames and may feature any one or more of the *Star Trek* characters. The judges shall include the editor of the Anthology, one employee of Pocket Books, and one employee of VIACOM Consumer Products. The decisions of the judges shall be final. All prizes will be awarded provided a sufficient number of entries are received that meet the minimum criteria established by the judges.

7) NOTIFICATION:

The winners will be notified by mail or phone. The winners who win a publishing contract must sign the publishing contract in order to be awarded the prize. All federal, local, and state taxes are the responsibility of the winner. A list of the winners will be available after January 1st, 2000, on the Pocket Books *Star Trek* Books website, www.simonsays.com/startrek/, or the names of the winners can be obtained after January 1st, 2000, by sending a self-addressed, stamped envelope and a request for the list of winners to WINNERS' LIST, STRANGE NEW WORLDS III, *Star Trek* Department, Pocket Books, 1230 Sixth Avenue, New York, NY 10020.

8) STORY DISQUALIFICATIONS:

Certain types of stories will be disqualified from consideration:

a) Any story focusing on explicit sexual activity or graphic depictions of violence or sadism.

b) Any story that focuses on characters that are not past or present *Star Trek* regulars or familiar *Star Trek* guest characters.

c) Stories that deal with the previously unestablished death of a *Star Trek* character, or that establish major facts about or make major changes in the life of a major character, for instance a story that establishes a long-lost sibling or reveals the hidden passion two characters feel for each other.

d) Stories that are based around common clichés, such as "hurt/comfort" where a character is injured and lovingly cared for, or "Mary Sue" stories where a new character comes on the ship and outdoes the crew.

9) PUBLICITY:

Each Winner grants to Pocket Books the right to use his or her name, likeness, and entry for any advertising, promotion, and publicity purposes without further compensation to or permission from such winner, except where prohibited by law.

10) LEGAL STUFF:

Look for STAR TREK Fiction from Pocket Books

Star Trek®: The Original Series

Star Trek: The Motion Picture • Gene Roddenberry
Star Trek II: The Wrath of Khan • Vonda N. McIntyre
Star Trek III: The Search for Spock • Vonda N. McIntyre
Star Trek IV: The Voyage Home • Vonda N. McIntyre
Star Trek V: The Final Frontier • J. M. Dillard
Star Trek VI: The Undiscovered Country • J. M. Dillard
Star Trek VII: Generations • J. M. Dillard
Star Trek VIII: First Contact • J. M. Dillard
Star Trek IX: Insurrection • J. M. Dillard
Enterprise: The First Adventure • Vonda N. McIntyre
Final Frontier • Diane Carey
Strangers from the Sky • Margaret Wander Bonanno
Spock's World • Diane Duane
The Lost Years • J. M. Dillard
Probe • Margaret Wander Bonanno
Prime Directive • Judith and Garfield Reeves-Stevens
Best Destiny • Diane Carey
Shadows on the Sun • Michael Jan Friedman
Sarek • A. C. Crispin
Federation • Judith and Garfield Reeves-Stevens
The Ashes of Eden • William Shatner & Judith and Garfield Reeves-Stevens
The Return • William Shatner & Judith and Garfield Reeves-Stevens
Star Trek: Starfleet Academy • Diane Carey
Vulcan's Forge • Josepha Sherman and Susan Shwartz
Avenger • William Shatner & Judith and Garfield Reeves-Stevens
Star Trek: Odyssey • William Shatner & Judith and Garfield Reeves-Stevens
Spectre • William Shatner

#1 *Star Trek: The Motion Picture* • Gene Roddenberry
#2 *The Entropy Effect* • Vonda N. McIntyre
#3 *The Klingon Gambit* • Robert E. Vardeman
#4 *The Covenant of the Crown* • Howard Weinstein
#5 *The Prometheus Design* • Sondra Marshak & Myrna Culbreath

Star Trek: The Next Generation®

Encounter at Farpoint • David Gerrold
Unification • Jeri Taylor
Relics • Michael Jan Friedman
Descent • Diane Carey
All Good Things • Michael Jan Friedman
Star Trek: Klingon • Dean W. Smith & Kristine K. Rusch
Star Trek VII: Generations • J. M. Dillard
Metamorphosis • Jean Lorrah
Vendetta • Peter David
Reunion • Michael Jan Friedman
Imzadi • Peter David
The Devil's Heart • Carmen Carter
Dark Mirror • Diane Duane
Q-Squared • Peter David
Crossover • Michael Jan Friedman
Kahless • Michael Jan Friedman
Star Trek VIII: First Contact • J. M. Dillard
Star Trek IX: Insurrection • Diane Carey
The Best and the Brightest • Susan Wright
Planet X • Michael Jan Friedman
Ship of the Line • Diane Carey

#1 *Ghost Ship* • Diane Carey
#2 *The Peacekeepers* • Gene DeWeese
#3 *The Children of Hamlin* • Carmen Carter
#4 *Survivors* • Jean Lorrah
#5 *Strike Zone* • Peter David
#6 *Power Hungry* • Howard Weinstein
#7 *Masks* • John Vornholt
#8 *The Captains' Honor* • David and Daniel Dvorkin
#9 *A Call to Darkness* • Michael Jan Friedman
#10 *A Rock and a Hard Place* • Peter David
#11 *Gulliver's Fugitives* • Keith Sharee
#12 *Doomsday World* • David, Carter, Friedman & Greenberg
#13 *The Eyes of the Beholders* • A. C. Crispin
#14 *Exiles* • Howard Weinstein
#15 *Fortune's Light* • Michael Jan Friedman
#16 *Contamination* • John Vornholt
#17 *Boogeymen* • Mel Gilden

Star Trek: Deep Space Nine®

The Search • Diane Carey
Warped • K. W. Jeter
The Way of the Warrior • Diane Carey
Star Trek: Klingon • Dean W. Smith & Kristine K. Rusch
Trials and Tribble-ations • Diane Carey
Far Beyond the Stars • Steve Barnes
The 34th Rule • Armin Shimerman & David George
What We Leave Behind • Diane Carey

Star Trek®: Voyager™

Flashback • Diane Carey
Pathways • Jeri Taylor
Mosaic • Jeri Taylor

- #1 *Caretaker* • L. A. Graf
- #2 *The Escape* • Dean W. Smith & Kristine K. Rusch
- #3 *Ragnarok* • Nathan Archer
- #4 *Violations* • Susan Wright
- #5 *Incident at Arbuk* • John Gregory Betancourt
- #6 *The Murdered Sun* • Christie Golden
- #7 *Ghost of a Chance* • Mark A. Garland & Charles G. McGraw
- #8 *Cybersong* • S. N. Lewitt
- #9 *Invasion #4: The Final Fury* • Dafydd ab Hugh
- #10 *Bless the Beasts* • Karen Haber
- #11 *The Garden* • Melissa Scott
- #12 *Chrysalis* • David Niall Wilson
- #13 *The Black Shore* • Greg Cox
- #14 *Marooned* • Christie Golden
- #15 *Echoes* • Dean W. Smith & Kristine K. Rusch
- #16 *Seven of Nine* • Christie Golden
- #17 *Death of a Neutron Star* • Eric Kotani
- #18 *Battle Lines* • Dave Galanter & Greg Brodeur

Star Trek®: New Frontier

- #1 *House of Cards* • Peter David
- #2 *Into the Void* • Peter David
- #3 *The Two-Front War* • Peter David
- #4 *End Game* • Peter David
- #5 *Martyr* • Peter David
- #6 *Fire on High* • Peter David

Star Trek®: Day of Honor

Book One: *Ancient Blood* • Diane Carey
Book Two: *Armageddon Sky* • L. A. Graf
Book Three: *Her Klingon Soul* • Michael Jan Friedman
Book Four: *Treaty's Law* • Dean W. Smith & Kristine K. Rusch
The Television Episode • Michael Jan Friedman

Star Trek®: The Captain's Table

Book One: *War Dragons* • L. A. Graf
Book Two: *Dujonian's Hoard* • Michael Jan Friedman
Book Three: *The Mist* • Dean W. Smith & Kristine K. Rusch
Book Four: *Fire Ship* • Diane Carey
Book Five: *Once Burned* • Peter David
Book Six: *Where Sea Meets Sky* • Jerry Oltion

Star Trek®: The Dominion War

Book 1: *Behind Enemy Lines* • John Vornholt
Book 2: *Call To Arms . . .* • Diane Carey
Book 3: *Tunnel Through the Stars* • John Vornholt
Book 4: *. . . Sacrifice of Angels* • Diane Carey

Star Trek®: My Brother's Keeper

Book One: *Republic* • Michael Jan Friedman
Book Two: *Constitution* • Michael Jan Friedman
Book Three: *Enterprise* • Michael Jan Friedman

1252.01